D0175483

From the Files of

Read all the books about Madison Finn!

Coming Soon!

Don't miss the Super Editions

From the Files of

Madison Finn

2C4W*
*Too Cool for Words

By Laura Dower

Books 1–3

HYPERION
New York

For Mom with love—always remember MTM,
sour cream & onion chips, and Warren Avenue

Special thanks to my editor, Helen Perelman

If you purchased this book without a cover, you should be aware that this book is stolen property. It was reported as "unsold and destroyed" to the publisher, and neither the author nor the publisher has received any payment for this "stripped" book.

Only the Lonely text copyright © 2001 by Laura Dower
Boy, Oh Boy! text copyright © 2001 by Laura Dower
Play It Again text copyright © 2001 by Laura Dower

From the Files of Madison Finn is a trademark of Disney Enterprises, Inc.

All rights reserved. No part of this book may be reproduced or transmitted in any form or by any means, electronic or mechanical, including photo-copying, recording, or by any information storage and retrieval system, without written permission from the publisher. For information address Hyperion Paperbacks for Children, 114 Fifth Avenue, New York, New York 10011-5690.

Printed in the United States of America

First compiled edition, 2006
1 3 5 7 9 10 8 6 4 2

The main body of text of this book is set in 13-point Frutiger Roman.

ISBN 1-4231-0040-9
Library of Congress Cataloging-in-Publication Data on file

Visit www.hyperionbooksforchildren.com

Only the Lonely

"Hnnnnnnugh! WHAT is your problem?" Madison grunted at her new orange laptop computer. She was smack-dab in the middle of downloading a picture of a super-cute *Ursus maritimus* (a.k.a. polar bear) when the screen just froze.

She knew her hard drive had plenty of memory.

She punched all the right keys.

But nothing.

Sometimes in the past, Madison's computer screen would freeze, but only for a blip. This was different. The computer wasn't *really* the one with a problem. Right now, Madison was frozen, too.

Madison Francesca Finn had a dreadful case of late-summer brain freeze. It was not the kind of

1

brain freeze you get when you drink a Grape Slurpee too fast. This was the kind of brain freeze that happens when your thoughts get stuck in a whirly swirl of loneliness, friendlessness, and total and utter boredom. This was the chronic, moronic, pain-in-the-brain freeze that happens when everyone you know is at camp but you're stuck at home with Mom; the summer reading list you were supposed to be finishing up hasn't even been *unfolded*; and you have no pool options on 95° days.

"Yikes!" Madison yelped, jumping up from her desk chair. "Why is it doing this to me, Phin?" She glared at her dog, Phineas T. Finn, who was curled up next to a giant metal file cabinet in the corner of her bedroom.

He poked up his wrinkly nose into the air and sneezed. "Rowroooooooo!" This pug hated it when his nap was interrupted.

"Well, I'll just restart it just to be sure everything's okay," Madison said out loud, groaning and hitting a few special keys, a trick her dad had taught her.

Dad was the one who had computerized Madison in the first place. He had shown her what DSL and HTML meant before most of her classmates even knew they even existed. He loved computer jokes, too, even though he told the same ones more than once.

"Hey, Maddie, why did the Net chick cross the road?" he would ask.

"I dunno, Dad . . . why?" Madison would say with pretend interest, even if it was the third time she'd heard it.

"To get ONLINE!" Dad would laugh.

And that was one of his better jokes.

Just this year, her parents had bought this new laptop in Madison's favorite color, along with a mega-pack of disks, special desktop-publishing software, and a slightly used scanner. Mom had crooned, "It'll be a great way to organize your thoughts, honey bear," as they unpacked the computer back in May. "Just think, you're on the cutting edge of technology. This fall, you'll be the smartest seventh grader at Far Hills."

Madison thought her Mom wanted her to be a computer genius or a writing genius or anyone who had "genius" potential. Madison didn't exactly feel like a "genius" *yet*, but she did know her way around a computer, especially on the Internet.

The computer beeped and zinged, and Madison's desktop page appeared once again. The polar bear was there in a document marked "recovered," and the desktop reappeared as a collage of white rhinos and mountain gorillas.

Madison always used pictures of endangered animals as her screen savers. In fact, she considered herself an official animal advocate both on the computer and off. She fantasized about working for the *National Geographic Explorer* TV show, or becoming a super vet, or maybe even becoming a documentary filmmaker like her mom.

With her computer unfrozen and ready to go, Madison logged on to bigfishbowl.com. Usually a chat room helped her break through a case of brain freeze better than most things. She knew meeting new people online wasn't the same as having actual, in-the-same-room friends whose hair you could braid or who could play hoops, but it gave her someone to talk to.

She'd logged on for the first time a year ago with Mom's permission. The people in charge of the site were sticklers for safety.

Madison's chat room screen name was "MadFinn," which was pretty funny, considering she was a "Finn" among the fishes, so to speak. Most of the people inside bigfishbowl.com were girls talking about girl stuff. Madison loved the way the home page looked like a real fishbowl, with seaweed, and even orange fish. She clicked on a rainbow fish to get into the Main Fishbowl, the waiting room where kids picked the chat they wanted to join. Madison scanned the list.

```
I am sooo bored! Hello!
(32 fish)

Tell me anything u want GRRRLS ONLY
(12 fish)
```

```
****animal lovers here*****
(3 fish)

Private! Wanna be keypals?
(28 fish)

Pictures of cute boyz can u help me
(11 fish)

only the lonely
(1 fish)
```

Madison picked "animal lovers here" and went inside. She was sure she must be in the right place. Maybe she'd meet a fellow polar bear admirer?

```
<Crazygal>: That is kool beans
MadFinn has entered the room.
<Crazygal>: Hiya!!!!!!
<Wayout>: Madfinn stats?
<MadFinn>: Hell
<MadFinn>: ooooo Helloooooo
<Iluvcats>: How r u? I love cats.
<MadFinn>: stats f/12/NY u?
<Crazygal>: f/14/DE
<MadFinn>: hey cats I love animals too.
<Iluvcats>: I LOVE CATS!!!
<Wayout>: :>) I loooove Jimmie J!!!!
<MadFinn>: Do you have cats?
<Crazygal>: GMTA I like Downtown
   Boyz 2!
```

Downtown Boyz was an all-guy singing group whose lead singer Jimmie J was pretty cute but . . . *wait a minute!* Madison wanted to talk about animals. This was the "animal lovers here" room. Why were they changing the subject? Who cared about Jimmie J? And why wasn't Iluvcats girl responding?

```
<Wayout>: (( )) :* they r sooooooo
   hot
<Crazygal>: IMO Jimmie is the
   hottest :-@
Iluvcats has left the room.
```

As soon as cat girl left the room, Madison left, too.

She went back to the room list in search of *someone* who would talk about animals or computers or something besides Jimmie J. She saw one other room that looked semi-interesting.

```
only the lonely (1 fish)
```

That was *exactly* how Madison felt. She missed her best friend, Aimee, who was away at ballet camp twirling around; and Egg, who was away at computer camp URL-ing around.

She clicked on "lonely" and hoped for the best.

Of course as luck would have it (and Madison's luck usually ran a little *slooooooow* these days), she entered and introduced herself with a quick "MadFinn" hello, but then nothing happened.

6

There was no "hello" back.

There was no "how r u?"

There was nothing. Madison waited almost three whole minutes before the "(1 fish)" responded in any way at all.

```
<Bigwheels>: ohhhh whoa i thought
    I was alone. My
<Bigwheels>: screen froze the
    computer is
<MadFinn>: hellllooo????
<Bigwheels>: wicked slow sorry
<MadFinn>: u r not alone! i saw
    how r u?
<Bigwheels>: ok. How are
<MadFinn>: how old r u?
<Bigwheels>: 12 and yoo?
<MadFinn>: 12
<Bigwheels>: my birthday was last
    wk
<MadFinn>: (:o!!!! no way! happy
    birthday!
<Bigwheels>: thank you where do u
    live?
<MadFinn>: NY are you at camp?
<Bigwheels>: no. I'm at home
    washington state
<MadFinn>: omigod you are all the
    way across the
<MadFinn>: country that is so
    cool WOW
```

```
<Bigwheels>: yeah but I'm lonely
   here u know???
<MadFinn>: me too
<MadFinn>: and bored too
<Bigwheels>: wanna be keypals?
<MadFinn>: ok what's that?
<Bigwheels>: like penpals only
   email like
<MadFinn>: o ok. What is your
   email?
<Bigwheels>: send me your em
<MadFinn>: tell me your email and
   I will write 2 u
```

Madison waited.

```
<MadFinn>: tell me your email and
   I will write u!!!
```

Madison waited a little longer.

```
<MadFinn>: r u there?
<MadFinn>: Helllllloooooo?????
<Bigwheels>: *poof*
```

Poof?
Madison felt even *more* alone than when she had
logged on, so of course she logged off immediately.
She wasn't in the mood to be lonely anymore.
   After that chat room fiasco, Madison went into her

super-special computer files. She accessed the files with a super-special password which was so super-special that even *she* forgot it sometimes. She had it taped inside the top drawer of her desk.

In the last few weeks (partly out of boredom and partly out of a desire to get her life together), Madison had begun a new system of personal information storage on the new computer.

She had been collecting magazine clippings like a pack rat for months. She'd stored them in multicolored rainbow folders up until now, but at last she was ready to load them online. Slowly, she was becoming computerized byte by byte.

The old scanner worked well, even if blue printed out more like purple. Dad said he'd eventually help her download more fun gifs from Web sites and teach her how to adjust the pixels properly, whatever those were. Madison was learning as fast as she could. In fact, she was certain she'd have her own Web page or even her own Web site one day. Maybe she'd be a Web site *genius*? Mom would love that.

In addition to downloading, scanning, and saving, Madison decided she would *also* keep an online record of her most important feelings and most important thoughts. Of course, most people would have called something like this a "journal," but Madison thought that sounded way too obvious. She briefly considered calling her writing a "diary," too, but that was just as obvious so she called it instead: *The Files of Madison Finn*.

She had friend files. She had homework files. She had nothing-in-particular files. She classified, collected, controlled, and computed *everything*. Here, inside this delightful orange computer, Madison was in the process of creating password-protected *miles* of files.

She opened one.

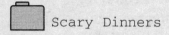 Scary Dinners

That made her laugh. On the screen before her was a graph on which Madison had plotted Mom's predictable fast-food dinners. After sixteen straight nights in a row of egg rolls, tacos, fried chicken, and other "scary" dinners, Madison was inspired to keep track. As of tonight, the graph showed pizza running neck and neck with Chinese food, with PB-&-J sandwiches lagging behind.

Tonight, Madison decided to open a brand new file in honor of her hour on bigfishbowl.com. She wondered what had happened to "Bigwheels" and why "Iluvcats" had just disappeared. Was it something she'd said?

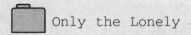 Only the Lonely

Madison closed her eyes for a second. She hoped in her heart of hearts that she'd get a hundred e-mails tomorrow. She longed for the speedy return of Aimee and Egg. She secretly wished that even Daddy would come home again.

Is absolutely everyone having a good summer except for me? I mean I went to Brazil for a nature documentary film location scout with Mom. Ever since she started working for Budge Films she makes nature shows. We saw lots of weird-looking tree frogs there. They were slimy and the truth is I was sicker than sick of the frogs and fast food and planes and strangers, especially strangers.

I wish Aimee and Egg were right here, right now, right away. I wish I had a brother or sister. I wish I wasn't only the lonely. I wish seventh grade would just start already. Of course, I probably won't be able to deal with the change. I never have before.

Rude Awakening: I'm allergic to change.

I mean, I know I'm allergic to pollen, grasses, and mold spores. But change makes me break out into big hives. Just the thought of seventh grade gave me a giant pink welt right here on my shoulder. *Gross.*

Last summer after fifth grade Aimee and Egg were not far away at stupid camp. They were here with me, dancing in the sprinklers on Aimee's lawn like we did every summer, getting cooled off, and laughing like we did every summer. We were laughing really hard about some things I can't remember but

I know they were great. I know we ate all
the Dreamsicles we wanted and we watched
scary old movies like *The Mummy*.

Not this summer.

Mom would probably say that at least
it's a good thing that I've identified my
bizarre allergy and maybe it just doesn't
matter if I fix it right now. All that
matters is acknowledging it, right? The
rest is just details, right? Mom says that
we learn things in steps. So this is just
step number one, I guess. This is just step
number one in learning about life.

Lucky me.

I can't wait for step number two.

The cursor blinked on the empty space. Madison
stopped and stared at what she'd written so far. The
screen went black.

It was frozen *again*.

Madison leaned down to scratch the top of Phin's
head.

So what if the screen was stuck! Madison
decided she just didn't care if she got the "safe to
turn off your computer" message or not. She just
pressed the power button and walked away.

As she turned, Madison crashed into a purple
blow-up chair in the middle of the room. It squeaked
as she landed on her backside.

She plucked open the little plastic thingie that
kept air in the chair. *Pssssssssssssss.*

She capped it again quickly.

Could Madison Finn really ever be saved from loneliness?

"Madison!" Mom yelled from downstairs.

It was time to go to bed. As she stood up, Madison lost her balance and fell backward. She groaned.

She wanted her friends, but thanks to camp they were gone.

She wanted her Dad, but thanks to the divorce he was gone.

How could she ever handle a switch into seventh grade when she kept slipping *backward*?

"Rowroooo!" Phin growled. He could always tell when Madison was upset.

She pulled her body up and into the bathroom, but her brain was stuck in REWIND. She wished she could just press FAST FORWARD and get through this moment.

At this point, Madison Finn wasn't sure she could survive the end of the summer, let alone the beginning of a new school year.

The next morning, Madison woke up to wet kisses from Phin. Smelly kisses of course. Dog breath.

"Oh, gross. Phin get off! Yeah, I love you, too." Madison gazed into his brown pug eyes. "Are you trying to tell me something, dog? Like W-A-L-K maybe?"

Phin danced on his back paws, jumping at the bed. Even Phin knew how to spell.

Madison wanted to lollygag around, but nature was calling—calling Phin, anyway. She pulled off her orange polka-dotted pajamas and slipped into short overalls so she and Phin could make a quick trip around the block.

Morning walks with Phin were the easiest. Madison walked out the porch door, down the corner to Grove Street, up a few more streets, and then around the block to the intersection before turning back home.

But for some reason this morning, Phin was being difficult. He wouldn't pee, so Madison took a detour onto Ridge Road, the scenic route.

It smelled like honeysuckle. Phin's nose started sniffing a mile a minute. Madison's eyes scanned the neighborhood. Everything looked different here from the way she remembered. She even saw a new-looking green house where the old Martin family had lived for years. Everyone thought that house was haunted. But today it was a whole new house, freshly painted and all.

Just as Madison was staring at the green house, a young girl walked out onto its front steps.

Madison kept staring.

The girl stared straight back.

Madison stared some more and she kept smiling—it was easy to be friendly at a distance. After a moment, however, the girl started to walk toward her. That's when Madison panicked. It was never as easy to be friendly up close. She felt the urge to run.

Madison wasn't quite sure where she was running *to*, but she sure knew how to run. She could have dashed away from that green house lickety-split too if it hadn't been for Phin, who tugged her right back to where she had started.

"Hi!" the stranger said, cheerfully. She walked right up to Madison and Phin on the sidewalk. "I'm Fiona. Do you live around here?"

Madison managed a feeble "Uh-huh," in response.

"Oh cool, do you live on Ridge Road?" Fiona asked.

"I live . . . uh . . ." Madison pointed behind her, in the general direction of Blueberry Street. It wasn't her most eloquent moment of all time.

Suddenly a woman called out from the door of the green house. "Fiona! Let's go, young lady!"

"Yeeps!" The girl smiled at Madison. "I gotta run! See you around the neighborhood?" She disappeared again up the path, almost as quietly as she'd appeared, waving the whole way. "Nice to meet you—sort of!"

Madison waved too. Then she waited a moment to see if the girl would reappear, but no one came outside. Madison stared at the big brown duck painted on the side of the family's mailbox and read the swirly letters: THE WATERS FAMILY.

As she and Phin made tracks back home to 5 Blueberry Street, Madison wondered when she would see Fiona again.

"Rowrooo!" Phin agreed.

As soon as they arrived home, Madison and Phin noticed an icky-sticky charred smell coming from the kitchen. The pug's nose was sniffing wildly at the air.

"Mom?" Madison hurried inside. "Is something burning?"

She stopped dead in her tracks. Had someone stolen Fast Food Mother in the middle of the night and replaced her with Cook-Me-Breakfast Mother? Mom was cooking? She was even wearing a tacky "Kiss the Cook" apron.

"Have a seat!" Mom announced, shoving a plate of very yellow scrambled eggs and very burned toast in front of Madison.

It was the morning of surprises.

"Gee, Mom," Madison said, a little stunned by the greeting, and the smell. Then she added, "They seem a little, well . . . gold, actually. What's up with that?"

Madison knew what was really up; Mom had forgotten to add milk again. One time Mom had tried to make lasagna, which came out more like red soup, but Madison had just slurped and said nothing. Madison didn't see the point in hurting Mom's feelings just because her pasta was a little runny.

Mom beamed. "Sweetie, today is a special day just for you and so I thought breakfast was a good way to start off. What do you think? Today we can go over to the Far Hills Shoppes and get you some new clothes for seventh grade. I know starting junior high is a big deal and I know I have been away a lot on business lately and, well, won't it be nice to spend a little time together?"

Usually Madison was good at predicting Mom's sudden bursts of "nice." But not this morning.

"Come on. What gives, Mom?" Madison laughed. "What's the catch?"

"Catch? There is no catch. Don't you *want* to go shopping?" Mom asked.

Madison scooped up a forkful of food and nodded. She would have said something, but she didn't want to gag on the eggs.

As soon as they'd cleared away the breakfast dishes, Madison filled Phin's water dish and waited for Mom to put on her eyeliner, lipstick, and concealer. That usually took a while, so Madison visited her computer keyboard in the meantime. She could check her e-mail, at least.

There was no mail. Madison was discouraged. She sighed, opened a new file folder, and began to type.

 Fiona

    Met this new girl over on Ridge Road.
She looked like the singer Brandy, like
with long braids and cool clothes. Her name
is Fiona Waters and she was very friendly
and I think she wanted to be my friend. Is
that possible? She looked my age and she
must have just moved in because I know the
house she lives in. Way, way long ago this
other family the Martins lived there.
    I wonder what happened to the Martins?

How can people just suddenly disappear and then appear in the neighborhood from out of nowhere? Everything really does change when you aren't paying attention.

I of course clammed up the minute Fiona said "hi" because I am useless around strangers. I wanted to run away. It's like I had the words to talk right here on the tip of my tongue, but no luck. I'm stuck. Sometimes I think there's this master conspiracy to keep me tongue-tied and friendless, for the rest of the summer. I wish Aimee would just come home, already!

At least I have Phinnie.

On their way out the door, Madison asked Mom if she would please drive to the Far Hill Shoppes via Ridge Road. She wanted to drive past the green house again, of course. As they passed, Madison saw that the Waters family car was no longer parked in the driveway. Fiona had vanished.

Madison and her mom cruised over a few blocks to the back entrance of the mall. There was a sign draped across the storefront: GOING-OUT-OF-BUSINESS BACK-TO-SCHOOL EXTRA-SPECIAL SUPER-SALE. Sales always sounded great to Mom, so that's where they started.

While Madison loaded her arms with cotton tees, embroidered khakis, and sweaters, Mom remained attached to her cell phone, waiting on a bench by the cash register. Some producer or director was always calling her about something.

"Mom, can I get these? Please?" Madison pleaded gently, trying to distract Mom from the phone. She held out a few shirts for Mom's vote. This was supposed to be *their* day together, after all.

"Well, try them on first, I wanna see," Mom said, grabbing a tank top out of the pile. She took the phone away from her mouth and frowned. "I don't know about shirts like *this* one, sweetie. People will be staring, don't you think?"

"Staring?" Madison suddenly felt self-conscious. Staring at *what*? Madison hardly had any boobs yet. She quickly gave Mom an "I could die right here, right now, if you ever, ever, *ever* refer to my chest again" look. She'd show Mom some *staring*.

Of course, Mom never noticed Madison's stares. She was too busy getting right back onto her cell phone or doing some work thing.

Madison pouted a little and proceeded into the dressing room. She felt hot with that special kind of embarrassment you only get when you're out with your mom. She felt hot from carrying all these stupid clothes. She felt—

Wham! She felt awful! She had walked right into someone on the way into the dressing area.

"Yikes!" Madison blurted out. "Are you okay?"

"Excuse me, I am so sorry," the girl said, suddenly bursting into a wide grin. "Hey, don't I know you?"

Madison's jaw slackened. It was Fiona. She was wearing the same yellow sundress Madison had seen her in earlier. Madison noticed Fiona's toenails were painted a perfect grape color and she had on an equally perfect pair of yellow jelly sandals. Madison had always wanted sandals like those.

Although she had an uncanny ability to process many visual details in a very short period of time, speaking was something Madison wasn't so quick about.

"H-h-howdy!" Madison stuttered. *Howdy?* Her cheeks turned the color of cherry tomatoes. *Howdy?*

"Hey, you were the one I met this morning, right? With your dog. He was cute." Fiona smiled again. "What's *your* name again?"

"Madison," she mumbled.

Fiona kept smiling. "I'm Fiona, but I think I told you that already, right? I'm new in Far Hills."

"Uh-huh," said Madison, listening. "New."

"Well, new because we just moved here and I don't actually know anyone here in Far Hills yet except my brother, Chet, he's my twin brother, so he doesn't count obviously as a friend-friend because he's not a girl and . . ." her voice trailed off.

She was good at talking—*a lot*.

"By the way, do people call you Madison or Maddie?"

"Most people call me Madison. Except my friends. They call me Maddie. But you can call me something else. . . . You can call me a complete moron for acting so dumb this morning."

Fiona chuckled. "You're funny! And you are so not a moron! I'm so happy to meet you. I was beginning to think I wouldn't have any new friends at all this summer and it can get pretty lonely around here, you know what I mean? It's like the whole world is away at camp or something."

Madison sighed again. The embarrassment of the previous seven minutes and twelve seconds started to wear off.

Fiona was pretty *and* she was so nice.

Fiona was even a little lonely.

Was Fiona Waters just like Madison Finn?

They cruised around the sweater racks and Fiona picked out a speckled blue cardigan while Madison grabbed an orange sweater set. In the blink of an eye a day of shopping was reduced to good-byes, the exchange of phone numbers and e-mail addresses, and a word or two about junior high jitters.

"So I'll see ya!" Fiona said as she walked out of the store with her mom.

Madison grinned. She wasn't so afraid to smile up close anymore.

On their way out of the mall, Madison and her mom stopped for banana splits. A little hot fudge goes a long way, especially when you've been shopping all day. Just the thought of seventh grade made Madison crave sweets. She knew that meant risking a zit, but today it was a risk she was willing to take.

In between bites Mom asked, "So who was that

girl you were talking to in the store?"

"I met her when I was trying stuff on." Madison volunteered the details of the dressing-room collision and Fiona and her twin brother and whatever else she could remember. "They live on Ridge Road."

"You know, Olga told me a new family had moved into the old Martin house." Olga was a real-estate broker friend who kept Mom in the neighborhood gossip loop. "Was she nice?" Mom asked.

"She's *really* nice, Mom. Is that weird?" Madison answered her own question. "Well, I'm a weird magnet, so it all makes sense."

"You are *not* weird, honey! You're perfect," Mom said. "I'm sure Fiona is going to be a wonderful new friend. That's how things happen, when you least expect them."

When they got home, Madison checked her e-mail right away. It *was* the day of surprises, after all. She had mail.

```
From: Eggaway
To: MadFinn
Subject: hi
Date: Wed, 23 Aug 3:21 PM
```
Hey Madison, whassup? Hey computer camp rocks so much I don't want 2come back 2 stupid Far Hills! i cant believe 7th grade is here in like a min. Hey anyway I miss yor stupid dog Phin. LOL!!! Is he still

FAT? I think you and me should defniteley take that cmpter class together in school by thewaynow that you have this ok talk L8R. Drew says hi BTW. Write back BYE!!!

Madison smiled. Egg was one of her best friends in the entire universe and she really missed him—*and* his stupid spelling mistakes. He didn't care about letters much; he was more of a numbers kind of guy. She liked that, of course. The funniest thing about Egg was how he had gotten his nickname. He didn't get it because he was a brain, although he *was*. When he was six, Egg got hit by a raw egg on Halloween. (He had the scar to prove it.) Egg's "real" name was Walter Emilio Diaz.

Madison clicked on REPLY.

From: MadFinn
To: Eggaway
Subject: Re:hi
Date: Wed, 23 Aug 5:05 PM
Egg it is sooooo good to hear from you!!!

How is computer camp? Do you have any other new friends? How is Drew? What else is new? I am here in Far Hills by myself (with Phin and Mom).

When are you coming home? Aimee is
coming back next week. I hope I see
you soon! TTFN

**Madison clicked SEND, smiling. She hoped her
friend missed her just as much as she missed him.
The next e-mail was from Dad.**

From: jefffinn
To: MadFinn
Subject: I'M COMING HOME!
Date: Wed, 23 Aug 4:40 PM
Hey sweetheart.

I am coming back begin. next wk.
Let's dinner?

I'll make you good food! Tell your
mother. I will call w/dates.

I love you, Daddy

p.s. got you a present! Call me
xoxoxo ;>)

**Madison grinned at the little hugs and kisses and
the winky symbol. Daddy always sent those.
No more mail. Madison looked at her list of files.
She opened the Fiona file.**

So does this mean the stars are aligned
for me? Two meetings out of the blue with

the new girl. I believe in coincidences.

I wish I had hair like hers, it is so shiny even in those braids. She just moved here from California and I think she looks a little like a model actually. I don't know. She has eyes that are a smoky green color and that is why I think she looks like a model. She was really nice to me even though I was acting so bizarre.

I hope she doesn't think I am the biggest loser for trying to run away this morning or for having like nothing interesting to say. I helped her pick out clothes for school. She actually asked me my opinion. No one ever does that.

I guess the reason I am acting all worried is because deep down I would like her to be my friend.

The moment Madison wrote the words "deep down I would like her to be my friend," she started over-thinking.

Dad always teased Madison about "over-thoughts." She would get one idea and then think about it over and over and over until she was completely muddled. Madison couldn't believe how much missing her friends was messing with her head. Egg was coming back soon. Aimee was coming home soon. She had to get ready to go back to everything the way it was before the summer started.

Now she had one guilty over-thought that would not go away.

If I want to be friends with someone new, does that mean that there's something wrong with me and my old friends?

Dad's voice echoed, "Don't over-think it, honey. Just let things be."
But it was too late.
Madison Finn had already way over-*thunk*.

Madison bolted up in bed. She was in the middle of a hazy, crazy nightmare about ice cream, orange sweater sets, and school. She was walking into the Far Hills auditorium followed by a hundred drooling pugs and tree frogs all barking and croaking the same thing because in this dream, Madison could understand the language of animals, of course.

"Rowroo! Ribbut!" This meant: keep away from Madison Finn!

Madison knew she had a good imagination, but this was ridiculous. She turned on her laptop. The monitor glowed in the half-dark of her bedroom.

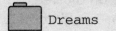 Dreams

I'm being chased by Phin clones and tree frogs like the ones Mom and I saw in Brazil! Maybe I shouldn't have had those cookies before bed? Mom told me I could get weird thoughts from sweet stuff too close to bedtime.

I think I am definitely weird.

Who dreams about dogs and frogs?

"Don't over-think it, honey. Just—"

Madison decided to "let things be" in an early morning bubbly tub. Mom had all these cool aromatherapy bubble baths and Madison loved the way they made the room and her skin smell. She couldn't believe that there had been a time in third grade when she didn't want to take a bath or wash her hair. Things had really changed since then.

Madison looked down in the bath water and traced the shape of her own body. Her shape was changing a lot these days, too—and it felt weird. Her hips were bigger. She grabbed at the fleshy parts of herself to see if they'd grown or shrunk.

Madison rubbed her hand across her shin. It was fuzzy. Had it always been this way?

"Good morning," Mom said all of a sudden, kicking open the bathroom door unannounced, arms full of warm towels from the dryer. "Mmmmm. Doesn't it smell nice in here?"

"Mom, I am so hairy!" Madison blurted out.

"Did you say *hairy*?" Mom couldn't help but chuckle.

"Yes, hairy. Right here. On my legs." Madison rubbed her calf. "I always knew I had little hairs but I never noticed how much they were growing before now and look! I'm as *furry* as Phin, Mom."

"No you're not!" Mom smiled. "Honey, human beings have hair on their legs and that's just the way it goes. We've talked about shaving before. It's not *disgusting*, it just is. I guess maybe we need to get you a razor."

"Mom, I'm not ready to shave!"

"Okay, girlie, stay hairy then," Mom joked.

Madison was over-thinking again—about razors and shaving and being hairy forever and ever and to infinity. Who else did Madison know who shaved her legs?

Mom did most of the time.

Aimee had also started shaving just last year, but she was blond, so you could barely see the hair anyway.

Madison wondered if Fiona had to shave.

"Okay, okay, give me the razor," Madison decided at last.

Mom pulled out one of her disposable plastic razors and a tube of aloe cream. "I promise it won't hurt, honey bear."

First, Mom demonstrated on herself. Then she shaved a strip on Maddie's leg.

Finally, Madison tried on herself, real slow. She only nicked herself twice, which Mom said was pretty good. Soon enough the leg fuzz was gone and little hairs were dancing on top of the bath water.

"Ewwwch! It stings," Madison said, dunking her legs back in the tub.

"Only for a moment," Mom sighed. "My big girl."

Madison rolled her eyes. "Yeah, Mom, whatever. I'm twelve, remember? You can cut out all that sappy stuff, all right?"

"Well, I'll let you finish up." She kissed the top of Maddie's wet head.

"Yeah, can you go now?" Madison asked. "Like *NOW*."

"Oh!" She pulled something out of her pocket. "I almost forgot. You got a letter yesterday."

Mom dropped an envelope on the counter, winked, and shut the bathroom door.

There on the sinktop was a letter written on deep-sea-blue stationery, Aimee's favorite color. The silver ink on the envelope was already a little smudged from water on the counter, so Madison ripped it open right away. It felt like opening her arms for a giant hug.

Dear Maddie . . .

Oh I miss you soooooo much!!!!! How are you doing at home? I am sorry that I haven't really

31

written except like twice this summer but I have been dancing every single day and I am sooooooo tired. I actually got on pointe last week, can you BELIEVE it??? The teacher says that the toe shoes will probably make our toes ache and bleed sometimes which is awful, but I want to be a dancer so I better just deal with that.

I miss you! Did I say that already? You would love camp sooooo much, Maddie, I know you would. There are the coolest people here. Of course it is a dance camp of all kinds so there are not just ballet dancers but jazz and tap too. Everyone eats together and we do other stuff like swimming and arts and crafts and have camp nights where we sing songs and tell stories and roast marshmallows and sometimes go on skunk patrol which is this game we play and oh it is the best ever. Did I say I MISS YOU??? I do.

I have made so many new friends too and I just know you would love them. This one girl Sasha is from Russia originally and she lives in New York City. She is so cool and I think we might see each other when I get back. Then there is this other girl Chelsea and she

Aimee had only been gone a month and already she

was making new best friends? Madison kept reading.

is TOTALLY cool, she's 15 and she has a tattoo! Can you believe that?

So the funnest part of the whole camp for me is this one counselor named Josh. OK, he is to die! He is such a total hottie. He teaches modern dance and I think he looks like he should be a movie star or something. Seriously!

Anyway, I decided for the last week of camp I am going to take his lessons as a dance elective and that way I get to see him <u>like every single day</u>. I know that he is like way, way older than me but I don't even care he is so, so cute!!! Can you imagine going out with someone like that? I think about him all the time. Sometimes I wish I was 16 already. I am like in love with him. Is that possible???? Maybe something could happen, you never know.

Well, I just wanted you to know that I miss you and all that. I will be back home a couple of days before school starts and I will call you like the very second I get home. Have you heard from Egg? I miss him too even if he is a total pain in the butt. I am so glad we are <u>finally</u> starting 7th grade. Now I can qualify to be in the Far Hills Junior High Dance Troupe and that is something I have wanted forever.

How are your Mom and Dad and the snuggly puggly?

Okay, I'm going now. I have Josh's class this afternoon and I am so psyched!!! I want to look just right and act just right, right?

Bye!!! I luv you more than ice cream!

Luv, Aimee

P.S. As soon as I get home I will call you I promise!

While Madison couldn't deal with the hives of change, Aimee was in a huge rush to change everything. How could she be crushing on a camp counselor? Madison hadn't even given boys too much thought lately. They all seemed pretty stupid and dorky to her.

"Camp must change the way you think about stuff," Madison mused, and put the letter in her desk for safekeeping. She'd scan it into her Aimee file later.

"Maaaaaadison," Mom suddenly screeched from downstairs. "Are you still in the bathroom? Get moving, I need your help."

Mom always needed something. Ever since Dad moved out, Mom needed help cleaning, gardening, organizing, and all that. She needed help so she could get her own film work done. Whenever Mom went away on an overnight business trip she said, "I need your help holding down the fort, honey."

Whenever Mom was going to be gone for more than a few days, she said, "I need your help while I'm gone. I want you be good for the Gillespies," or whomever Madison was staying with during that trip.

The truth was, "help" was Madison's real middle name.

Madison Francesca *Help* Finn.

"In a minute, Mom!" Madison screamed back. Of course, she should have said "In twenty-six minutes, Mom," because that was how long it took Madison to actually get downstairs. But once they started cleaning up, the two of them accomplished a lot. She and Mom washed the kitchen floor and repotted some of Mom's orchids.

After the general house "summer cleaning" was done, Mom raised her eyebrows and in her best Wicked Witch from *The Wizard of Oz* voice, said, "Weeeell, my pretty . . . now it's time to clean your ROOM!"

Officially, she didn't bug Madison about cleaning her bedroom until the laundry factor got out of control. Unfortunately, today was that day. Madison's hamper was overflowing onto the floor and Mom had seen it. Mom had a mantra: Clean up your mess, say bye-bye to stress.

"Madison, my pretty," Mom whined like the Wicked Witch again. "Go pick up your room now before I lock you up in it forever!"

Mom was such a weirdo sometimes. That's where Madison got her weirdness—definitely.

All joking aside, Madison was happy to straighten up the piles of clothes and books and magazine clippings in her bedroom. After an hour or two, she'd even finished a collage card for Aimee.

Inspired by Aimee's letter, she pasted a picture of some cute guy on the front of the card and drew a big arrow with the words *Josh & Aimee 4-Ever*. She even found a clipping of some ballerina that made it look better and more Aimee-like, too.

Madison wondered what Josh *really* looked like. She assumed he must be cute, because the cute boys always liked Aimee best.

Finally, Madison signed the card, "I love you more than chocolate shakes, Maddie." They always signed letters with stuff that way. One day back in fourth grade, when they were on the swing set in Aimee's backyard, they had decided to be best friends forever and to love each other forever more than absolutely anything else. That "anything" included ice cream and chocolate shakes, of course. Once Aimee had even sent Madison a card that said, "I luv you like a sister." That meant a lot.

Later on, Madison went online. She'd cleaned, she'd organized, and now she figured it was a good time to check out bigfishbowl.com again.

On the home page, Madison scanned the list of names currently logged onto bigfishbowl.com. A bigfishbowl.com moderator (also known as Shark) led off the list. (The sites were required to have some Web police person who tried to keep people from cursing or saying nasty things to the other members.) This site prided itself in being super safe. Mom liked that—and so did Madison.

```
        Shark
      Cuteguy87
       Mystake
      Wuzupgrl
       PC_cake
     Bethiscool
      Imagoodie
      Peacefish
       HelPer
      Bigwheels
```

Bigwheels?

Madison couldn't believe it. Her "only the lonely" chat buddy was somewhere on the site—right now. That meant Madison could IM her. IM stood for Insta-message. It was like having a live conversation on the computer.

```
<MadFinn>: heybigwheels remember me
   only the
<MadFinn>: lonely?
```

In less than ten seconds, a message back popped up.

```
<Bigwheels>: Hello!!! Oh WOW its u!
   2K4W!! HIG?
<MadFinn>: 2K4W? HIG?
<Bigwheels>: 2 kool 4 words! Howz
   It Going? LOL
<MadFinn>: ya LOL
<MadFinn>: I thought about what u
   said B4 about being alone I am
   alone a lot too
<Bigwheels>: when does your school
   start????
<MadFinn>: next week and my friend
   is comin home
<Bigwheels>: I cantbelieve u looked
   me up sooo KOOL
<MadFinn>: ;>) I WANNA BE KEYPALS
   OR WHATEVER oops sorry I hit
capslock
<Bigwheels>: ok em me it's just
   bigwheels@email
<MadFinn>: madfinn@email too
<Bigwheels>: hey BRB
<MadFinn>: Hello??
<MadFinn>: Are you AFK?
```

BRB meant "be right back."
AFK meant "away from keyboard."
Madison had learned a lot of online lingo from Egg.
But Bigwheels stayed away for longer than BRB.
She was AFK for at least five minutes! Madison was
forced to log off again.

That night, after Mom's takeout sushi supper, Madison returned to her file.

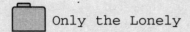 Only the Lonely

Alone once again. Big surprise. This will be the file that gets filled the fastest, no doubt.

Dad called again. He thinks he might be coming home a lot later than he said in his e-mail and he was checking to make sure we were on for dinner as soon as he got back. He doesn't want me to feel left out but he sure sounded so far away. Then again, everyone feels far away to me these days. I guess Dad's new Internet company start-up is going well, though. He has his fingers in a lot of different pies; that's what Mom always says. He calls himself an entrepreneur (that is a huge word, I had to look it up to spell it!). Maybe Dad can help me find Bigwheels online?

I couldn't believe that Mom and I had sushi tonight. It's a little more interesting than pizza even though I think raw fish is maybe the grossest thing on the entire planet except headcheese and pig's feet, which I saw at the butcher's once. I must admit that I did like the California roll sushi a teeny bit. It was just vegetables and rice and a little bit of seaweed, which wasn't so bad. But forget the tuna roll!!! That wasn't anything like

tuna from the cans (Mom lied) so I spit it
right out right away. Not even Phin the
animal garbage disposal would eat that!

If I don't like tuna rolls, does that
mean I am not an adventurous person? If I'm
not an adventurous person, does that mean
that I am going to be snubbed in junior
high as some kind of loser? If I am branded
as a loser, does that mean I'll be alone
forever?

For Madison, all over-thoughts led back to one
place: the lonely, looming doom of seventh grade. It
was less than two weeks away.

Madison wished she could see Fiona again.

She needed a real friend real fast.

They had swapped phone numbers, but who
would be the first to call?

Chapter 4

The next day, while Madison was taking a predictable walk around the block, something quite unpredictable happened.

Phin took a sharp corner, got loose, and ran full speed ahead, tongue wagging along with his curlicue tail.

Naturally, he was chasing a C-A-T.

"Stop! Phin!" Madison shouted, almost catching up with him. That's when she saw the car. Phin was on a one-way collision course with—

"STOOOOP! Phiiiiiiiiin!"

Someone in the car must have seen Madison darting down the street like a cartoon character, hands waving in the air. The car screeched to a stop.

Phin stopped too, collapsing at the curb.

"Are you okay? Phinnie?" Madison rushed over. He sputtered and sneezed, stunned by all the activity. He was probably mad that he'd missed the cat, too. Madison wrapped her arms around his furry body and guided him onto the sidewalk. He licked her hand.

The girl who had jumped out of the car rushed over, talking too fast. "Oh, Madison! Is he okay? Oh, my dad didn't see him. He just came out of nowhere—"

Madison looked up. "Fiona?"

"Is your doggy okay?"

"Phin's fine." Madison smiled.

By now Mr. Waters had pulled his car to the side of the street so the rest of the traffic could pass.

"Young lady, you have one lucky dog there," Mr. Waters said, as he also got out of the car. "I turned my head for a moment and—whammo—we almost hit the little guy. You just can't be too careful these days, can you? Hey there, little fella."

Phin wagged his tail, shaking his whole butt. He got excited around strangers. No one could have guessed that Phin just missed crashing into a car. He was loving all this attention.

"Dad, this is Madison. We just met the other day, actually. We're going to be in the same grade at Far Hills this fall."

Madison couldn't believe she was sitting on the

pavement, holding Phin and talking to Fiona and Mr. Waters. Now she *definitely* believed that some kind of cosmic forces were pulling her together with this new girl.

And now no one had to worry about who called whom first.

"Well, Miss Madison," Mr. Waters continued, "how about we give you and that pooch a lift back home? He's shaking like a leaf."

Fiona's Dad helped lift the dog into the back seat of the car.

Madison showed him the way home.

It took thirty seconds.

"What a pretty house," Fiona said as the car tires crunched up the gravel driveway.

"Thanks," Madison shrugged from the backseat.

"It was very nice meeting you, Miss Madison," said Mr. Waters in a very low voice. He sounded like Darth Vader's brother. "And you too, little doggy."

"Rowrooo!" Phin howled back.

Fiona called out cheerily from the car window as they pulled away, "Maybe we can hang out later? I don't really have any—well—it would be fun, do you think?"

"Do I think?" Madison laughed and then quickly added, "*Way* too much. Wanna hang tomorrow maybe?"

"Yeah! Come to my house around twelve," Fiona cried. "You know where I live! Bye!"

As the car made a turn onto the street, Mr. Waters honked his horn good-bye.

Madison hardly ate any dinner that night. Suddenly life had gotten interesting, or at least she hoped so. It was better than TV or bigfishbowl.com, and Phin even deserved some of the credit.

"What a good dog," Madison cooed at him that night when she went to bed. "I am sorry you almost got run over, Phinnie, but thanks to you I get to hang out with Fiona again."

The next day, Madison knocked on her new friend's door around lunchtime. She got there at twelve noon *exactly* because she didn't want to risk being late, early, or in between. It was twelve on the dot.

A boy answered the bell. He was at least a foot taller than Madison.

"Hey!" he grunted. "You here for Fiona?"

Madison guessed he was Fiona's twin brother, Chet, since they looked exactly the same. The only difference was that he had fuzz on his face, and was a lot taller.

Chet was just back from band camp and he was in a bad mood. He yelled upstairs for his sister and then flopped back onto the sofa in front of a giant TV set until Fiona came down the stairs a minute later.

"How was camp?" Madison asked.

"Camp is what it is," Chet said in a monotone.

Madison was certain this conversation was going nowhere. Thankfully, Fiona appeared.

"Madison! I am so glad you came! Do you wanna go for a walk and maybe get an ice-cream cone or something?"

They spent the next hour walking into the old town part of Far Hills, near the train station, past the ice cream Freeze Palace, of course; a discount shoe-repair place; a bakery; Wink's Pet Store; and some other places. Madison gave Fiona a neighborhood tour.

"I go to Wink's when I'm feeling bummed out," Madison admitted. "They have cool tropical fish and actually it's where I got Phin when he was just a baby. He's almost four now."

"I don't have any pets," said Fiona. "I'm so jealous of you. Phin is a total cutie. I love those snorty noses."

It was the beginning of a great week.

On the second day, Madison and Fiona went to Freeze Palace for two scoops of Raspberry Bliss, a new homemade flavor.

On the third day, they skipped the cones and bought an entire pint of Cherry Garcia at the store and sat on the Waterses' porch to eat it spoonful by yummy spoonful right out of the container. These days, for Madison and Fiona, life was just a bowl of Cherry Garcia.

Of course, day three wasn't all cherry ice cream.

That was the day when Madison saw a *very* different side of Chet Waters. He threw a fit at his sister. "You're such a mega-loser, Fi-moan-a!" he screeched. Madison thought at first he was a major crybaby, but then she realized that maybe he was just jealous because his sister had a new friend and he didn't. Maybe he was only the lonely, too?

Fiona was not as sympathetic. "My brother Chet is not lonely—he's just a load. Ever since he got home from camp, all he can do is play Age of Empires and pick on me. He won't even let me online when he's home."

"You go online?" asked Madison.

"Of course! I totally love computers. I gave you my e-mail, right?"

Madison made a mental note: send Fiona an e-mail soon. She didn't want Fiona to think she'd lost her address.

On the fourth day, Madison and Fiona went clog shopping, because clogs were comfortable and Madison loved them.

On the fifth day, they sat on Fiona's porch and made friendship bracelets from string.

On the sixth day, they went for a long bike ride and Madison met Fiona's mother.

Mrs. Waters kept insisting how thrilled Madison must be to be starting those junior high school years.

"Aren't you just overjoyed?" Mrs. Waters gushed.

Madison didn't really know how to answer that one.

On the one hand, of course she was excited about leaving middle school and starting a whole new life adventure with new friends and new teachers and new after-school activities. On the other hand, she was "run for the hills and don't look back" *terrified*. She was afraid of getting lost on the first day of school. She was afraid of getting swallowed up by all the popular people and trapped in study hall with all the geeks.

Time was flying and suddenly she had this strange feeling like she didn't want the summer to end. Had Fiona changed everything?

"Overjoyed." Madison finally answered Mrs. Waters with middle-of-the-road enthusiasm. "I guess."

And on the seventh and final day of the week, Madison Finn and Fiona Waters had their best afternoon ever together. That was the day when Madison spent the entire day hanging out in Fiona's bedroom. She'd seen it before, of course, but not for such a long time. Madison was learning a few of Fiona's secrets.

Fiona was a collector, too. Madison noticed that right away. Up on a top shelf in Fiona's room, Madison saw a far-out, enormous collection of Beanies.

"I'm really over them," Fiona had to admit, even

though they were dripping off the shelves. "Except for Halo and maybe Mooch, I don't like any of them anymore. I guess I'll just put them in the attic or something."

"You must have like a thousand animals here," Madison said.

"One hundred and fourteen, and they all have tag protectors, too." Fiona said. "They're pretty stupid, though, right? Mom said we should sell them on eBay, but I don't wanna do that yet."

Elsewhere in her room, Fiona had tacked up all sorts of postcards and pictures on a piece of flowered fabric that hung over her bed. Madison leaned in to read some of the cartoons. She pointed to one photo in the center. It showed Fiona and a red-headed girl. They were standing by the ocean.

"What beach is this?" Madison asked. "Who is that?"

"Pacific Ocean, Debbie," Fiona said. She sounded a little sad.

Debbie was Fiona's best friend from where the Waters family used to live in Los Gatos, California. Unfortunately, Fiona's parents only let her call Debbie on weekends, because it was too expensive to talk at other times.

Fiona knew all about Aimee being at ballet camp, too. Madison told her about Egg at computer camp; about Mom and Dad's divorce; about hating chunky peanut butter; and about loving romantic movies on cable. So far *Love Story* was the top flick on Madison's list. It was an old movie from the '70s that was really romantic *and* really sad. After all, if something made you cry, that meant it was meaningful.

Fiona agreed. In fact, Madison and Fiona seemed to agree on most things.

"Don't you hate it when you miss someone and then you get, like, so bored? Do you know what I mean?"

Madison knew *exactly* what Fiona meant.

"And Mom tells me to just get over it and she and Dad don't understand *anything*," Madison added. "They forgot what it's like to be twelve—"

"Almost thirteen!" Fiona laughed.

They were practically finishing each other's sentences.

On the walk home from Fiona's, Madison's mind buzzed a mile a minute: new friends, new school, new EVERYTHING.

Madison powered up her laptop as soon as she got home.

 Fiona

Can new friends swoop in and take the place of old friends? I don't miss Aimee and Egg as much as I did a week ago. I don't even miss Dad that much, even though it's been a month since I saw him.

```
    Okay, I miss Dad but only a little bit
and only because you're supposed to miss
your parents, right?
    I'm happier than happy about almost
every little thing this week, even walking
Phinnie, and that is just plain BIZARRO. I
haven't even been back into these files in
almost
```

As she thought about what to type in next, Madison realized a very important thing. Her mailbox was blinking.

She hadn't even been back into these files in almost *three* days.

Madison had ten e-mails, but of course eight of them were stupid spam or ads or unimportant chain letters. But she had two real e-mails.

The first one was from her new keypal. She was beginning to think Bigwheels and MadFinn would really stay K4E (Keypals 4 Ever).

```
From: Bigwheels
To: MadFinn
Subject: I'M ALIVE ARE U?
Date: Sunday 27 Aug 4:42 PM
I hope you aren't MAD! My uncle
finally got me a stupid modem that
works right. That is why I kept
getting disconnected for the last
week so I O U an apology. I really
did like meeting you in the
```

bigfishbowl. Maybe we can be keypals after all?

BTW I'm in 7th grade now too. We started already though because I think schools start earlier out west and down south or something like that.

Write back soon or else!
Yours till the butter flies,
Bigwheels

The second one was from her old school pal.

From: Eggaway
To: MadFinn
Subject: hi
Date: Wed 30 Aug 10:01 AM

Hey Madison, where r u? I am now at my gramp's lake house. I am totaly bored. Did you see that new movie Tidal Wave? Say hi to your Mom and dad. See u SOON! I'm leaving tomroow then back in Far Hills on Friday.
p.s. oh yeah does Aim have a bf at camp? She wrote me this queer lettr about some dude. Wuzup?
p.p.s. don't wrtie back i will see you SOON
p.p.p.s. Drew says hi.

Madison was happier than happy that she'd finally heard from her online chat buddy *and* that Egg was on his way home Friday.

Now Aimee would be back on Sunday and then the three of them would be together again and then school would be starting and they'd be best friends all over again just like last year.

Madison opened a file.

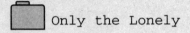 Only the Lonely

Just when you think change is like the worst thing ever, it turns into a good thing all of a sudden.

Mom and I are getting along good for a change (considering the fact that we argued through most of sixth grade).

Even Daddy is coming home soon. Well, not to *this* home exactly, but he's coming back to his loft in downtown Far Hills.

The stupid cliché is so true. There are gold linings in almost every cloud. Or silver linings, whatever. I just know that things are good at this very moment.

I'm not totally alone anymore.

Madison read the words on her screen. For the first time all summer she was happier than happy.

Chapter 5

Madison looked at the *Simpsons* calendar Mom had stuck up on the fridge. Exactly four days from today junior high was starting. Madison had drawn a giant red circle around the date: September 5.

Madison dialed Fiona's number, but hung up right away. She decided it was Fiona's turn to call her instead. She didn't want to appear like a clingy friend, after all.

Now that Madison was going to be a seventh grader, things like when-to-call etiquette had taken on greater importance. Aimee had always been the one who paid attention to stuff like that, but Madison was trying to figure it out on her own now.

Distractedly, Madison flipped through a copy of a

teen magazine Mom had picked up at the super-market checkout, staring at the pictures of girls in mini-skirts and super-high platform shoes. How did they stand in those for more than five seconds? How did they bend over?

All the models were wearing glitter makeup and gobs of lip gloss. Madison thought about wearing lip gloss on her lips. Strawberry-Kiwi Smooch was the best flavor and it tasted like candy when you chewed it off. Madison liked Root Beer flavor, too, of course, but that was harder to find.

She wondered if boys liked the way lip gloss tasted when they kissed a girl. Did lip gloss flavor taste different if you chewed if off someone else's lips? Madison had never kissed anyone, so she didn't know from personal experience.

Who else wore lip gloss? Aimee didn't. She hated makeup of all kinds. (Her family, including all four older brothers and their basset hound Blossom, were into granola and all-natural *everything*.)

Did Fiona wear lip gloss? Madison couldn't remember. Had Fiona ever *kissed* someone (besides her parents, of course)? Madison would have to ask her about that.

A few pages after the platforms and lip gloss spread, Madison randomly opened up to a quiz titled "Are You Friends to the End?" She grabbed her favorite orange pen, the one with a Florida navel orange–shaped eraser on top.

1. You have a big algebra test and you haven't even cracked open a book! The night before the test you call your best friends and ask them:
   a) If you can sit nearby and cheat off their test the next day!
   b) To come right over and help you cram for the exam!
   c) If they will help you make up an excuse so you don't have to take the test!

Madison couldn't imagine who would ever pick a) or admit to picking a). She didn't cheat. In fact the entire quiz seemed stupid and obvious. It wasn't exactly the kind of "are you friends?" quiz Madison had hoped for. She was looking for some concrete advice. She also wouldn't make excuses as c) suggested, so Madison selected b).

2. Your mom grounds you and you're stuck at home on the night of the coolest party of the year. You:
   a) Call your friend and beg her to blow off the party and stay with you instead.
   b) Call your friend and wish her a good time at the party! You can't wait to hear all the details!
   c) Call your friend and cry into the phone. Your friend will listen to anything.

Madison selected b) again. She could tell already how this quiz was turning out. She was a "b)" type, which probably meant something like: honest, caring, straightforward, and all that. Sometimes (like right in the middle of this quiz) Madison turned into the "nice" friend. She was sick of that. Sometimes she wanted to be "wild" or "spontaneous" or even a little outrageous. She knew she *must* have those qualities in her somewhere, even though she was the person who always got too embarrassed to even *speak* and usually ran as far away as possible when confronted with any kind of conflict whatsoever.

"Maybe seventh grade will be when I finally take a few more chances," she said hopefully, moving to the next question.

3. Your best friend is away at camp, and you're so bored! Then you meet a new friend in your neighborhood and you start hanging out. Do you:

Madison reread the question *slowly*. What were her choices?

a) Kick your best friend to the curb!
   There's a new friend in town!
b) Tell the new friend that you like her
   but you already have a "best" friend.
c) Try to see if the two friends might like
   each other so you can be a trio instead
   of two against one.

Madison started to over-think *every* answer. This was a question pulled from the pages of her life.

What really would happen when Aimee did get back? What would happen once school started? What if Fiona and Aimee hated each other?

Answer a) was definitely out. Madison didn't have a mean bone in her body, and she wouldn't kick anyone to any curb.

Was c) was the right response? Madison wasn't sure.

She played it safe and circled b). After all, she told herself, she and Aimee had been best friends forever and *that* was that. You can have a lot of different friends but you only have one really, truly, madly, deeply, true-blue friend. That was Aimee Anne Gillespie, not Fiona Waters. Not yet.

Madison's head hurt from thinking so much, so she went online to check her e-mail again. This e-mail checking was addictive!

Today the list was longer than usual but it wasn't all friends. dELiA's clothing was having a sale on platform shoes Madison would never, ever wear. Some Joke-A-Day service addressed their message to Attn: Mr. Madison Funn. She deleted them both.

Madison decided to send a few e-mails instead of just sitting around waiting for everyone to write her. She dashed off a note to Dad and sent Egg an e-mail asking how camp was just to annoy him (because of course, camp was O-V-E-R). Finally, she started a note back to Bigwheels. She hadn't written her terrific bigfishbowl.com friend an "official" e-mail yet. Bigwheels seemed pretty hip. Maybe she had some friendly advice to share?

```
From: MadFinn
To: Bigwheels
Subject: me with a question
Date: Fri 1 Sept 10:41 AM
Hello? I hope this is the right
e-mail address. Thanks for your
message the other day. I think this
whole keypals thing is a good
thing.

Okay so I'm having a not-so-great
day so maybe you can cheer me up? I
hope so.

The funniest thing about keypals is
that for some reason I feel like I
could tell you anything. Do you
feel that? You really have to know
me to know how incredible that is
because I am the kind of person
who turns beet red and can't form
complete sentences when I'm
embarrassed. But the jitters go away
on e-mail. Like now. Okay, so what
else do I wanna say?
```

What is school like 4 u Washington?
Why do they start so early there?

If you can believe it I have no
idea what my school is even like
b/c I have only seen it from the
outside. I told you it's Junior
High. How do you stop yourself from
being so nervous about all the new
school things? Do you do something?
Do you have any pets? Do you have
any brothers or sisters? Do you
believe in God?

I guess I have a lot of
questions. You don't have to answer
any of these, of course, but it
would be cool if you did. I guess
if we're going to be keypals we
should be honest with each other.

Yours till the chocolate chips,
MadFinn

p.s. write back or else!!!

**As Madison finished her e-mail, an IM box
popped up on her screen.**

Insta-message to Madfinn
<<Emily114>>: Wanna talk?

Madison didn't recognize the screen name. It was some random person online. Both her Mom and Dad told her never to respond to people she didn't know. Madison deleted the dialogue box and then clicked offline.

Right after she closed down her computer, the phone rang. Madison nearly jumped out of her skin. Madison did the phone call math inside her head. This call was definitely from Fiona.

She had *said* she would call, after all.

"Got it, Mom!" Madison yelled, catching it on the fourth ring, gasping into the receiver, "Hello?"

"Ma-di-son?" a boy's voice taunted.

That wasn't Fiona. That was . . .

"Egg!" Madison exclaimed, happy to hear his voice but unable to totally mask her disappointment. She'd been crossing her fingers for Fiona.

"Whassup!?! I am back as of like twenty minutes ago thanks to my dad busting the speed limit all the way from Vermont and we are so hanging out today! Yes we are, you and me and—"

"Egg?" Madison tried to get a word in. "Why don't—"

"Hey, hey, hey! Maddie, you didn't say anything about my e-mails! Did you get my e-mails? I have so much to tell you and I have the coolest new thing to show you and—"

"Egg? Why don't you just come over!" Madison barked.

"Okay," Egg barked back.

She threw herself across the living room sofa. From where she was draped, she could see the kitchen stove's digital clock readout: 11:11. She made a wish on the numbers. (When four ones lined up like that, your wish was supposed to come true, or at least that's what Egg's older sister Mariah always said.) Madison wished Fiona would just call already.

"Hey, Mom, did anyone call this morning?" Madison cried out.

"The phone just rang, dear, didn't you pick it up?"

"No, like maybe when I was asleep late and you just forgot to tell me?"

"No, honey. No one called. Check the caller ID."

Now the clock said 11:14. Madison had spent the entire morning playing the waiting game.

The doorbell rang and Madison jumped.

How would she greet Egg? A smack on the *head*? He deserved it! She opened the door, laughing.

"Fiona?"

Fiona rocked from foot to foot, hands in her cargo pants pockets. Madison could see Mr. and Mrs. Waters and even Chet waiting out in the car so she quickly used the door as a shield. She didn't feel like waving or smiling or dealing with parents in any way right now.

"Oh, Madison, I'm sorry to just show up like this,"

Fiona said. "I forgot to tell you about my mom taking me and Chet over to the mall again today to get some more clothes for school. I told her you and I said we'd hang out today since I've never been over to your house, but I really have to go shopping again because she said so."

"Okay," Madison said, a little numb from the surprise.

"But you can come along too, if you want. She said that was okay too. Do you wanna?"

Madison looked at her feet. "Fiona, I look awful in my sweats."

"That's okay. We can wait for you to change. Come on . . ."

"W-w-well . . ."

"It'll be so much fun," Fiona blurted again, "even if my pain-in-the-butt brother does have to come along."

"W-w-well . . ." Madison said again, "the truth is that I can't."

"Oh," Fiona seemed genuinely disappointed. "Oh, well. Are you sure?"

"It's just that one of my friends, Egg, is back from camp and he's coming over like right now and—I can't. Look, I'm really sorry."

"Oh, well, I'll call you later, maybe?"

"That would be cool. Let's talk later."

"You're sure you can't come?"

"Sorry." Madison shook her head.

"Okay, I'll call you!" Fiona bounced down the stairs and across Madison's lawn into her family's car. She actually looked like she was running away. Of course Madison knew she wasn't running away. *Madison* was the only one who ran away from things.

" 'Bye!" Madison cried out after her, a little too late.

Mr. Waters honked the horn good-bye. The car pulled away. Madison walked back inside and flopped back onto the sofa.

"Is Fiona mad at me?" she wondered aloud.

Phin just snored.

She suddenly felt very alone again.

Chapter 6

"Surprise!"

Egg screeched and made a ridiculous piggy face at Madison. He did this gross thing where he pushed his nose up so his nostrils looked like pig nostrils and then he made this awful sucking noise against his top teeth.

"I'm baaaaaack!" he yelped.

Madison couldn't help but giggle. "Egg! You doof! You freaked me out."

Egg smacked her shoulder with a loud *Slap!* "You're a doof, DOOF!"

He bounded inside and quickly whipped off his backpack.

"Maddie there is the coolest thing ever invented

I have to show you right now! Look at this—"

Mom walked into the living room at that exact moment.

"Well, Walter! Welcome home! You look like you had a good time at camp. You also look taller."

Egg was panting like Phin at this point, hot from the summer heat. Madison noticed that he was taller and had even more freckles than usual.

"Yeah, Mrs. Finn," Egg said. "Grew two and a half inches. Lost four pounds. Camp was okay. At least I didn't get picked on or anything. It was a whole bunch of us computer-heads. What's up with you?"

"You are such a major computer EGG-head, Egg!" Madison laughed.

"Am not!" he snapped back.

"Are too!" she retorted.

"Am not!" he snapped back again.

"Well, it's nice to see you again, Walter. Don't get into any trouble. No fighting." Madison's Mom cautioned with a big grin. "I mean it."

"Mom, why would we get into a fight? I haven't seen Egg in forever!"

Egg hurriedly unzipped his backpack. Phin was sniffing around the varnished wood floor where he'd put it down.

"Is that some kind of calculator?" Madison asked when he pulled out his latest toy.

"No, no, it's not a calculator, it's like this miniature computer. Here, look, look at how cool this is."

He showed it to Madison, who oohed and aahed.

"This is way cool," she said.

Egg patted Phin's head a little too hard. "Yeah, yeah, get lost, doggy."

"Hey! Don't talk to Phinnie that way! Come here, Phin."

Egg teased, "He is still fat! Ha-ha-ha! Ugly pugly!"

"Cut it out." Madison bonked the top of Egg's head. Then she punched a few buttons on his computer. "This really is very cool, *Walter*."

Madison was glad to have Egg back home, even if he teased her. She could, after all, tease him right back. That's what friends were for.

He showed Madison how he'd downloaded an entire copy of some kids' science encyclopedia off the Internet.

"Why would you do that?" she asked.

"Uh, I dunno. Because I could?"

Madison wanted to tell Egg about her new computer, too, but at that moment Mom walked back into the room with a tray of toasted blueberry Pop-Tarts and Egg's eyes got as big as saucers.

Egg was easily distracted by TV, computers, and *any* kind of food.

"Pop-Tarts! Mrs. Finn, you are like the best cook ever!" Egg exclaimed.

Madison couldn't believe anyone would call her mother the best cook ever.

Egg had eaten two tarts before he noticed what time it was. "It's 11:34! Hey Maddie, you still have cable? Wrestling is on now! I missed WWF so much when I was at camp. Madison, can we put it on?"

This was predictable too: Egg wanted to watch wrestling every time he came over. The Diaz family didn't believe in cable television. They stuck to broadcast channels only. They had barely even managed to put an antenna on the roof.

So Madison flicked on the tube. Egg beamed.

"I'm going upstairs to change, okay?" Madison said.

"Huh? Yeah. Okay." Egg's eyes were fixed on the screen.

A whole summer had gone by, and Egg was still a wrestling freak! Madison thought shows like *RAW* were so dumb, but she couldn't exactly tell Egg that. What was the point to wrestling? It was so fake. She pulled on a pair of shorts and an orange halter top and went back downstairs.

Egg was *still* in a TV coma. Madison seriously began to question her motives in ditching Fiona and keeping the plans with Egg.

"The Rock is so cool! Stone Cold Steve—WOW! Look at them. This is AWESOME," Egg cried out, engrossed by the action. "Check that OUT, Madison!"

Madison squirmed into her seat. She and Egg hadn't seen each other in over a month, and already things were back to the way they had been before. *Why* was that? They were doing that hanging-out-but-not-really-hanging-out thing that they'd been doing since Miss Jeremiah's kindergarten class.

Spending an afternoon with Egg almost always meant doing what Egg wanted. Boy stuff.

Madison picked up Phin and put him onto her lap. "Good dog," she cooed into his ear. It twitched. Pugs have sensitive ears.

"Look at that! Look at that!" Egg shrieked. He was shouting nonstop, sitting on the edge of Madison's sofa, eyes glazed over. "Go, go, slam him! Awwww!"

Phin jumped off Madison's lap and scurried into the other room. Even Phin didn't want to put up with *this*.

Madison had one of her over-thoughts.

Here she was, having spent the past few days believing she'd developed an allergy to change, believing that her entire universe was in a state of constant flux, but right here and now she realized that she was experiencing a hundred-percent "allergy-free" moment.

I guess there really are some things that never change, Madison thought.

Here she was, sitting in her living room with one of her oldest, best-est pals, watching the same show as always, saying the same things she and he always said, eating the same snack foods she and he always ate. Even Phin was bored; he'd already left the room.

"Hey, Egg, do you mind if I go up to my room for a minute?" Madison interrupted his wrestling show.

"What? Yeah. Sure." Egg was so distracted.

"Just come up when it's over." Madison said and walked upstairs. It was better this way.

 Egg

Wrestling is the stupidest thing on the planet and I am so glad that Fiona is not a wrestling fan. At least, there were no wrestling posters hanging in her room anywhere. I wonder if Chet is a wrestling fan?

Rude Awakening: Be careful what you wish for. I wished for Egg and now I'm just not sure I feel like hanging around to do *this*. I don't feel like watching *RAW*, Egg! Ha ha. Very funny.

Why is it when people go away for the summer that you remember friends differently than they really and truly are? Like Egg, for example. Why are things always better when

"You got a new computer!" Egg sneaked up behind Madison. "How much memory you got?"

"I remember plenty of things," she quipped.

"Ha, ha—very funny," Egg made a face and sat down next to her.

"Hey!" she covered up the computer. "Egg, this is private."

Egg made a face. "I don't care what you're doing. Come on and just close your stupid files. Let's go online and play a game. I hear there are download-able versions of some great arcade games like Space Invaders or Frogger. You'll love it. Those are so easy."

"But I'm in the middle of something, Egg."

"Come on, wrestling's over. I'm bored. Let's go online. Hey, I know this awesome gaming site. Let's go," he said, leaning over to type in the Web address. "We could play *Who Wants to be a Millionaire* or they also have this wrestling game that is so cool."

"Wrestling? I don't think so."

"Please?" Egg begged.

"No way."

"Oh, Madison, pretty please with sugar and cherries and a bucket of whipped cream on top . . . please?"

"Oh, whatever," Madison sighed, half smiling at his pathetic gestures. "What's the Web address?"

He'd only been over for an hour, and already Madison wondered what it was that she had missed about Egg.

He was rude and he was obsessed with stupid wrestling! A game site with a *wrestling* game? Madison rolled her eyes.

Egg found the site. "Yeah! Okay, I'm gonna be The Undertaker. Who do you want to be? Lemme just download this and enter my password. . . ."

Egg wanted to be The Undertaker.

Madison wanted to be . . . *anywhere but here!*

She used to think Egg's computer games were fun. Now, they seemed so stupid.

"Egg, are you ready to start seventh grade?" Madison asked while he was punching away at the keyboard.

"Wha?" He was too busy getting ready to rumble. "What did you say?"

What had happened to the Egg who played night tag until the mosquitoes got too hungry and the streets got too dark? Where was the Egg who dressed up as a kangaroo three years in a row for Halloween and who thought wrestling was too *violent*?

"Get ready to . . . RUMMMBLE!" Egg was laughing hysterically at the announcer's voice and the mayhem on the computer. He'd also turned up the volume so Madison had to talk louder in order to be heard a little bit.

"Egg! I asked what you were thinking about starting at Far Hills. Have you thought about junior high?"

"YES!" he screeched without even flinching. Madison could not tell if he was answering her question or smacking some other wrestler down with a metal folding chair.

Madison crossed her arms. "Egg, did I tell you

71

that I'm blasting off for Mars and that planet Earth is about to explode and that little aliens are coming to take you apart piece by piece . . . ?

"YES!" he screeched again.

Egg was hopeless.

But thankfully, after a few more rounds of Smack Down! and one more Pop-Tart (for the road), Egg left. As happy as she had been to see him, Madison was even happier to see him leave, at least for now.

She made a note to say "NO WAY" next time he asked to watch wrestling.

After Egg had left, Madison called Fiona's house, but no one was there. The machine picked up.

"Hey, Fiona, it's Maddie and I'm sorry about today. I wasn't sure if—well, call me and we can talk. I just wanted to make sure you were—"

Beeeeeeeep.

The machine clicked off.

Madison opened her computer.

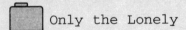 Only the Lonely

I think everyone in my life took an annoying pill. For whatever reason, Egg is just the most annoying boy I have ever met in my entire life. Okay, maybe he's not different at all, maybe he just is exactly the same and I just forgot how ANNOYING he was! What's the deal with the wrestling anyhow?

Walter Egg Diaz is a BIG GEEK. And I feel bad even thinking (let alone writing that down) because I don't want to be the kind of person who puts people into boxes and judges them for stupid stuff like what they wear or who they hang with or what they watch on televison like WRESTLING. I don't *want* to but somehow I always end up doing just that.

I guess when it comes right down to it, people could stereotype me, too. I mean I am a little bit of a computer geek myself. But the truth is I am NOT the Nutty Professor or some kind of genius or anything with a label on it. I am just Madison Francesca Finn who happens to like computers and happens to like science and math and who happens to be good at remembering things. I like animals, too but that doesn't mean I want to live in a zoo.

Am I being unfair? I know. Egg just happens to be a regular guy who happens to like computers and (groan) wrestling. And I need to stop being so harsh. He's my best *guy* friend.

Sometimes when everything around me is changing, it feels like the world is so different and I wonder when and how did this all happen to me? Why did everyone go and change like this?

Then I realize that it's really not Egg or Aimee or Mom or Dad or even Phin that is doing all the changing.

It's just *me*.

Chapter 7

"Yo, who's this?" Chet was the one growling into the phone.

"Is Fiona there?" Madison asked. "Uh, is this Chet? Is your sister there? This is Madison."

She heard him grunt another "yo," and then scream for his sister, who picked up a second phone.

"Madison?" Fiona chirped.

"Hey, Fiona, I called to say hi. And . . . well, I thought you were going to call me back yesterday. I left a message—"

"Oh really?" Fiona paused. "I did? You did?"

Fiona was a little spacey, which bugged Madison more than she thought. How could she have *forgotten*?

Fiona glossed right over any questions Madison was asking. She was on to the next thing already.

"Hey, Madison, wanna hang today? Mom and Dad have to go do something in the city and I would do anything to get away from evil Chet and his stupid new friends—they are so GROSS. Can I come over to your house for a change?"

Madison invited her over. For some reason, Fiona hadn't hung out at the Finns' yet.

When she arrived, Fiona was wearing another cool outfit, just as nice as the pretty yellow sundress from the mall. She had on a flowered top and capri pants, and her braids were pulled back with a purple ribbon.

"Rowrroooo!" Phin greeted her at the door, his tail wagging a mile a minute. Madison saw this as the best sign yet that in spite of her spacey self, Fiona was a BFTB (best-friend-to-be). Phin was an excellent judge of character.

"Why did you ask me to bring a picture of myself?" Fiona blurted as soon as she entered Madison Finn's front hallway.

"I can't tell you yet," Madison answered. "FIRST . . . I made us smoothies. Hungry?"

"I'm always starving," Fiona said as she took a huge slurp of shake. She spit it out right away. "Is this banana?"

Madison nodded. She had blended together vanilla yogurt with frozen bananas. It was her favorite recipe.

"Oh, bananas make me puke," Fiona said, sticking her tongue out and looking for a glass of water. "Sorry. I'm not really into fruit."

Madison apologized and made a plain vanilla smoothie. She made a mental note, too, for the Fiona file: no fruit—EVER.

"Wow, you have such a nice place, can I see your room?" Fiona asked.

Madison took her upstairs.

"Is that *her*?" Fiona pointed to a photo of Aimee tacked to Madison's door. "That's Annie, right?"

"Annie who?" Madison looked. "You mean Aimee?"

"Your friend, the one who's at camp?" Fiona queried again. "She looks so nice. Is she nice? Duh. Of course she's nice—she's your friend. That was a stupid question."

Madison nodded, but it didn't really matter. She noticed how sometimes Fiona started and finished a conversation all by herself.

"Who's *that*?" Fiona asked, pointing to a second photo with Egg in it.

"Oh, that's Egg—well his real name is Walter. Walter Diaz. He'll go to Far Hills too. He's a nice guy even if he does like wrestling more than life itself sometimes. Well, you'll probably meet him soon."

"Yeah," Fiona snickered. "He's pretty cute, isn't he?"

Madison stopped the tour. Had Fiona actually used the words *Egg* and *cute* in the same sentence?

"Fiona, did you just say Egg was *cute*?"

"He is, Madison. He's like totally my type. You said his name was Walter?" Fiona was actually *staring* at his picture.

In that brief moment, Madison realized that she had SO much to learn about Fiona if they were going to be friends. She had to learn about bananas and other foods that made Fiona puke. She had to learn when Fiona was being a space case and when she was really ignoring Madison. She even had to learn that sometimes Fiona might just see someone like Egg as a cutie. Being a friend with someone new suddenly meant learning lots of new stuff.

From the moment Madison had said "Make yourself at home" inside her room, Fiona had started snooping around like a kid in a toy shop. First she picked up Madison's stuffed Beary, an oversized Teddy Bear with bald patches from where he'd been loved a little too much.

"Is his eye missing?" Fiona asked.

Madison grinned. "I chewed it off when I was two, I think."

Fiona examined Madison's glitter nail polish, picked over a basket of junk on her dresser, and read every CD case and book spine on the bookshelf. Meanwhile, Madison just stood by and let herself be *inspected*. She had been nervous about sharing her house and her stuff, but now Madison wanted Fiona to know everything.

"Oh, do you like Calvin and Hobbes too?"

Madison nodded.

"Is orange your favorite color or what?"

Madison grinned.

"Who's this guy? Is he your boyfriend or something?"

Madison grimaced. "NO WAY!"

Fiona was looking at a framed photograph of Madison with Hart Jones, a gross-out geek from her class. It had been taken on a second-grade field trip to Lake Wannalotta upstate. The only reason Madison had it on her shelf was because she and Hart were holding up this humongous sunfish between them. It was funny, so she'd kept it. Now she realized she'd better replace it. She didn't want people to get the wrong idea, especially people like Fiona.

"Lucky thing this Hart guy left at the end of second grade. He was like a walking zombie, always tagging along with me and Aimee and Egg, and pestering me. Ugh. His family moved." Madison said quickly.

"Hey, what's *this*?" Fiona asked when she saw a framed collage over Madison's bed.

Madison explained that she liked cutting out words and images from magazines and pasting them all together to make a picture. The collage hanging over her bed was themed around the subject of "family." She'd glued pictures of babies next to words like *Need You* and *Comfort.* There was a border of lace around the edges.

"You are a wicked good artist, Madison," Fiona smiled when she said that. "I mean it. You should take art in school. Have you ever? I can't draw to save my life. I'm so jealous!"

"Gee, thanks." Madison shrugged again. She figured Fiona was just trying to be nice since they were only starting out as friends. "I don't really consider myself to be any kind of real artist, but I like it. I mean it's not *drawing*, exactly . . ."

"Maybe we should take an art elective or something *together* this year?" Fiona suggested. "You can help me with art!"

"What are your hobbies, Fiona?" Madison asked.

"Hmmm. I know I'm gonna try out for soccer this year. Does sports count as a hobby? Chet plays basketball and everyone usually tries to get me to do that too because I'm tall, but I think I'm going for seventh-grade soccer."

"You're into sports?" Madison plopped down on her bed.

Fiona smirked, "Oh yeah, I am *totally* into sports. Big time." She sat down next to Madison.

They decided to sign up for art class *and* try out for soccer together when school started the following week. Maybe soccer could help Madison get rid of her klutziness? She hoped so.

Madison clicked her computer on. She wanted to

show Fiona her computer and all the stuff it could do, including a special program Mom had given her. This software called *Makeover Magic* could morph Madison's—and anyone else's—face into a whole new look.

"Now . . . *this* is why I wanted you to bring a photo," Madison admitted, "so we can make us both over. I have a photo of me, too. Wanna try?"

Fiona and Madison loaded the program. Once their photos were scanned, they started to play.

First, they tested a blond wig on Fiona's head. She looked like a cross between Brandy and Christina Aguilera.

"I look like a clown!" she cried. "Can you imagine if I dyed my hair blond for real? My parents would KILL ME!"

Madison gave herself brown eyes and a crew cut. "Ha! Look at me! I look like my brother—if I had one!"

They laughed. Fiona tried the full-figure makeover with a whole new style. She put herself into a teeny-tiny, itsy-weenie polka-dot bikini.

"I look like an even bigger fool with this look!" she shrieked. "Would you ever wear something like this in public? I don't think so!"

They both tried to cut and paste on the same exact blondie wig, dress, and shades. They looked like *Charlie's Angels* rejects.

"What else do you have on your computer?" Fiona asked.

"Lots of things," Madison said, feeling a little protective of her files. She really wanted to show off all her stuff to Fiona but decided at the last minute that it was much better *NOT* to share files.

Madison decided there was no harm in *describing* the files though.

"The thing is, I started out keeping real files of pictures of clothes, sunglasses, cool shoes, temporary tattoos and stuff like that, like from all the teen magazines." Madison showed Fiona the stacks of colored folders. "I cut stuff out and keep it in folders and I organize it all by categories so if I need to make something like a card I know where to look and find it."

"You are so organized." Fiona gasped.

"I guess so," Madison tilted her head to the side. "I like to make stuff. Actually, I LOVE to make stuff. And I really like being organized."

"Can I see what's on the computer?" Fiona asked.

Madison shrugged. She suddenly felt *very* protective of her online files. But Fiona didn't ask again. She just kept talking.

"I need to get organized in a BIG way," Fiona continued. "I still have all these boxes to unpack from our California move! Plus, my Mom and dad expect me to be like a straight-A student in junior high. They have me like on the advanced placement list at Harvard University already."

"What?" Madison was shocked. "College?"

"Well, not really of course," Fiona said. "But my

dad is like this super achiever and I think he expects us to be the same way. Since Chet is such a lump, I guess that leaves me. I have to do well."

Madison couldn't believe Fiona had even given a single thought to college. It was five years away! But she admired the fact that Fiona wanted to do well in school.

"Hey, Madison, you should store our makeover picture in a new and improved Fashion File," Fiona joked, hitting a few computer keys. "Why am I worried about Harvard for? We can be maw-dells!"

"You really could be a model, you know," Madison said earnestly.

Fiona laughed so hard, she spit. "NOT!"

Madison decided to save the picture of them as "blondie twins" as a screen saver. She'd e-mail it to Fiona, too.

Fiona walked back over to the photo of Egg. "You know, Madison, I really, really, really would love to meet your friend."

"Egg?" Madison gawked. "You may change your mind when you see him up close, Fiona. He's like a real wrestling freak and—"

"I like sports!" Fiona squealed.

Madison laughed.

"Can I ask you a question?"

Fiona shrugged.

"Hey, have you ever kissed a boy?"

Fiona smiled coyly. "Sure. Twice. Two different boys."

"Two? You have to tell me about it."

"Well." Fiona thought for a minute. "There was this guy I was in love with in California and we were boyfriend and girlfriend for a year. We really were in love, I swear. His name was Julio and we saw each other at the beach for this school volleyball squad and then we saw each other every single Thursday for a year. In the beginning we were just like smiling at each other. But this one time after a scrimmage, I got a point in and he grabbed me and kissed me, right there in front of everyone."

"Were you embarrassed? I would have been so embarrassed!"

"A little bit. I was more embarrassed by the fact that everyone started clapping and hooting. But whatever. I was secretly hoping he would do it again. It wasn't a long kiss, the first one, but it was just so nice."

"Did he kiss you again?"

Fiona dropped her head. "Yeah. A lot."

"So what happened?"

Fiona frowned. "He kissed my friend Claire, too. A lot."

"Uh-oh." Madison made a face. "What about the other guy?"

"Okay, that guy was just a dare. Maybe it doesn't count exactly, but it was a dare and I kissed this eighth grader, Clark Cook, on the last day of school last year. He wasn't even that cute. But we kissed. I swore I was going to die because I felt his tongue

83

and I almost lost it and all I can say is thank goodness I don't have to go back to school and face him. It was like kissing a dog, seriously."

"Wow." Madison was impressed, even if one of the kisses was bordering on gross.

"I guess leaving those guys in the dust is one good reason for having moved here to Far Hills, right?" Fiona laughed. "No more DOG kisses, except for Phinnie, of course!"

"Wow, I'm jealous of you. I haven't really ever done *anything* with a guy. Well, I accept the fact that no one likes me."

"That can't be true, Madison! You are so pretty! You're just not paying attention, I bet."

Madison was embarrassed, as usual. She fought the urge to get off her bed and run away.

"It is so true, Madison," Fiona repeated. "I bet *lots* of guys like you. Didn't you say that Hart guy was chasing you around?"

"Yeah, but he's a loser."

"Still, he's a loser who's a GUY!"

"Come on, Fiona, this is so embarrassing. I get too nervous around guys. I'm the person who runs away from people, remember? Besides, the only boys who even look at me are all into wrestling and stupid boy stuff."

Fiona laughed. "Yeah, I know. Like Chet, my brother."

Fiona stayed all day long until the sun went down. It was the best day of the summer so far. It was better than Brazil. It was better than shopping. It was better than *anything*.

When Mr. Waters came by to give his daughter a lift home, Fiona whispered good-bye in Madison's ear: "Thanks for being my friend."

 Fiona

We are official friends.

She has said so three times including today right here in this room. She told me when we went for ice cream last Thursday and I dropped my scoop of Raspberry Bliss on the ground. She told me in her living room the other day when we were looking at her family's old photo albums. And she told me just now. Three time's a charm, right? Mom always says that.

I think Fiona Waters is perfect and she has such a funny sense of humor and she's a little spaced out and forgetful but I forgive her. And she's experienced, too. She's kissed 2 boys! Maybe she can help me in that department?

We talked for a while today about the whole boy thing. I admitted to her that I always get crushes on older boys like the ones Mom says to stay away from. She laughed at my story from last year when the ninth grader Barry Burstein who lives up the block asked me out and I had to tell him I was still in sixth grade. Mom called his mom she was so mad but of course I was

flattered. Sometimes I see him around the
neighborhood but he's still embarrassed
about thinking I was older than I am.

Anyway, Fiona says that boys are no big
deal and that when we're in school I'll see
that for sure and even I, Madison Finn,
will have a boyfriend some day.

I think the rest of the kids at Far
Hills are all gonna be soooooo jealous of
me because the new girl who is so cool is
already MY friend. She and I will take
electives and try out for soccer together.
Fiona said so. And we'll sit next to each
other at lunch. We'll maybe get into the
same homeroom if we're super lucky. I hope
we're lucky.

Fiona Waters is like the friend I have
been waiting for all summer. She is the
antidote to all this loneliness.

Madison stared at what she had written and then
turned off her computer. Phinnie had fallen asleep
at her feet.

"Maddie!" Mom called from the kitchen. "Your
father's on the phone."

Madison hadn't even heard the telephone ring.
Her mind was someplace else. On her way downstairs, she suddenly remembered something. Something important

Aimee was coming home tomorrow.

Chapter 8

Madison looked at the clock. It was just after eleven.

Aimee would be pulling into her driveway any moment now.

And Madison was still trying to sign Aimee's homemade card with just the right words. She was stuck.

She scribbled down the saying from the Girl Scouts: *Make new friends and keep the old; One is silver the other gold.* But that sounded goofy. In fact, everything Madison thought of writing just sounded terrible. It was like "Return of the Brain Freeze."

She wanted to say something important. She knew that much. Finally, she knew what to write.

This is just a card to say I missed you and I hope we will never have to be apart like this summer ever, ever again. I am lucky to call you my BFF.

Love,

Madison

P.S. I hope you missed me as much as I missed you.

She folded the card, licked the envelope and waited for Aimee's call.

There was a group of birds feeding just outside the kitchen window. The male cardinals were bright red. They were biting off the ends of sunflower seeds to feed the gray birds with the tufts on their heads, who must have been the females. They were sharing perfectly. Madison always marveled at how birds worked together to eat and talk and fly—and just *be*. She wished her mom and dad knew how to do that.

The phone rang. Madison spied the clock: noon. On the dot. Aimee was never late. Not even for phone calls.

"Is this you? Is this really and truly and absolutely YOU?" Aimee screeched. "I am just going to unpack my duffel bag and then I'm coming RIGHT OVER!"

Of course, she didn't come right over. She didn't even hang up the phone right away.

She had to say that she missed Madison when she was at camp.

Then she said that she had so many stories to share from camp.

Then she said she wished so much that Madison had been at camp.

Camp! Camp! Camp!

Madison wanted to kick "camp" in the head. First, it took her friends away from her for half the summer and now what? Were all those same friends coming home—and camp was following them back?

Madison didn't really feel like hearing about camp tents and lake trips and marshmallow roasts anymore. She had her own stories to tell, right? It wasn't as if camp had a corner on the market for making new friends. Madison had met someone new and she hadn't had to go live in a tent in the woods or attend some fancy dance camp to do it. She had met a new friend right here in Far Hills, and she was going to tell Aimee all about it.

But of course, what Madison *actually* said to Aimee was, "Cool! Can't wait to hear all about your CAMP!"

Madison felt excitement and guilt and weirdness churning inside her belly. She sat by the window to wait for Aimee's arrival. Was Aimee's hair going to be longer? Had she gotten any skinnier? Aimee didn't really eat all that much to begin with, plus she was a ballet dancer, so that made her like a total skinny-mini. And then there was that Josh guy. Madison knew Aimee would talk about the camp counselor and of course, Madison had no boy stories of her own to compare with JOSH. What if Aimee had actually *done* something with that Josh guy? What would she say *then*?

That would be weird.

Of course, thinking through every possible hello and good-bye did Madison no good. The exact moment Madison saw Aimee cross the street, every nerve in her body stopped being nervous. She was just THRILLED.

Madison Finn exploded into a chorus of high-pitched shrieks.

"OH MY GOOOOOOOOD!"

She ran out the front door and Phin followed, barking.

Aimee and Madison practically squeezed each other to death on the front lawn.

"You look sooooo good, Maddie!" Aimee screamed. "I missed you so much!"

"So do you! I missed you so much too! Your hair is so long! You look so good, too!" Madison screamed back.

Their arms wrapped around each other like twine.

"Maddie, camp was like the best experience of my life so far I have to tell you absolutely every sin-

90

gle solitary detail you just won't believe how great it was oh I wish you could have been there. . . ."

Madison grinned from ear to ear. What had she been so worried about? She could survive a few of these camp stories. With Aimee in her living room again, Madison felt so much better about everything.

Seeing Aimee again, on that muggy Sunday morning after such a long dragged-out summer, was like winning first prize on a game show. It felt as good as ice cream.

"Okay-doh-kay," Aimee clucked, "so there I was and I was so afraid I wouldn't make any new friends or anything and OH MY GOD Madison I swear I was like one of the most popular dancers by the end of the summer I swear can you believe it—*me*?"

Madison didn't ever remember Aimee being so full of herself, but she kept listening. Aimee looked so happy. She was glad to know her friend was proud of being a good dancer. Everyone was allowed to toot their own horn a little, right?

Aimee was dancing around the room while she talked. "So I got the lead in *Swan Lake* there can you just die? And there was this boy dancer named Willem and he was so cute and I almost forgot!"

"What?" Madison was enraptured by what Aimee was saying and by the fact that Aimee was literally pirouetting in the living room.

"You are NOT going to believe this but Roseanne Snyder was at camp too!"

"Rose *Thorn*? Get OUT!"

"Yeah, she came for the last session. I forgot to put it in my letter." Rose *Thorn* was a nickname Madison had given to one of her classmates. Roseanne was friends with *Phony* Joanie Kenyon. They were both sidekicks to Class Enemy #1, Ivy Daly.

Ivy Daly was probably the meanest girl in Far Hills. She'd been hated by Madison, Aimee, and Egg for—well, for*ever*. She would be attending Far Hills Junior High, too.

"Rose Thorn is such a snot! Was she in *Swan Lake* too?"

"She thinks she is all that and she is NO swan," Aimee taunted.

"And what about that Josh guy you wrote me about?" Madison asked.

"Josh? Oh well he was a counselor so that was never like a real deal or anything. And the truth is I didn't really like him after all, he just turned out to be well, not a good teacher either. SO! Forget him. Like I was saying there was this other guy Willem and he was the best dancer in the entire place. He was there when I was on pointe for the first time and he picked me up . . . I think I told you that in my letter that I started pointe, right?"

"Uh-huh." Madison nodded. She could barely get a word in. Aimee kept on talking for another ten minutes at least. Actually, she had been talking for fourteen minutes and thirty-three seconds. . . .

Thirty-nine seconds . . .

Fifty-six seconds . . .

Fifteen minutes!

Madison hated to admit it, but at a certain point she was wishing Aimee would just shut up already. It must have showed on her face.

"Is something wrong?" Aimee suddenly asked, stopping to take a breath.

"Huh?" Madison snapped back to attention. "Keep going, Aimee. I'm listening."

"But you have this weird look on your face. Are you *really* listening? I've been waiting all summer to tell you about this and OH MY GOD you would have liked all these people and the place it was so beautiful Madison it was soooooo beautiful!"

"Aimee, of course I am listening. Go ahead. I wanna know what happened, all right!"

"Okay!" she said, and spun around on her heels. "Fine!"

Madison figured Aimee must have been saving up all these words about camp. Madison *had* to let her talk or else Aimee would just bust a gut right in her living room.

I just have to be patient, Madison told herself. Aimee will listen right back when it's my turn.

And the truth was, she did.

"SO!" Aimee said after another eight minutes and ten seconds, "What about YOUR summer?"

It now felt like *hours* after Aimee had arrived and

she was finally ready to hear from the other side. Of course, Madison wasn't really sure what to say. She could tell Aimee about Brazil and the frogs. But instead, she gently said, "Well, I missed you. It was lonely here without you."

Aimee looked like she was about to bawl. She threw her arms around Madison. "OH MY GOD, I missed you too! You are so much like a real sister and I don't know what I would do if I didn't have you here. Thank you so much for listening to me. Thank you so much for being SUCH a good friend."

Madison hugged her and squeezed. When Aimee said that, it made all the "camp" talk and all the pirouettes around the living room worth it.

They spent the rest of the day together, talking. Madison eventually *did* get a chance to fill Aimee in on the different kinds of South American poisonous frogs and how not to approach a snake in the rain forest. Aimee kept telling Madison how sorry she was for monopolizing the conversation and sorry she was for being a little overly consumed by camp, but somehow, Aimee never left that subject far behind.

While they were eating wafer cookies Aimee said, "We used to have these in the barn when it rained at camp."

They painted their toenails with Madison's special brand-new orange glitter polish and all Aimee could say was, "My feet are so callused from dancing at camp."

They watched Madison's favorite love story on cable TV and Aimee said, "Did I tell you that the guy Willem was the best dancer in the entire camp?"

Madison wanted to shout back, "CAMP—SHMAMP!" But she didn't.

There was one good part about Aimee doing all the talking. The subject of Fiona never came up.

Until the phone rang—and *Aimee* picked it up.

"Hello, Finn residence," Aimee answered, laughing as she put on a fake butler voice. "Hello? You want Miss Madison? And WHOOOO may I ask is calling?"

Madison held her breath. She got all tense about Aimee answering the phone, as if Fiona meeting Aimee were *Godzilla Meets the Smog Monster*.

Madison had a feeling they wouldn't get along.

"It's Fiona. For you," Aimee handed the phone to Madison. "So who's Fiona, Maddie? Huh?"

Madison's stomach went flip-flop as it always did under pressure.

"Fiona, hey!" she grabbed the phone. Unfortunately for Madison, Fiona was in a talkative mood too. She couldn't hang up right away.

Aimee just stared and listened.

"What? Oh, you wanna hang out? . . . Well I can't. . . . Well, my friend Aimee . . . Yeah, she was the one who answered. . . . Well, she's back from dance camp and I . . . Well, we're kind of hanging out together alone right now and . . . Fiona? Look, I'll call you later."

No sooner had Madison hung up the phone than Aimee asked her for a third time, "So are you gonna tell me who Fiona is?"

Madison couldn't understand why she felt so guilty about Fiona *vs.* Aimee, but she did. She didn't understand why she always felt she had to take sides with everyone: with Mom and Dad, with friends, with *everyone*. It was always about picking sides and picking the people you liked more than other people.

Like now.

"Well, Fiona's my new friend," Madison admitted. "I met her when you were at camp."

Aimee brushed it off. "Oh, okay. Well, is she nice?"

"Yes. Very nice."

"Oh, that's cool. I can't wait to meet her." Aimee twirled around. "Anyway, you know, Maddie, I think I should probably go home now. Do you wanna get Egg and hang out tomorrow like we always do the night before school starts?"

"Yeah, I guess."

Madison was dumbfounded. Aimee wasn't asking any more Fiona questions?

"So, later, 'gator!" Aimee squeezed Madison good-bye as she made her way to the front door. She yelled out, "GOOD-BYE, MRS. FINN!" and skipped away. She really *skipped* too, which annoyed Madison a little. Aimee was a dancer.

Madison smiled and shouted out, "I'll see you tomorrow, then!"

Of course, she realized five minutes too late that she had forgotten to give Aimee her collage card. She stuffed it into her backpack so she wouldn't forget it tomorrow on the occasion of their pre-school party.

Right before bed, Madison opened up her Aimee File.

 Aimee

I thought that I was doing all the changing around here, but Aimee has changed, big-time. She's not the same and she's a talking hog all of a sudden and she's not the same person I remember. I don't ever remember her being such a blabbermouth. Am I being mean by even *thinking* that?

Another change I noticed is her boobs! They are getting like really big. I didn't say that to her face, but I could see them through her T-shirt. I wonder if they hurt? She always said big boobs were like doom for a dancer. I wonder if that's true?

I hope that Aimee and Fiona can be friends. If we three get along, does that mean we have to leave Egg out? Does that destroy, like, the whole Three Musketeer thing with me, Aimee, and Egg? I had this two-second wish that maybe we *four* could be best pals, but I don't know. Maybe I'm being a hog, too. I want things my way all of a sudden.

Sometimes I just want to keep Fiona to myself. Does that make me the *friend* hog? Or is Fiona just one of those summer friends? I am confused.

Madison realized that was a topic better discussed in her Fiona File, and quickly switched back to the subject of Aimee.

I know that Aimee is my best friend in the universe and that we did the soul sisters pact thing in fourth grade and it's stupid to worry about our friendship. Right?

Madison wondered if maybe she really was still "only the lonely."

What would Bigwheels do at a time like this? She looked at her empty mailbox and felt extra lonely.

Chapter 9

It was 1 A.M.

Mom was fast asleep.

Phin was fast asleep.

But Madison was wide awake. Madison couldn't remember being up this late since the year Mom and Dad let her stay up for New Year's Eve when Mom was on the road making *Documentary of a Documentary*, or something like that.

My mind is racingracingracing, Madison thought to herself. It was super-hot, too. Mom had turned down the air-conditioning because she claimed it was supposed to rain. The bedroom fan wasn't working properly. Madison felt sweaty and way too conscious. She'd much rather be dreaming than facing this reality: it was the early morning before the night before the start of seventh grade.

SEVENTH GRADE.

It was all Madison could think about. Her insides were jumping beans. Her head thumped. She swore she could smell smells stronger than before. It was like the whole world was changing.

SEVENTH GRADE.

Wasn't that enough to keep anyone awake?

Madison had spent the last part of the summer worrying about her parents, her friends, and her slow death from boredom, and just now—with twenty-four hours to go—she realized that the thing she was probably most worried about all along was junior high.

Around 5 A.M., Madison finally did fall asleep. At long last she was wiped out by all her thinking. She slept for almost six hours, too, but then Mom finally woke her up.

The first thing sleepy Madison did was check her e-mailbox. To her surprise, she discovered a bunch of messages from a bunch of people she hadn't expected to hear from.

FROM	SUBJECT
✉ dELiA's	Super Savings—PLUS!
✉ jefffinn	I'M HOME!

✉ wetwinz   is this you???

✉ Bigwheels   sorry

The message from dELiA's was an even bigger discount promise on their latest sale. Madison was psyched, until she deleted the message by mistake.

JeffFinn, a.k.a. Dad, sent news from his Far Hills apartment. He was home at last and he wanted to take Madison to dinner the first night of school on Tuesday. It would be special in honor of his junior high school girl. Sometimes Daddy said the sappiest things. Madison couldn't wait to see him. It had been a month, after all. She missed his hamburgers almost as much as his hugs.

The next message was from Wetwinz. *Fiona* had sent mail—*finally!* Fiona and Chet both had screen names that were variations on the words "we twins." Chet's screen identity ended in *s* and Fiona's ended in *z*.

From: Wetwinz
To: MadFinn
Subject: is this you???
Date: Mon, 4 Sept 9:31 AM
Happy day before school, Maddie.

Can I call you that now that we're friends?

I have a lot to do w/mom and Chet
before school but I'll see you
tomorrow at Far Hills okay? I am so
SCARED for everything that's new but
I am also so excited. Do you know
what I mean? I am more excited
because we are friends now, too.
Have fun with Aimee and Egg
tonight. You said you guys always
celebrate together on the night
before school, right? Sorry I can't
be there with you!

Bye, Maddie!!!
Love, Fiona

Madison wished Fiona could be here, even if that
meant breaking tradition a little bit. She wondered
how Egg and Aimee would react if Fiona turned
their threesome into a foursome. It wouldn't be fair,
of course. Egg had wanted his pal Drew officially
included in a lot of things, too, but Drew usually got
left out. The three best friends wanted to hang on to
their trio for as long as possible with no strangers
included or invited.

Was seventh grade going to change all that?
Madison's last message was from Bigwheels.

From: Bigwheels
To: MadFinn

Subject: school
Date: Mon, 4 Sept 10:32 AM
I think maybe you sent me a
message too last week and it got
zapped. Sorry. Lemme know. And
resend it if you still have it.

BTW I start school government next
week so I may actually be a little
busy so please don't mind if I
can't e-m right away. I promise
will write ASAP. Bye!

p.s. pls. Are you angry about something? Why is your screen name MAD?
Bye!
p.p.s. Oh, did I tell you that I
like to write poems? Ok, here is
one for you for the first day of
school. I'm always scared about new
things. RU?

<u>Scared</u>

When toes curl
When hands sweat
When eyes twitch
When you're not set
Scared of people making fun
Scared of summer being done
Scared of new

Scared of old
Scared of always being told
What to do and who to see
Do you agree?
Are you scared like me?

Madison couldn't believe that other people out there in the middle of the world were as freaked out about starting junior high as she was.

Was Far Hills Junior High just a bunch of scaredy-cats like her?

She closed the window on her computer. She couldn't think about being scared now. She was sure Aimee and Egg weren't scared! She made a mental note to send Bigwheels an e-mail later on. She wanted to thank her for the poem.

Ever since they had gotten out of kindergarten, Madison, Aimee, and Egg had been celebrating together on the night right before school and here it was all over again. Their moms were the ones who had really started the tradition and the three friends had picked it up a few years back.

One year they went roller-skating. Another time they camped out in a tent in the backyard. After such a long tradition, they had gotten superstitious about the whole thing.

Egg got to the Finn house first tonight. The dog jumped him.

"Phin you are a bad, bad doggy! Get back!" Egg joked, but then he tickled the spot behind Phin's sensitive ears and Phin turned to Jell-O.

Egg definitely had a love-hate-love relationship with Phinnie.

"Hello there, Walter Diaz!" Madison greeted Egg at the door with a smack on the back.

"Hello there, Madison Finn."

Egg was about to smack back, even harder, when Aimee rushed up and threw her arms around him instead.

"Get off me!" Egg screamed. Of course, he was happy to see her, he just wasn't into any kind of squeezing or hugging. "You're sick," he added.

Aimee laughed and hugged Madison instead. Then she twirled around, waving her arms down toward the ground. She was wearing her pointe shoes.

Madison gasped. "That's them?"

"Aren't they magic?" Aimee got up on pointe and showed off her balance on one toe. She was good at showing off even in the strangest places.

Egg made a face at Aimee's feet. "That's just messed. How do you get up on your toenails like that? Gross me."

Aimee and Madison laughed and threw their arms around each other again.

It had been three months since they had last hung out. Madison, Aimee, and Egg were back together again at last. For a split second Madison considered whether she really should have gotten

105

Fiona to join them, but Fiona had said she had other plans and Madison left it at that. This was no time to feel guilty.

Outside, it was a perfect summer night, so the trio parked their butts on the Finn patio as Mom lit a few citronella candles, and passed out popcorn and root beer.

Madison made Phin do a few stupid pet tricks like fetching the hose, rolling over in the grass, and sitting on the command "park it." Basically Phin did whatever Madison wanted him too. It was entertaining.

"So what are you guys most nervous about this year?" Aimee asked all of a sudden.

Silence. The bug zapper zapped, but no one seemed to have an answer for Aimee's question.

"Nothing, *nada*, not a thing," Egg finally replied. "What's to be nervous about? Bunch of losers mixed in with another bunch of geeks. I'm not different from the rest of the crowd, right?"

Madison chuckled. "Except that you're King Geek, remember?"

"Oh yeah. Where's my crown, Miss Loser? Did you borrow it again?"

"You guys are out of control," Aimee said, interrupting. "I was talking about school stuff like classes and, you know, teachers, and I have heard some scary stories about the amount of homework—like we thought sixth grade was bad but I have a feeling seventh grade is just worse. My brothers say that it's evil."

Aimee had four older brothers: Roger, Billy, Dean, and Doug. They had all been through seventh grade and survived just fine, so Madison imagined they were exaggerating for Aimee's benefit.

"What's their definition of *evil*, Aimee?" Madison inquired.

Egg spoke up, "Uh, I do believe that next to the word *evil* in the dictionary you will find a picture of Aimee herself, yeah."

Aimee faked being mad for a minute and then she hauled off and gave Egg a knuckle noogie.

"Owwwwwwch!" Egg screamed, kicking her in the shin.

"Boys and girls, please stop this fighting," Madison announced like a flight attendant. "In case of emergency, your seat cushions can be used as flotation devices."

They all cracked up.

"Hey, has anyone seen Ivy Daly this summer?" Egg asked out of the blue.

"Oh, puke me!" Madison yelped. "Are you kidding me?"

"I hung out with Ivy's BFF for a week," Aimee said. "Roseanne can't *jeté* or pirouette to save her life!"

Madison faked a scream. "POISON Ivy? Aahhh!"

"I don't know how it's possible but I almost

forgot about her," Madison said. "*She* is the one whose picture is in the dictionary next to *evil*, Egg."

"Madison *vs.* Poison. Sounds like a good wrestling match." Egg snickered.

Hating Ivy officially had started in fourth grade, a year after Ivy moved to town and moved into their elementary school. As third graders, she and Madison had totally bonded. They spent every afternoon together doing homework and playing at the park and all the things that new friends do.

Then things changed.

Egg pulled on Ivy's braids one day in recess and she tripped him in the corridor and then he beaned her in kickball and things got *way* out of hand. Madison tried to stick up for her new friend, but no one listened. And that was when Ivy spread an awful rumor that Madison had cheated on a math test and soon everyone in the fourth grade was whispering and after that the principal got involved. . . .

Any mortal enemy of Madison's automatically became a mortal enemy of Aimee's and Egg's, too.

The worst backstabbing kicked in the year before when Madison went so far as to nickname Ivy "Poison." Of course she never said that to her face.

"I never thought about this before but Poison Ivy just might ruin seventh grade," Madison complained. "She and her stupid sidekicks Rose *Thorn* and *Phony* Joanie."

"Ivy won't ruin *anything* if we have anything to

say about it," Aimee said. "I mean I know I'll whup her and Roseanne in dance troupe tryouts. And you're way smarter than they are, Maddie. That's something to be glad for, right?"

"Yeah, Ivy's hot but she's a major math moron, too," Egg said.

Madison and Aimee said at the same time, "EGG!"

"She is a hottie! I may be against her politically speaking, but I'm not blind!" Egg argued. "She's good-looking."

Aimee jumped all over him. "Those three witches are off-limits for friendship and crushes. Egg, you don't mingle with the enemy no matter what, got it? I mean it, Egg. You are totally not allowed to crush on any of them."

Why was Aimee being so bossy toward Egg? Madison wondered. Egg didn't seem to mind, so she laughed it off, too. Still, it seemed that Aimee really had changed a little. And here, on the night before seventh grade, she was changing a little bit *more*.

"So what homeroom are you in anyway, Maddie?" Aimee asked.

"2A." Madison said.

Egg piped up, "Hey, I'm in 2A too."

Aimee was bummed out. "Then why did they put *me* in 2B?"

The very logical Egg answered her. "Alphabet,

Aimee. A through F is in Room A. Then G through O or something is Room B, and the rest are in Room C. Something like that. They do it all on the computer."

"How do you guys know?" Aimee asked.

Madison joked, "Hey, I think they stuck you in 2B just to torture you, Aimee."

"They finally figured out how to separate you two!" Egg added.

"That isn't funny, Egg. I don't want to be in a different homeroom than you guys. That isn't fair."

"We'll live, Aimee," Egg said. "We'll probably have all our other classes together. Besides, you should feel lucky you're not in Room A. The lovely Poison Ivy is in there!"

Madison put her hand on Aimee's shoulder. "We'll have every other class together, I bet we will."

"I guess," Aimee agreed halfheartedly. She seemed dejected.

Everyone was a smidge more worried than they wanted to admit.

"You're not really upset, Aimee, are you?" Madison asked.

"Yeah, I am. I'm bummed."

Madison wanted to make Aimee feel better. That's what BFFs were for, after all. She remembered Aimee's collage card, the one she'd been making for most of the month of August. It was still in her backpack.

"You made this?" Aimee whimpered. "You made this for me?"

Madison nodded and Aimee sniffled. She was *almost* crying.

"You guys, I feel like I have been waiting for this moment all my life, waiting to get older, to get into junior high, to start dating finally and become a good dancer and get smarter and just start moving up in the world in general. All my brothers are major successes in everything they do and I have to be that way too.

"Now the day is here. Seventh grade is here. We're like, grown-up now. We have to deal with things now. My brothers are telling me that in seventh grade all your friends change and no one likes you. Junior high is all about being popular."

Madison took a deep breath. "Aimee?" she asked quietly.

"Mmm-uh-huh."

"Well, what are you wearing tomorrow?"

"What?"

"What are you wearing tomorrow, Aimee?"

"I dunno. Clothes."

They couldn't help but laugh at that one.

"Well, I'll probably wear my capri pants and that yellow shirt I got last spring with the embroidery, you know the one with the little ties? Or maybe my flower skirt and a T-shirt."

Madison told Aimee that she would wear the

111

same exact shirt, only in lilac. Then they could be alike but not exactly the same so no one could accuse them of being copycats or anything.

"You should wear those cool sandals, too, with the red straps," Madison added. "They would look so good with that shirt."

Egg was not especially interested in his friends' fashion plans so he said his good-nights.

"See you in the land of the lost," he said, joking about the halls of Far Hills Junior High, where they'd meet up again tomorrow. "Thanks for the eats, Maddie. Too bad all the Pop-Tarts were gone."

They laughed and waved and then Aimee stayed for another hour with Madison planning their outfits and outfitting themselves with a plan.

Madison typed up their list into a new file.

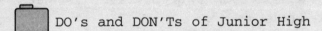 DO's and DON'Ts of Junior High

```
        Do's and Don'ts: Day One
        by Madison Francesca Finn
          and Aimee Anne Gillespie


DO coordinate your new school outfit with
your BFF the night before 7th grade starts.

DON'T wear anything see-through and don't
wear a dark-colored bra under a white
shirt. No glitter barrettes either or
anything too flashy. Blending in is the
best plan.
```

DO put your clothes out the night before school so you don't have to run around like a freak on the next morning looking for something cute to wear.

DON'T wear anything white on the first day unless of course you have a good tan in which case you should wear white on the first day and every day after that until the tan fades away.

DO bring most of what the faculty put on the school supply list: new notebooks, sharpened pencils, and pens. You will feel like a big loser if you don't have something to write with.

DO put all your stuff into a knapsack or backpack or whatever you call it.

DON'T use the same backpack as you did in sixth grade. People will notice.

DO eat breakfast before school starts on the first day but make sure you don't get food on your new outfit.

DO bring lunch money or a lunch bag. You need food to keep awake on the first day of junior high. There's a lot of important stuff to pay attention to.

DON'T eat anything that looks like it's moving.

DON'T chat with the lunch lady or lunch
guy.

DO write down your school locker combination
on your palm so you don't forget it.

DON'T move into your school locker until you
have been at school for at least a week.
Test the locker area to make sure that you
are okay with your locker location, after
which you can paste up pictures and whatever
else you need to paste up.

Madison kept typing their list right up until the
moment when Aimee's ride came to take her home.

"Madison! Aimee!" Mom yelled out after the
door buzzed.

Aimee's oldest brother, Roger, was standing at
the front door.

"Hey, Maddie Finn, what's up?" Roger smiled
from the porch step. His teeth sparkled. Madison
didn't remember him being so . . . *cute*. Had something about him changed too? He had the same
thick blond hair and brown eyes that Aimee had. But
he looked different. Very different . . .

"So we'll meet in the morning and walk to
school, right?" Aimee gushed. "I missed you so much
Maddie and I'm so glad to be back and right here."

Madison choked a little. Aimee was squeezing
pretty hard.

"Okay, break it up you two." Roger joked,

pulling on Aimee's arm. "Mom wants you to get a little sleep before school, Aim."

Aimee threw her arms around Madison's mom, too. "Thank you, Mrs. Finn! I missed you too. 'Bye!"

She skipped down the stairs, as usual.

"See you tomorrow, Aimee!" Madison waved back. "See you in seventh grade!"

Chapter 10

The first person Madison spotted in seventh grade homeroom was Ivy Daly.

Of course.

Since 2A was last name letters A through F, Ivy Daly belonged there, just as Egg had said. She was standing at the classroom door chatting with some blond guy Madison didn't recognize. He had probably attended the other middle school and probably was named Biff or Boff or maybe Doof. Madison was trying hard not to stereotype other people too much—but it was a challenge. Mere moments into the first school day, Ivy was moving in for the kill on the cutest boy in school.

The first bell hadn't even rung yet.

"Look at her, trying too hard as always," Egg

coughed. He whispered in Madison's ear, "But she looks good, right?"

"NO!" Madison punched him. "Shhhh!"

Madison never understood why Ivy had been voted Princess of the Middle School Dance last spring, since as far as she could tell every single girl in school hated her guts. Egg claimed Ivy had bribed fifth graders with chocolate to cast their votes for her.

Madison hated Ivy for a million reasons, but there was a teeny-tiny part of her that was a teeny-tiny bit jealous, too. She was jealous of the way Ivy knew how to get all the attention. It was like she could walk into a room and suck out all the energy. She was always the teacher's pet. People listened to her, and she never looked lonely.

"I am sorry, but she is just a tease." Egg elbowed Madison, shaking his head. "She's popular like . . . in her dreams."

Madison looked at the clock. It was 8:04 and seventh grade was two bells away from starting. As kids rushed into the classroom, Madison and Egg said "hello" and "how was your summer" to everyone they'd missed since June. Egg's friend Drew was in this homeroom 2A too, and he and Egg started chattering about Palm Pilots and RAM as soon as they spotted each other. The entire classroom was a flurry of activity. Plus, no one knew where their lockers were located yet, so everyone had piles of stuff to carry around with them.

The first bell rang.

Madison wondered how Fiona was doing on her first day at Far Hills. She hadn't spoken to her since the other night. Of course Fiona and Chet were probably together, so Madison didn't think Fiona would feel totally alone.

Egg poked Madison's side to get her attention. "Drew's having a party Friday," he said.

"Well, my parents are," Drew continued. "Like a start-of-school-and-end-of-summer party. A barbecue. It's the third year we've done it."

"Oh that's nice," said Madison, flashing a smile. "Is that an invitation?"

Drew smiled. "Yuh. Of course. Yeah."

Egg chimed in, looking at his neon watch as he always did. "Second bell will go off in exactly three seconds . . . three . . . two . . ."

The second bell rang.

By the time homeroom had ended, teachers were running back and forth, up and down the aisles handing out dittos and schedules and maps. Far Hills Junior High was big, probably about four times the size of Far Hills Elementary. The kids needed a major map to find their way. Even with directions, most seventh graders wandered down the wrong hallways and found themselves trapped on the opposite side of the building from where their next class was being held.

Madison thought her map looked like it had been written in Japanese.

"I can't read maps to save my life," Madison moaned when she got her pack of multicolored pages. "I have no sense of direction—EGG!"

There was so much to learn and absorb. Where was she going to be going? How would she get there?

Madison's schedule said: ENGLISH, Room 407. Egg had math on the second floor with Drew, so when homeroom bell rang, they waved good-bye.

Of course, there was no elevator, so Madison went immediately to the jam-packed stairwell, grabbed the banister, and inched her way up two flights. When she got up there, she looked high and low for the classroom.

"Hey, Finnster!" a voice called out from down the hall. Madison's eyes searched for the source.

A very handsome guy with little black glasses, hair that swept up off his face, and dimples, walked up to her and smiled. He was *awfully* cute for a seventh grader, Madison thought. *Awfully* cute.

"Madison, is it you? How are you?"

Madison thought she recognized the voice, but she couldn't place the face. "I'm sorry. . . ." she started to say, blushing a little bit.

"It's Hart. Hart Jones! Remember? When we caught that sunfish? My family moved but we moved back again. Funny, huh?"

Madison froze. *This hunk was HART?* Finnster should have been a dead giveaway. Hart called her that in second grade.

"H-h-h-hello, H-h-h-hart," she stuttered, barely getting the words out. "Gee . . . uh . . . see ya!" she made a U-turn in the opposite direction. She told herself she was speeding off to first period, but of course she was just running away as she always did.

"Hola, Señorita Finn!" another voice called out. It was Mrs. Diaz, the best Spanish teacher in the world and mother to Walter, otherwise known as Egg Diaz.

"Hello . . . uhhh . . . *hola*, Mrs. . . . uhhh . . . Señora Diaz." Madison said with a lot of effort. She knew maybe ten Spanish words and most of those didn't even count because they were curse words she'd learned on cable TV.

"Cómo era tu verano?" Egg's mother wanted to have a conversation in Spanish in the middle of the hallway and Madison was NOT prepared.

"Uh . . . see you later, Mrs. Diaz. I have class. . . ." Madison fumbled for the words. *"Ahora . . . class . . . Oh, hasta la vista, Señora!"*

The first bell rang.

Madison's eyes scanned the doorways for her classroom number. She saw 4D. Then she saw 4C. These looked like language labs, not English classrooms.

The clock was ticking. The hallways were emptying. Madison felt her stomach doing its usual flip-flop as she desperately looked for the right room. These were all letters! Where were the *numbers*?

"Excuse me," she suddenly asked a male teacher

who was about to lock his classroom door, "Excuse me, where is Room 407?"

He chuckled and said "Ooooooh" and Madison knew she was in deep trouble. "Oooooooh," he said again, "Miss, that's over in the other building."

"The *other* building?"

"Yes. You go down those stairs there, all the way across the quad out there, and then through two sets of glass doors, and then up the middle stairwell, and then across the top floor, which is four, and then there are a whole bunch of rooms sort of kitty-corner. . . ."

Madison's head was spinning.

The second bell rang.

"Good luck!" he trilled, slamming his classroom door.

Madison realized that she was the only person left standing in the hallway—without a hall pass.

"Great going, Madison," she said out loud to herself, on the verge of tears. Then, she ran. She ran fast, too. So fast, in fact, that she got grabbed by another teacher in the other building who gave her a warning for running.

"Just because you're in junior high school now young lady doesn't mean you can break all the rules and do whatever you please," the woman said. Madison prayed this crabby lady wasn't going to be one of her teachers. She just grit her teeth and kept moving ahead.

By the time she finally did make it to 407, class

was already underway. She was the last to arrive.

Madison was convinced that *her* nightmares were coming true. At least this one didn't involve dogs and frogs.

On the upside, English class looked promising. The teacher went out of his way to get Madison to relax once she finally took her seat.

"Why don't you take a few breaths and get your bearings. Class, I'm Mr. Gibbons and this is seventh-grade English."

Madison wasn't sure she knew *where* her bearings were right about now. She didn't see Aimee anywhere. And Egg wasn't here, either. Madison was alone in this English class with none other than Poison Ivy and a bunch of her followers.

Mr. Gibbons handed out the "syllabus." Madison glanced at it, expecting to find the usual grammar page assignments, vocabulary lists, and all that razzamatazz. But what she saw was something very different. At the top of the page was "Mr. Gibbons," and the class unit number, and then in the very center of page three:

Expect the unexpected.

"Okay, class, who can tell me what we'll be studying this year," Mr. Gibbons asked. He was parading around the room looking for guinea pigs disguised as seventh graders.

Madison blinked at the page and . . . of course . . . started to over-think.

Seventh grade had already thrown her about four curve balls and it was only nine in the morning.

And that's when Fiona walked into the room.

Madison almost blurted her name out, "Fi—" but she stopped.

As Fiona took a seat in the next row, Madison leaned over to hand her a copy of the page Mr. Gibbons had passed out.

Expect the unexpected.

"He seems cool," Madison whispered.

"Seeing you in my English class is unexpected," Fiona said, pointing down at her page as if she was answering a question. "I guess I already expected the unexpected here."

Brrrrrrrrrrrring!

"Huh?" Madison smiled. As far as she could hear, the only thing that could be expected at Far Hills were the bells. Every time Madison got comfortable in a seat . . .

Brrrrrrrrrrrring!

These twenty-minute first-day classes were giving her a headache.

Chapter 11

After English, Fiona and Madison blabbed between bells and agreed to meet later in the lunchroom. They'd be serving some kind of snack to keep the kids' motors running.

"This new school is so weird! California was way more mellow." Fiona tossed her head back and the beads on her braids clinked. "So I'll see you later, then? Meet me at one of the tables."

Fiona was one of the few people Madison was seeing in classes. It seemed like Aimee and Madison had been officially "separated." Her BFF was nowhere to be seen.

Madison went to the computer tech labs next, where she saw Egg and Drew again. Of course, they were goofing around at their adjacent terminals and paying absolutely no attention to her. Madison doodled on her tech schedule, drawing little stick people with giant heads.

"Hey, Maddie," Egg elbowed her from the side, "Can you believe we're really in junior high? Just look at these computers!"

Their new computer teacher Mrs. Wing was telling the class "to be super-careful with the 'mice' and the keyboards."

Mice?

"Isn't she cool?" Egg said as they walked out of the tech lab. Egg always fell for every new female teacher he ever had. He had been doing that since Miss Jeremiah's kindergarten class.

Madison was grateful that at least someone was having a good day, even if it was Egg. Today was not turning out the way she'd planned it inside her head.

Madison sighed and looked at her map again. Lucky for her, computer and her next class, science, were near each other, so she probably wouldn't get lost again. But first, she had to eat.

The bell rang.

Madison walked into the cafeteria. It was as busy as the mall on Saturday. Kids were everywhere, talking, screaming, hugging, and eating little containers of yogurt, bagels, and fruit cups. Madison searched the sea of faces. Where was Aimee? Where was Fiona?

From across the room, she saw Fiona sitting at a

table with some other people who Madison couldn't see—*at first*. As soon as Madison started walking closer to the table, her stomach flip-flopped.

Fiona was gesturing for Madison to sit in a seat next to—*Poison Ivy*?

"Hey, Madison! How was your day so far!" Fiona blurted. "Sit here!"

"Yeah, Madison sit here," Poison Ivy groaned, not moving over. Rose Thorn and Phony Joanie laughed but Fiona didn't catch what was going on. She kept right on talking, unaware of what was happening. She was being a little spacey again.

"Madison, do you know Ivy and Roseanne and Joan?"

Madison stared and nodded. "Yes, yes, and yes."

By now, Ivy was grinning. "Fiona, we've known each other since third grade, actually. Right, Madison?"

Madison's head screamed, "RUN AWAY!" Fortunately, it was at that exact moment that Aimee bumped her from behind.

"We saved you a seat over here, Maddie."

Madison looked at Fiona and then at Aimee. Poison Ivy was ruining everything about lunch.

"Look Fiona, thanks for the invite, but I have friends waiting for me over there. I'll see you around, okay?"

"Madison?" Fiona's jaw dropped. "Madison? Where are you going? I thought you said . . ."

She stood up to stop her, but Madison had already hustled away.

"Check you out! Talking with the enemy!" Egg teased as Madison passed by his table.

"Hey, Madison," Drew called out sheepishly, "What's up?"

Madison didn't even hear Drew. She made a bee-line for the long orange table at the back of the room.

"Was *that* the Fiona girl who called you the other night?" Aimee asked, sliding in beside her.

Madison nodded. "How can she be sitting with Ivy, Rose, and Joan?"

"You won't believe this but that girl Fiona's in my science block. Maddie, she is a major poser. I wouldn't be so worried if I were—"

"Excuse me?" Madison couldn't believe Aimee would say something like that, especially when she knew how Madison felt about her newest friend. "What do you mean by 'poser'? She is not a poser. She's nice. She's my new friend, Aimee."

Aimee rolled her eyes. "Well, I don't know. She just is. Look at her. Why do you think she's sitting with *them*?"

Madison sneaked a look back at Poison and the gang. Fiona was drinking a juice.

"What about the way she looks?" Aimee said.

"Since when did you judge people like that? What are you talking about, Aimee? She's new. She doesn't know Ivy is poisonous."

"Hey, I'm not judging her! Come on, Maddie!"

Just then, Egg walked up to the orange table. "Hey, Maddie, can you set me up with that one with the braids? If you ask me, she's pretty cute."

"No one asked you anything, Egghead." Aimee threw a grape at his head.

Drew didn't say much. He just laughed whenever Egg laughed.

Madison turned her body a little so she could spy on Fiona's table some more. What was going on?

It was like this whole other Fiona was sitting there with Ivy.

It was like this whole other Aimee was sitting here with Madison.

Aimee, as usual, kept right on talking, changing the subject, too. She was good at that. "Okay Maddie, you have to tell me about your classes. I am so bummed that we don't have English or science together. How did that happen? Who did the stupid schedules and let's go complain!"

"I don't know," Madison mumbled.

Aimee told Madison about her science teacher who she claimed was close to a hundred. "I swear! She can barely stand at the front of the classroom to write on the marker boards. And her element chart looks like it was made in 1950 or something, it's falling off the wall. And she wears those orthopedic shoes you know the ones I mean. . . ."

"She's really old," Drew added, simply.

This time, Madison was the one who rolled her eyes. "Well, old doesn't mean anything except that she knows a lot more. So that's good, right? You guys are so obnoxious."

Aimee ignored that comment and kept right on talking. "Hey, Egg, who do you have for science?"

"I haven't had science yet," he grunted, devouring a sesame bagel.

"Hey, Maddie, you won't believe who I saw in the hallway by the way!" Aimee said.

"Hart?" Madison couldn't keep herself from grinning even though Aimee had her a little annoyed.

"Did you see him too?" Aimee shrieked.

"Hart *Jones*?" Egg asked.

"Hart Jones?" Drew repeated.

"Yes, are you deaf? Hart Jones." Madison said, not revealing any more information than that. She lowered her voice. "He looks *really* different though."

"Different?" Aimee shrieked again. "He's a babe!"

"Shhhhhh!" Madison shushed her. "What if he's around here?"

"If you don't want him, I'll take him," Aimee joked. "Drew, don't you remember that drip who used to always follow Madison around and stuff? He was even nerdier than Egg!" She threw another grape at Egg's head.

"Of course I know Hart Jones, Aimee," Drew piped up. "He's my cousin."

Egg laughed, hard. "Ha! Nice one, Aimee!"

"Oopsie!" Aimee gasped and covered her mouth.

She and Madison burst into peals of laughter. "NO WAY!"

Egg picked up his snack tray and pulled on Drew's shirt. "Let's go. They've crossed over into the girl zone. I can't handle this."

Aimee smiled again. "Mad and Hart, sitting in a tree, K-I-S-S-I-N-G."

Now Drew was the one who looked a little confused.

Madison grabbed a grape and threw it at Aimee. Of course, Madison's typical luck caused the grape to ricochet off Aimee's shoulder and into the assistant principal, Mrs. Bonnie Goode, who happened to be walking by at that exact moment. She shot a look in the direction of the orange table and Egg almost laughed milk out of his nose, it was so funny.

"Nice way to start the school year, right?" he cracked after the A.P. had walked away. Drew chuckled too.

Aimee finished up her yogurt and the four of them went off to the Assembly Hall. One more double period and the Far Hills seventh graders were free. Seventh grade had started with a whoosh and a bang.

Of course, Fiona had eaten lunch with THE

ENEMY, but the more she thought about it, the more Madison realized that Fiona had no idea *who* was enemy and who was friendly in this war zone. All's fair in lunch and war, so if Fiona had no facts, she had no way to know that girl was evil.

It was up to Madison to help Fiona see the poison in Poison Ivy.

She'd send Fiona an e-mail later on about it.

Chapter 12

Madison, Aimee, and Egg walked home together after school let out. Drew lived on the other side of town.

It was one of those hot and humid days that makes you sweat behind your knees. Egg complained, "Why did I wear long pants?"

"So no one would have to look at your ugly legs, obviously," Aimee laughed. They chased each other up the street.

Madison had searched for Fiona before leaving school, thinking maybe they'd walk home together too, but she was nowhere to be found. Madison hadn't seen Chet anywhere in school today, either. Far Hills was a big place. Of course, lucky

Madison had seen Ivy in every single hallway, class-room and girls' bathroom. Poison Ivy was really con-tagious.

Aimee dropped Madison off on her porch and continued up the street, skipping.

Phin was at the front door the moment Madison entered the house.

"Wanna go O-U-T?"

They were just going to cruise around the lawn for a quickie, but Madison walked a little farther up the street. Soon she found herself at the corner of Ridge Road, right by Fiona's.

"Hey, look where we ended up, Phin," Madison said with mock surprise. "Should we go see Fiona?"

"Rowrrroooo!" he howled. Madison took that as a "yes." She needed to see her new friend. She wanted a chance to apologize for her behavior in the cafe-teria. She hadn't meant to run away that time—but she *had*.

As Madison approached number five Ridge Road, she saw Fiona sitting on her front porch. She was alone, which was good. Madison didn't feel like deal-ing with her twin brother in the middle of this mess.

How would Madison apologize? She figured that Fiona might be extra-understanding, because Fiona knew Madison was in the habit of fleeing when things got weird and that had definitely been one of those weird moments.

"Fiona," Madison practiced what she would say.

"Fiona, I am very sorry for leaving you there today with the enemy. You see, Ivy Daly is not exactly a friend of mine. She—"

Madison froze.

Ivy Daly was standing there on Fiona's porch.

Poison Ivy must have been inside or out of sight when Madison had first glanced that way.

She turned around and ran home as fast as she could. No one saw her great escape.

"Hey! My junior high schooler!" Mom cheered as Madison rushed inside. "Well, how was it?"

Madison was flushed. She dropped into a chair.

"What is it honey? Are you okay? What happened?"

Madison's dramatic entrance had Mom worried she was sick or something.

"Mom, do I have a sign on my head that says 'Keep Back 100 Feet'?"

Mom leaned in closer and gently grabbed Madison's arms. "What happened, sweetie? What happened at school?"

Madison looked up at her mother. She didn't want to cry. She told herself not to cry. She didn't want to yell, either, not now. Her feelings were jumbled and the words wouldn't come out like she wanted them to come out.

Madison had never, ever lied to Mom before now. In fact, she always shared *everything* with Mom. But right now, she couldn't tell her the truth.

Madison was too embarrassed by today's events. So she lied.

"Nothing's wrong, Mom, not really. School was okay. I like it. I like my classes. My teachers are okay. I saw everyone. I'm gonna go now."

"Madison?"

She just didn't feel like getting into it, not one little bit. She was too ashamed, too devastated, too woozy. She went up to her room and curled up in a ball with Phin.

An hour or so later, the phone rang.

"Mad-i-son!" Mom bellowed from downstairs. From the pinched sound of her voice, Madison knew who was on the line. Dad.

"Hey," she cooed as she took the receiver. Madison needed Dad badly.

He told her to be out front by five o'clock. Tonight was their very special dinner and Madison missed Dad so much and she needed his moral support—now more than ever. Plus, Dad was making Madison's favorite thing on the planet: french fries and steak. She'd first had it last year when she went to Paris with her parents—before the big D. She kept a postcard of the Eiffel Tower up on her wall to remind her what it was like when they were all together.

"I can't believe he makes you *steak frites*!" Mom groaned. Mom hadn't eaten meat in four years, a fact she was happy to share whenever the subject of beef came up. She didn't understand how Madison could be an animal lover and eat meat, too, but Madison usually avoided that conversation. She liked animals but she just wasn't willing to give up burgers—what was the problem with that?

Because Madison hadn't seen Dad in so long, she tried to fix up her hair to look extra nice. She borrowed Mom's yellow sundress, too.

"Why do you want to wear this, honey? It's too big for you," Mom stated, zipping up the back. Madison had to wear a white T-shirt underneath so you couldn't see anything.

"I dunno, Mom," she answered. "I just feel like wearing a yellow dress, that's all."

"It actually looks like the sundress Fiona was wearing the other day," Mom observed. Of course, Madison had known that when she picked it out of Mom's closet.

Dad arrived a few minutes after five, but Madison wasn't phased. Dad was always late. It made Mom unhappy that he didn't understand "being on time."

Mom had staked out the front porch with Phin at her side.

So as soon as he pulled into the driveway, Madison ran for Dad's car. She liked it much better when Mom and Dad didn't have to talk to each other face-to-face. Right after the divorce, for about a month, Madison wanted nothing more than Mom and Dad to get back together. Now, she'd rather see them on two separate islands in the middle of the Pacific Ocean.

"Gee, Maddie, your hair looks so pretty," Dad said as soon as Madison hopped into his car. "And isn't that a nice color yellow dress."

Daddy always noticed those things. Madison smiled. She wouldn't admit that the dress was really Mom's. As usual, she went way out of her way to avoid the subject of "Mom."

When they got to Dad's apartment, it smelled funky, but Madison didn't say anything. He was never there, after all. In Dad's townhouse loft, Madison actually had her own room, so she rushed in to visit it. She didn't have many things, just a photograph of her, Aimee, and Egg taken the summer before at the beach; copies of *The Phantom Tollbooth* and *Harry Potter and the Sorcerer's Stone*; a Magic 8-Ball; and one of Gramma's hand crocheted afghans.

Dinner was served about an hour after they arrived. Daddy talked nonstop about his new Internet start-up company. Sometimes Dad would get so caught up in talking about himself and his job that he would throw out all these big computer programming words Madison did not understand. She kept listening though. She really wanted to know what the words meant.

Madison felt so safe in Dad's house, watching him cook. He was a better cook than Mom, at least.

The steak was yummy and Madison over-salted her fries too, as always. Of course, they had ice cream for dessert. It was Madison's favorite flavor: Cherry Garcia.

"So, honey, I have been doing all the talking tonight."

Of course this was nothing new. He *always* did a lot of talking. Just like Aimee.

"Maddie? It's your turn to talk now. Tell me about Brazil."

Madison told Dad how they went on a big plane; then a smaller plane; and then by boat all the way out to this small village.

"Mom's making that frog-u-mentary, eh?" Daddy joked.

"Yeah," Madison laughed out loud. She realized they were discussing the untouchable subject of Mom, but she continued. "I think Mom has to go back in a week or something, too. I dunno. You guys are both out of town a lot these days, I guess."

"Yeah, well, it's not forever, Maddie. Hey, so tell me all about your new school. How's junior high?"

Madison said something about "too many people" and "too much work." Daddy grinned and handed her a small, wrapped gift. "Here's a little something for the *second* day of school. Maybe it'll be a little less overwhelming. And a toast, of course, to my big girl. I really can't believe you're in junior high school. Your old man feels *old*."

Madison opened the box. Inside, Dad had bought her a pair of earrings with teeny moonstones in the middle of teeny silver-wire flowers. They were beautiful. Madison modeled them immediately.

When Madison was ten, Daddy had given her a moonstone necklace because, he said, moonstones had special powers. She had worn it everywhere until one day she lost it in the Far Hills public pool. Egg had tried to dive in after it, but the pool filter sucked it up like a leaf. She'd cried for weeks.

Now she had two new moonstones. Maybe these earrings would give her *new* power? They would be her seventh-grade lucky charms, for sure.

After they had cleaned up all the dishes, Madison started to tell Dad about everything she'd been doing on the new computer.

"I have these files, you see, so I can like, well, get my thoughts organized and all that. I think it's working so far. Of course it's only been two days."

Dad thought the file idea was fine. "As long as you don't have a 'Things I Hate About Dad' file," he joked.

Madison gasped. "Never! Daddy, of course I wouldn't."

Of course, Madison knew she should probably never say *never,* but she said it anyway. She couldn't imagine not liking her Dad. He was the one who always came to her rescue. He never said bad things about people. Even tonight, for a few hours, it was like he washed away all the yukkies of the previous few days. Madison found herself talking on and on about nothing at all and yet it all seemed so important, the way Dad listened. He was maybe the best listener in the entire world.

"Well, it's funny you should mention all that stuff about going on the computer, Madison, because . . ." Dad handed her a rather large box before he finished his thought. It wasn't wrapped or anything, just taped shut. "I have this for you, too."

"Daddy, what is *this*?" Madison was perplexed. She opened it and found herself face to face with a brand-new, high-resolution computer scanner. "No way!"

"I thought it would be a good thing for you to have. I know you have my old dinosaur of a scanner, but now you can scan and design all that new stuff. You can make screen savers, too. See, I stuck a photo of you and Phin right there. Put it up on your screen. I hope you like it, sweetheart."

Madison felt like crying. Daddy hadn't even really known about the files yet, but he was already on that wavelength. She was amazed at how Daddy always knew what to get, what to say, and what to do. Now the files of Madison Finn had *unlimited* possibilities.

Madison went on to tell Dad about her new friend Fiona and not-so-drippy-anymore Hart Jones and even Poison Ivy.

"Hey, Daddy, did I tell you that I think I'm also going to take a computer class with Egg this year?"

She and Dad swapped computer stories until they both noticed the clock. It was already ten.

Dad sighed. "Time flies when you're having . . ."

". . . dinner with the best dad on the planet," Madison finished his sentence.

Of course, Mom was expecting them back home a half-hour earlier. Madison pictured her out on the porch on Blueberry Street, playing tug-the-chew-toy with Phin, exhaling something not so nice about Dad under her breath. Mom hated when people were late more than anything else.

"We'd better go, Dad." Madison decided for the both of them.

When they arrived at the house, Daddy walked Madison as far as the front-door threshold and kissed her on the top of her head. He walked back to carry her computer scanner up from the car.

Madison liked it when Dad walked her up to the door. It made her feel safe. Of course, Phineas and Mom were waiting up on couch. Mom opened the door.

"Hello, Jeffrey," she said coldly. "Right on time, as usual."

Dad didn't seem to mind the chill. He jumped at the opening in the conversation. "Hello, Fran. I heard your trip to Brazil was a success? Hearty congratulations."

"Yes, well, we'll see you later, then." Mom looked at Madison and then walked back inside.

Madison tugged Dad's arm. "Thanks again,

Daddy. The earrings are cool and the new scanner is cooler than cool."

Through the living room bay window, Madison watched as Dad drove away. Rain started to pitter-pat against the sill. She pulled another one of Gramma's afghans over her toes and watched her breath on the cool glass.

Upstairs, Madison slid into her favorite Lisa Simpson T-shirt and sat down at her computer. She opened yet another new folder and named it.

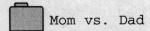 Mom vs. Dad

She certainly had a *lot* to say on this subject. Of course, it was all stuff she could never, ever say out loud. She wouldn't even tell Aimee some of this stuff—and she told Aimee absolutely everything. After the lists were typed, she returned to another file.

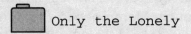 Only the Lonely

    My school psychologist told me last year
that I had to be patient. He told me I had
to let Mom and Dad figure out their own
lives again. So I am trying. Sometimes it's
hard to imagine how two people could ever
have let themselves get so mad at each
other the way Mom and Dad did, but it
happened and that's that I guess. I still
keep their wedding picture on my file
cabinet just because it makes me think of

when they were trying a little harder to be nice. They must have loved each other once, right?

I know I get mad at Aimee sometimes, but the truth is that she is still my best friend and I have to keep reminding myself of that fact. Besides, I can't be mad at my BFF just because she talks too much, can I? What qualifies as a good reason to stay mad at someone?

There are no reasons good enough to stay mad forever. I mean, if I wanted to be mad at anyone it would have to be Egg because he is the most obnoxious boy who ever lived, but the truth is I am NOT mad at Egg. For one thing, he always remembers my birthday and for another thing, he sticks up for me in gym class even when I can't make it on base in kickball.

Staying mad is a huge waste of time.

Some people have it so hard and my life is not that hard at all, even though I act like it is. What's so hard about this? I can handle it. I will handle it.

Tomorrow I will find Fiona.

I will find Fiona and I will say I'm sorry.

I will not let Poison Ivy or *anyone* get in my way.

Most of all, tomorrow I will stop obsessing about this lonely stuff once and for all. And even though my nickname just happens to be Maddie, tomorrow I will get un-mad.

Chapter 13

Science "block" in Room 411 felt more like cell block 411. The fourth day of school was practically over and Madison found herself alone again.

Mr. Danehy's class was a collection of people Madison wasn't sure she really wanted to be with.

Madison sat across from Poison Ivy, who was sitting next to the blond guy she'd been talking to in homeroom. Phony Joanie was across from him. Across the room, Madison caught Chet Waters picking his nose but he didn't seem to care about getting caught and in the back of the class Hart Jones had his attentions focused on a redheaded girl who Madison had never seen before. Plus, there was a bunch of other kids from her old middle school and the other middle school in town scattered here, there, and everywhere.

"Hey, you were hanging with my sister, right?" Chet said.

Madison nodded and stuck her nose into her notebook.

It wasn't that people weren't *friendly*. Everyone was comparing summer tans and asking questions and Madison was in the mix. It was just that out of all the classrooms in all the schools in all the countries of the world, Poison Ivy and the others had walked into hers.

"Hey, Mad! Have you seen Walter?" piped a voice from behind

"My name is not *Mad*," she snapped back. But as soon as she turned, she realized that she had just snapped at Egg's friend Drew. "Oh, it's you."

Drew sighed, "No prob."

But Madison felt awful. "I didn't mean to yell, it's just that—"

"No prob," Drew repeated. "Really."

A kid from the back row yelled out, "Yo, Drew! Isn't your BBQ today?" and the entire class started buzzing. He'd invited the entire seventh grade section to his house for a barbecue—and *everyone* was planning to go.

Madison wondered how 300 people would fit into Drew's house. Did his mother know he'd over-invited by about 250 people? Madison figured the reason for the massive invite list was simple: Drew was the kind of kid who couldn't say no to anyone. He didn't want anyone to feel left out.

After waiting past the second bell, the science teacher, Mr. Danehy, finally rushed into the room and quickly handed out a list of things they'd be studying.

"I am sorry to be late, class," he said "The copy machine busted down and I had to wait. How is everyone today? As you know, I'm Mr. Danehy."

The class was whispering like a chorus of crickets—about science, Mr. Danehy's ugly brown tie, and most of all about Drew's upcoming barbecue, which was scheduled to begin in less than three hours.

"Okay, now quiet down, please," Mr. Danehy said. "We need to get going since this period is going to be really short today."

Madison read the top of the page the teacher had passed out. The words *ozone*, *waste*, and *parasites* jumped out at her.

Sounds great, she thought. It's all dead stuff. What about living, breathing *animals*, Mr. Danehy —huh?

"In addition to the items on this page, we will also be dissecting a frog," Mr. Danehy announced. "A *virtual* frog."

Madison grimaced. *Virtual* frog? She didn't want to cut open anything, not even on a computer screen. What animal-lover Madison Finn really wanted to study was penguins and puffins, as they had in third grade. Why couldn't they study arctic creatures all over again? Why couldn't she just be *in* third grade again, when life had been so much easier? In third grade, Madison didn't have to worry about enemies like Ivy. Everyone liked everyone else.

After the bell rang, Madison met up with Aimee at the lockers. They'd gotten their locker assignments in homeroom that morning.

"I saw your friend Fiona in class," Aimee said as soon as she saw Madison.

"You did? Where?" Madison couldn't believe Aimee had found Fiona today before she had.

"In our science block the teacher paired us up as lab partners. Pretty scary, huh, how things work out? She's cool though. We talked a lot."

Madison couldn't believe it. "Well, what did you talk about? What did she say? What happened?"

"What are you getting all worked up about?" Aimee snapped. "You new friend barely said anything except how nice you were and that you guys had fun over the summer. I asked her about that. What's the big deal, Madison?"

"Is she going to the barbecue today?" Madison asked. "What did you talk about?"

"Why don't you just ask her?" Aimee answered. "She's coming down the hallway right now."

147

Of course, what Aimee neglected to say was that Fiona was walking down the hallway with Poison Ivy, Rose *Thorn* and *Phony* Joanie.

Madison turned away.

"Madison!" Aimee poked her. "Fiona's coming right . . ."

But Madison's head was stuck into the locker, where she emptied her bookbag and stayed as still as she possibly could.

"Madison?" It was Fiona's voice calling her name this time, but Madison still didn't move.

Everything with Fiona was different now that they were in school. There was no way she could associate with Fiona and Ivy together. It wasn't the same as over the summer. Maybe they were meant to be summer friends and that was that. Madison Finn was cornered, so running away was out of the question. This time, she just froze.

After a few seconds, Fiona just walked away.

Ivy made a face at Aimee and blurted, "Nice friends you are."

Madison's stomach flip-flopped.

"What was *THAT*?" Aimee said as soon as Fiona and Ivy and the rest of the gang were gone. "Madison Finn, that was so strange. I don't think I have ever seen you blow someone off like that before. I can't believe she was standing there trying to talk and you just . . . *ignored* her? That is so mean. I can't believe—"

Madison finally interrupted her. "Just leave me alone, Aimee."

Aimee shook her head with disbelief. "Fine, be that way." And she walked away.

Madison ran into the girls' bathroom to cry. She felt sick and now she hated seventh grade more than before and it was only the FOURTH DAY! There was no way Fiona would ever talk to her again. Even Aimee was probably going to stay angry for a little while. Madison had started the day wanted to be everything but mad, and ended up alienating half her friends.

Drew saw her as she walked out of the bathroom.

"Madison, don't forget about the party," he said, handing her a slip of paper. On it he'd written, *BBQ Party at Drew's*. It had the address and phone number of his place.

But Madison just shoved it into her backpack and headed home—*alone.*

Since Mom was still off at work by the time Madison got back to Blueberry Street, she took her laptop out to the porch to wait around.

It was a beautiful sunny day. The clouds were practically invisible, just wisps of gauze across the blue sky. There was even a soft breeze in the air.

It was a perfect day for a barbecue.

Madison logged on to bigfishbowl.com almost immediately and was amazed to discover that

Bigwheels was online. She sent her an IM and arranged to meet in a "private" fishbowl.

```
<MadFinn>: help
<Bigwheels>: how was the first week
   of jr hi???
<MadFinn>: right now evryone is @ a
   bbq except me
<Bigwheels>: y??? y do u nd help?
<MadFinn>: I am all alone
<Bigwheels>: no ur not
<MadFinn>: yes didn't you read evry
   one is @ a party
<MadFinn>: except 4 me
<Bigwheels>: STOP
<MadFinn>: :-@!!!!!!!!!!!!
<Bigwheels>: ic
<MadFinn>: :-@!!!!!!!!!!!
<Bigwheels>: quit screaming it can't
   be so bad
<MadFinn>: I am so stupid :'>(
<Bigwheels>: do u wanna talk ?
<MadFinn>: Y
<Bigwheels>: is that yes?
<MadFinn>: Y
<Bigwheels>: ok so were you not
   invited is that
<Bigwheels>: what the prob is????
<MadFinn>: nonnono
<Bigwheels>: ok so what???
<Bigwheels>: are u there?
```

150

```
<MadFinn>: Y
<MadFinn>: I am a loser
<Bigwheels>: ur a loser if u blow
   off the party YBS
<MadFinn>: YBS?
<Bigwheels>: You'll be sorry!
<MadFinn>: u think :~/
<Bigwheels>: look I dontknow u that
   well but here
<Bigwheels>: is the deal I think
   that ur just
<Bigwheels>: nervous about school
   startin we all r
<Bigwheels>: that way and u should
   be nice to
<Bigwheels>: ur friends NOT :~/
<MadFinn>: hw bout :-|
<Bigwheels>: LOL that's better
<MadFinn>: so I should go 2 the
   bbq???
<Bigwheels>: DTRT
<MadFinn>: ??????
<Bigwheels>: Do the right thing!
<MadFinn>: tx
<Bigwheels>: send me EMSG when u
   get home from the
<Bigwheels>: bbq GL
<MadFinn>: TTFN
<Bigwheels>: *poof*
```

Bigwheels had logged off and Madison did too.

She closed her laptop and went upstairs to pick out an outfit.

She had a barbecue to go to—and a lot of explaining to do.

Chapter 14

Madison had been staring at her reflection for at least ten minutes.

"Phin, what am I gonna wear?" she was hoping maybe the dog could tell her the best look for end-of-summer barbecues, but he was too busy sucking on a rawhide chewie to offer fashion advice.

Madison tried on the plaid jumper with her pink T-shirt. *Nope.* She looked sicker than sick in pink.

She tried on the blue striped tank with matching skort—a skirt-and-shorts outfit her mom had gotten for her last summer. *Skort? No self-respecting seventh grader would be caught dead in a skort!*

She tried on the yellow sundress from last night. *Too risky. What if Fiona had on her yellow sundress, too?*

Finally, Madison decided on denim shorts, a plain white T-shirt and sneakers. She pulled her hair up into her signature ponytails.

"Whaddya think, Phinnie?" she asked her pug. "Might as well call me Plain Jane, right?"

She did look a little boring, but maybe nondescript was a good way to sneak into the party, apologize to Fiona, have a few laughs with Aimee, Egg, and Drew, and sneak right back out again?

Madison dug her hand into her backpack and pulled out the slip of paper Drew had handed to her at school earlier. He lived all the way across town in Falstaff Fairway, a giant mansion with its own tennis court, pool, and a bunch of other stuff that cost a bunch of money. Drew's great-grandad had invented some little washer or screw or something that every single plumber in America and all over the world used in plumbing.

Translation: Drew's family were bazillionaires. Who else could host a barbecue for over 300 screaming twelve and thirteen year-olds?

Before dashing out the door, Madison applied a layer of Strawberry-Kiwi Smooch. She had no plans to kiss anyone at the party, but she wanted to look good. She figured that if she looked good, she'd feel good, and if she felt good, she'd do good.

Madison needed to do *real* good in order to get Fiona's forgiveness.

Then she put on her new moonstone earrings from Dad for good luck.

The bus ride over to Drew's place only took fifteen minutes. All the way up Drew's front walkway were different colored balloons. He even had orange balloons. Madison liked those the best.

Naturally, the entire Far Hills seventh-grade class *was* in attendance.

There were people in the pool (and lifeguards, too, thanks to Drew's parents).

Next to the pool, a dozen or more seventh-grade girls were lying out to get suntanned. Madison hadn't even brought her bathing suit.

A group of guys were playing Frisbee on the massive lawn.

Another group of guys were sitting in a semicircle checking out the seventh-grade girls who were sunbathing.

There were even a few people milling around who definitely looked like eighth graders.

There was, however, no immediate sign of Fiona or Aimee.

"Hey, yo!" Chet Waters said with a mouthful of potato chips. He walked over to Madison before she had a chance to escape.

"Hey, yo back!" she said.

"You seen Fi-moan-a around here?" he asked. "That Ivy girl was looking for her."

Madison frowned. "No."

"Did you come with Fiona?" Chet asked.

"No, didn't you?"

He shrugged "no" and walked away.

"Weirdo," Madison mumbled under her breath. She couldn't believe Chet and Fiona were twins. They may have looked alike, but they were total opposites.

Someone reached for Madison's arm. "So you came," a voice said softly.

It was Drew.

"Drew!" Madison turned. "What a party! Wow."

Madison had known Drew for years, but she'd never actually been to his place.

He nodded. "Thanks. I'm glad you came."

The music blared. There was a band in the middle of the yard and they were playing at top volume.

"I like your earrings," Drew said.

"What did you say?" Madison yelled.

Drew just smiled. "Cool earrings, Madison," he said again.

"What did you say?" Madison yelled louder. She leaned in closer "I can't hear."

"Great party." He nodded, and took a sip from his can of soda.

"Have you seen Aimee?" Madison asked, looking around for her BFF in the pool, on the lawn, on the patio.

"Inside," he answered. "Aimee's inside with Egg and that new girl, Fiona, I think."

Jackpot! Madison thanked Drew and headed into the house.

"Madison Finn?" Drew's mother greeted her as she walked through the sliders. "I haven't seen you since sixth-grade graduation!"

"Mrs. Maxwell! Thanks so much for inviting me to the party."

"Well, I'd say Drew outdid himself again, inviting the whole school, for goodness sake." She laughed and walked into the crowd. "Off I go! Have fun, my dear!"

Across the giant kitchen, Egg, Aimee, and Fiona were laughing.

Madison approached. At first, she could almost feel her sneakers turning to run in the opposite direction, but she resisted.

She moved *forward*.

"Maddie!" Egg screamed and slapped her on the shoulder. "How nice of you to come!"

Aimee just grunted "Hello." Whenever Aimee was even the littlest bit mad, it showed all over her face. Her lip curled, her nose wrinkled, and her eyes got all squinched up. She looked that way now.

Fiona just smiled. "Hi, Madison."

Everyone stood around for a few seconds in silence.

After ignoring Fiona in the lunchroom and turning her back to Fiona at the lockers, why wasn't Madison getting told off?

Aimee finally made a face. "Look, Fiona, you don't have to be nice to her just because we're standing here."

Egg chimed in. "No way! Let's be mean to Maddie! It's mad fun!"

Madison took a deep breath. Now she was going to get it.

"I really don't want to be mean to anyone," Fiona said. "I mean this was all some kind of weird misunderstanding, I think."

Madison felt so guilty. "Fiona, let me explain—"

"Madison, I don't expect to change everything in your entire universe just because we hung out for a little while this summer, right?"

Aimee made another face. "Are you for real?"

Fiona nodded. "Of course I'm for real, Aimee. Are you?"

"Whoooooo!" Egg shrieked.

Madison interjected. "Look you guys, I am so sorry. I don't want to hurt your feelings, Fiona. And of course I don't want to hurt yours either, Aimee."

Aimee huffed. "I know."

Madison added, "It was a misunderstanding, all of it. So can we just go back and start again?"

"Oh, get a room!" Egg cracked. "All this girl stuff makes me want to hurl. Where's Drew?"

Aimee crossed her arms a little tighter when Madison and Fiona leaned in to hug and make up. Madison hoped this hug wasn't fake. Like wrestling was fake. She really wanted the three of them to be friends.

Egg put on a high-pitched girls voice. "What about *me*?"

Fiona laughed and teased. "What *about* you?"

Fiona was definitely flirting and Madison was weirded out. She remembered how Fiona had said Egg was a cutie.

Aimee put in her two cents. "Egg, you are such a dip. And you know where dips belong? With the chips!"

Fiona smiled. "I don't get it."

"You know, potato chips and dip, get it now?" Aimee said helpfully.

"Oh, sort of." Fiona grabbed Madison's arm. "Wanna play Frisbee?"

"Sure!" Madison grabbed Aimee's arm. "What about it, Aimee?"

"Yeah," Fiona said. "Come on, Aimee."

Madison looked at her friend as if to say, "Come on, let's just go play Frisbee and act stupid and forget about everything else today, okay?"

Aimee had other ideas. "Nah, you two go ahead."

"No," Madison said. "Aimee, we can't play without you."

Fiona tapped her foot. "Are we playing . . . or *staying*?"

Madison shook her head. "I think that I'll pass, Fiona."

Fiona shrugged and walked toward the lawn. "Okay. See you later then! Call me, okay?"

Madison nodded. "See you later!"

"You didn't have to not play just because of me," Aimee blurted out. "When I was at camp I was actually a good Frisbee player, but right now I just don't feel like it for some reason, but that doesn't mean you have to stop. I didn't mean to upset you or get in between you and Fiona and—I feel like a big doofus right now. Jeesh."

Madison grabbed Aimee's arm. "You're my BFF, Aimee. That means forever, remember. Who cares about Frisbee?"

They decided to go hang out by the pool instead.

Mom picked the Three Musketeers up sometime after ten o'clock, which was late, but okay because it wasn't a school night. Phin was in the car of course, and Egg teased him mercilessly all the way home.

"Dawg foooooooood!" he tickled Phin on his soft, spotted pug belly.

"Leave my dog alone!" Madison punched Egg right in the arm.

"Ouch! That hurt!" he yelled.

"Rowroooo!" Phin howled.

Mom dropped off Aimee last. She and Madison made a pact to see each other tomorrow, Saturday. It was supposed to get *really* hot.

Later that night, after Mom thought she had already turned out the light and left her daughter in the land of Nod, Madison pulled her laptop computer into bed with her.

She owed Bigwheels a note.

```
From: MadFinn
To: Bigwheels
Subject: BBQ
Date: Fri 8 Sept 11:11 PM
```
I went. It was on this big estate
and everyone was sunbathing and
smiling and I waltzed in and made
the friend thing work like you said
I could.

Thank you for your long-distance
advice.

I couldn't have BBQ-ed without you.
You know if you ever need advice
from me, I'll try to give it!

Yours till the root beer floats,
MadFinn

p.s. write back sooner than soon!

Lastly, Madison went into her favorite file.

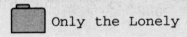 Only the Lonely

Today was Drew's BBQ.

161

He had one in fifth grade, the first one
he ever threw I think, but I had a cold
and had to stay home from school that day.
He had one last year, too, but I can't
remember exactly why I wasn't there. I seem
to remember being in the middle of some
kind of personal crisis seeing as that is
the time when Mom and Dad got the big D.
Yeah that was definitely it. The big D got
in the way a lot last year.

All I can think about is the way things
used to be and how that won't ever *change*.
What I mean is that no one can ever take
any of that away from me. No matter
whatever happens in the future, I own every
little thing that has already happened in
the past—all the food fights, the pop
quizzes, all of it.

Maybe worrying about being only the
lonely was TOTALLY normal??? Maybe everyone
is a bit lonely.

How can I possibly be lonely when everything that makes me and Aimee BFFs has
already happened? No one can take that. So
no matter how many Fionas I meet, no matter
how my body changes, no matter how time
flies, Aimee and I will never change what
makes us close. No one can take away the
soul sisters pact from fourth grade or the
fact that I know all her secrets and she
knows all of mine, right? Why is it that I
can't ever seem to

Madison's eyes were getting very sleepy. She

162

tried to keep writing, but she just couldn't, so she turned off her computer and pulled up the blankets, patting the bed a few times so Phin would leap up and under the covers. Of course the dog jumped in immediately. He licked Madison's nose. That was his puggly way of saying nighty-night.

Madison had been afraid she wouldn't make it through the summer.

But she had—all the way through to September.

She was scared about starting seventh grade.

But here she was—and the giant pink welt on her shoulder had already disappeared.

She closed her tired eyes dreaming about how she and Aimee would spend Saturday afternoon tomorrow in the middle of the Indian summer heat wave, dancing in the sprinklers on Aimee's lawn, getting cooled off, and laughing the way they did every summer—just like last year and all the years before that.

From now on, Madison Finn would be only the lonely no more. She was ready to expect the unexpected.

Mad Chat Words:

```
:>)           Smile
(( ))*        Hugs and Smooches
:-@           I'm screaming!
;- )          Winky-wink
*poof*        Has left the chat room
GMTA          Great Minds Think Alike
IMO           In My Opinion
LOL           Laugh Out Loud
BTW           By the Way
L8R           Later
2K4W          Too Cool For Words
TTFN          Ta Ta For Now
BRB           Be Right Back
```

<u>Madison's Computer Tip:</u>

Whenever you are online, you have to be smart and safe, especially when you're in chat rooms. **<u>Never give out information about you or your family online.</u>** This means no phone numbers, addresses, passwords, or credit card numbers. I always tell my Mom or Dad where I surf online and who I talk to. You should too.

Visit Madison at www.madisonfinn.com

Book #1: *Only the Lonely*

Super Quiz

Now that you've read the story . . . how much do you *really* know about Madison and her friends?

1. What is Madison's screen name?
    a. MadAboutYou
    b. MadFinn
    c. Maddie

2. Where does Madison live?
    a. Ridge Road
    b. Blueberry Street
    c. Far Hills Avenue

3. Where does Fiona live?
   a. Ridge Road
   b. Blueberry Street
   c. Far Hills Avenue

4. What is the first day of school?
   a. September 1
   b. September 2
   c. September 5

5. Where does Bigwheels live?
   a. Washington, D.C.
   b. Washington State
   c. Wyoming

6. What does Madison do for the first time early in the book?
   a. Cut her hair
   b. Bake a chocolate cake
   c. Shave her legs

7. How does Madison refer to her parents' divorce?
   a. The Big Disaster
   b. The Big G
   c. The Big D

8. What is Egg's real name?
   a. Walter Diaz
   b. Antonio Diaz
   c. Walter Eggman

9. What does Egg like to do in his spare time?
   a. Go bowling
   b. Play computer games
   c. Wrestle with his sister, Mariah

10. In which ballet does Aimee perform at camp?
   a. *Swan Lake*
   b. *The Swan Prince*
   c. *Nutcracker Crack-Up*

11. Which one of these items can be found in Madison's room at Dad's?
   a. A smelly old pair of sneakers
   b. A magic eight ball
   c. A collage featuring the words *need you* and *comfort*

12. What/who else is pictured in the second-grade photo of Madison and Hart that Fiona spots on the shelf?
   a. Ivy Daly
   b. Phin
   c. A sunfish

13. What special software does Madison show Fiona on the computer?
   a. "Makeover Magic"
   b. "Make Me a New Room—NOW"
   c. "Making Friends and Slamming Enemies"

14. What thoughtful statement does Madison's English teacher, Mr. Gibbons, write on the board?
    a. "Expect to be challenged."
    b. "Expect the expected."
    c. "Expect the unexpected."

15. When did Madison and Aimee make their soul-sisters' pact?
    a. First grade
    b. Third grade
    c. Fourth grade

16. What kinds of images does Madison prefer to use as her screen saver?
    a. Pictures of her BFF
    b. Pictures of endangered animals
    c. Pictures of her dog, Phin

17. Who lived in Fiona's house before the Waters family moved in?
    a. The Smiths
    b. The Martins
    c. The Walters

18. What is the name of the camp counselor Aimee has a crush on?
    a. Josh
    b. Matt
    c. Colin

19. What is Madison's middle name?
    a. Maria
    b. Tiffany
    c. Francesca

20. What is Egg's favorite sport to watch on television?
    a. Professional Hockey
    b. Professional Wrestling
    c. Professional Golf

21. What fruit makes Fiona want to puke?
    a. Banana
    b. Raspberry
    c. Grape

22. What are Madison's nicknames for Poison Ivy's two best friends?
    a. Rose Thorn and Phony Joanie
    b. Nosy Rosy and Clone Joan
    c. Red Nose Rose and Joanie the Clown

23. What screen name does Fiona use on the Internet?
    a. Wetwinz
    b. Wetwins
    c. Fi-Fi

Answers:
1b, 2b, 3a, 4c, 5b, 6c, 7c, 8a, 9b, 10a, 11b, 12c, 13a, 14c, 15c, 16b, 17b, 18a, 19c, 20b, 21a, 22a, 23a

How well do you know Maddie?

20–23 correct: You might as well pack your bags and move to Far Hills, because you are a *Madison Finn* fanatic!

17–20 correct: You could totally be Madison's BFF, because you know her inside out!

14–16 correct: You think Maddie's pretty cool, and you'd have fun hanging out with her.

10–13 correct: You know a few things about Madison, and you're interested in finding out more about her.

12 or fewer correct: You didn't quite catch all those details about Maddie, but don't worry— there's still lots of time to learn.

From the Files of
Madison Finn

Boy, Oh Boy!

For my brother, Andrew MacTaggart, who is destined for great things

Fifteen minutes into the start of the school day, and Madison Finn had already chewed off all the orange glitter polish on her left hand. It was one of Madison's thirty or so nervous habits, right up there on the list next to sweating when she tried to play the flute and fleeing the scene when she was embarrassed. She was *very* skilled at fleeing.

Mrs. Wing stood in front of the classroom. "Welcome to the twenty-first century, where technology teacher and librarian morph into one being. Well, online librarian, anyhow. I'm your happy cybrarian, at your service."

"That's *Mrs.* Cybrarian to us, right?" Egg (a.k.a. Walter Diaz) said aloud, his voice warbling.

"Last week we talked about some basic facts about computers," Mrs. Wing said, lecturing from the front of the class. "We covered how hardware is assembled and how chips are made. And Mr. Diaz was kind enough to explain to us how a chip works."

She glanced over to Egg's desk and he grinned a real Grinchy grin.

"No prob', Mrs. Wing," he said.

Madison flared her nostrils. The only thing she hated more than Egg's constant crushing on teachers was when he was being extra cocky. Ever since Madison and Egg were kids, he had crushed on pretty female teachers. First it was kindergarten's Miss Jeremiah; now it was the seventh-grade cybrarian.

Mrs. Wing fit into Egg's crush category perfectly. She was prettier than pretty, Madison thought. Her long hair was swept up into a French twist and she wore a long plum-colored skirt, a neat white blouse, and a red bead necklace. She moved around the room as if she were walking on cotton balls, floating from computer station to station, beads *plink-plink-plinking* together.

"Now, what I'd like to try out with the class this week are some basic programming skills," Mrs. Wing continued. "I think we're all ready to move ahead, am I right?"

Lance, a quiet kid who always sat at the back of the classroom, raised his hand and shook his head, dejected. He didn't get computers and felt *way* left out. He was *not* ready. Not by a long jump. Or was it a shot put?

Madison shot Egg a glance, but, thankfully, Mrs. Wing said she'd explain it again *later*.

"Learning Basic," Mrs. Wing went on, "means that every one of you in this room will be able to program a computer. Just think about that. Think about what that could do for all of you. And looking around, I can see already that I have a classroom filled with technological geniuses . . . even *you*, Lance."

As soon as she said that, someone on the other side of the room snorted. Madison realized it was Egg's best friend, Drew Maxwell, who laughed when he heard the words *Lance* and *genius* uttered in the same breath. And as soon as he snorted, Egg snorted too. And then this kid P.J. Rigby snorted. And then Jason Szelewski, Beth Dunfey, Suresh Dhir—*everyone* snorted.

It sounded like a pig farm.

Mrs. Wing didn't get mad, though. She just sort of snorted right back.

"Well, I can see we'll be having a lot of fun in here, class. Just let's make sure it's not at someone *else's* expense, okay?"

Madison saw Egg making puppy-dog eyes at the back of Mrs. Wing's head when she said that. Turning away, Madison reread her onscreen notes.

```
Dim strTemper As String
Const strNormNumbers$ = "0123456789"
Exit Function
End If
End If
OnlyNumericTextInput = strSource
End Function
```

After reviewing her page of code about strings and substrings and lots of little dollar signs, Madison popped in a disk and booted up her own personal file.

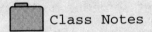 Class Notes

Nothing at Far Hills Junior High is what I expected. I thought it would be way different than middle school. NOT. I figured there was no way the same people from Far Hills Elementary would be geeks or popular but that is just the way it is, like the same thing as last year but in a different building. Dad says I always overthink this kind of stuff but it's just so hard to hold back a thought sometimes.

Mrs. Wing is sooo smart, so she probably will catch me right now writing personal stuff, and not school stuff but oh well. She's all the way on the other side of the room.

I like the way her beads look like red jelly beans. I wear a ring on almost every single finger, but I don't go for necklaces so much. Maybe I should?

Something about seventh grade was inspiring Madison. With a new laptop and a brand-new scanner, maybe she could become a techno-queen for a change.

"She's so cool, right?" Egg nudged Madison and stared as Mrs. Wing flew around to the other side of the classroom.

"Egg," Madison whispered back. "Aren't you bored? We know this stuff already."

"Bored? Not me," Egg replied, pie-eyed. "Why ask for more work? Are you crazy, Maddie? You want *more* work?"

Madison sneered. "Gimme a break. Egg, don't you want to learn something new?"

"Learn? Geesh, you sound like my mom," Egg's pal Drew butted in.

"Yeah, Maddie," Egg said, copying him. "You sound like *my* mom, too."

"Yeah, Maddie," Drew said again.

"Hey, quit it!" Madison snapped.

The two boys laughed and high-fived each other softly.

"At least I don't have a crush on someone who reminds me of my mom," Madison said, looking in Mrs. Wing's direction. She crossed her arms in front of her chest, daring him to respond.

"Put a lid on it, guys," Drew suddenly warned, yanking Egg's fleece.

Mrs. Wing was headed back toward their computer stations.

"Mr. Diaz. Miss Finn. Problem here?" Mrs. Wing said.

Madison and Egg looked at their monitors and grunted at the same time in the same monotone. "No, Mrs. Wing. No problem."

Then she looked over at Drew.

He tried not to react. But it's hard to hold back a snort.

"Do I need to separate you three?" Mrs. Wing said, tapping her foot. Madison thought she would stay like that forever, huffing and puffing and looking disappointed, but in less than a minute she gave up. Mrs. Wing had to help Lance, who was lost in Basic again.

Madison glared at Drew and Egg. "Don't get me in trouble, guys!"

"Maddie, you are a stress puppy," Egg said. Drew nodded in agreement.

Madison gave them both another nasty look and they all went back to their computer screens.

Of course Madison was overly sensitive these days to begin with. She missed her parents.

Dad was out of town on business, all the way across the country. He was meeting with the design firm that had helped set up his Web site. He was launching a new business *again*. Madison couldn't remember what exactly it was going to be.

Mom was also gone. She'd left yesterday to head overseas on a business trip for Budge Films, a movie production company that made small nature documentaries. During the summer, Madison had been able to travel along with her mom on another journey—to South America—to film rare tree frogs. But there was no more traveling allowed together now, not during *school days*.

Mom always said, "You have more important things to take care of during the school year, Maddie. Like getting your junior high diploma."

So while Mom was meeting with lots of French people and eating plates of *pommes frites*, Madison stayed put in Far Hills. She and her dog, Phin, were camped out for the duration at Aimee's house.

Staying at Aimee's was a treat. Aimee Anne Gillespie wasn't just Madison Francesca Finn's best friend. Madison liked to think of her as a sister. They had known each other since birth.

"Um, Mrs. Wing? Could you help me out with this?" Egg was mooning in the teacher's direction again. Madison wanted to gag. He may have acted all tough and smart, but in computer class Egg was *definitely* soft-boiled.

While the rest of the class continued working on their Basic assignment, Madison tried to sneak on line. The system connected, but she couldn't get on to her favorite site, bigfishbowl.com.

No Access! See your Cybrarian!

On these classroom computers, there were built-in blocks preventing students from online access except at designated times. Madison knew Mrs. Wing had put up all the blocks. She knew how to keep everyone focused on the assignment and only the assignment—didn't she?

This was going to be a long week.

Madison could feel the low dull ache that burns inside when you really, *really* miss someone.

And it wasn't just Mom or Dad.

Madison missed her purple blow-up chair, her file cabinet, her miles of files, and all her other *stuff*. Madison missed the way her bare feet felt on Mom's wood floors and the way the kitchen table rocked on one side when you leaned on it. She missed the way her pug Phinnie liked to curl up in front of the dishwasher during the dry cycle.

Right now, thinking about it too much, Madison missed everything about home. Or at least about the way home had used to be, when Mom and Dad were still together.

"Psssst!" Drew suddenly whispered over to Madison. "Are you having trouble getting online?"

Madison nodded. She was having *all* kinds of trouble. But she was glad to know she wasn't the only one bored with the assignment.

"I know a secret back entrance," he said, still

whispering so Mrs. Wing couldn't hear. "I can tell you the secret password that only the teachers are supposed to know."

"Oh really? Then how do you—?"

Madison dropped her head down a little because Mrs. Wing was slowly making her way over to their desks.

Brrrrrrrrring.

The cybrarian code would have to be cracked later.

"And we are outta here!" Madison's brain whirred as she zipped up her orange backpack.

"Uh, Madison Finn, could you hold on a moment?" Mrs. Wing held up her hand for Madison to wait around. Everyone else who was still in the room stopped and stared.

"Oooo, you're in trouble now!" Egg whispered.

"Oh, shut up," Madison grunted under her breath. She scratched her cheek. It was so hot. Everything was happening in slo-mo.

"Later for you, Maddie." Egg was ready to walk out.

"Want us to hang outside?" Drew said to Madison. "I mean, we can wait here in the hall."

Egg was getting impatient. "Come on, Drew-fus. Let's make like a tree—"

"Don't leave!" Madison buzzed. "What do you guys think she wants? Do you think she knows I was trying to get online? I mean, I know I shouldn't have

9

been working on my own disk in class, but do you guys think—"

Madison had never *ever* been asked to stay after class. And she had never ever *ever* been asked to do it in front of a whole bunch of kids either, let alone ones who didn't know her. It was the worst moment of seventh grade so far. Madison was panicked.

Drew shrugged. "Maddie, it's probably nothing."

Egg looked over at Mrs. Wing. "I wish she was keeping *me* after class."

Oh boy.

Chapter 2

Madison slumped into a blue chair near Mrs. Wing's desk.

She felt blue, too.

"Madison, I noticed you seemed a little distracted in class," Mrs. Wing began.

"Distracted?" Madison repeated with concern. She gazed over Mrs. Wing's head so she wouldn't have to look her in the eye. As usual, she expected the worst kind of news.

"Well, you seem bored," she said, beads clacking again.

Madison frowned. "I do?"

"And I don't like seeing that," Mrs. Wing continued.

11

Madison sighed.

"Well, why would I? You are obviously good at computers. And I'm your teacher. I want to keep you challenged. Not bored."

Madison tilted her head to the side. "You do?"

"Of course," Mrs. Wing chuckled, which broke the tension a little. She sat on the edge of her old metal desk. "I want this to be your favorite class, of course. Isn't that what all teachers are supposed to say?"

Madison smiled. "But this is my favorite class. And I am not just saying that. Really. Truly."

"Madison, are you interested in doing something special with the Computer Center this year? Usually I ask eighth graders to do this—"

"Something special?"

"Class elections are coming up and I'm the faculty advisor. I am responsible for getting the elections up and running on the Web. The school wants your classmates to vote online for the very first time this year. Far Hills just got a brand-new proxy server over the summer!"

"Proxy *wha*?" Madison asked.

"Server. It's a computer that will support our own special network right here in the building. And what I need is someone to help me to maintain the site— download photos, results, and other new information on a regular basis. Then we will have everyone in seventh grade vote online."

12

Madison didn't know what to say.

Mrs. Wing just grinned. "So, Madison, what's the verdict? Would you be interested in helping out?"

Madison nodded, but no words came out.

"I take that as a yes?" Mrs. Wing joked.

"Yes!" Madison said at last.

"As you know, we have less than two weeks until the election, so I will need you to stay after school to work on the site, answer e-mails, and other work. We can talk specifics tomorrow. Does that sound like something you might be able to do?"

Madison nodded with delight. She felt as if someone had just handed her a winning Lotto ticket. She really could be techno-queen.

"So." Mrs. Wing held out her hand to shake. "Are we a team then?"

"Yessss!" Madison gushed again. She grabbed her backpack and started for the door. "I can't believe this, Mrs. Wing. I can't. I swear I will be the best, best, best Web-site person ever."

Mrs. Wing laughed. "I'm sure you will be. See you tomorrow."

On her way out of the room, Madison's mind turned to mush. She had never been asked to do something like this by a teacher before.

"What did she say?" Egg said, leaping out from a bank of lockers.

Madison jumped. "Oh, Egg you scared me—"

"We were waiting for you all this time," Egg said. "Spill it."

The first bell was ringing. Aimee and Fiona walked up to the lockers.

Fiona Waters was Madison's newest best friend from over the summer. She and her family, including twin brother Chet, had moved to Far Hills from California. Even though she was a little bit spacey, Madison liked Fiona a lot.

"Hey, Maddie," Fiona said, "what's going on? Were you just in computer?"

"Yes, she was," Egg chimed in. "And Mrs. Wing kept her after class. She was about to tell me."

Madison scowled at Egg. "What is your problem?"

"Hey, Walter," Fiona said coyly. Of course Egg was too busy bugging Madison to give Fiona a hello or even a smile.

"Did you say 'Walter'?" Aimee asked, shaking her head. She laughed. "Fiona, his name is Egg. Nobody calls him Walter except his mother."

Fiona looked a little embarrassed.

"Maddie, are you gonna tell me or *what*?" Egg asked again.

"Well, gimme a chance, all right?"

Madison was busting to tell Egg and everyone else what Mrs. Wing had said to her after class. But everyone else wouldn't shut up.

14

"Hold it!" Aimee said. "Is this because something happened in computer class?"

"Is everything okay? Did you get into trouble?" asked Drew.

"Why won't you just tell us?" Egg yelled again.

"I am TRYING!" Madison yelled and then quickly lowered her voice. "I am trying to tell you but you guys keep talking. Okay. What happened is that Mrs. Wing says she wants *me* to help her run all of the online elections for Far Hills Junior High. That's it."

"She *what*?" Egg wasn't smiling.

"Hey, that's pretty cool," Drew said.

Madison continued, "She wants me to be Election Web Manager or something like that for the school Web site."

"You?" Egg slapped his forehead.

"Yeah, *me*. What's wrong with that?"

"What about *me*?" Egg said.

"You can't have everything your way, Egg," Aimee snapped.

"That is so awesome, Maddie!" Fiona chimed in.

"Yeah, way to go," Drew added.

Aimee grinned. "Maddie, you will totally be the best person for the job."

Egg backed himself up against a bank of lockers. "But I am the one who taught you how to go on-line, Madison. It should be me who gets this, not you!"

"Egg, just chill out," Aimee said. "It is no big deal."

"It is a deal," Egg said. "This is a big, fat, *hairy* deal."

"I'm sorry, Egg." Madison stood there for a moment waiting for Egg to say something else, but he didn't.

The second bell rang, echoing in the hall.

"Look, you guys, I gotta run!" Drew waved as he wandered away. "Got a class . . ."

"See ya, Drew." Madison waved back. "Egg?"

Egg was already walking in the other direction.

"What a pain," Aimee said.

Madison hated the fact that Egg was annoyed, but she also knew that no matter what was said right now, tomorrow he would get over it and they'd be friends just as before. She hoped.

As she, Aimee, and Fiona moved off toward their next class, a voice called out from near the water fountain.

"Hey, Finnster!"

Finnster was a nickname Hart Jones had called Madison way back when they had been in first grade. It was a dorky name and she hated it, but he did it anyway. After second grade, Hart had moved away, but now he was back and the name was back, too.

Aimee chuckled under her breath. She elbowed

Madison in the side. "Hey, I think he likes you."

Fiona was giggling.

"Hart?" Madison groaned. "Get real."

"Just like a fairy tale," Aimee laughed. "Once he was a frog and now he's a prince."

"Ribbit." Fiona laughed some more.

Madison walked faster. She heard Hart call out again, "Hey, Finnster!" but breezed on by pretending not to hear.

Aimee and Fiona heard and responded at the exact same time, however.

"Hi, Hart. 'Bye, Hart."

"Isn't Hart cousins with Drew?" Fiona asked Aimee as they walked away.

"You know he really has gotten sooooo cute." Aimee teased Madison some more.

"And he's really tall for a seventh grader."

"Yeah, whatever," Madison moaned. "I don't hang out with him anymore."

"Maybe you should," Fiona said.

"No thank you very much," Madison replied.

"I forgot you think all boys are just idiots," Aimee said.

Fiona laughed. "Maybe that's true. I know my brother Chet is."

Aimee stopped and grabbed one of Madison's hands. "Maddie, what are you gonna do if this boy really does like you? What then?" She looked down at Madison's fingers. "Hey, what happened to the nail polish I put on last week? It's all chewed off."

"Oh, that," Madison said, glancing down at whatever was left of the glitter polish. "It was delicious," she said walking toward study hall.

 Boys

Is something wrong with me? I cannot believe the way life works these days. I spend all summer stressing out about being a seventh grader. Now that I'm here I am just stressing out about something else.

Is Egg right? Am I a total stress puppy? No wait, my dog, Phinnie, is the stress puppy. I'm the stress *person*. Ha ha.

I'm just not like Aimee or Fiona. I just don't see the point in wasting time trying to get some stupid boy to like me. Every time Aimee likes someone she always changes her mind anyhow. It's not real. I don't want to pretend. I want the real thing when I have it. I would rather just stay friends anyway. That is easier.

Aimee doesn't even know what it's like because she always can talk to boys. And Fiona is good at flirting too, even if Egg is the one she flirts with.

NO BOYS FOR ME.

I have to worry about other stuff like

the election Web site and not boys. I have to make sure the school election is the best ever. Mrs. Wing is counting on me.

Madison spent the entire study hall period working at the lone computer station up in the library. Students were allowed to work in the classroom, the library, or the media center. Madison liked to escape to the top floor of the school's main building whenever she could. It seemed like no one else ever came up here, so Madison had it scoped out as *her* secret place—a place where she could go to hide, think, do homework, and even update her files. Mr. Books, the librarian, knew Madison by sight, since she came up at least twice a week.

After study hall, Madison wandered into the newspaper office to pick up some photos and bios of class presidential candidates. It was for the Web site, of course. This was Mrs. Wing's first "official" assignment for her.

Madison loved the way the newspaper room smelled like ink and glue and copy paper. Maybe she should try out for the newspaper staff? Madison was having trouble figuring out which after-school activities were the most important. She loved the computer, but Madison wanted to try other things, too.

There on the desk at the front of the room was a rubber-banded pile of envelopes with a simple note: "For Mrs. Wing: 7th-grade candidates."

Madison picked up the envelopes.

In envelope number one was a photo of Madison's enemy number one, Ivy Daly, also known as Poison Ivy. Madison had been calling her that for a few years now, ever since they had their major falling-out in third grade.

So far, Ivy was the only girl at Far Hills Junior High running for class president. She was going to win. Everyone knew Ivy.

For one thing, Ivy was pretty smart.

For another thing, she was pretty pretty.

Ivy was also wicked good at talking to boys. She was even better at it than Aimee, which was saying a lot. With those talents, how could she lose a seventh-grade election?

Ivy also surrounded herself with influential sup-porters like Roseanne Snyder and Joan Kenyon. They were two drones who stuck to Ivy like superglue and made fun of all the people who weren't just like them. Rose and Joan were intimidating even when they didn't speak. Madison knew deep down they were fakers. She called them Rose *Thorn* and *Phony* Joanie behind their backs. But even if they were obnoxious, they would still help Ivy win. Safety in numbers.

As she stared at Ivy, Madison got less excited about her new Web assignment.

At first it seemed so exciting, being picked to be in charge of the election site. Madison could be the boss for once. But now, looking at Ivy, Madison felt discouraged.

How could she enjoy any election when she *hated* the number one candidate?

Chapter 3

"Miss Finn, you'll be working with Miss Daly."

In science class, Mr. Danehy was assigning lab partners.

Madison got Poison Ivy.

"So is it true that you're like in charge of the election?" Ivy asked as they paired off together and sat on their stools at the lab counter.

"It's true," Madison mumbled, trying to say as little as possible.

"I heard from Mrs. Wing that you're the one doing the school Web site or something."

News travels fast around junior high, Madison thought, pasting on her best plastic smile. "Yes, I am in charge of the Web site. Mrs. Wing asked me."

"Oh," Ivy said with a perplexed look on her face.

"Why should you care, Ivy?"

"Care?" Ivy said. "Because I am only like the number-one candidate for seventh-grade president. Like, where have you been? Didn't you see my posters in the cafeteria?"

Madison pretended like she'd swallowed something the wrong way and cleared her throat. Ivy kept talking.

"So far it's just me and Montrell Morris and Tommy Kwong. Should be an easy election, really."

Madison stared down at the lab's black countertop, feeling like she'd been drop-kicked. Everything seemed so rosy first period. Now she had gone from being singled out by Mrs. Wing to being *bummed* out by Poison Ivy. What fun would it be working on an election when the enemy had the distinct advantage?

"You *are* gonna vote for me, right?" Ivy said.

"Well," Madison said, gritting her teeth. "I'm not sure who I'm voting for yet."

"Whatever," Ivy said, opening her science book.

The clock said 11:22. Could Madison make it through the other forty-eight minutes until science class ended?

She wasn't so sure.

Right now Madison Finn wanted to slam her science teacher Mr. Danehy for putting her in this position, at this table, with Ivy Daly. She would have preferred being matched up with *anyone* else on the planet. Even Hart Jones would have been an okay lab partner.

Madison looked across the class at Hart. He and Fiona's twin brother, Chet, had been paired off together. They were becoming fast friends, Madison could tell by the way they goofed around. Madison looked at Hart's hair, combed back off his face. His black glasses were slipping down his nose and he looked nerdy, but he also looked cute.

Was he really the same Hart Jones who used to chase her around at recess and try to pull her hair? Madison suddenly realized she was staring.

"And one more thing! You will *NOT* leave science lab early under any conditions," Mr. Danehy's voice boomed. "If you and your partner finish up an assignment, simply move along to the extra-credit questions. I do not encourage loafing, is that clear? This is not a place to have conversations, this is a place to learn science. Clear?"

Mr. Danehy had set up microscopes all over the room. Lab partners were asked to record their simple observations as they viewed a series of slides.

Of course, Ivy didn't feel like looking. "I'll just copy your answers?" she said to Madison. "After all, we are partners, right?"

Madison bit her lip. She looked into the micro-scope and adjusted the magnification knob.

"What you are looking at right now," Mr. Danehy said, "is a slide of human spit."

A couple of girls and guys said, "Eeeeeew" but then leaned in to get a closer look. Madison took a look, too, while Ivy drummed her fingers against the lab table, impatient.

"This is so stupid. Spit? Gimme a break. What about cells or something a little more scientific?"

Madison pushed the microscope toward Ivy. "Why don't you see for yourself? There's science going on there. Science like *cells*, you know."

Ivy scoffed. "I don't think so. Get that spit away from me."

Madison ignored Ivy and looked into the microscope. She adjusted it once again for the next slide.

Ivy jumped off her stool and walked to the front of the classroom. She needed a hall pass to use the bathroom. She said she had to pee, but Madison suspected she was going in there a) to apply more lip gloss; b) to make a call on her cell phone (a little pink phone she carried everywhere); or c) to get away from the spit slide once and for all.

Mr. Danehy handed Ivy a hall pass and then disappeared into the science closet. Once he was gone, everyone started talking and moving around. Hart Jones wandered over to Madison's table.

"Hey, there," he said gruffly.

Madison rolled her eyes but didn't speak.

"Uh, I seem to have lost my fruit fly. Have you seen him?"

Madison was mortified. Was anyone else listening? She couldn't help but laugh a little bit at Hart's stupid attempt at a joke, but she certainly didn't want anyone else to hear it.

Hart cracked another joke about someone's fruit fly being open.

Madison laughed a little more. She liked the way his hair twisted on top of his head. This was the first time she'd ever noticed that he had a cowlick. It looked like a wave of dark chocolate. She wondered why he had come over to talk to her. Why was he just standing there making jokes?

Mr. Danehy pulled out a large container from the closet. It was filled with hundreds of *living* fruit flies. Quickly, he dropped in a cotton ball with chloroform. In two minutes all the flies were knocked out. Chet yelled out, "Fruit flies dead! Details at eleven!" Everyone laughed.

When Mr. Danehy was almost done showing the flies to the room, Ivy walked back in. She walked in just in time to watch Hart slip off her stool and make his way back to his own seat as the class settled down.

"Did I miss much?" Ivy said, eyeing Hart and Chet across the room, and pushing Madison to the side a little bit so she could squeeze back into her chair.

Madison grabbed at the counter edge, but she lost her balance. She fell forward, knocking into a cardboard tray of glass beakers.

Crash.

"What did you do that for?" Ivy screeched. "I can't believe you!"

The beaker of stunned flies survived. Unfortunately, Madison's pride did not.

Mr. Danehy rushed over. "Nobody move. I'm gonna sweep up this mess. Watch the glass, girls."

From across the room, Hart yelled out, "Way to go, Finnster!"

Madison turned beet purple as the class laughed.

"Finnster?" Ivy laughed. "Nice name, Madison. For a circus act, maybe."

The last thing Madison wanted to do was to call attention to herself, and yet here she was, the center of the chaos. Everyone was staring and laughing. Ivy was pointing. And Hart was calling her Finnster.

She couldn't believe it.

"Miss Finn, Miss Daly," Mr. Danehy said as he plucked up the glass shards. "This is absolutely not your fault—"

"Well, I *KNOW* it's not *my* fault," Ivy interrupted.

"I should not have had the containers here . . ."

"Oh, well, Madison probably didn't mean to make a big mess," Ivy said. "I mean I tried to grab the materials for her but she fell off the chair—"

Madison's jaw dropped.

"Madison, you really have to be careful in science class," Ivy went on, smirking. Mr. Danehy believed every word.

He patted her on the back. "Well, it's no problem,

Madison. We all make mistakes and get caught off balance, don't we?"

All at once, Madison felt tears coming but she sucked on her top front teeth, inhaled deep, and held them in. She wanted to flee—*badly*.

If Ivy Daly did not shut her trap in T-minus-30 seconds, Madison was ready to do the fifty-yard dash down the hall. She tried to hold on.

By the time science class finally ended, Madison's stomach ached from holding on so long. She watched as Ivy, Rose, and Joanie exited class at the exact same time as Hart and Chet.

"Aren't you Bart Jones?" Ivy said, tossing her hair.

Chet grunted. "Who wants to know?"

Hart just smiled. "Yeah, I'm Hart Jones. With an H."

Madison could hear every word.

Ivy tossed her hair again. "Oh yeah, H for Hart. Do you remember me?" She cocked her hip to the side and twirled a strand of her red hair. Her jeans were cut low on her waist so that Madison could almost see her belly button.

Madison wasn't sure why, but she didn't want to see Hart with Poison Ivy. As they were standing there, Hart turned around once and caught Madison's eye. But then he looked away again.

"Madison!" Mr. Danehy said loudly.

"What?" Madison said, stunned.

"Don't forget your books."

Madison grabbed them and pushed her way over to the door. For a brief moment, she was stuck right between Ivy and Hart.

"Excuuuuuse me." She nudged Ivy and walked through.

Ivy clucked her tongue. "Way to be pushy, Madison."

Hart stared at the floor.

On the way home, Madison talked with Aimee and Fiona about the day's events: the good, the bad, and the ugly. The good news about the election Web site, the bad news about the tiff with Egg, and the ugly—Poison Ivy Daly.

"*OH MY GOD*, she can *NOT* win this election!" Aimee exclaimed. "She is such a kiss-up."

"Who else is running?" Fiona asked. "Is that Montrell guy?"

"Yeah, Montrell Morris. He's funny."

"And Tommy Kwong, too," Madison added. "He's one of the leads in Drama Club."

"Ivy Daly *MUST* not win," Aimee said again with emphasis.

Fiona nodded. "I really didn't think she was so bad at first, but I really see what you mean about her being a little too—"

"Two-faced?" Aimee shouted.

"Yeah, well, if you put it that way, I have to agree," Fiona joked.

"Did you guys see the way she was acting in school assembly last week?" Aimee pointed out. "She was kissing up to Principal Bernard after he made another one of his stupid speeches." Aimee moaned, doing her best Ivy imitation. "Ooooh, Mr. Bernard, you're sooooo funny!"

"She's disgusting when she hangs all over the teachers. That's how she is in science, too. She was even flirting with Hart Jones today."

"Hart?" Aimee screeched. *"NO WAY!"* Aimee, as usual, was being a little dramatic.

"Yeah," Madison groaned. "And Ivy was doing that thing she always does. That guy thing."

Fiona asked, "What *guy* thing?"

"Hey, *do* you like Hart or something?" Aimee said.

Madison blushed. "No."

"You do like him!" Fiona screeched. "Look at you!"

"I do *NOT* like Hart Jones. Will you guys just stop, already." Madison sighed.

Aimee started back in on the subject of their least favorite classmate. "You know, for once I wish things would not go Ivy's way."

"She's eviler than evil," Madison said.

"I don't think any of us will be signing up for an Ivy for President fan club," Aimee said.

"Not me," Madison agreed.

"Well then, me neither," said Fiona.

If there had ever been any doubt at the start of seventh grade about what new kids were friends with what old kids, that doubt ended here. Fiona was with Madison and Aimee all the way.

Continuing up the street, Madison felt the quick breeze in the air that announced fall was really on its way. Gone were the afternoons of running through freshly cut lawns and sprinklers and all things summer. The sky was getting dark earlier now. Gone were the sidewalk smells of lilacs and honeysuckle, replaced by the sweet scent of firewood and damp, cool air. Soon all the trees in the neighborhood would blend yellow, red, and *orange*—Madison's favorite color in the whole world. Maybe the breezes could blow away all the bad vibes of school?

Madison hoped so.

"So does Egg have a girlfriend?" Fiona said all of a sudden, switching to a new subject.

"Egg?" Madison laughed.

Aimee stopped short.

"He really is a cutie," Fiona said shyly. "I know I said that before but—"

"Fiona Waters, did you just say Egg was *CUTE*?" Aimee laughed out loud.

"Don't you think so?" Fiona said. "I don't know why but he is just so—"

"Are you nuts?" Aimee asked seriously. "No, Fiona, I mean it. *ARE YOU NUTS?*"

"Noooo." Fiona grinned. She was a little

embarrassed, but she didn't stop talking about it. "I just think he's cute."

Aimee doubled over with laughter. Madison had to hold back her own attack of the giggles, too. How could someone *really* like Egg, the same Egg who had burped "Yankee Doodle" at field day last year?

Aimee and Madison were practically keeling over in hysterics, but Fiona wasn't going back on what she had said.

"Go ahead and laugh," Fiona said. "Whatever."

"We're not laughing at you, I swear," Madison said.

"You really have boys on the brain, don't you?" Aimee smiled.

"Don't you?" Fiona asked.

Fiona didn't get a chance to hear their answers. From across the front lawn where the girls were standing, someone suddenly howled.

"Fi-moan-a, you're *LATE*!"

It was Fiona's twin brother Chet.

Fiona yelled back, "Coming!" and looked down at her silver watch. "Oh! I am soooo busted! Tonight is my Dad's birthday and I gotta make a cake and Mom's gonna—'bye!"

She dashed across the lawn.

Madison tried to say, "Wanna walk to school tomor—?" but it was too late.

Fiona was already inside the house.

As Madison walked inside Aimee's house, Phineas T. Phin, Madison's snuggly pug, rushed the front door.

"Phinnie!" Madison squealed, chasing him into the family room. His little pug tail squiggled. He was allowed to stay at the Gillespie house too when Mom was away because he could hang out with Aimee's dog, Blossom, a sad-looking girl basset hound with bloodshot eyes.

Her arms full, Madison chased Phinnie into the next room to get his personalized dish, which said PHIN FOOD on the side.

"Whoa, there!" Roger jumped back. "You're about to crash into me!"

Roger was the oldest child in Aimee's family. At twenty-three, he was busy helping Mr. Gillespie with

The Book Web, the family bookstore, while he saved up money for graduate school. He had thick blond hair like his sister. Madison liked the way it waved. He was really smart and talented.

Older brothers were so great. Aimee was so lucky. She had *four* of them.

"Hey, Ma says keep it down in here you guys and, oh yeah, dinner is in like an hour," said another one of Aimee's brothers, Billy, coming into the room. The soles of his sneakers were peeled back to reveal ratty yellow socks. He was an undecided sophomore at Briarwood, the local community college. Billy couldn't decide what TV show to watch, let alone decide on a major or minor.

He clicked past ten channels, which annoyed Aimee.

"Billy, don't be a jerko," she yelled, looking disgusted. "You are such a—"

"Bonehead, just give sis the remote." Roger flicked a finger on the back of Billy's head.

"No way," he responded. "Quit poking me."

Roger poked him again. The two brothers started a slap fight.

Aimee, as usual, was not amused.

"Roger! Billy! Can't you be a little bit more normal? What is your problem?" Aimee's voice increased in volume with each word. "Maddie, let's go up to my room before dinner. My stupid brothers are soooooo embarrassing."

Madison picked up her bag and laptop computer case, followed closely behind by panting Phin and Blossom. She caught one last look at Roger and Billy, sprawled across the couch as she left the room. Aimee had her brothers all wrong. These boys seemed perfect.

Half an hour later, everyone was gathered together again at the Gillespie dinner table for a health food feast.

This is a long way from one of Mom's Scary Dinners, Madison thought as she and Aimee silently devoured their platefuls of delicious homemade spaghetti and tofu meatballs. Madison hoped chewing quickly would help make the tofu taste more like real meatballs. Healthy dinners could *also* be scary ones in their own way.

The boys chattered and chewed and burped, seated in an arc around one side of the table. Madison caught herself staring a few times. She hoped no one else caught her doing it. It was like a piece of her brain had become fixated on boys, even boys who were Aimee's brothers.

She didn't know why. It just was just one of those things.

Before they got ready for bed, Madison found a little downtime to go online. She hadn't been on her computer since yesterday.

FROM	SUBJECT
✉ BUSTER	Sk8ing Message for You
✉ finnrpalzyfg_gogo	Earn $$$ at Home
✉ ff_BUDGEFILM	bonjour!
✉ BUSTER	Sk8ing Message for You

Dad always warned Madison about opening unexpected e-mails and attachments in her mailbox. Tonight she deleted them without even opening the files. She figured the BUSTER Special Message was some kind of advertisement and she wasn't interested in "earning $$$ at home."

That left one *real* message.

Getting Mom's e-mail tonight was like getting tucked in via long distance.

```
From: ff_BUDGEFILM
To: MadFinn
Subject: bonjour!
Date: Mon 11 Sept 2:06 PM
Bonjour mon amour! Comment va
l'ecole? I love you so much,
sweetheart, and I miss you already!
I thought you might have fun
figuring out the little bit of
French here.

The weather over here is rain,
```

rain, rain. Have to get me a new
parapluie. That's umbrella, by the
way. We're on site all week but I
promise to write and call. You must
be having fun with Aimee.

Au revoir!
Love you, Mom

ff_BUDGEFILM

Ms. Francine Finn
Vice President of Research and
Development
Senior Producer
Budge Films, Inc.

"Hey, can we turn out the lights, Maddie?" Aimee
grumbled in a sleepy voice. She put down her copy of
The Outsiders and rolled over. "Good night."

It was getting later than late. The clock said 10:25
P.M. Madison punched a few keys to save Mom's message and then typed one last e-mail, a note to her
brand-new keypal, Bigwheels, whom she had met in
a special chat room on bigfishbowl.com. Bigwheels
was starting seventh grade too.

From: MadFinn
To: Bigwheels
Subject: School elections and stuff
Date: Mon 11 Sept 10:32 PM

Sorry FTBOMBH that I haven't written! Well, I actually cannot believe a week has passed. How r u???? School is getting to be a little bit weird. I should have written sooner. HELP!

We're in the middle of school elections right now and it feels like total chaos. I'm not running for president or class rep or anything but I am in the middle of it all. I feel like I am ALWAYS in the middle of SOMETHING!

The computer teacher asked me to help her put all the school elections onto the computer and I'm soooo nervous. What if I make a mistake?

Actually, I wonder sometimes what's the point of the whole thing. It's all decided already. Did I mention that my sworn enemy is probably gonna win and rule the school? I just don't know what magic power she has over everyone so they like her, but they do. How come the people you like the least end up being around you the most? And the

people you love the most go away
when you need them? It's a drag.

All I can say is TAL, PAL! Just for
being out there in the Web world. I
feel not so alone just writing now.

Oh—I have 1 more very important
question!!! Is it possible to
suddenly like someone when you
didn't like him AT ALL yesterday?

Do you have a boyfriend?
Yeah, I know that was two
questions.
Yours till the nail tips,
MadFinn

After she sent the message, Madison yanked on
her favorite Grrrilla Power T-shirt with the ape on
the front and crawled silently into Aimee's trundle
bed. She loved the way the sheets smelled like cin-
namon at Aimee's house.

Once again that creepy yellow hall light clicked
on, casting an eerie glow that danced and bobbed
along Aimee's wall. Madison thought for a moment
how funny it was that *everything* in Aimee's world—
even the shadows of her bedroom—danced.

Aimee's room was so quiet Madison could hear
herself blink.

"Maddie?" Aimee whispered from under the covers.

Night vision kicked in as Madison rolled over on her side to see her friend's face. "Yeah?"

"I can't sleep."

"Sorry."

"No, I've been thinking about our conversations today. You know, about Ivy and all."

"Yeah?"

"Why do you think we want her to lose so badly?"

Madison shrugged but then realized, of course, Aimee couldn't see her in the dark. "I dunno. Because we do. Because we want to see her lose, for once."

"Because sometimes, I dunno. I feel bad about being so nasty. Like I'm so mean or something—"

"Well, you're *NOT*," Madison said. "And neither am I. She had her chance to be our friend, and she totally blew it."

"Ivy always gets her way, doesn't she? She always wins."

"Yeah." Madison yawned. She was getting a little sleepy, but she made herself stay awake to talk some more. "Well, she won't win this time."

"She's the only girl running, Maddie. Of course she'll win."

Madison yawned again. "Yeah, I guess."

"I just wish we could get back at her in some way. Not like revenge. Just something to show her that—"

"To show her that she is not the queen of the universe?"

"Exactly."

Madison scrunched her toes up under the covers. It was cold in Aimee's room.

"Maddie, I think I know. I have an idea.

"Tell me," Madison whispered. "Just say it."

"I think that the way to get back at Ivy for everything she's ever done to us," Aimee said softly, white teeth flashing a sudden smile in the dark, "is to make sure she has some *real* competition in the election.

"Yeah," Madison agreed, "I guess Montrell Morris and Tommy Kwong don't have a chance."

"Like you said, they're gonna split the boy vote."

Madison wondered aloud, "Too bad there isn't a way to split up the girl vote, too."

"There is. I'm gonna run against her," Aimee said matter-of-factly.

"You're what?" Madison propped herself up onto one elbow.

Aimee sat up in bed and clicked on the lamp on her nightstand. Madison squinted.

"I'm gonna run against Poison Ivy in this class president election," Aimee said with growing confidence. "And I'm gonna win."

Chapter 5

"Is she loony-toons?" Fiona said to Madison at lunch.

They were standing on line in front of the hot food counter.

"Do you honestly think she can win?" Madison asked aloud. "Do you think Aimee even has a chance?"

"Baked beans, cheezy macaroni, or smashed potatoes?" the cafeteria server asked. Her stained name tag read GILDA Z and she liked to crack jokes as she ladled out the food.

"Macaroni, please," Madison said politely.

"Good for your noodle." Gilda laughed, scooping out the pasta. "Now, skedoodle!"

"She freaks me out," Fiona whispered.

"Hey, you guys." Aimee arrived, breathless. She twirled up to her friends like the perfect ballerina she was and slid in behind Madison and Fiona with an empty tray.

"No cutting," a kid yelled.

Aimee snapped back, "They were saving my place."

"Where were you?" Fiona asked.

"Class." Aimee's eyes scanned the tub of neon-yellow-colored macaroni. "Hey, Maddie, did you know that that tub of food has more fat in it than—"

"Aim! I'm eating that," Madison yelled. "Shhhh!"

Gilda Z. slopped vegetables onto Aimee's tray.

On the way to the orange table at the back of the room (their *regular* lunch table), Madison, Fiona, and Aimee passed Ivy and her drones, Rose and Joan. The enemy was seated at their usual yellow table, chatting away.

"Hey, Finnster!" Hart Jones called out from nearby.

Madison groaned under her breath but didn't say hello.

"Why does he call you that?" Fiona asked.

Madison shook her head, and sat down to eat her lunch. Sitting there, looking out across the student body, Madison felt herself shrinking—and over-thinking.

Why did Hart keep calling her Finnster?

How could she figure out a way to help Aimee win, help Ivy get beaten, and still work on the Web site fairly?

43

How did she get herself into this mess?

With each bite of cheezy macaroni, Madison was feeling more and more conflicted about her role in the upcoming election.

"Maddie, did you hear what I said?" Fiona slurped her milk.

"Wha?" Madison was acting more spaced-out than Fiona. Apparently, her friends had been trying to get her attention for a minute or so.

"I was just telling Aimee that I really think she can win," Fiona said. "If we help."

"I guess so."

Aimee made a face. "Hey, you're supposed to be on my side! Whaddya mean, 'I guess'?"

Madison snapped back to attention. "Sorry. I was just thinking."

"Oh! I almost forgot," Fiona said. "The coaches told us they would put the soccer lists up today. We can find out if we made the JV team, Madison." She slid out from behind the orange table.

"I can't believe Fiona got you to try out for a sport, Maddie."

Last weekend, Madison had joined Fiona at soccer tryouts. Fiona had been on four different soccer teams back in California before she moved to Far Hills. Everyone who tried out was blown away by Fiona's running and passing and overall soccer skills.

"Of course *you* made it. You were born wearing soccer cleats, right?" Madison dragged her fork across her plate. "Fiona, you'd better give up on me. I just don't have a chance at getting on."

"It would be fun to do it together, though." Fiona was still hopeful. "Maybe you can get picked as an alternate."

"Well, you check the list. I'm too scared to look," Madison said.

"Okay, then." Fiona was standing up, slinging her bag over her shoulder. "But you should think positive."

"I am positive," Madison said, "positively sure I didn't make it."

"Well, if I don't see you after school, I'll IM you later, 'kay?" Fiona said. "'Bye, Aimee."

Madison knew she hadn't made the team because during tryouts, she'd passed the ball to the wrong person *twice* coming down the field and she had touched the ball with her hand like four times. That was a no-no.

But deep down, she didn't mind. The whole reason for trying out wasn't so Madison could become the next soccer star. It was just a way to get closer and have something else in common with Fiona. With soccer practices happening practically every afternoon, Madison wouldn't be seeing very much of Fiona during the fall, especially not on weekends with out-of-town games.

"Don't worry about soccer, Maddie," Aimee said, trying to make her friend feel better.

Madison picked pieces of coconut off the cake on her tray. She said nothing.

"Hey, did you see what Ivy was wearing today?" Aimee said. "She thinks she is so *all that*. Please."

Madison glanced over at Poison and her drones. Ivy had on a tight pink T-shirt that said FAR OUT and a long camouflage-patterned cargo skirt. Madison recognized it from the pages of her favorite online catalog. She hated the way Ivy looked good wearing anything. It wasn't fair.

Just as she was looking that direction, Madison also saw Ivy motion to Hart Jones to come over to her table. Chet and Hart sat down there together for a moment or two.

"Don't look now," Aimee leaned into Madison, "but there's a teacher headed right this—"

"There you are!" Mrs. Wing rushed up to Madison's table carrying a clipboard and a cup of coffee that looked like it was about to spill. "Oh! I have been looking for you all over. We need to talk about the election site. Mr. Bernard is so pleased that you will be helping out. Can you come by my class-room after school?"

Madison shrugged. "Okay."

"Of course!" Mrs. Wing said. "Now, I should tell you that I have two other students helping out, too. Andrew Maxwell and Walter Diaz."

"Drew?" Madison wasn't sure she'd heard Mrs. Wing correctly. "Walter?"

"They'll be working with me on data entry. You know, candidate profiles and that stuff. They volunteered to help. Said they just really had to be involved in some way. Isn't that nice?"

Aimee stood up. "Look, I gotta go, Maddie. Sorry to interrupt, Mrs. Wing." She disappeared before Madison had time to respond.

"Well, then, I'll see you and Drew and Walter after classes then," Mrs. Wing said. Then she disappeared, too, out the door going in the direction of the teachers' lounge.

Madison looked up to see that three-quarters of the 12:00 cafeteria group had left. Madison stood up. No one sat in the lunchroom *alone*! She dumped her uneaten food.

"Hey, Maddie!" Drew caught up with Madison in the hallway on his way to social studies class.

"Hey," Madison said. "So I wanted to ask you—"

"What?" Drew asked.

"Okay." Madison bit her lip. "I wanted to ask you. . . . Since when are you and Egg signed up to help with Mrs. Wing's thing?"

He stammered. "H-h-help? Well, I don't know. We just figured it was a cool thing to do. After yesterday, we got to talking. That's all. We wanted to be a part of the Web site."

Drew usually got to be a part of whatever he wanted. His father was a richer-than-rich inventor who always gave his son the newest, coolest gadgets.

47

Once Drew had an actual spy pen with a teeny-weeny camera inside it, as if someone had slipped James Bond's toy into his pocket.

Madison made a face. "Did Egg put you up to this?"

"Egg?" Drew acted surprised. "Like I said, we thought about it together."

"Yeah, but it's really him," Madison mumbled. "He's so competitive."

"Maybe a little," Drew said. "But he's also smart. Don't you think it will be fun if we all do it together?"

"I guess," Madison sighed. She wasn't totally convinced.

After school, by the time the three of them met up together in room 510 to start the Web site project, Madison was getting used to the idea of Egg and Drew helping. She had to admit that the boys were as good as she was (if not better) with computer stuff. Especially Drew. Even though Egg was a bigmouth about his skills, Madison knew for a fact that Drew had a much higher score at Age of Empires than Egg. He was just a lot quieter about what he knew and didn't know.

Mrs. Wing walked into the technology lab, arms filled with folders and envelopes. "Walter, could you help me here?"

While Egg rescued the folders from Mrs. Wing's arms, Madison and Drew logged onto their computer stations. They went to the text prompts first. There was information to be input on the site. It was the information Madison had retrieved from the newspaper room.

"I'll be right back," Mrs. Wing said. "I need to run back to the office. Start inputting this information and I'll be back shortly."

"Did you read this?" Drew was typing in Ivy's profile and statement of purpose. "She says, 'I promise that when I am elected, I will make this the best junior high in the world.' Is she kidding? In the *world*? Talk about making stuff up. She doesn't even say *how* she's going to do it."

Egg looked at her photo. "Yeah, but she's still a hottie."

"Egg!" Madison groaned. No matter how evil Ivy acted, all Egg really seemed to notice was how she *looked*.

"She comes off like a total robot," Drew said.

"Aimee isn't a robot," Madison said. "Read something from her profile."

Drew shuffled the pages. "'I, Aimee Gillespie, promise that when I am elected, I will make this the best junior high in the world.'"

Egg cackled. "Hah! She says the exact same thing as Poison Ivy!"

"Maybe we should change that," Drew said. "You have to fix what Aimee says."

"That wouldn't be fair," Egg said.

"Yeah, but Aimee is a way cooler candidate," Drew insisted.

Madison just listened as the boys bickered back and forth. She was busy scrolling through the pages of programming code to make sure the information had all been input correctly.

"Do you like Aimee or something?" Egg asked.

"Aimee?" Drew replied. "I like her. She's nice. She's a good dancer."

Madison jumped into the conversation. "No, he means *like* her, like her."

"Yeah, Drew, do you like her, *like* her?"

"What?" Drew was taken aback. "Well, not exactly," he gulped. "I mean, not in the *like* like kind of way." He was very surprised by this new line of questioning. "No way, Jose. I don't like Aimee. No."

"Who do you like?" Egg prodded him.

"Yeah," Madison chimed in. "Who?"

Drew shook off the question. "We should input this before Mrs. Wing comes back."

At first Madison had wanted this election project all for herself, but she felt different as time passed. Maybe it wasn't so weird with the three of them working on the site. Madison had always assumed Egg and his pals were abnormal. But Drew and Egg could set up the Web pages faster than fast.

Madison remembered that Drew was a cousin of Hart Jones's. Maybe she could ask him questions about who Hart liked, too?

"Hey, Drew, what's the deal with your cousin Hart?"

"Hart? What does Hart have to do with anything?" Drew looked confused.

"Oh, I was just wondering—"

"Hart's a fart," Egg interrupted. Drew snorted. Madison just rolled her eyes. Sometimes boys could really be so immature. She'd save her questions for another time.

"Just forget it," Madison said.

She was glad to drop the subject. Madison had no logical reason whatsoever to be asking about Hart. She didn't want Egg or Drew to get the wrong idea about her interest. She didn't want them to get *any* idea.

When she got home to Aimee's, Madison found her e-mailbox icon blinking.

Seeing that she had mail lifted her spirits.

From: ff_BudgeFilms
To: MadFinn
Subject: Phone Call
Date: Tues 12 Sept 1:21 PM

Hello, sweetie. I tried to call you before sleep tonite (we're 6 hours ahead, remember?) but the line was busy for an hour! Aimee's brothers are always on that phone, I'm sure. Well, I just wanted to say that I miss you very much. Are you okay at

51

school? I'm sorry to be gone for so
long. I promise, no more long
trips.

Did I mention that it is very rainy
here?

Je t'aime, ma cherie.

Reading the mail left Madison disappointed. She
wanted to hear Mom's voice for real. She wanted
someone to tell her that the election would turn out
okay. But this would have to do. Calling France was
way too expensive, Madison told herself, especially
from someone else's house.

A new note from Bigwheels popped up after
Mom's. Madison had hit the e-mail jackpot.

From: Bigwheels
To: MadFinn
Subject: Re: School elections and
stuff
Date: Tues 12 Sept 5:01 PM
Yes, I think boys are all weird.
No, I do not have a boyfriend. (I
used to have a pen pal in Spain
named Robbie, but he moved and I
never got his new address. I met
him through my parents. My Dad had
a client who lived there. Robbie

was so nice but he made me a little
nervous and in general I think boys
make me nervous.)

I never feel like myself when I
am with boys. Do you? I do have
crushes on movie stars sometimes
though. Do you?

Do you like a person at your
school? Is that why you feel weird?
I am sure whoever you like will
like you right back if you are just
honest with him. I may not be the
best person to ask for advice, but
I definitely think you need to be
honest. Honesty is the best policy.
Just don't be nervous if you can
help it.

I actually meant to tell you that I
was just elected last week as class
rep in my class, so I know EXACTLY
what you mean by annoying elections.
Good luck with yours! Why aren't u
running for class prez? You sound
so smart.

I have a question for you: do you
have brothers and sisters? I have
one sister and one brother who are

both younger than me. My brother is
only four. He is a pest.

Yours till the moon beams,

Bigwheels

p.s. If your mom is away, y don't u
call ur Dad? My dad always makes me
feel much better. Yesterday my daddy
got me flowers.

Madison's Dad got her flowers sometimes, too.
But today, when Madison dialed his cell phone, she
only got Dad's recording.

Please—leave—message. Beeeeeeep.

"Uh, Dad . . . this is Maddie and . . . I am calling
because I need . . . well, I miss . . . when you get this
please call me back I don't know when . . . I just
wanted to say hi and good-bye so . . . hi . . . and
good-bye. Okay, that's all. Don't forget I'm at
Aimee's house."

No sooner had Madison rested the phone back
into its cradle, when Mr. Gillespie screeched from
downstairs.

"Soup's on!"

So far they were having dinner every night at six
o'clock on the dot. Tonight there was baked whole-
wheat bread (all-natural and organic, of course),
grilled vegetables, and some other macrobiotic food.

Madison wasn't too sure what half of the food on her plate was. She was now eating the exact *opposite* of Mom's Scary Dinners.

Aimee's other two brothers, Dean and Doug, were the only ones at the table tonight and they didn't talk much. It wasn't the same as the previous night's burps and urps. Mayhem tonight was minimal.

Dean was a senior in high school who worried and talked more about his Camry and hot girls than anything else. Doug was a ninth grader who Madison sometimes saw at school but who never said much of anything, let alone "Hiya, Madison." He didn't seem to care about anything more than his high-tech calculator and baseball. Tonight Doug and Dean were arguing about catchers. Madison tuned right out.

Blossom brushed Madison's foot and she sneaked a grilled piece of zucchini under the table. A second later Blossom woofed it up. Even the dog liked vegetables in this house.

"Mmhey, Mmmaddie." Aimee chewed with her mouth full sometimes. "Mmmell my dad—"

"Pass the pepper, please," Mr. Gillespie said.

"Mmhow mmis the mmelection mmmweb site?"

Madison looked at Aimee for a moment like she had three heads, and then finally figured out how to translate her mouth-full-of-food lingo: *How is the election site?*

"Fine," Madison answered, picking at the couscous on her plate. It was brown bulgur wheat, Mrs. Gillespie had said, but it looked more like coarse sand. *Sand?* She would have given anything in that moment for a cheeseburger. Why would anyone want to eat sand?

It always grossed out Madison that Aimee loved brussels sprouts more than burgers. Aimee liked eggplant, okra, and lima beans, too! She was already on her second helping of sand.

"Madison," Mrs. Gillespie said, "have you heard from your mom?"

"Yes, she wrote me an e-mail." Madison shrugged. "I miss her. I mean, I *missed* her. She tried to call and the line was busy."

"Well, I bet she'll call again either late tonight or tomorrow, depending on her schedule." Mrs. Gillespie's radar was up. She could tell Madison was homesick. "I'm sure your mom is having a great old time over there. I am so envious of her traveling around the world. That must be so—"

"Pass the salt, please," Mr. Gillespie interrupted.

"Mmddad!" Aimee groaned, giving her Dad an evil look.

Mrs. Gillespie kept right on talking, about how smart Madison's mom was, and independent, and adventurous. . . .

And never home, Madison thought. By now, Blossom and Phin were begging under the table. She

56

shoved another grilled pepper downward. There was a collection of all-natural food scraps under the table.

It seemed that feeding dinner to the dog was only increasing *Madison*'s appetite. Madison realized she would have to ask Aimee for a peanut-butter sandwich after dinner. Her stomach grumbled and she prayed no one else had heard it.

"You know, Mrs. Gillespie," Madison said as they helped clear the sand and sprouts off the table. "I really appreciate your having me stay here. And Phinnie, too."

Mrs. Gillespie ran her hand over Madison's shoulder and squeezed. "I know. Maddie, you're like family here. You and Aimee have been friends since you were *born*."

Phinnie growled, "Rowrrooo!" It was like he knew what people were saying. Or at least knew when people were talking about him.

Aimee picked a sponge fight in the kitchen, and the two pals were throwing wet dishrags around, putting on fake accents, when Mrs. Gillespie called Maddie back into the dining room.

"Oh my gosh!" she cried, as she walked in.
Too late.
Mrs. Gillespie was down on her hands and knees picking up the mess.

"Oh, Mrs. Gillsepie, I am so sorry, I am—"
Aimee's mother just grinned. "Next time, you tell

57

me what you want, okay? No more secret dumping on the carpet. I don't think Phin or Blossom is much of a vegetarian. And neither are you."

"I like vegetables," Madison stammered. "It's just that—"

She didn't know what else to say. She could feel her feet telling her to run away, as always. But of course she didn't go anywhere. She kneeled down and picked up a soggy carrot. Phin had half-chewed it and dragged it across the floor.

"Maddie," Mrs. Gillespie said again, "you don't have to pretend around here. So you can talk to me if you want. You can tell me things . . . I meant what I said before. I think of you like my second daughter, okay?"

Mrs. Gillespie always knew how to say just the right thing. It really *was* like having a substitute mom when Mom was out of town. Madison couldn't decide if that was weird or if she was lucky or both.

When Aimee and Madison had finished up their social studies homework (from the one and only class they *did* have together), they sneaked out Aimee's bedroom window onto the roof. This was their secret place. It was the flat part of the roof, more like a patio where you could lay on your back and watch the stars. Aimee's dad had built a little lip around the roof to keep people away from the edge and close to the window.

"Gee, it smells like rain tonight, doesn't it?"

Aimee said as they lay back on the shingles.

Madison lay back again and searched the sky for the moon. Even with some stars, it was so dark out tonight that looking for a crescent moon was like searching for a fingernail paring in the sky.

"So, Maddie, tell me about the Web site," Aimee said.

Madison explained how she downloaded photos and information and Mrs. Wing helped them to code the information in a special way. Aimee was the biggest chatterbox, but she could also be a great listener.

"Oh, is that what happened to those election pictures I gave in when I announced I would run?"

Madison told her those had been uploaded, too. "Oh, did I tell you that Egg and Drew are part of the team now, too?" Madison added.

"Drew *Maxwell*?"

"Yeah." Madison nodded. "Mrs. Wing said they asked to be a part of it. They volunteered. Weird, huh?"

"Oh, really?" Aimee said. Madison detected a funny tone to her voice. "Do you think Drew did that to make sure I win or something?"

"What?"

"I'm just joking. Of course I know he's probably only doing it so he can—" Aimee cut herself short. "Well, I'm sure that's nice for you, having Egg and Drew around."

"It's okay."

Aimee pointed up into the sky. "Hey, is that yellow thing a planet or a UFO?"

"UFO. Totally! Aim, remember that alien dream you used to have as a kid?"

Aimee covered her eyes. "Why did you have to remind me? Now I'll never sleep tonight. Alien abductions. Spaceships. Weird machines. That gives me the jeebies."

Suddenly, a shooting star zipped past.

"Did you see that?" they said at the exact same time.

Then they laughed and made a wish with their eyes shut.

Madison felt serious all of a sudden and so she said, "Aimee, I want to make sure you know that I want you to win this election. I really, really want you to beat Ivy. I just wanted you to know that. I'm on your side."

"I know that, silly!" Aimee laughed. "I want to win, too. Not that I have any idea about how to be class president. Well, I have an idea about what I *could* be like. I guess I just did this because someone had to show Ivy she can't always have it *her* way."

"Too bad there isn't a talent contest as a part of elections. You could dance and win all the votes just like that."

"Just like *THAT*!" Aimee snapped her fingers.

"I think it's between you and Ivy, for real. Are you nervous?"

"*SO* nervous," Aimee said, hugging her knees.

The two stayed huddled under the chilly, speckled night sky for a while longer, enjoying their "slumber party." It was one of those moments you gulp and swallow to keep in your belly, in your heart, for always.

Then the phone rang.

"Hey, maybe it's your mom calling from France," Aimee yelped encouragingly, lunging back inside through the window to answer it.

Madison's stomach flip-flopped at the idea—but of course it wasn't Mom.

It was one of Aimee's brother's girlfriends.

"Dean has like ten different girlfriends," Aimee said. "He's so hideous. Who would date him? Someone else hideous, I guess."

Madison giggled. "Doug's still a hottie!"

Aimee lightly punched Madison's shoulder. "Get *OUT*! Quit looking at my brothers! That's like . . . you shouldn't even joke about that kind of stuff." She was half-yelling and half-laughing. "Oh my *GOD*, can you imagine?"

Madison teased, "Maybe I'll marry one of them, Aimee, and we could be sisters for real. What do you think?"

Aimee made a face like she would throw up. "I think I'd rather be friends."

As they turned off the light to sleep, Madison imagined a day when she would be the one getting a late-night call from a boyfriend. Maybe boys weren't so terrible.

"Aimee?" Madison whispered after a few minutes in the darkness.

There was no answer.

"Aimee, are you there?" Madison asked again. She wanted to talk about boys and parents and family and the Far Hills elections for just a little bit longer.

But Aimee was already fast asleep.

Madison wished talking in your sleep meant having *real* conversations with each other. That way she and Aimee could keep on talking until the sun came up again.

She reached over the edge of the bed and placed her hand on Phin's back. His side heaved with little, fast breaths, like the kind you have when you're in the middle of a doggy dream.

Chapter 6

Dad

Dad called this morning. He and I are ON
for dinner tonight and I cannot wait. I
can't wait for so many reasons. First,
because I want to see my dad of course.
Then, because I want to eat meat or
something that isn't sand. And also because
I just want to be somewhere that really is
my family. Even though the Gillespies are
the best and they take good care of me it's
not the same.

I told Dad all about the election Web
site and stuff. He sounded really excited,
so we'll probably spend all of our reunion
dinner talking about that. I like these

dinners because it's our special time just him and me. Oh, and Dad says he has a big surprise for me. I love surprises.

At 6:28 on the dot, Dad pulled into the Gillespies' driveway.

Dad had said he would show up at Aimee's at six o'clock to pick Madison up. Madison knew that really meant he'd be there at 6:30, of course, but she didn't mind. He was always late.

Madison smoothed out her peasant skirt (she had borrowed it from Aimee, and it was a little snug, but so pretty), checked her hair in the mirror (she wore it down tonight with her sapphire-blue barrettes), adjusted her favorite moonstone earrings (the same ones Dad gave to her when school first started), and smelled her armpits, of course. She always did that just to make sure she wasn't sweating too much. It was a gross thing to do, but it was *way* less gross than being a stink bomb in the middle of dinner. Luckily, even though it was humid tonight, Madison smelled like Lovely Ylang-Ylang. She'd borrowed some of Aimee's all-natural perfume.

"'Bye," Aimee yelled out as Madison walked down the porch steps. "You look great! Nice skirt."

"Ha ha!" Madison joked back. But she really did feel great.

For the first time in a few days, she felt like she was finally going to get some of her own family TLC. She needed some of that.

64

Dad was always so sweet, and she needed sweet. And he said that he had a surprise. Maybe he had another present? Madison couldn't believe she'd expect that, but the thought whizzed through her mind. The only benefit to Mom and Dad being away a lot was the fact that they sometimes got her cool stuff. As soon as she thought that, Madison felt guilty. What was she doing thinking about "stuff"? She told herself that she shouldn't—

Stop over-thinking, a voice echoed in her head. Voice of Dad, of course.

"Well, don't you look lovely," Dad said in person a moment later. He opened his arms to give Maddie a great big squeeze as she approached his car. It was really dark because the side lawn light was broken, but Dad still noticed what she was wearing. He *always* noticed.

"Isn't that a nice skirt," he said. "Mmm, you smell lovely, too."

"Lovely Ylang-Ylang, actually." Madison smiled.

"What?" He laughed. "Wang wang?"

"Eelang-eelang, Daddy! Like the letter L."

"Oh."

From inside the front seat of the car a strange voice said, "Ylang-ylang is an essential oil, Jeffrey."

Madison stopped in her tracks. Her stomach did a *GIANT* flip-flop.

"Uh, hello? Do I know you?"

"No, but I have heard so much about you." A

woman opened the door and stepped into the half-light in the driveway.

Madison turned to her dad and then turned to the woman.

"I haven't heard *anything* about you." Madison looked right at her father. "Daddy?"

"Madison, meet Stephanie," he said suddenly, clapping his hands together. "She's going to be joining us for dinner. Isn't that great?"

"Great? Um . . . Daddy?"

The woman stuck out her hand. "I'm Stephanie Wolfe," she said. "I'm a friend of your father. It's so nice to meet you. As I said, I've heard—"

"What's nice about it? I didn't know you were coming." Madison abruptly opened the back door, slid inside, and pulled it shut.

From where she was sitting inside the car she could just make out the figures of Dad and Stephanie talking in the shadows. She couldn't hear what they were saying, but they were talking very fast.

Madison smoothed out her skirt again. It was hot inside that car. Her legs itched. Madison smelled her armpits again just in case. Nothing but ylang-ylang.

How could Dad have forgotten to tell her he was bringing someone to dinner . . . to their special *reunion* dinner? How could Dad be with another woman besides Mom? Was this his idea of a surprise?

Madison *hated* surprises.

Stephanie got into the front seat again. Madison could smell her hair spray. Madison hadn't been shoved into the backseat of this car since she and Mom and Dad took Phin to the vet more than a year ago. She always rode shotgun. *Always.*

A droplet of sweat ran down the back of Madison's neck.

"So your dad tells me that you're a real computer whiz, is that true?" Stephanie said in the half-darkness, turning her head to catch Madison's eye.

Madison avoided all eye contact.

Stephanie paused. "Look, Maddie, I know you're surprised by my being here. And I don't feel all that comfortable either, Maddie, to tell you the truth—"

"Steph!" Dad said, a little surprised.

"But, Maddie, let's try to make the best of it? I could leave if that would—"

"Then leave," Madison cut her off. "Leave. And stop calling me Maddie. No one calls me Maddie except people who are my friends. I don't even know you."

"Now, wait just a minute!" Dad yelled. "Do you have any manners, young lady? I want you to apolo—"

"Jeff, look out!"

Dad swerved to miss hitting a cat in the middle of the road.

"Stupid animal!" Dad barked.

Madison spoke up from the backseat. "Animals are NOT stupid."

Dad sighed, exasperated. Even from where she was crouched into the backseat, Madison could see Stephanie put her hand on Dad's knee. She just wanted to turn around and go right back to the Gillespies.

No sooner had they parked the car than Madison jumped ten paces ahead, rushing across the parking lot, taking two steps at a time up to the restaurant lobby, praying that Le Poisson would be air-conditioned. Of course it was nice and cold inside. Nice and *ice* cold.

Be careful what you wish for, Madison mused, shivering.

The maitre d' sat the threesome at a table near a giant fish tank. Madison was grateful. Fish could focus her *away* from Stephanie. She named a yellow-finned one Phin 2 in her mind and watched him swim behind a fake treasure chest to hide out. Madison wished she could hide out. It was like being in the real-life bigfishbowl.com.

When the waiter came to take their drink order, Madison asked for root beer, her favorite drink on the planet.

"No root beere," he said. "This eez French restau-rahn."

"No root beer? Then I'd like . . . a cream soda?"

"No creamy soda," he said, shaking his head.

"Ginger ale?" He nodded. *Finally.*

"One, please."

The waiter smiled as Stephanie ordered a wine spritzer on the rocks and Dad got his usual seltzer with lime.

All the Frenchy French waiters and the French words on the menu reminded Madison of one thing.

"You know, my Mom's in France," Madison said, staring right at Stephanie. "She's a really, really important film producer and she's making a documentary there. Right now she's scouting locations."

"Oh, really?" Stephanie pretended to be nice. "That sounds interesting."

"She's really, really important. Did I mention that?"

"Yes, you did. You did mention that," Stephanie said. For the first time, Madison noticed that Stephanie was actually kind of pretty. How annoying. Madison searched Stephanie's face for moles and wrinkles.

"Maddie," Dad started to say when it seemed like things had calmed down a little bit, "I really am sorry that I didn't tell you first about—"

"Whatever, Dad. No biggie, right?" Madison shrugged.

Dad was fumbling to speak, but Madison wouldn't even let him finish a sentence. She told them both about the election Web site start-up, Mrs.

Wing, and how Aimee was running for class president.

Stephanie acted interested. "Is that glitter nail polish you're wearing?" she asked Madison.

Madison frowned. "Yeah, but I ate most of it off." She saw that Stephanie had perfectly manicured pink nails.

"This dinner is turning out just great," Dad said. "And here I thought—" He laughed and grabbed a sesame roll out of the bread basket on the table, mumbling to himself a little.

That's when Madison caught Stephanie putting her hand on Dad's knee again. At least that's what it seemed like. They were sitting very close. *Too close.*

But Madison knew what to do.

When dinner was served, Madison watched and waited until Stephanie was ready to take the first big bite of her fish dinner.

That's when Madison said, "Um, Dad, did I tell you about Phin?"

Dad was laughing nervously at everything by now. "No, honey bear, what about him?"

"Well." Madison stared right at Stephanie as she started the story. "It's just that Phin has that stomach thing again, you know the bad sick thing where he can't stop pooping."

Stephanie made a disgusted face.

"Maddie!" Dad said, but Madison kept right on talking.

"Yeah, it's really gross. It was all over the carpet this morning and he just makes this awful noise when he's doing it and it smells and—"

"Madison!" Dad said again, a little louder.

Stephanie gulped and put down her fork.

"Oh!" Madison covered her mouth. "I'm sorry, Stephanie, were you eating?"

As Stephanie took a sip of water, Madison took a huge bite of her own dinner. Her "Le Poisson" hamburger was well done, just the way she liked it.

 Dad

There are not enough words in the entire Webster's Dictionary to explain what I am feeling right now but I would have to say that CRUSHED is it. I came home right after dinner and I feel disgusting. How could Dad have done that to me? I was so freaked out during dinner I ordered eight ginger ales and drank every single one! I had to pee the whole time. And I don't even like ginger ale. How could we go to a restaurant that doesn't serve root beer?

Now I really wish Mom were home. I wish I could call France. I wish I had a brother or sister to share this with. Aimee is downstairs right now watching the end of some movie with Roger and I just can't go in the TV room all sad and depressed and make this scene and call attention to

myself. I just can't. I hate Daddy for
this. No, I hate Stephanie more. Now I hate
this feeling of hating people!

Madison closed the file, plugged her modem line
into the phone jack, and dialed up the Internet.
She needed to chat—NOW.
In the bigfishbowl.com main lobby, or "fish tank"
area, Madison searched the room lists and eaves-
dropped on a few rooms. Where was Bigwheels? She
needed Bigwheels in a big way—NOW.

```
SHARK (Moderator)
GottaWIN
2good2be2
TellMeAStORY
Iluvrich
Intoredgiant
Screammeem
JimD71068
URPrincess
NvrSAYNvr
Pokemenow
654aqua
```

```
<Screammeem>: 12345
MadFinn has entered the room.
<URPrincess>: NO!!!!!
<Screammeem>: Anyone from WV?
<NvrSAYNvr>: Hey MadFinn A/S/L?
<Screammeem>: Anyone from WV HELLO
```

```
<Iluvrich>: How r u?
<654aqua>: heymeem, GAL
<Screammeem>: Wuzup with skool/>?
   It's kool
Intoredgiant has left the room.
gonefishin has entered the room.
<URPrincess>: LMSO School is SO NOT
   :~/
<MadFinn>: :—0
<MadFinn>: What is 12345?
<NvrSAYNvr>: Hey gonefishin A/S/L?
<Screammeem>: anyone play soccer?
<Gonefishin>: 13/M/NY
URPrincess has left the room.
<TellMeaStoRY>:Have u seen Tidal
   Wave the movie?
<NvrSAYNvr>: anyone wanna private
   chat
<TellMeaStoRY>: it is soooooo good
   and so scary
<Screammeem>: am in soccr leage
doggydave has entered the room.
<gonefishin>: ^5 meem! How r u?
<screammeem>: IM Me
<gonefishin>: c ya sucka
<SHARK>: Watch your language, please
<MadFinn>: *poof*
```

Bigwheels must have been asleep or something even though it was only dinnertime where she was. Maybe she was doing her homework?

She definitely wasn't in this chat room. She wasn't even online.

Madison checked her e-mail just in case.

`Mailbox Empty`

As soon as she saw the word "empty," the heaviness in her ribs pushed up into her throat. It was like nausea, only she knew she wasn't sick. Madison shut down the computer, shut off the light, and buried her face into one of Aimee's pillows. She hated crying in a strange place.

After ten seconds, her nose was running and she was drooling, too. Madison always drooled when she cried. Phinnie heard her and jumped onto the bed too. He was licking the salty tears off her face and wiggling his curlicue tail.

Dogs always can tell when people are really sad. Madison was glad that Phinnie was around. Blossom was at the bottom of the bed the whole time, jumping, but basset hounds aren't so good at getting onto high places.

"Maddie?" The light clicked on all of a sudden and Aimee rushed over to the bed. "Maddie, I heard you . . . what happened? Are you okay?"

Madison sniffled but no words would come out. She tried to catch her breath in between hiccups and tears. She was crying hard by now.

"Aimee?" Mrs. Gillespie walked into the room

next. "Is everything all right in here? I heard—"

Aimee shrugged. "Maddie's all bummed out. Her Dad brought a date to dinner and she didn't know about it and—"

"I—was—so—up—set—"

Madison coughed each syllable and Aimee's mother sat down on the edge of the bed and rubbed her back. "Take a deep breath, Maddie. You'll be okay, dear. I know it's got to be hard. All this change."

Madison gasped and sniffled and choked on her own words.

"Change—Steph—stink—Dad—"

She wasn't making any sense.

Mrs. Gillespie ran a cool hand across Madison's neck to get her to stop crying. Her hands were as soft as the satin edge of a blanket. "Maddie," she asked, "Should we call your mom?"

Madison wiped her eyes and blinked. "In Paris?"

"I think we should." Mrs. Gillespie pulled a few strands of hair out of Maddie's wet eyes. "I know your mom would want to be right here, right now, giving you a hug and telling you everything is okay. You should call her."

Madison sniffled. "You mean it?"

"Yes, let's call her. Right now."

Madison's could feel her heartbeat quicken at the prospect of hearing Mom's voice. Together, Mrs. Gillespie, Aimee, and Madison dialed the international operator and called Mom all the way over in France. It was 5:30 in the morning, but Madison didn't care about waking Mom up.

Madison Finn was caught between a dad and a date and all she needed was to know that her Mom was there, somewhere. She needed to know she wasn't crazy for feeling all knotted up inside. That everything with Dad and Ivy and school and elections would all work out. That feeling like a baby was an okay way to feel right now.

Sometimes only a mom can tell you things so you believe them.

Chapter 7

From: MadFinn
To: ff_BudgeFilms
PRIORITY MAIL
Subject: Last Night
Date: Thurs 14 Sept 7:19 AM

Mom I am so sorry I woke you up.
But I slept so well after we got
off the phone. I didn't realize I
missed you so much. Is that weird?
I mean, last night I was just so
sad. And it wasn't Dad's fault. I
don't want to make it sound like
he's bad, because I know you think
that sometimes. No, it was just
everything happening all at the same
time.

Phinnie slept under the blankets
with me for a little while, too,
just like you said. Until he got
hot and started snoring like he
does. Oh well. Now Aimee's bed
smells like dog.

Thanks again Mom. I am really sorry
again for getting you up to the
phone at like 4 your time or whenever it was. I know you are busy
and that the movie is
important too.

By the way, Dad called this
morning first thing to check on me.
He says no more surprise dinners so
that's a good thing, right?
Please come home soon.
Love, me :>)

After all the excitement of yesterday, Madison made
like a zombie and zoned out through her morning
classes. She didn't come out of her trance until noon,
when she, Drew, Egg, and Mrs. Wing spent lunch
period huddled over a computer monitor inside the
tech lab, checking out the day's progress on the Far
Hills site. Despite her anxiety from yesterday, it felt
good to Madison to be working on the election Web
pages again with the boys. Plus, serious computer

work got Madison's mind off any and all "bad" subjects: last night's dinner with Dad and Stephanie; Hart calling her Finnster (four times so far that week); and Poison Ivy, of course.

The home page was looking good.

```
WELCOME TO FAR HILLS JUNIOR HIGH
       1753 Far Hills Avenue
       Far Hills, New York

School Principal: Mr. Joe Bernard
Assistant Principal: Mrs. Bonnie Goode
Web page designed and created by FH
          Faculty and Students

Elections coordinator: Madison Finn
       Data entry: Drew Maxwell
     Online programs: Walter Diaz
  Student adviser: Mrs. Isabel Wing

Note: Please adjust your screen to 640x480
          full window for optimal
                 viewing.
```

The Web page layout was a basic model, devoted to helping direct students to the polling areas, but Madison knew it had big possibilities. She hoped that the school Web site could change the way *everything* was done and how everyone communicated at school. She had the entire Web site menu mapped out in her imagination.

Homepage
Schedules
Assignments & Calendars
Clubs & Organizations
Sports & Teams
The Far Hills Journal
Faculty
Links
The I Don't Like Ivy Daly at All Club

Sometimes she got a little carried away.

Faculty and students were logging on to the Web page on different computers all over school. Not just in the tech lab, but in the library media center, the administrative offices, the reading room, and even in the school newspaper headquarters.

After being up only two days, it was already a huge success. The word was out.

Madison and her friends felt so proud.

Thanks to Mrs. Wing, all of this was happening. Madison noticed how Mrs. Wing's iridescent shell earrings shimmered like magic each time they caught sunlight. They reminded Madison of the moonstone earrings Dad had bought her for seventh grade good luck. Working on computers was working magic on Maddie.

One of the most important tasks of Mrs. Wing's election Web site team was to get the online voting tabulation system to work properly. A Far Hills ninth-grade math teacher named Mr. Lynch installed more memory in all computers to make the election program work faster. He stayed around to help supervise the HTML coding, the special Web site-making language. Neither Madison nor the others knew HTML very well. Madison realized that even a smarter-than-smart teacher like Mrs. Wing needed help sometimes. Things really happened when they all worked together.

They didn't have a lot of time to do it. Mrs. Wing was pulling out all the stops. Next week was the election assembly and they had to be ready.

Drew and Egg worked together during their free period to get the student polls in order. The first poll results were already in.

```
What school issue is important to
you in this year's election? Please
check off your #1 choice.

1. Homework 51%
2. Cafeteria food 16%
3. After-school activities 14%
4. Sports 10%
5. Computer science 7%
6. Other 2%
```

One by one, the three of them checked through other grades' Web pages for the status of all the candidates for the offices of president, vice president, class treasurer, secretary, and class reps.

Everything looked fine, especially the seventh grade pages.

Drew brought up the Montrell Morris candidate page. Montrell had written a poem for his page that ended with the lines: "How do you spell Montrell? W-I-N-N-E-R."

Then Drew glanced over the Tommy Kwong page. Tommy just had one banner across the top: "TOTALLY TOMMY." Both Tommy's and Montrell's photos were a little blurry, but the links on their pages all worked.

Egg opened up to the page marked Ivy Daly. Everything looked in order there, too, especially Ivy's perfect red hair. He had to comment on that.

"You can't tell me this girl is not hot," Egg said.

Madison just rolled her eyes. She leaned over Egg's shoulder and clicked NEXT. It moved along to Aimee's page.

"Whoa!" Egg said with a start.

Madison stopped, blinked, and clicked the refresh button to reload the page.

"Wait! Hold up!" Egg squirmed around in the chair. "Did you see that?"

Madison punched at the keys frantically.

"What is THAT?" Drew added. He was now looking over Drew's other shoulder as the page reappeared. "Maddie, that is not Aimee."

Madison shook her head. She couldn't believe what she was seeing.

The image up on the screen next to "Aimee

Gillespie" was most definitely *not* Aimee. Not at all. On the computer screen, in the spot where Aimee's photograph had been, was a photograph of an ugly, spiny, old lizard.

"A heloderma!" Madison shrieked. "How did a helo—"

"Hello—*huh*?" Drew wrinkled his nose.

"A heloderma! A gila monster! A LIZARD!" said Madison.

"How do you know that?" Egg asked.

"Is this some kind of joke!" Madison squealed a little louder. "Did one of you guys do this?"

"Don't look at me!" Drew was *very* confused.

Egg shook his head. "Hey, I know I cause trouble, but this is like way beyond me."

"Then who put a gila monster up there? This is AWFUL!"

"Since when do you know gila monsters, Maddie? What, did you see one when you and your mom were in Brazil or something?" Egg blurted out.

Madison didn't like the way he was asking her questions. She pointed at the monitor. "Are you responsible for this, Egg Diaz? Is this how you get back at me?"

"Get back at you for what?" Egg said. "You know, Drew, I think Aimee and gila actually look a little the same. Whaddya say?"

Madison almost laughed—but she didn't.

"Put a lid on it, Egg," Drew said. He pinched Egg's arm.

Egg winced in pain. "Owwwch. What did you do that for?"

"Quick!" Madison tapped at the keyboard. "You guys, how many hits has the page received today?"

Egg read the number off the screen. "Two-hundred and ninety-one. Jeez, that's a lot of gila monster lovers."

"EGG! I'M SERIOUS!"

Mrs. Wing dashed back into the classroom at that exact moment and rushed over to help. She knew exactly how to fix the screen with all joking aside.

In only a few minutes the four of them were able to remove gila and get back Aimee.

Madison just kept shaking her head. "I don't understand. Yesterday we were here. We were here and everything seemed fine. . . . Aimee *looked* like Aimee, not like some—"

"Lizard?" Egg interjected. Madison shot him a look.

"Well, when was the last time you checked the site?" Mrs. Wing asked Madison. "This is a breach of the site. We need to look into it."

"Breach?" Madison let out a huge sigh. "I'm sorry, I'm sorry," she kept apologizing. She was crushed by the thought that somehow she'd failed. "This is all my fault. I must have done something— I'm sorry!"

"Madison, calm down. Now, we've deleted the photo of the—"

"Lizard," Egg piped up again. Madison shot him another look.

Drew gave him a noogie on the side of his arm.

"Stop!" Egg said.

"Would you two please relax?" Mrs. Wing said.

She made it clear that she would file a memo to administration, but that it was probably an "isolated incident," so no, they didn't have to cause a big fuss.

"However," Mrs. Wing added, "I think you three need to keep a closer watch on these pages just to make sure that we don't have any *more* funny stuff, okay? People like to play jokes, especially around election time. Be sure to let me know if anything else comes up, will you?"

Madison nodded emphatically, relieved that no more would be said about the lizard. She never wanted to see its spiny little body again, and she hoped that Aimee hadn't seen it—*ever*.

Unfortunately, by the end of the day, most of the teachers and students, and even Principal Bernard had seen it. Everyone *including* Aimee.

A wisecracking eighth grader had found the messed-up page and printed out a hard copy that got stuck up on the elevator bulletin board. Another kid posted a copy in the girl's bathroom with a note written in pencil: "Liz" Gillespie for Class Prez.

It was a disaster.

"Maddie, how could this have happened? I thought you were in charge of the election Web site! I thought you were helping with my campaign! I thought you were MY FRIEND!" Aimee shrieked as she confronted Maddie in a deserted stairwell. Her voice ricocheted off the walls and windows.

"Aimee, pleasepleaseplease let me explain," Madison pleaded. "I am so so so so so sorry that it ever happened. But we fixed it. I mean we didn't do it on purpose. . . ."

"I don't think you understand how embarrassing this is," Aimee said, shaking a little. Usually she looked graceful, but now she was sputtering. "Look, you're responsible for the Web site, right?"

"I know, I know. I feel awful." At this point, Madison was tempted to get down on her knees. She didn't want Aimee to be mad or sad.

"Maddie, who would do this? Are you gonna find out who? Oh my GOD I am so embarrassed. I AM MORTIFIED."

Aimee didn't want *anything* to get in the way of her race to whup Ivy Daly in the school election. Madison knew a thing or two about awful embarrassing moments. She was often on the run from embarrassment.

"Can we please stop yelling?" Madison said softly. She saw imaginary steam steaming out of Aimee's ears, she looked *that* mad.

Suddenly, a fire door opened one flight up. Aimee and Madison clammed up. They waited to hear a second door creak open and slam shut.

"Wait!" Aimee shouted when the door slammed.

"What?" Madison was surprised.

"It wasn't you!" Aimee cried out, coming to a sudden realization. "Maddie, wait! I know who did this. This isn't *your* fault!"

"That's what I've been saying." Madison's eyes glazed over.

"And if it isn't your fault and it isn't Egg's fault and it isn't Drew's fault . . ."

"Then who?" Madison wondered aloud.

"This is Ivy Daly's fault! Of course! It has to be Poison Ivy! Think about it, Maddie. She probably did it because she was annoyed at me because my profile was better and she just *knew* I would win. So she logged on to the site, went online, and ruined my photo."

Madison thought for a minute.

"Doesn't that sound just like her?" Aimee said accusingly.

"Well . . ." Madison took a deep breath. "I dunno."

"Maddie!" Aimee insisted. "It has to be her! Who *else* would do this?"

Madison sighed again. She wanted Ivy to lose the school election as much as Aimee did, but she didn't want to accuse her of something like this—*did she*?

"Aimee, do you really think she would think of something like this? It seems a little shady, even for her."

"Absolutely. And now the joke is gonna be on Ivy. I'm gonna tell *everyone* at school tomorrow about what she did."

"Wait. I think we should find out for sure if she did it first," Madison said.

"Wait? Geesh, Maddie, whose side are you on?"

Madison was never on someone's "side." She was in the middle, as usual. "After all," she wanted to scream to Aimee, "accusing Ivy doesn't even make sense."

As the night wore on Aimee became more and more convinced that Ivy was the culprit. Madison silently grew more and more convinced that Ivy *wasn't* responsible. First, Ivy was so good at computers. Second, Ivy was the kind of meanie who said stuff to your face—not behind your back. Some other hacker had to have done it.

But *who*?

It was an election Web site mystery.

 Roger

Sometimes I wish I had an older brother
like Roger Gillespie. Does Aimee know how
great it is to have someone listen and
really listen, not the kind of listening
moms and dads do because they want to
protect you and play it safe? Roger listens
like he wants to really help.

This morning Aimee had to leave for her
dance practice at like 6:30 and I was
talking to Roger at breakfast about the
problems we had with the election Web site.
I asked him what I should do since Aimee was
saying Ivy had put the lizard on the Web
site but I didn't think so. I don't think
Ivy even knows what a gila monster is.

Roger says don't put myself in the middle.

He says maybe being in the middle is why I feel crushed by different things, like being the meat in a sandwich or something.

Rude Awakening: I'm sandwich meat? No wonder boys don't like me.

After adding to some pages in her files, Madison ducked into her favorite online shopping site. It was a place where you could buy clothes and books and candles and other cool objects. She wrote down the online code and inventory numbers for a few things she desperately wanted. She knew when Mom came back home, the items would probably never get ordered, but she still liked to think about having them.

```
SWTTLK09214Q   Zipper Sweater with
               Flower Appliqué
SWTTLK09203Q   Cargo Pantskirt
               Camouflage Pattern
SWTTLK09239Q   Fuzzy Scrapbook
SWTTLK09218Q   Baby Tee (Orange Neon)
```

By the time Madison got into school that morning, her head was overflowing with over-thoughts about boys and clothes, and, of course, the election. She headed straight for Mrs. Wing's classroom.

"Madison!" Mrs. Wing cried out as soon as Madison walked into the room.

Egg was in the room, too. Drew wasn't in school yet.

"Madison, we have a problem," Egg said in an announcer's voice.

Madison's stomach flopped. She imagined Aimee's Web page again: *Attack of the Gila Monster, Part Two.* She was afraid to look.

"See?" Egg pointed to the computer screen. "Problem."

Madison's heart sank.

"What is this?" Mrs. Wing asked, pointing at Ivy's page.

There, under the flashing name IVY DALY was not a photo of a seventh grader with picture-perfect long red hair, but a photo of a skunk.

"A skunk?" Madison said with disbelief. She covered her face with her hands.

Egg chuckled. "Really smells, doesn't it?"

Madison frowned. "Not the time to be funny."

"Now I think we need to take this seriously, you two. I think I have to let Principal Bernard know what is happening now."

"Mrs. Wing, I swear we triple-checked all the pages, the scans, the HTML code you and Mr. Lynch showed us how to input. I swear."

Mrs. Wing nodded. "I'm sure you did."

Drew walked in on the mess. He couldn't believe his eyes. "Oh no. Look! Ivy's a skunk, Maddie."

"No kidding, smart guy!" Egg said.

"Oh, Mrs. Wing I know that I double-checked the scans yesterday, too. We all did. I just don't—"

"Madison, I don't blame you. I don't blame any of you. But now this is a problem I have to handle from here." Mrs. Wing took over.

Madison stared at the monitor. Seeing the skunk on the page meant that her ideas about Ivy being the true hacker were all wrong.

So who *was* it?

The mystery plot thickened.

"Mrs. Wing, I want to figure out who did this." Madison decided on the spot that *she* had to be the person to find the source of the problem—even if she didn't know where to begin.

"Well, I am still filing a report with the principal. But I'll let you look into this immediately. Tomorrow we'll meet again to talk about it."

The three of them spent the next half-hour eliminating Miss Skunk and putting Ivy's real photo back online.

The remainder of the day passed by in a kind of haze. At every corridor turn, at the door to each class, Madison kept expecting some kind of showdown with Ivy, just as she'd had a showdown with Aimee. No matter what Mrs. Wing said, Madison felt responsible.

Madison didn't see Ivy in science class. Did her absence mean she hadn't seen it yet and she was just late to class? Had the skunk been safely removed in time? Or *had* she seen it and run screaming from the building?

A little after three o'clock, after the second bell, Madison got her answer. And the only screaming Ivy was ready to do was in *Madison's* direction.

"Hey, Finnster," a sarcastic voice howled from behind Madison as she went through her locker.

She twisted around.

"Madison Finn, I want an apology and I want it RIGHT NOW!" Ivy was standing there with hands on her hips, lips drawn into a mean pout.

"Apology for what?"

"For messing with my campaign. For messing with ME!" Ivy tossed her red hair back and a little fell into her eyes. She poked Madison in the breast-bone with her pointy finger. "YOU can't get away with this."

"Don't touch me," Madison pushed the finger away. "Ivy, I'm trying to figure it out, I swear."

"I heard that you put a certain picture of a certain animal up on my page of the school site. I heard that you're trying to trash me and my chances to win class president. I heard—"

"Well, you heard WRONG," Madison asserted. "Who tells you this stuff?"

"None of your business!" Ivy snorted. "You don't play fair."

"I play fair, Ivy, even with you."

"What's up with *that*?" Ivy pressed her palm up

against the locker so Madison couldn't get in to get her last book. "I wonder what Principal Bernard will say about all this. I wonder what *he heard*," she added in a mocking tone of voice.

"Quit it, Ivy. I won't let you scare me."

"You are the scary one, Madison Finn."

"When did you get so mean, Ivy? You used to be so nice."

"What are you, Queen of Nice?"

The two enemies were practically spitting on each other. A few lockers away, a small crowd was gathering.

"Madison Finn, you don't know what nice is."

"Ivy Daly, you don't know what *friendship* is."

"Don't be stupid."

"*You're* stupid."

"No, you are."

"Liar," Madison said without thinking.

"You are the liar," Ivy yelled.

"Takes one to know one."

"You're the one who backstabs and runs away from friends."

"Shut up!" Madison felt her skin get all clammy. This had become so personal all of a sudden. It wasn't really about the skunk anymore and they both knew it. Suddenly Madison felt like she was back in third grade with her scratchy kneesocks and braids.

Ivy yelled a little louder. "So why should I believe *anything* you ever say?"

"Believe whatever you want," Madison shot back. "I didn't put the picture up there. Go ahead and tell the principal. I don't care."

"I think I *WILL* tell!"

"You know what, Ivy? You're no skunk. You're a RAT!"

"Well, you're a—" For a split second it seemed that Ivy didn't have a response. She gave Madison an evil stare and took a deep breath. "You're a *COW*."

One of the bystanders laughed out loud and suddenly Madison got very nervous. She looked up at Ivy.

"Well?" Ivy barked. "No more answers from the brainiac?"

Madison had to run. She cut to the left and took off down the hall.

"Crybaby!" Ivy shouted after her. By now the rest of the kids had dispersed. Ivy turned in the opposite direction. She had won.

Madison disappeared into the girls' bathroom around the corner. She couldn't face anyone right now, especially not eighth graders milling about in the hall. She couldn't even look into her own reflection in the bathroom mirror.

She wished Bigwheels were here right now to tell her what to do.

```
From: MadFinn
To: Bigwheels
Subject: What Do I Do?
Date: Fri 15 Sept 3:19 PM
```

Hello? Are you out there? I haven't heard from you.

Hasn't been a great week. HELP!

I'm @ the school media center right now. I have an English paper due and I have not even picked the book I'm writing a report on. Can you help with that? Help (x100) is basically what I need on that and some other stuff I'd rather IM you or chat about.

Please write again. Is something wrong? I'm worried.

Yours till the ping pongs,
MadFinn

p.s. Thanks in advance.

In the corner of the Waterses' living room, Chet, Egg, and Drew were firing weapons onto a target—a computer target. They were busy playing *Commando Missiles*, a new CD-ROM that Chet had bought the day before.

"Hit it! Yes! No! Hit it!" Egg was jumping up and down. Drew had control of the joystick.

Chet groaned. "You shoulda cut out. Now you're gonna die, man."

Drew looked a little flustered. "I don't even know how to play this. Aaaah!"

"WOULD YOU GUYS PLEASE SHUT UP?" Fiona screamed. "We're trying to get organized over here."

"Egg, are you gonna help with posters?" Aimee asked. "Or are you chained to your computer games?"

"Yeah, I'm thinking of a slogan."

"Thinking of a slogan?" Madison laughed out loud. "Tell us."

Egg put his hands on his hips. "Well, how about 'Aimee Rocks'?"

Aimee made a raspberry noise with her lips. "That's my vote on that slogan. Are you serious?"

Egg made a serious face. "Always, Aimee."

"How about *that*?" Fiona spoke up. "For a slogan, I mean."

"What?"

"'Always Aimee.'" Fiona thought it was a great idea.

Aimee wasn't too crazy about any of the slogans on the list so far.

Aimee's Awesome
Aimee 4-Ever
Aimee Aces the Prez!
Have You Voted Aimee Yet?
Aimee's Alright!
Awake and Aimee
Ready, Aimee, Fire
Honest Aimee

Everyone had all gone to the Waterses' house for snacks and poster preparation. It was the end of a long week and Fiona, Chet, Egg, Drew, Aimee, and Madison were rolling up their sleeves to make Aimee's last-minute round of campaign posters.

They needed more to hang in the hallways for the week of the election. It was time to get out the poster board and Magic Markers.

The other two candidates, Montrell and Tommy, had hung a few posters here and there, but *no one* could match Ivy's poster invasion.

"I think we should put posters up all over the gym, too. I mean *all over*. Maybe we should try gym sayings or something," Aimee said. "Like 'Vote Aimee: It's a slam dunk!'"

"That's cool," Drew said.

"You really think so?" Aimee sounded happy to hear that Drew liked her ideas.

"And the library too, don't forget," Madison reminded them of another place where students would be sure to *read* the posters.

"What about the dance studio?" Chet spoke up. "You're a dancer, right?"

"Everyone in the dance troupe says they're voting for me already," Aimee said.

"Cookies!" Mrs. Waters came into the living room all of a sudden with a tray of homemade gingersnaps. Everyone grabbed as many cookies as they could stuff into their mouths.

"Not too many at once, guys!" Mrs. Waters said.

Twenty gingersnaps each and twenty minutes later, Chet, Drew, and Egg got bored with the slogans and word games. They went back to playing *Commando Missiles*.

Then the doorbell rang.

"Hey, Maddie, can you get that?" Fiona yelled out. Madison was closest to the door.

Madison opened it quickly without thinking. She had cookie crumbs all down the front of her shirt.

"Finnster!"

She jumped. Behind Door Number One was none other than Hart Jones.

"Madison, what are *YOU* doing here?" Hart asked.

"There's a bunch of us here making posters for the election. You know, for Aimee." She took a breath. "You wanna help out?"

"Maybe another time—hey, what's with the cookies?" He chuckled.

Madison brushed off the crumbs and gave him a dirty look.

"Sorry," Hart said sheepishly.

"Okay, then." Madison fumbled for something else to say. "Okay?"

"Yeah, okay, then." Hart fumbled too.

"Yeah, well . . ." Madison grinned and turned to go back inside.

"Finnster?" Hart took a step to follow her, but by then Chet had air-boxed his way over to the door, screeching, "Watch it, Jones! Watch it! J-O-N-E-S!"

"See ya, Finnster," Hart was still calling after Madison.

"Feeeenster?" Chet mimicked him.

All four boys vanished outside together to shoot some hoops.

As Fiona shut the door, Aimee wailed, "What about the posters? Who's gonna finish up?"

"We are!" Fiona laughed. "Did you really expect those guys to do anything real? They were total loads, as always. Especially Chet."

Aimee curled up on the sofa. "Hey, you guys, I have a confession to make."

"What?" Fiona asked curiously.

Aimee tilted her head back. "I think I like someone. A little."

Madison rushed over to the floor next to her. "Who? Oh Aimee, who? Why didn't you tell me?"

Aimee rolled her eyes. "Because."

"Who is it?" Fiona asked. "Is it Hart Jones, because he's pretty cute—"

"No, you can't!" Madison blurted out.

Aimee and Fiona looked at her in silence, stunned.

"What do you mean, 'No!' Maddie?"

Madison chewed on her lip—and lied through her teeth. "No, of course not! He's a freak. He always calls me Finnster. Please. No, I only yelled that because—"

Aimee and Fiona nodded. "Okay, Maddie. If you say so."

"I don't like *anyone* and no one likes me. That's okay with me," Madison said.

"You know, we should finish election posters," Aimee said, "before it gets too late. We can talk about boys later." She had brought up the subject suddenly and now she suddenly wanted to change it.

"But you didn't tell us. . . . Who do you like, Aimee?" Fiona wanted to know.

"Well, I dunno. I don't really like anyone."

"Okay." Fiona gave up. "Then I don't like anyone either."

"That is such a lie! You're crushing on Egg, you admitted it!"

Fiona smiled. "Egg who?"

The three girls laughed.

 Hart

Rude Awakening: Crushing can be hazardous to your health.

OK, so I saw him this morning in the library media center. Is it to be or not to be??? He was wearing a nice brown sweater. I swear I don't know how it is possible that I like him. I know I do. I like Hart. I CANNOT TELL ANYONE. Aimee would die. Fiona would probably say "Way to Go," but then she'd find something wrong with him. Friends do that a lot.

Of course I saw him today at Fiona's too. And it feels like I ate something funny just to think or talk about it. The little hairs on my arms all stand up. Is that weird? Part of what makes Hart hard to handle is that he can be so *mean* to me. Does that make any sense that a guy who likes you would dis you? He was ok @ Fiona's actually, but around other school peeps he is obnoxious with a capital O.

I just don't get boys. One minute they're so nice and the next minute they're so not. Does crushing on someone also mean MY heart is gonna get squashed?

Back at the Gillespies' later on, Madison tried to finish up her science homework before the weekend. Of course it was hard to get through any science assignment without thinking about Poison Ivy, her esteemed lab partner, but Madison tried. She typed up all her lab notes from class.

As soon as she clicked off her laptop, Madison sat on the floor so Aimee could french-braid her hair. Aimee was the best braider *ever*—even better than Egg's older sister Mariah, who had hair all the way down to her waist.

"Maddie," Aimee said as she pulled the hair back, "I hope you find out tomorrow what loser is ruining your Web site. That is so messed about what happened with Ivy's picture."

"Yeah, it stinks."

A second later Madison realized what she had said. The whole *skunk* thing stank. The two friends laughed. Madison started to laugh so much she almost forgot about the election Web site. . . .

Almost.

"Stop twitching," Aimee said. "Hold still."

"You're *pulling*!"

"Not me. It's you. HOLD STILL."

Madison had too many tangles.

"I still have to write my campaign assembly speech, Maddie. Can you help me do it before the assembly?"

"You're gonna be great, Aim, I know it. You're not worried, are you?"

Aimee shrugged and twisted Madison's hair into the tail end of the braid, while Phinnie curled into Madison's lap. He wouldn't stop kissing her hand and every time he did, Madison saw the little black stripe on his pink tongue. This dog was so cute. Cute and homesick, too. Madison could feel it. When she scritched behind Phin's ears, he hummed like a motor.

"Madison?" Mrs. Gillespie knocked softly on Aimee's door and peered inside. "There's a phone call for you."

It was almost eleven.

"Hello, honey." Dad's voice sounded like a low hum over the phone line, too. He was calling to check in because he hadn't heard anything in a day or so. "Is everything good?"

Madison yawned. "Yeah, I guess."

"I was thinking all day today about you but I got stuck in this meeting and—"

"Daddy?" He had been talking about his latest business venture, when Madison interrupted him.

"I lied."

"What did you say, honey?"

"I'm really not so good. Well, I'm better now, but school is just really tough."

"Oh, Maddie, why didn't you tell me? Should I speak to someone—"

"No, I don't want to make a big deal out of it or anything."

"Okay, well, you know, maybe you should leave the Gillespies' and come stay with me for the next day or so. Your mom gets back when?"

"Soon."

"Why don't you come over until she gets back?"

"Is Stephanie there?" Madison asked.

Dad took a moment to respond. "Uh, no. Why would you think that?"

"Because. You guys seem pretty close already. I just imagined that she was moving in or something major."

"Maddie, *no*." Dad put all the stress on the word "no."

Madison wanted to see him, but the truth was that she wanted to stay with Aimee *more* right now.

"Daddy, I think I'm just gonna stay here so I can cheer on Aimee in the election, okay? And Phinnie's here, so I'm okay. I can see you on Sunday, maybe. Is that okay? You probably want to do stuff with Stephanie then, right?"

"Maddie," Dad crooned, "what's with all this Stephanie stuff? You know honey, *you're* the apple of my—"

"Eye." Of course, Madison knew. She was just playing it safe. Just in case Stephanie *did* show up unannounced.

Just like that, the conversation was over.

Dad didn't argue with Madison's decision to stay at Aimee's rather than go. He wasn't an arguing kind of guy. If Mom wanted something she'd ask for it twelve times until she got it. Dad was different. He gave up easier. Of course, that made him easier to understand, too. In many ways, Dad was probably the only "boy" in Madison's life who was the least bit predictable. He was the only boy she understood.

She couldn't say *that* about Drew, or Egg, and especially not Hart Jones.

Madison didn't get Hart one itty-bitty bit.

Chapter 10

"Hey, mmwill you help me fix mmup my mmam-paign speech tonight?" Aimee asked through a mouthful of brown rice. "I have some ideas but I could mmreally use your super-brain. I mmam so worried about the mmassembly."

Madison looked down at her lukewarm vegetar-ian burrito and shrugged without taking any kind of bite whatsoever. "Okay. Sure."

It was Sunday. She'd spent the weekend raking leaves in the Gillespie yard, working on her English essay, and playing Age of Empires online with Egg. (She wasn't very good—but then, Egg beat almost everyone.) Madison had a page of vocabulary words to memorize and now she had to help craft an elec-tion speech?

Madison didn't want to do *anything* with the

election right now, not even to help her best friend in the universe. She couldn't get the gila monster and skunk episodes out of her head.

From: MadFinn
To: Bigwheels
Subject: This Weekend
Date: Sun 17 Sept 3:53 PM

Where r u?????? How is your life? I am living a life of HELP! Did you get my other emails????? I was waiting for a response. I hope you r ok.

Weekends are like Roswell or Twilight Zone and I can tell you why. There are these moments in time when people sort of float in and out of your life and set your head spinning a little. Do you know what I mean? Here is my proof:

1. Dad was supposed to come by this weekend to take me and Phinnie (my dog) out for a long aftenoon. But then he couldn't at the last minute because of work and he said he was so sorry. I say something came up with this new girlfriend he has.

2. I saw one of the other election candidates @ the mall, Tommy and some friends who were loud and not so nice to me. He thinks he's so cute but he is wicked fake. And his friend Brendan is even worse. He called me stupid. Boys can be such DORKS.

3. My Mom is still in Paris.
I think I have now told you my entire life right now. I am mainly checking in because I haven't written much and haven't heard from you. You give good advice, did I ever tell you that? So please do. Okay? Maybe we can have another online conversation one of these days? I remember last week we met in the room GOFISHY.

Your IM name is the same, right? Mine's MadFinn like everything. C ya.

Yours till the candle sticks,
MadFinn

No sooner had she hit SEND, than Madison saw her mailbox icon blinking. She and Bigwheels had sent e-mails to each other at *exactly* the same time.

From: Bigwheels
To: MadFinn
Subject: I Wonder
Date: Sun 17 Sept 3:53 PM

I had a cold and wasn't on the computer for almost three days. I had 16 e-mails when I logged on today. Three were from YOU.
I hope you are not mad at me. Well, I know you are, MadFinn, but you'll just get over it, right?

How is the election going? I wonder about other things too. I know you asked me about boys before. Are you going out with someone?

Did I ever tell you I like fish? That's why I first joined bigfish-bowl.com. Well, 2 of my very own tropical fish died this weekend. My father says they caught my cold. I think he wanted me to feel better about it but I don't.

I wish you would write me again, too.

Yours till the dandy lions,

Bigwheels

110

Madison turned on her IM Buddy List to see if maybe Bigwheels was online right now. But she wasn't. *That was weird.*

Another name popped up, though.

```
INSTA-MESSAGE to MadFinn
<Wetwinz>: Hellooooooo Maddie!
```

It was Fiona, also known as Wetwinz.

Fiona and Aimee didn't know about Madison's online friend Bigwheels, but they did know about the bigfishbowl.com site. It was kind of hard to keep that a secret. It was the most popular chat site at Far Hills Junior High.

Aimee never went on the computer because she thought Insta-Messages were annoying. Aimee didn't chat much. She thought why type when you could just talk? Wasn't it way easier to just pick up the phone? Aimee didn't even have a screen name.

Fiona had only started her online chatting. Her Mom had been nervous about giving her permission to do things online before junior high had started. Now, she decided to give Fiona and Chet online access.

```
INSTA-MESSAGE REPLY to Wetwinz
<MadFinn>: Hey you. Meet me in room
STARFISH.
```

Madison liked the way that sounded, so she picked it as her private chatroom destination.

```
<Wetwinz>: What is happening is
something wrong?
<MadFinn>: I'm fine
<Wetwinz>: At my house Fri. you
seemed a littlebummmed out 2 me
<MadFinn>: not really
<Wetwinz>: How was today
<MadFinn>: I had squishy vege
burritos 4 dinner!
<Wetwinz>: LOL
```

Fiona had heard daily updates on the wacky dinners Madison was eating—and not eating—while staying with Aimee and her family.

```
<MadFinn>: yuk but seriously
<Wetwinz>: is school bumming you out
maddie???
<MadFinn>: not school no
<Wetwinz>: then what??? I can tell
don't lie 2 me
<MadFinn>: remember that fight
onFriday???
<Wetwinz>: Ivy???
<MadFinn>: Y
<Wetwinz>: IMS! U know Chet told me
too he saw and heard it did you
know?
```

```
<MadFinn>: that is sooo embarrass-
ing. He did? Who else
<Wetwinz>: AFK
```

Fiona was Away From the Keyboard.
Madison scrolled back up to reread what they'd
said so far.

```
<Wetwinz>: sorry!! stupid Chet
walked in just then
<MadFinn>: maybe we should talk F2F
in skool
<Wetwinz>: r u bummed because Ivy
is mean?
<Wetwinz>: I'm ur friend . . .
```

Madison grinned and nodded at the computer
screen.
Fiona was a *good* friend, too.

```
<Wetwinz>: r u there?
<MadFinn>: THX, F
<Wetwinz>: n e time
<MadFinn>: <Hugs back> (())**
<Wetwinz>: c u tomorrow in class?
<Wetwinz>: <:D
```

The next morning, Madison left for school extra
early so she could tally and present the latest poll on
the school site. After the conversation with Fiona,
she decided once and for all that she really could

leave the whole Ivy episode behind. She could get back to her computer duties and get back into gear.

There was no need to feel embarrassed, either. Madison had real friends where it really mattered. Not only that, but today the Web site looked sabotage free, thankfully. And the online poll taker was working perfectly.

As of today's tally, girls *ruled*.

9/18 CURRENT STANDINGS:
What candidate will do the most for
Far Hills?
48% Ivy Daly
32% Aimee Gillespie
12% Montrell Morris
8% Thomas Kwong

Unfortunately, girls named Ivy ruled better than girls named Aimee. But Madison told herself to ignore that gigantic lead. She had to focus on the good stuff, not the bad stuff. Aimee still had a chance to win.

The bell for homeroom rang.

In the middle of roll call, Madison realized she had done all her homework for the day except science. Why hadn't she finished her science reading? She'd have to sneak into the girls' room before class to skim-read the chapters. Sometimes Madison would hide out in a stall to finish math problems or read through essays before class started. That way she could show up a little late and say she was "in the bathroom."

Unfortunately, as Madison discovered that afternoon, the science reading had a lot of new vocabulary. And Madison read so fast the chapter wasn't making much sense.

There would probably be a pop quiz today, too.

It was several moments after the bell had rung, and still Mr. Danehy had not shown up. Some kid poked his head into the classroom.

"Mr. D's stuck in a meeting and he'll be late."

The class began humming. From all corners of the room, different conversations started up like chain saws.

Bzzzzzzzzzzzzzzzzzzzzzzzz.

"Hey, Finnster," Hart whispered loudly across class. "You okay? I mean, considering . . ."

Madison made a face. "Yeah," she said. Of course she was okay. Why would he ask her that? Considering *what*?

"You have a lotta nerve," Rose Thorn said not-so-nicely from her seat at the front of the room.

Another kid mumbled, "Show-off."

Madison turned toward her seat.

What were they talking about?

"Nice Web site!" a boy from the back of the room yelled. The rest of the class laughed, especially, Poison Ivy.

115

"Now, settle down." Chet banged on Mr. Danehy's desk, pretending to be the teacher. "I will not stand for these reee-diculous deee-sruptions!"

Hart was laughing so hard his face turned all pink.

Were they laughing at her?

"Hey, Maddie," Phony Joanie called out. "How does it feel to be a screen star?"

Madison shook her head. "What are you all talking about?" She flipped through her textbook frantically, trying to ignore everyone and study more.

Ivy let out a big "HAH!" She was doodling "class president" all over her science book cover.

"Ivy, is there something going on that I don't know about?"

Ivy adjusted her skirt and crossed her legs. "Oh, Madison, poor you. Don't you get it?"

The tone in Ivy's voice told Madison that something was *definitely* wrong.

Madison knew it must have to do with the Web site. "Is this about the skunk again?"

"What do you think?" Ivy said.

Madison wanted to run to the nearest computer just to check and make sure the skunk wasn't back again, but no sooner had she stood up when Mr. Danehy came into the classroom. He was waving papers in front of him.

"Pop quiz, kids!"

Everyone let out a dejected "Awwww" even though they had all seen the quiz coming.

Madison clutched at her throat. Panic was working its way up, faster now than before. She felt hot all over. She had to get to a computer—NOW.

Every bit of classroom chatter sounded ominous.

"Messed . . . Web . . . she . . . joke."

She only could catch a few words here and there, but she was sure that they were targeted directly at her.

"Mad . . . Wing . . . site . . . can't . . . bad . . . Madison."

There was more whispering and rustling as Mr. Danehy passed out the quizzes—and funny stares all around.

Madison looked down at the pop quiz. It was a gray blur.

"Class, you will have fifteen minutes to complete . . ." Mr. Danehy explained what the quiz was about.

"Gee, Madison." Ivy leaned in close to her. "Don't you have the scientific data to fill in this quiz?" Ivy laughed softly and twirled a piece of hair around her finger, waiting for Madison to take the bait.

"Ivy, your idea of scientific data," Madison said, "is a scientist who likes to go on dates!"

It was a good answer, but it didn't count for much. Ivy was still laughing.

Madison's skin flushed. Her neck was sweating.

She could feel the room starting to spin a little.

And when Hart bellowed, "Way to go, Finnster!" Madison *really* lost it.

"Yeah, GO Finnster!" Ivy cried a little louder. "GO take a look at the election Web site."

Everyone got very quiet. Even Mr. Danehy stopped explaining for a split second. Dozens of eyes landed on Madison's hot skin.

She wanted to scream. She wanted to cry. She wanted to . . .

RUN.

"Miss Finn?" Mr. Danehy was surprised and more than a little rattled. Science teachers were not typically trained to deal with freaking-out seventh-grade girls. "Miss Finn? Are you all right?"

Madison bolted out of her chair.

What was she doing?

She ran out the door, down the hallway, down past the girls' room, past the hall monitor, down the stairs, all the way to Mrs. Wing's classroom.

No one was following her. She gasped for air.

Feelings are like fuel that jet-propel you into places and situations you don't even expect.

"What's wrong?" Mrs. Wing asked as Madison rushed into the technology lab, breathless. "You're purple!"

Madison's felt the tears and anger making her face all blotchy.

"We have to check the Web site, Mrs. Wing," Madison gasped again.

"Oh dear, I think you need to see the nurse," Mrs. Wing said.

But Madison had already logged on to the computer station and punched the right keys.

"Madison, I really think you should slow down and tell me what it is that you are looking for," Mrs. Wing added.

"Oh no." Madison turned to look up at her teacher.

Mrs. Wing stared back at the monitor.

There was the home page for the school's election site—but with one big difference. The photo of the *school* was gone.

In its place, there was a picture of Madison Finn with three little words: FINN FOR PREZ.

Chapter 11

Madison learned later on that day that thanks to her crying and fleeing, Mr. Danehy had lost all sense of order in his classroom and thereby decided to forget about the science pop quiz. So what had started out as the most embarrassing thing that could ever happen to anyone, ironically ended up winning Madison more *friends*. Her entire science class was ready to high-five her, as if Madison's freak show had somehow turned into the perfect pop-quiz-blocking method of all time.

Nothing made any sense anymore.

"Are you okay, Maddie?" Drew asked her later on in Mrs. Wing's tech lab. Madison was fixated on the screen image: FINN FOR PREZ. She couldn't even delete it this time.

"What IS that?" Drew asked.

The photo of Madison kept shifting in and out of focus. Mrs. Wing walked over to the classroom phone and dialed the Administration office.

"Do you think someone is doing this on purpose?" Drew wondered out loud.

"Don't you? Or maybe it's just a coincidence that they put FINN FOR PREZ? I don't think so."

"Principal Bernard is coming up right now, you two," Mrs. Wing said as she clicked a few more keys. Madison watched Mrs. Wing jump from computer screen to screen, checking in once again on all of the other pages. Madison wanted to be like her almost as much as she wanted to be like Mom. Mrs. Wing was so smart, Madison thought again. She wanted to be smart, and wear iridescent earrings, and sip hot coffee in the morning.

Madison wanted a lot of things.

"Where is Mr. Diaz?" Mrs. Wing asked. She was smart, but she was also very annoyed. She didn't like the way this computer prank was turning out. It was jeopardizing the entire school election.

No sooner had she asked the question than Egg appeared.

"Sorry I'm late, Mrs.—check that out!" Egg spied the sabotaged home page screen. "Maddie, you're on the home page! Hey, Mrs. Wing, do you—?"

"Walter, would you please just sit down. This is a serious problem."

Egg was surprised by Mrs. Wing's stern tone of

voice. His crush had just dealt him a crushing blow.

"Walter, take a seat please," Mrs. Wing repeated.

He collapsed into a chair. "She hates me," Egg whispered to Drew.

Meanwhile, Madison kept trying to figure out everything Mrs. Wing had been explaining about strings and substrings and things. She looked at what was typed up on the screen.

```
Source of message.
Proxy server location.
Time of use.
```

"Is Mrs. Wing in here?"

Principal Bernard was at the classroom door. Mrs. Wing got up to speak to the principal "privately" for a moment.

Drew had a blank look on his face. He didn't want to get into trouble with the principal.

Egg wore a look of devastation. The wisecracker had cracked.

Madison tapped a few more keys and finally found the "history" of the Finn photograph flashing up on the screen. She was surprised to see that the photo had been downloaded *last Friday*.

The source of the message was a serial number.

Madison turned to Mrs. Wing, Principal Bernard, and the rest of the room. She grinned proudly. "I know where the photo was sent from."

"Madison?" Mrs. Wing smiled. "You do? Well, good for you. You were paying close attention, I see."

"Miss Finn, I am impressed," Principal Bernard said. "Does this mean you can tell us who the prankster is?"

"Way to go, Maddie," Drew pumped his fist in the air.

Egg looked up, too. "Can you really tell who did it just by looking—"

"Maybe!" Madison nodded. "The photo here was sent from a computer up on the sixth floor," she explained. "See, I figured out that each computer has its own code based on its location."

Mrs. Wing was smiling wider now, as if she was *proud*. She gave Principal Bernard a sidelong glance.

"So computer 611FH is the only unit with a six in the code," Madison continued. "The older main building is the only building with a sixth floor. And the only computer on the sixth floor is in the library."

Mrs. Wing was genuinely impressed.

"Whoa," Egg said. "You figured all that out from looking at that code?"

Principal Bernard piped up. "Don't they keep logs so people who use computers have to sign in and out of the media center?"

Mrs. Wing held up her hands as if to say, "This is your ball, Madison Finn. Run with it."

So Madison ran all the way up to the sixth floor.

She wondered what she'd find in the log. Maybe the culprit was Rose Thorn or Phony Joanie?

Mr. Books was just closing up the library as they climbed the stairs.

"Hello, there. What is the big rush?"

"We may have a little computer problem happening from your station up here, Mr. Books. I know it's hard to believe, but quite true. Miss Finn here seems to have found the source."

The library computer logbook was laid out on a wooden table near the station. Madison rushed over to it, followed by Drew, Egg, Mrs. Wing, Mr. Books, and Principal Bernard.

"Okay." Madison searched in a frenzy. She flipped back to Friday's entries. "I know the download happened at ten-forty P.M. So, that means I'll find it right here."

Madison ran her finger down the list of sign-in names—and stopped.

She took a step backward.

"Who is it?" Mrs. Wing asked with concern. "Madison, is it someone you know?"

"Worse," Madison groaned. "Drew, look."

There was nothing listed for a 10:40 download. There was no one in school then. No one had used the computer over the weekend, either.

But on the list was a very familiar name.

Madison Finn.

"I guess that's not who you expected to see, right?" Egg said.

"Very funny," Madison grunted.

Drew elbowed Egg in the side.

Everyone else was tongue-tied.

And Madison was right back where she had started.

Which was, basically, *nowhere*.

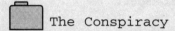 The Conspiracy

Rude Awakening: Sometimes it's easier to believe your enemies than your friends.

I am at the center of a Far Hills Junior High conspiracy, I swear. Of course, I shouldn't be talking about it so much. That's like whammying myself to have even worse luck. But I can't help it.

When Aimee got back from her dance troupe tonight I told her everything. She almost died when she heard. She said it was like a REAL conspiracy. Like a movie. I sent mom another e-mail too and told her about it, since she is the movie person, after all. And Fiona and Bigwheels know too, of course. I couldn't leave them out.

At least this election Web site is only

accessible at school. But I don't think I
will ever recover from the embarrassment.

That evening, Maddie set up her laptop in a
corner of Aimee's bedroom to do her homework.
But she just didn't feel like studying. What was the
point in attempting to solve a tough math equation
when she couldn't even figure out who had invaded
the school Web site?

Madison wanted to work more on her files. She
wanted to get to the bottom of the Web site mystery. She considered the suspects.

```
Poison Ivy Enemy #1
Rose and Joanie
The other candidates: Montrell? Tommy?
Definite not Aimee, Egg, Mrs. Wing, or
Fiona
Hart Jones?
```

After she typed Hart's name for the first time
Madison got a little distracted. She entered it a few
more times.

```
Hart Hart Hart HART hart
Maddie + Hart
Madison Jones
```

When Madison realized what she was
really typing, she pressed DELETE. What if her file
got into the wrong hands?

Plus, Gramma Helen had always told Maddie

126

never to write anything that she wouldn't want someone else to see. "Think before you ink, Madison," Gramma would say.

Madison figured the same rule had to be true about stuff keyed in on the computer. She didn't want *anyone* to know the way she felt about the guy who called her Finnster. It was way too embarrassing.

When Mrs. Gillespie screeched from downstairs, "Frittatas! Come and get it!" Madison wasn't sure what to expect.

Would tonight's dinner selection be better or worse than the sand or vegetables from the nights before?

Phinnie was, of course, waiting in the dining room. He was such a little beggar. Madison poured kibble into the PHIN FOOD dish, and he muscled in for his chow. Blossom howled too. Together they looked like they were performing a doggy comedy routine.

Dinner was unusually quiet. Mr. Gillespie made dinner conversation with the "girls," since none of his four sons was eating at home tonight. Things were definitely less interesting without the boys around.

"Aimee, have you written your campaign speech yet?"

Aimee chuckled. "I'm working on it, Daddy."

Madison added, "It's going to be great, Mr. Gillespie."

"Maddie's gonna help me write it, Daddy."

"Yeah," Madison continued, "Aimee's saying really smart stuff. Better than Ivy Daly anyway."

Aimee nodded. "That's for sure."

"Ivy Daly? You mean Jack Daly's girl?" Mr. Gillespie said. "Now, weren't you girls all friends at one point?"

"Only like a million and a half years ago, Daddy!" Aimee swallowed a mouthful of lentils. They were little brown beans piled high on a platter in the middle of the table, a platter that Madison was avoiding at all costs. Maddie opted for extra helpings of potatoes instead.

"I could have sworn you three were still friends." Mr. Gillespie was perplexed.

Madison thought about how funny it was that parents could fall so far out of the loop of friends and acquaintances sometimes. There was a time in life once when everyone's moms and dads knew everyone's friends, those friends' parents, and all the friends' pets. But things were different now. Way different.

"We were friends in elementary school," Madison said to clarify things. "When we were kids."

"Oh," Mr. Gillespie said, surprised. "And now you are—?"

"In junior high, Dad. Gimme a break. We are not babies anymore. Things are just different."

"Watch your tone, Aimee, please," Mrs. Gillespie reprimanded her.

Aimee sulked a little.

"Madison, I thought Ivy Daly always seemed like such a nice girl," Mrs. Gillespie continued, "and you used to have so much fun together."

Madison laughed out loud. "Well, you should see Poison Ivy now."

"Poison *who*?" Mrs. Gillespie was lost. "What did you call her?"

Mr. Gillespie just shook his head. "You girls change friends like you change the cable-TV channels. I can't keep up."

"But Maddie and I are still here," Aimee crooned. She stood up and danced her way into the kitchen with the dirty dishes.

"I stand corrected then," Mr. Gillespie said. "You only change *some* of the channels."

After dinner, while Aimee watched a TV show about jazz dancers, Madison went looking for an e-mail from Bigwheels in her mailbox.

Her heart leaped.

Maddie's bigfishbowl.com friend had written back sooner than soon—as requested.

Phin jumped onto the bed next to Madison. Since her orange laptop was taking up *his* usual spot on her lap, Phinnie snuggled into Madison's side, snorting and scratching at the sheets to make just the right spot for his little body.

From: Bigwheels
To: MadFinn
Subject: Poem and other stuff
Date: Mon 18 Sept 9:24 AM

Yes I am writing again! I'm writing
from MY school media center. Ha!
I decided that the best way to
cheer you up was to send you a poem
I wrote when I was feeling like a
total outsider when it seemed like
the world was after me and against
me. It happens to everyone I think.
People can be so mean and hurtful.
Even though my poem says so, you
are not alone!!! NO WAY! You know
that these poems are not how I am
always, right? I feel good mostly.
But when I don't it just comes out
like here. 'Bye.

Frown

I am bugged by some of the people
Just who do they think they are?
I am crushed at school near and far
Sometimes I feel it like a squeeze
that won't end
I want to stop the crush
I want to have a normal friend
I like to talk on the phone
It keeps me from being alone

```
If you are having a hard time too
Do not worry just tell someone
about it
Like your mom or teacher too
Don't ever let anyone get you down
And most of all don't frown

Write back soon and tell me what
happens with the election this week.
Bye.

Yours till the gum drops,

Bigwheels
```

As soon as Madison read the poem, she knew that maybe she could believe this friend—*way* more than any of her enemies. Bigwheels' e-mail energized her.

Tomorrow Maddie could find out who the culprit was, and she could make the election Web site work. Then Mrs. Wing would *really* be impressed.

Chapter 12

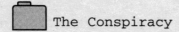 The Conspiracy

Rude Awakening: Objects on the calendar are closer than they appear.

Two more days left.

Suddenly the election is here and I am no closer to finding the computer hacker than I was yesterday or the day before that. Of course I never wanted to be Nancy Drew, but I could do better than THIS. I always guess the wrong rooms when I play Clue and hit all the dead ends in all the video games. Sometimes it's like all the signs are here, there, and everywhere and I'm wandering aimlessly in the middle of it all.

And I'm Aimee-less, too. At least for

now. She's off dancing somewhere as usual.
I'm slumming in the technology lab. Mrs.
Wing isn't saying much.

I haven't seen much of Ivy. Right up
until yesterday I actually thought she
could still be guilty of the Web site
problems STILL. Esp. when the FINN FOR PREZ
thing came up. But now I know that's not
so.

It's kind of bad, because if Ivy *had*
been the one responsible and I had proved
she *was* the one responsible then I could
know for sure right know that Aimee Anne
Gillespie would win the election.

Madison couldn't stop thinking either, about conspiracies and homework and ice cream.

"Maddie!" Drew ran up to her later in the hall-way after lunch.

"Drew, where were you?"

"In the other building . . ." He coughed. "I had to find—you—to show . . ." He stopped to catch his breath.

"Drew, what's going on? Is this some kind of freaky joke again? Because if it is, it really isn't funny—"

Drew shoved a folded-up piece of paper in front of Madison. "I think you should read this."

Madison made a face as she grabbed the paper. She wasn't sure what kind of game he was playing. All week long Drew had been everywhere she was, like a computer virus himself. He and Egg both.

The page was all scribbles and hard to read, but Madison could make out a few key phrases. She decoded its message.

```
Network passwords:  CSXRUNNING
                    ELECTIONBASE
                    ELECT891WING
File/words:         A:/GILA.BMP
                    A:/SKUN.BMP
                    A:/FINN.BMP
                    A:/WING.BMP
                    FLASH: TOMMY RULES
MF(locker combo)    658
```

"Where," Madison gulped. "Where did you get this?" She almost dropped the torn sheet onto the floor.

Drew explained, "I was sitting there in social studies class and—"

"THAT'S MY LOCKER COMBINATION!" Madison shouted. She pointed to the note, shocked by its discovery. "Did you hear what I said?"

Drew nodded politely. "I think the whole hallway heard you."

Madison quickly glanced over at the locker banks to make sure no one was listening or watching the two of them anymore.

"Pretty bad, huh?" Drew rocked from foot to foot.

"*Where* did you get this?"

"Like I said, I was in social studies class and these kids got up to leave and—"

"Drew! Someone has written down all the files and the combination to my locker and the network codes assigned by the school and Mrs. Wing. This is MAJOR."

Drew nodded.

"This is like get-suspended-from-school MAJOR."

Drew nodded again.

"Don't just stand there—tell me what happened!" Madison said.

Drew sighed a heavy sigh (since he'd been trying to get a word in edgewise for the last five minutes). He had seen a group of kids hanging out before class with Tommy Kwong, one of the other candidates. They all sat together in social studies. This one kid dropped the sheet of paper on his way out of class.

"He didn't feel it or see it or stop to pick it up," Drew added. "So I picked it up for him. It was Brendan Lo."

"Who's Brendan Lo?" Madison cried when she heard his name. After a moment, she realized maybe he was in her science class. Or was it English? She couldn't be sure.

"You don't know him?" Drew asked. "That's weird. Why would he—"

"I know!" Madison cried. "Tommy's friend. The one who was a jerk at the mall. Whoa."

Madison wondered why Brendan was stupid enough to let himself be discovered. How could someone who had been so computer smart, who had gone to all the trouble to hide his tracks, even signing her name, and who had been so clever about scanning photos and sabotaging the site . . . would then let himself get caught with a handwritten note? Madison remembered her Gramma Helen's old saying once again: *Think before you ink*. It was truer than true right now.

Drew adjusted the paper and pointed to the page where it listed files: GILA (for the lizard), SKUN (for the skunk), FINN (for Madison), and then WING.

"Do you see that? He was even gonna put up something online with Mrs. Wing's picture or something. That's what that means, right?"

Madison slid down the wall and hugged her knees.

This was it.

This was the proof Madison needed to show that *she* had not been responsible in any way for what had gone wrong on the Web site.

It was too good to be true.

"This isn't some kind of joke, is it, Drew?"

"What?" Drew wrinkled his forehead. "Are *you* kidding?"

"I mean, you and Egg aren't playing some mean trick on me, are you? Please tell me this note is real and that this kid Brendan really wrote it."

Drew pulled the note back. "Look at this. Does it look fake? Anyway, how would we know your locker combination?"

In her heart, Madison knew Drew was telling the truth.

She rolled forward on one knee to get up and Drew extended his hand to help her. It was clammy and cool when Madison grabbed it. (She made sure Drew wasn't looking when she wiped off her hand on her pants a minute later.)

"You know, if you're gonna write a note or a letter or a journal, you'd think a person would keep it under lock and key or password-protect himself," Madison thought out loud.

"Yeah." Drew said.

"Sometimes people can be smart and stupid at the exact same time, you know?"

"Yeah." Drew shrugged. "So now what do we do?"

Madison shrugged back.

"Let's go tell Mrs. Wing. She'll know what to do."

Chapter 13

From: MadFinn
To: Bigwheels
Subject: Re: Poem and other stuff
Date: Wed 20 Sept. 3:29 PM

I have huge news so I should just
spill it.

The Election Web Site Mystery is
SOLVED.

Turns out that the person I told
you about who was putting up all
those pictures on the Web site has
been suspended from school. It was
this kid who was friends with one
of the other candidates, Tommy. He
was actually in my SCIENCE CLASS—can
you believe it? He was good at

computers and wanted Tommy to win
soooo much that he decided to mess
with MY site. I guess Brendan
wanted to embarrass me and the rest
of the candidates so Tommy would be
the only person left to pick.

What a weird twist. It also turns
out that Brendan wasn't really a
part of Tommy's crew, he just
wished he was. So he figured doing
this would make people like him
more. It's like a bad movie of the
week on TV!!! I feel so bad for
this kid.

Tommy says he didn't know anything
but he got pulled from the election
anyhow. AND he got suspended for a
week. SO harsh.

By the way, you are maybe the best
poet I have ever read for a seventh
grader. I mean, how are you so
good? I have read your poem over
and over and it is so like my life!
I think the title could be
"Crushed" maybe—something like
that.

Please please please keep your

fingers crossed for my friend Aimee.
I think she really could win this
school election tomorrow w/one
candidate gone now. Here's hoping.

Yours till the web links,

MadFinn

Brrrrrrrring.
By the time Thursday's 1:10 bell rang and the
announcement for the election assembly came over
the loudspeaker, Madison was ready to scream for
joy. What would Ivy's drones Rose Thorn and Phony
Joanie say when they realized their crowned princess
Ivy was an L-O-S-E-R?

Classes were excused from seventh period so kids
could hear the candidates' speeches and vote.

All of a sudden election day was here—and
almost over.

"Attention! Students?" Principal Bernard tapped
on the mike once everyone had taken seats in the
auditorium. "Now, you know why we are all here?"
Mr. Bernard's voice lilted so he sounded as if he was
always asking a question.

Madison rolled her eyes as the lights were
dimmed to show *Campaign USA*, one of those edu-
cational, how-to videos principals and social studies
teachers liked to show in assembly. During the video,
kids were whispering, rolling spitballs, and even

zapping messages to each other on their Cybikos (which should have been confiscated, of course, but weren't).

Madison sat up in her seat a little taller.

She could just see the top of Hart's head.

After seven minutes, when the lights went back up, Mr. Bernard cleared his throat. As always, he spoke into the microphone a little too closely.

Sqweeeeeeeeee.

Everyone cringed from the feedback.

"Now, let's announce Far Hills' candidates for class president, starting with class—"

Sqweeeeeeeeee.

Half the room clapped and stomped on the floor while the other half fanned themselves with flyers. The teachers had handed out a Far Hills Junior High Elections Guide, so everyone knew the rules, but of course no one had really read it. It was carefully attached to a printout of the candidate profiles Drew and Madison had posted on the Web. Tommy's section had been whited out.

Thankfully, Madison noticed that *these* flyers carried real photos of candidates and not pictures of lizards or skunks or Madison Finns.

Madison glanced around. A few rows back, Drew Maxwell caught her eye and waved. She waved back but then turned around again, suddenly embarrassed even though she didn't know why.

Was he smiling at her?

Madison looked back once more, but Drew was talking to Egg by then.

"As you know, we take elections at Far Hills very seriously, students," Mr. Bernard said, demanding everyone's undivided attention. "Would you please give this year's candidates your warmest welcome."

Onto the stage walked Montrell, then Poison Ivy, and Aimee.

Mrs. Wing was up near the stage fiddling with both a video camera and an instant camera. She was getting footage and photos for the Web site.

Montrell talked about how the school needed to give way less homework and throw pizza parties every Friday. Of course, he was a basketball player, so team sports was his main focus.

Madison groaned when Ivy stepped up to the microphone. It was because of the way she did it, with a sweep of her hand and a toss of her head, as if she were posing for a modeling shoot.

She acted like a winner and no one even had voted yet.

"I think Far Hills Junior High needs to bond together. We should all look out for each other and be friends." Ivy's voice was earnest but Madison knew *she* wasn't. How could the Queen of Mean call "bonding" and "friendship" her goals as class president?

Between Tommy's scandal and Ivy's attitude, Aimee *had* to win this vote.

Finally it was Aimee's turn. She pirouetted onstage, making an entrance, of course. She had written her own speech the night before with the help of Maddie, Roger, Mr. and Mrs. Gillespie, and Fiona (over the phone).

"Go, Aimee!" Fiona shouted in Madison's ear. She was crossing her fingers. She was as superstitious as Madison.

Madison clapped loudly, pinching her eyes shut just so she felt a little less nervous. This was her best friend and her best chance to stop Poison Ivy before Far Hills turned into her kingdom. Madison didn't want Junior High to turn out just like elementary school.

Aimee's voice was a little shaky at first.

"Let me begin by saying how much I love running for class prez. I love it. You guys are all really great. Doing this has given me the chance to meet lots of you and I think that being class president is so important. . . ."

She warmed up after a while. Madison was trying to pay attention throughout, but she kept getting distracted by Hart's head again each time he shifted in his seat.

"So I promise I will do my best. Even better than the rest . . ."

Madison knew this was near the end. She clapped—hard.

"Go, Aimee!"

The rest of the audience clapped, too. Even Egg and Drew circled their fists up into the air. "Woo! Woo! Woo!"

As soon as all the candidates were done, a loud kid sitting behind Madison said, "Let's get outta here already." She was painfully reminded that not everyone *really* cared as much as she did about school elections. Then again, Aimee didn't need *everyone*'s vote to win. She just needed enough to whup Ivy Daly fair and square.

Up on stage, Madison watched as Montrell shook Aimee's hand and then Ivy's. But Aimee and Ivy took a moment before they shook, smiling their plastic smiles. People who didn't know they were enemies never would have been able to tell what was *really* going on. Only Madison and Fiona knew.

The applause for candidates continued right up until the moment when the vice-presidential hope-fuls came out, but Madison stopped paying atten-tion altogether by then. She craned her neck to see what Hart was doing and kept her eyes on him.

Once all seventh-grade reps had been presented and given their chance to speak, Mr. Bernard's voice boomed again over the microphone. "Thank you, students it's time to vote." He leaned into the mike and the sharp, metallic sound of feedback blared up once again.

Sqweeeeeeeeee.

Kids covered their ears. Principal Bernard quickly

144

turned the microphone over to the best computer teacher on the planet, Mrs. Wing. Today she was wearing a scarf instead of beads. Madison could see multicolored numbers all over it.

"Weren't those speeches great?" She led the auditorium in another burst of applause. "Now, thank you all for paying attention to our candidates. I know most of you have visited our exciting new Web site. This year is very special because for the very first time we are voting online. I would like to take a moment to thank a few people who have helped make this election Web project possible. First, Mr. Lynch in ninth grade, who programmed the basics and got us up and running. Second, Principal Bernard who graciously gave the technology area a new proxy server over the summer. And of course to Madison Finn, Walter Diaz, and Andrew Maxwell who have worked very hard—"

"Yeah, Finnster!" Madison heard Hart yell from the front row. Everyone in the auditorium clapped and laughed at the same time.

Egg went "Woo! Woo!" again.

Madison shrunk into her seat. Running was not an option. Fiona tried to get her to stand up, but she would not budge. It felt like an eternity between the moment Mrs. Wing said her name and the moment the applause and laughter ceased. In that moment Madison Finn realized that maybe—no, *definitely*—she didn't like the spotlight.

Principal Bernard took back the microphone. "So now students will be dismissed in small groups to vote. You will go to Mrs. Wing's class and vote at the computer stations. Do I need to ask this again? Vote nicely—"

Sqweeeeeeeeeee.

"And that's all folks!" He pounded the lectern with a happy fist.

Everyone stood up now, waiting for their turn to vote. It was after 2:45 by the time Madison shoved her way out the door of the assembly hall with Fiona. Egg and Drew were walking down the hall in the opposite direction.

"Who are you gonna vote for, Maddie?" Egg teased as he walked by with Drew.

"Uh . . . that's a hard one, Egg," Madison faked. "I just don't know!"

"The site looks good," Egg said. "I admit it."

"Thanks," Madison said.

Fiona smiled at Egg. "Hey, Walter, I mean . . . Egg."

For the first time ever, Egg smiled right back. "Hey, Fiona. Whassup?" He walked away with Drew following closely behind, as usual.

Mrs. Wing's classroom was chaos. People were everywhere.

Some groups of kids were sitting at terminals to punch in their votes while other groups were shuffling around the classroom floor in lines that stretched in a circle.

"Everyone is voting really quickly," Fiona said. "Is that a good sign or a bad sign?"

Madison didn't know. She crossed her fingers inside her pockets just to make sure she was doing everything possible to secure an Aimee victory.

Mrs. Wing saw Madison inside the lab and rushed over to thank her in person. "Well, Madison Finn, we did it. And the voting program seems to be tallying everything up in fine order."

"I'm so glad," Madison mumbled. She was overwhelmed.

Mrs. Wing touched her shoulder. "I am very proud of how hard you worked and how you handled the Web problems, too."

Madison's shoulder drooped into an "Aw, shucks!" pose. She was embarrassed by Mrs. Wing's compliments.

"So, you are staying after school today to help with vote tallies, aren't you?"

Madison nodded.

She would be the first person at Far Hills to know whether or not the election winner would be her worst enemy or her best friend.

What kind of Rude Awakening was in store?

"It is not possible!" Madison said as she scrolled down the page of election results. They weren't good.

```
        9/21 VOTE TABULATION
     Class Seven: 312 students
  Ivy Daly                    114
  Aimee Gillespie              87
  Montrell Morris             111
  Thomas Kwong                N/A
```

Not only had Aimee lost to Ivy Daly, but she had come in *third* place after a second-place Montrell Morris.

Ivy had run away with this election. Madison wanted to run away from its results.

The computer automatically did a third vote count to make sure the results were right. It came up the same. Winner: Ivy Daly.

"Mrs. Wing?" Madison asked nicely as could be. "Could I be the one to tell Aimee the bad news about losing?"

Mrs. Wing decided it would be fine on one simple condition. "You can share the news with her tonight, but let's keep the rest of the school in suspense until morning announcements, okay?"

Madison agreed.

The next morning Principal Bernard would get on the announcement speaker to announce all class presidents in grades seven through nine, as well as names of all the vice presidents, class treasurers, and class reps. Madison wanted Aimee to know *before* she heard that announcement.

Aimee had dance practice that day, so Madison didn't get a chance to talk to her alone until after dinnertime. Mrs. Gillespie had made hamburgers, real *meat* ones, in honor of Madison's last night dining and sleeping at their place. It was a full house tonight, with Roger, Billy, Dean, and Doug all home for good eats and good talk about their sister.

"Here's to the next president of Far Hills Junior High." Aimee's dad raised his water glass.

Everyone cheered except for Madison, who gulped her water down and barely spoke.

"Maddie, you're so quiet, what's the problem?"

Aimee asked her when they were waiting for Mrs. Gillespie to bring out dessert.

"Tell ya later," Madison said. She could feel her knee jumping. She was trying to figure out the right time to talk.

It took a few minutes of after-dinner playing with Phin before Madison finally told Aimee.

Aimee grabbed a pillow and screamed into it when she heard the news.

"Aimee?" Madison didn't move. "Aim? Are you okay?"

Slowly, Aimee rolled over to one side. She looked more mad than sad. "Ugh!" she cried out. "She always wins. I can't STAND it!"

"I'm sorry you lost, Aimee, I really am," Madison continued. "And I didn't want to ruin tonight. I just didn't want you to find out at school tomorrow. I wanted to tell you now so you wouldn't be—"

"I know, Maddie," Aimee groaned. "Hey, I tried, right?"

"Yeah," Madison said. "But you deserve it so much more. You really, really, really did."

"Did Ivy really win by that many votes?"

Madison nodded.

"The popular girl always wins, doesn't she?" Aimee grumbled.

Madison thought about that for a moment. She agreed that Ivy seemed to get her way most of the time.

"I think people voted for Ivy because they think they'll be cool or something if she wins."

"Like they'll become a part of her little club or something," Aimee added. "You know, it just makes me so mad!

"I'm gonna go talk to Roger," Aimee sniffled. "Maybe one of my brothers can cheer me up. I am so bummed out. Those guys are always good with this kinda stuff, ya know?"

Madison knew firsthand. Roger gave *great* advice.

As soon as Aimee walked out, Madison started up her orange laptop immediately, hoping to catch Bigwheels online. She needed a big-time mood booster.

The bigfishbowl.com server was a little slow. Too many other people were online at once. When she finally did get on, Madison scrolled down the alphabetical list of people who were in the "fishtank."

```
2good2be2
654aqua
7thheavn4
A+student
Abadabadoo
allurluv
Bethiscool
Bhurley
Bigphat88
Bigwheels
```

She was there! Bigwheels was online! Aimee had lost at school, but here was a smaller victory. Madison felt her stomach flip-flop—but in a *good* way.

```
INSTA-MESSAGE to Bigwheels
<MadFinn>: R u there?
```

She waited for only a split second before her answer popped right up.

```
INSTA-MESSAGE REPLY to MadFinn
<Bigwheels>: MADISON! Meet me in deep
sea chat area, ok 4 private chat???
<Bigwheels>: Oh yeah u know my fave
room is GOFISHY
```

Madison was so excited she kept hitting the return key before her message was typed, but she finally got through.

```
INSTA-MESSAGE REPLY to Bigwheels
<MadFinn>: C
<MadFinn>:
<MadFinn>: SORRY! C u there
<MadFinn>: GOFISHY
```

Chatting in private was the next-best thing to being right next to someone—and MadFinn and Bigwheels hadn't chatted in a whole week.

<Bigwheels>: S^?
<MadFinn>: election OVER
<Bigwheels>: WHO WON?????????
<MadFinn>: My frind Aimee lost
<MadFinn>: I mean friend
<Bigwheels>: [:>(
<MadFinn>: ⊥ know boohoo
<Bigwheels>: Big smile 2 her
<MadFinn>: 88
<MadFinn>: POAHF
<Bigwheels>: did that other girl
win?
<MadFinn>: Yes IVY
<MadFinn>: THAt makes me maddddd
<Bigwheels>: Hey I know an Ivy
<MadFinn>: WHO???
<Bigwheels>: JK
<MadFinn>: LOL
<MadFinn>: I shldnt say stuff rigtht
<Bigwheels>: She could read this
<MadFinn>: Not good to write stuff
down like
<MadFinn>: Her name
<Bigwheels>: whatever she wont see
<MadFinn>: Howz school?
<Bigwheels>: RL is no fun
<MadFinn>: I decided to like someone
<Bigwheels>: { :O You did?
<MadFinn>: :>&
<Bigwheels>: STOP Just tell me who
is it?

153

<MadFinn>: Hart
<Bigwheels>: Like HEART? LOL
<MadFinn>: Yeah I guess
<MadFinn>: FC he likes me
<MadFinn>: but I dunno
<Bigwheels>: Is he in ur class?
<MadFinn>: I knew him b4 in 2grade
& then he moved but now he's back
and he is way dif I dunno no one
knows but you so don't tell n e one
<Bigwheels>: LOL who would I tell?
<MadFinn>: oops GMBO
<Bigwheels>: Does he know?
<MadFinn>: He HATES me I think
<Bigwheels>: Do u have classes
2gether?
<MadFinn>: Y r boys so clueless
soemtimes?
<Bigwheels>: Boys are annoying
<MadFinn>: u said it!!!
<Bigwheels>: #1 reason: only think
of 1 thing
<MadFinn>: what
<Bigwheels>: Hookups
<MadFinn>: Have u ever?
<Bigwheels>: Not xactly
<MadFinn>: 404
<Bigwheels>: Ask the blowfish

"Ask the Blowfish" was a special area on bigfish-bowl.com where you could go to ask advice on matters of the heart and head. It only answered yes and no questions, but Madison swore it was always right.

```
<Bigwheels>: Hey PAW!!!!
<MadFinn>: what
<Bigwheels>: let's talk tomorrow
<MadFinn>: what
<Bigwheels>: PAW!!
<MadFinn>: ok bye :>)
```

Madison was about to turn off her computer when she noticed that her mailbox had mail in it.

```
Fm: Wetwinz
To: MadFinn
Subject: THE ELECTION!
Date: Thurs, 21 Sept., 8:44 PM
```
Maddie! Chet just told me the worst thing ever I am sooo sad. He says Aimee lost the election. I guess Drew told Egg and Egg told Chet who let the news slip when we had dinner. Oh no what does Aimee think? Please please tell her I am soooo bummed out. I sent an e-m just in case she doesn't know and also I can't get thru on the phone which I can't. I've been trying since 8.

I wanted her to win sooo much. WoW.

Anyway bye.

Madison quickly deleted Fiona's e-mail. She couldn't believe all that had happened in the past week.

Bigwheels had been right about boys. They were so annoying. How could Drew confide in Egg, who had the hugest mouth in all of Far Hills? If Chet knew, that meant that Egg had probably told the rest of the class. Even Ivy probably knew. She would be gloating about her victory before Friday announcements even happened.

But Friday wasn't the drama Madison anticipated. No big surprise that Ivy was her winning self, poisonous as ever.

There was one very important thing that made Friday *very* nice, however, in spite of the election results. Mom had flown in from France that morning, so Madison was going home to her *real* home after school. At *last*.

Madison smelled cloves when she walked through the door. Mom was boiling potpourri and airing out the living room.

"Hello?" Madison said, dumping her orange bag in the front hall. "Are you here, Mom?" She kicked off her sneakers and slid across the wood floor.

Phinnie came running. The Gillespies had

dropped him off already that day, along with all of Madison's overnight bags.

"Rowrooo!" he howled, happy to be back home where he belonged, too.

Mom appeared from behind the kitchen's swinging door, arms outstretched. "Honey bear!" she cried.

Madison squeezed. It felt good to be called that name in person rather than just in e-mail. Mom wrapped her arms around Maddie's middle.

"I missed you!" she said. Madison hugged her even tighter.

Phinnie wanted in on the clinch, too. He jumped up and tried to get Madison's attention as if to say, "Stop holding that human and start hugging ME."

Madison saw a wrapped package on the dining room table with a card: *Je t'aime Madison*.

"That's for you." Mom smiled.

Madison opened the wrapping and saw a wooden box covered with decoupage animals varnished on the surface. She'd never seen anything so beautiful. Inside that box was another surprise: a shiny silver ring with a moonstone top. The band of the ring was little daisies linked together.

"Mom!" Madison burst into happy tears. "I love it. I love it SO much!"

"I thought since your Dad gave you the earrings, this would be a nice match. I picked it up on the Place de la Concorde."

157

Madison's smile turned downward. "Uh, can we not talk about Dad?"

"Maddie, what is it?" Mom pulled out a kitchen chair. "Is something wrong with your father?"

"No," Madison replied. "Forget it."

"Do you want to talk? Tell me," Mom said. "What is it? Are you upset about Dad's girlfriend?"

Madison didn't answer. Her parents both had a sneaky way of needing to talk and then making it seem like *she* was the one who had something to say.

"You know, I did a lot of thinking while I was away," Mom said, trying to get Madison to talk, too. "I did a lot of thinking about my work and you and—"

Madison stared at the ceiling. She wanted to run, but she stayed put.

"Okay, I get it. You want to talk about this another time." Mom sensed Madison's discomfort and changed the subject. "Are you hungry? Wanna order pizza for dinner? "

"Pizza is perfect!" Madison cheered.

No more sand or soggy vegetable burritos or tofu meatballs.

"Ggggrrrrowrrooooo!" Phin growled. Even the dog was ready to chow down some real food. Mom called in for an extra large pie with extra-cheese.

During dinner, Mom stayed away from the topic of Dad, as requested. But then she started asking other questions Madison liked even less.

"Why are you asking if I like any boys at school?" Madison said.

"Just curious," Mom replied. "I have been gone a while, honey bear. I don't want to miss anything. Now that you're in seventh grade."

"I don't like *anyone*, Mom," Maddie said firmly.

"Okay." Mom kissed the top of Madison's head. "Okay. I get it. That subject is off-limits too." She went off to clean the dinner dishes.

Of course, Madison *did* like someone. She just didn't want to say his name out loud, not even to Mom, because once it was out there in the universe her chances of getting crushed increased. And she had been crushed enough this week with elections, the Web site and Dad's new girlfriend. Plus, if she said her crush's name out loud, then people would know. Madison wasn't ready for that—or the *Hart* ache. Boy, oh boy.

Mad Chat Words:

[:> (	Serious Frown
:o	Shocked
:>&	Tongue-tied
FTBOMBH	From the Bottom of My Broken Heart
TAL	Thanks a lot
12345	Talk about school
GAL	Get a Life
LMSO	Laughing my socks off
>5	High Five
s>	What's Up?
88	Love and kisses
POAHF	Put on a happy face
JK	Just kidding
404	I have no clue

Madison's Computer Tip:

If you're reading e-mail or surfing the Web and you see something weird, speak up. **<u>Always tell an adult if you see *anything* online that makes you uncomfortable.</u>** Don't be afraid to tell parents or teachers, even if you're embarrassed by it. I had to tell Mrs. Wing, my computer teacher, about the problems with the school site and I was mortified. Safety comes first!

Visit Madison at www.madisonfinn.com

Book #2: *Boy, Oh Boy!*

Super Quiz

Now that you've read the story . . . how much do you *really* know about Madison and her friends?

1. Who calls Madison "Finnster"?
   a. Egg
   b. Hart
   c. Aimee

2. Who are the drones?
   a. Roseanne Snyder and Joan Kenyon
   b. Fiona Waters and Egg Diaz
   c. Ivy Daly and Hart Jones

3. Who is the Far Hills "cybrarian"?
    a. Mr. Books
    b. Mrs. Wing
    c. Mr. Wing

4. How many older brothers does Aimee have?
    a. Four
    b. Three
    c. Two

5. Why does Madison stay over at Aimee's house?
    a. Because Aimee's mom is a better cook
    b. Because Madison ran away
    c. Because Mom is away in Paris on business

6. What's one of Madison's worst habits?
    a. Picking her nose
    b. Chewing her nails
    c. Spitting at people

7. Where does Madison have dinner with Stephanie for the first time?
    a. A French restaurant
    b. Dad's apartment
    c. At the local diner

8. What is Madison's official title on the school election Web site?
    a. Online programmer
    b. Data-entry clerk
    c. Elections coordinator

9. What's Aimee's dog's name?
   a. Buttercup
   b. Blossom
   c. Boomer

10. Which one of these is *not* on the school Web site?
   a. *The Far Hills Journal*
   b. Assignments and calendars
   c. The I Don't Like Ivy Daly at All Club

11. What animal shows up on Aimee's face on the school Web site?
   a. A dinosaur
   b. A gila monster
   c. A chameleon

12. According to a school poll, what is the number one important issue for students during the Far Hills election?
   a. Homework
   b. Cafeteria food
   c. After-school activities

13. *I am crushed at school near and far / sometimes I feel it like a squeeze that won't end.* Who says this?
   a. Madison
   b. Poison Ivy
   c. Bigwheels

14. Who gets kicked out of the Far Hills Junior High school election?
    a. Montrell Morris
    b. Tommy Kwong
    c. Ivy Daly

15. What is Madison's locker combination?
    a. 9-8-9
    b. 8-7-8
    c. 6-5-8

16. What computer language is Mrs. Wing going to teach Madison's computer class?
    a. Basic
    b. Pascal
    c. Computer programming

17. What is the name of the production company that Madison's mom works for?
    a. Budget films
    b. Universally Pictures
    c. Budge films

18. Which would be the most likely dinner menu at the Gillespie house?
    a. Hot dogs and potato chips
    b. Whole wheat bread with grilled vegetables
    c. Meat loaf

19. If Madison's dad organizes to pick Madison up at 6:00 P.M. from school, what time is he most likely to arrive?
    a. 6:00 P.M.
    b. 6:10 P.M.
    c. 6:30 P.M.

20. Who helps Mrs. Wing install more memory in the school computers right before the class election?
    a. Mr. Lynch
    b. Mr. Gibbons
    c. Mr. Wing

21. What animal shows up on Ivy's face on the election Web site?
    a. An elephant
    b. A spider
    c. A skunk

22. What is the name of Madison's science teacher?
    a. Mr. Brown
    b. Mrs. Daly
    c. Mr. Danehy

23. What advice does Madison remember getting from her Gramma Helen?
   a. "Always do your homework."
   b. "Always believe in yourself."
   c. "Think before you ink."

24. How many students voted in the seventh-grade class election?
   a. 312
   b. 400
   c. 650

25. What do Madison and Ivy have to look at through a microscope in science class?
   a. A dissected frog
   b. The cells in human spit
   c. A blade of grass

BONUS QUESTION:

Why did Madison's mom buy her a moonstone ring?

    a. Because moonstones are expensive

    b. Because Madison's dad already got her moonstone earrings

    c. Because Madison asked her to buy it in Paris

Mad Chat Madness

Can you match the correct definitions of these Mad Chat words? Draw a line to the correct answer.

[:>(	I have no clue
:o	Laughing my socks off
:>&	Tongue-tied
FTBOMBH	Put on a happy face
TAL	Talk about school
12345	Thanks a lot
GAL	Just kidding
LMSO	Shocked
>5	Love and kisses
s>	What's up?
88	High five
POAHF	From the bottom of my broken heart
JK	Get a life
404	Serious frown

Answers:
1b, 2a, 3b, 4a, 5c, 6b, 7a, 8c, 9b, 10c, 11b, 12a, 13c, 14b, 15c, 16a, 17c, 18b, 19c, 20a, 21c, 22c, 23c, 24a, 25b

Bonus Question: b

How well do you know Maddie?

24–25 correct: You might as well pack your bags and move to Far Hills, because you are a *Madison Finn* fanatic!

20–23 correct: You could totally be Madison's BFF, because you know her inside out!

17–20 correct: You think Maddie's pretty cool, and you'd have fun hanging out with her.

14–16 correct: You know a few things about Madison, and you're interested in finding out more about her.

13 or fewer correct: You didn't quite catch all those details about Maddie, but don't worry—there's still lots of time to learn.

Play It Again

For all my drama teachers

Special thanks to Kim R. and the New World Players
at Isaac E. Young for your inspiration

"I want a dance solo," Aimee Gillespie announced at lunch. "What about you, Maddie? What part do you wanna get?"

Madison Finn shrugged and took a sip of her chocolate milk.

The Far Hills Junior High administration had decided to organize a special cabaret in honor of the school's assistant principal, Mrs. B. Goode's, twenty years of distinguished service. They were planning three separate nights of entertainment—one for each class in the school. Everyone in the seventh grade was expected to try out for selected scenes and songs from *The Wiz*.

But Madison didn't want to. *She couldn't.*

Madison couldn't get up on stage to sing some lame rendition of "Happy Birthday" in the key of C.

She couldn't face having other classmates with their eyes fixed on her every onstage move.

And she absolutely couldn't dance.

Just the thought of auditioning made Madison woozier than woozy.

Even worse, Madison couldn't tell her friends that she didn't *want* to audition, especially her best friend, Aimee. Being afraid is one thing, but having to admit that to other people is another thing.

"Maybe I'll just be one of those creepy trees that talks," Madison finally told Aimee, trying to change the subject. "You know, like on the way to Oz."

"Yeah, Maddie, like that's the part you'd get." Aimee made a face.

"I'm serious," Madison said, flicking her straw at Aimee. Chocolate milk splattered across the orange lunch table.

"Don't get—ahh! My new top," Aimee cried. The milk just missed her.

She and Madison burst into a goofy fit of laughter.

"Morons," some kid with a buzz cut at the next table grunted. He looked like a ninth grader.

"Takes one to know one," Aimee muttered bravely under her breath.

Madison covered her face with her hands and turned back to the comfort of her lunch: two slices of bread, peanut butter, and a neatly peeled orange on the side. Orange was Madison's favorite color and her favorite fruit.

"Hello, superstars," Fiona Waters teased, sliding onto the lunch table bench alongside Aimee. Fiona was the new girl in town and at school, and Madison and Aimee were happy to have her as a new part of their group, along with their guy friends Walter "Egg" Diaz and his shadow, Drew Maxwell. Fiona's twin brother, Chet, usually hung out with them, too.

"Did you check out what Ivy's wearing today?" Fiona whispered.

The three girlfriends twisted their heads to catch a glimpse of Ivy Daly's showy blue-flowered dress.

"That's a Boop-Dee-Doop dress," Aimee sneered. "I saw it in a magazine this month. Figures *she'd* get it."

"She looks good, though, don't you think?" Fiona said.

"Whatever." Aimee's voice bristled.

Once upon a very long time ago, way back in third grade, Madison had been a best friend with Ivy, but things had changed a lot over the years. Now Ivy was known as *Poison* Ivy, enemy number one at Far Hills.

Aimee glanced over at the enemy again. "She'll probably get the lead in the play, just like always. She always gets what she wants."

"Uh-huh," Madison agreed, chewing an orange section.

Across the cafeteria, Ivy tossed her red curly hair and looked around the room. No matter how poisonous she acted, Madison thought, she always managed to get noticed. That was how she won the election for class president and how she won the attention of most boys in the seventh grade. She didn't have to worry about being liked by the popular crowd because Ivy Daly *was* the popular crowd.

"Let's talk about something else, please," Aimee pleaded. "Are you trying out for *The Wiz*, Fiona?"

"Will rehearsals conflict with soccer? I have team practice almost every day after school and—" Fiona paused. "Well, I can't miss soccer. I want to make a good impression with the coach, you know?"

Fiona and Madison had tried out together for the school soccer team, but only Fiona had actually made the team. Fiona had been a soccer star last year when she was living in California, so her making the Far Hills team was no big surprise. And Madison wasn't much of an athlete, so *not* making the team was no big surprise for her, either. Madison considered it a minor success, actually. She hadn't run away from team tryouts. That was something.

"Do you guys think I can do both at the same time?" Fiona asked.

"Totally," Aimee said. "We're only doing a few scenes, so we won't have rehearsals all the time. Mr. Gibbons schedules them in between normal after-school stuff—I think that's what I heard."

"I want to do both," Fiona said. "I love singing."

"Wait a minute. You play soccer, go to Spanish club, and you *sing*, too?" Madison said, a little surprised. She kept learning new things about her new friend. It seemed like Fiona was good at everything she tried to do—and she tried to do a lot. "When do you have time to do homework?"

"In between," Fiona said.

Madison stared down at the table, not saying much. She poured a molehill of sugar onto her lunch tray and traced a path with her fork. She didn't want Aimee to ask questions about the audition.

But it was too late. Aimee reached across the table for Madison's wrist.

"You still haven't said what you're gonna sing at auditions, Maddie!" Aimee cooed.

Before Madison could admit to being *all* nerves, Egg appeared out of nowhere. He stuck his head in between Aimee and Fiona.

"Are you guys talking about the show?" Egg said.

"Who wants to know?" Aimee growled back.

Egg swiped an apple off her tray and took a big bite. "After tomorrow's audition, everyone can call me *The Wiz*ard."

He put the apple back onto Aimee's tray.

"Wizard? You wish!" Aimee swatted at him. She glanced down at the bitten apple, dripping with his spit. "Soooo gross."

5

Drew, who was standing there, too, laughed. He stuck his hand up in the air and waved a silent hello to the rest of the table.

"Drew thinks I have a good shot at the part, so there," Egg said.

Fiona giggled. "You'll probably get the part, Walter," she said softly. "I mean, Egg." She bowed her head, and the beads on her braids clinked. Madison and Aimee both knew that Fiona had a giant, inexplicable crush on him.

Unfortunately Egg ignored her. Chet had walked up by now, and the three boys sat down in a cluster at the other end of the table.

"Whassup?" Chet mumbled.

"We're talking about auditions for *The Wiz*," Fiona said.

"Yeah," Madison jumped in. "Egg thinks he can be cast as—"

"A Munchkin," Aimee interrupted. "And I think that's a safe bet."

Chet cracked up. "Hey, fool! She got you."

Egg smirked. "And I'll get her back—when she least expects it."

"Well, I don't know what you guys are doing, but we're *all* trying out for the play tomorrow," Aimee said as she pointed to herself, Fiona, and Madison.

Madison leaned across the table, whispering, "Aimee, I'm not sure that I want to—"

The bell rang for the next period. In an instant

the group dumped their trays, grabbed their books, and exited the cafeteria doors.

"Ex-cuse me," Ivy said to Madison as she pushed her way to the door. "Watch it."

Ivy's annoying drones, Rose Thorn and Phony Joanie, followed close behind, pushing past Madison, too. They always traveled in a pack.

A rat pack, Madison thought as they scampered away.

Later that night, Madison asked her mom what she should do about *The Wiz*. She hoped Mom had the instant cure for all this audition anxiety, the way she poured eucalyptus oil in the bathtub when Madison had a cold.

"Gee, honey bear," Mom said gently, tickling her daughter's back. "No one says you have to audition."

"I have to be a part of the show, Mom." Madison sighed. "I can't just sit back and be scenery. I'm in junior high now."

"It could be a lot of fun. . . ."

"What's so *fun* about standing onstage while everyone and their parents stare at me?"

"William Shakespeare says, 'The play's the thing,'" Mom said. She paused. "You know who William Shakespeare is, right?"

"No duh, Mom. We read *Romeo and Juliet*, remember?"

"Rowrooooo!" Madison's dog, Phin, agreed.

The pug rushed over toward them, tail wagging in excited circles. His whole butt jerked as he huffed and puffed.

"Good doggy," Madison said as she bent down. Phinnie licked her chin. "What do *you* think I should do?" she asked him sweetly.

Mom came up with another suggestion. "If you don't want to act or sing, then why not try something else to help the show? You don't want to be a part of the scenery, but you could *paint* the scenery, right? You could paint a castle or something. Is there a castle in *The Wiz*?"

"I think." Madison shrugged.

"Well," Mom reached out to hug her daughter. "I know whatever you decide to do, it'll be great."

Before bed that night, Madison and Phin curled up in bed with her laptop computer. She punched in her secret password and opened a brand-new file.

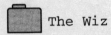 The Wiz

Rude Awakening: The play is definitely *not* the thing. I don't care what William Shakespeare says.

Or what Mom says.

Tomorrow they're holding auditions and tomorrow I am doomed. And of course Aimee won't understand when I tell her I can't try out. She'll say I'm just being chicken. It's so easy for her. And Fiona too.

Who knew that she could play soccer, look great, *and* sing? Well, she can. No one will understand why I'm so scared to try.

I remember one time when I had to sing Christmas carols onstage at school and I passed out, fell right there on the floor like a lump. Some teacher in a Santa suit had to carry me out of the assembly and everyone was staring.

What if that happens again? What if I faint or worse—throw up in front of the world?

What if *Hart Jones* sees me do that?

The whole time Hart followed me around in second grade he was SUCH a pest. Now why do I feel like following him? I saw him today in the hall when we left science class. I pray he didn't notice me staring.

If he tries out, I really think I should try out.

Madison decided her online keypal might know what to do. She hit SAVE and logged on to bigfishbowl.com, her favorite Internet site, looking for Bigwheels.

Usually Madison was suspicious of people she met inside the fishbowl since they sometimes made up facts about themselves. The Web site rules said you had to be "100% honest" about your facts, especially age and sex, but some kids weren't so honest. One time there was a boy in a chat room who pretended he was a girl. The moderator kicked him off for using dirty words.

Bigwheels was way different. Madison had met her over the summer in a room called ONLY THE LONELY. They now met back regularly in their own private room, GOFISHY. Bigwheels liked computers just like Madison. She gave great advice, too, which had come in handy since seventh grade started. They were kindred spirits in the virtual world.

Madison could share things with her online friend that she couldn't tell her other friends, not even Aimee or Fiona. Like her files, Madison still kept most things secret from the rest of the world.

Her crush on Hart Jones was one.

Bigwheels was another.

When she didn't find her keypal online, Madison wrote an e-mail to touch base.

```
From: MadFinn
To: Bigwheels
Subject: HELP
Date: Wed 27 Sept 9:46 PM
Thanks for your message from the
weekend. I wanted to write back
sooner, but I had like three hours
of homework. And now there's this
school play. Yikes. My friends don't
understand, but I don't want to
```

audition. I need your AMAZING
advice.

Yours till the curtain calls,
Madfinn

Madison hoped a megadose of "amazing" from Bigwheels would help her to make it through tomorrow's auditions.

"Your alarm went off twice," Mom shouted. She tugged Madison's quilted comforter off the bed. "Now, up!"

Madison rolled into a ball. She *had* hit the snooze button on her combination CD-stereo-clock twice. Mom was right about that.

She would be late.

Madison pushed herself down, down, down into her mattress and pillows, where it was warm and safe from things like tests and teachers . . .

And auditions.

Phinnie licked Madison's nose as Mom appeared at the bedroom doorway again. "I am not going to ask you again, honey. I said get—"

"Up, up, I'm up," Madison groaned, finally lifting

herself into a sitting position. She pushed Phinnie out of the way and rubbed her eyes.

"Fifteen minutes and I want you ready to go." Mom dragged Phin out by the collar and shut the door behind her. "I'll get your breakfast ready."

"What would Aimee wear to an audition?" Madison asked herself a moment later as she posed in front of her closet. She sighed, pulling sweaters off the top shelf and throwing jeans, then corduroys and a long skirt into a pile on the floor. She finally decided on khakis, a white oxford shirt that she left untucked, and her favorite pair of orange sneakers. MADFINN was doodled in ballpoint pen on the left sole.

Madison stared at her reflection in her dresser mirror. Postcards and photos and ticket stubs wedged under the edge of its frame stared back. There was Aimee in jazz shoes; Phinnie at the beach; a close-up of a Brazilian frog from last summer's trip; Mom's business card for Budge Films; a receipt from Byte City, a nearby computer store; a pink ribbon from Lodge 12 at Camp Chipachu, where she'd won "Most Creative Camper" the summer after fourth grade; other pictures of Dad, Mom, and her newest pal, Fiona . . .

"Ten minutes and counting!" Mom screamed again. "I mean it!"

Phinnie was scratch-scratch-scratching at the door.

On her way out, Madison tripped over a pile of

files on the floor and then bent down to gather the colorful clippings that had slipped out. She'd been collecting files on all sorts of subjects for the last year: animals (she loved animals more than anything), cool words, clothes she wanted, singers she loved, flowers, and more. Madison had hopes of scanning all the words and images onto her computer and then onto her very own Web page.

What a mess, Madison thought. The more she tried to pick up the clippings, the more they went flying.

"Five minutes!" Mom screeched.

It felt like the beginning of the *worst* possible day.

When it was time for the afternoon seventh-grade auditions for *The Wiz*, Madison felt even more nervous than ever. In a study period, she went up to the library media center computer to check her e-mail, just in case Bigwheels had sent a message. But her mailbox was empty.

Nothing worse than an empty mailbox, Madison thought.

On top of everything else, she hadn't really seen much of Aimee or Fiona during the day. Everyone was way too busy thinking about *The Wiz* auditions to talk about other subjects. Tryouts had a wacky way of sucking everyone into the acting twilight zone so that suddenly even the quietest kids in school got stars in their eyes.

At the end of the day, as Madison entered the half darkness of the school auditorium, she felt a bolt of panic surge through her body like electricity. She zapped into a middle row of seats where Egg and Drew were sitting and sank down so no one could see her. It was almost like sinking under the bedroom covers this morning at home. Under those covers had to be the safest place on earth. Why wasn't she back there instead of in here?

"Has everyone filled out one of these?" Mr. Gibbons, Madison's English teacher and the drama advisor, waved a light blue piece of paper in front of the kids. "I want you to indicate what parts you want to play and what songs you'd like to sing. Put down your name and homeroom, too. Okay?"

Fiona came up from the seat behind Madison and whispered, "Did you see Hart Jones, Maddie? He told me he was looking for you. Oh yeah, do you have a pencil I can borrow?"

Hart?

Madison sunk deeper into her seat. The last person she felt like seeing right now was Hart Jones. She was in the middle of an audition freak-out. What possible reason could he have for wanting to see her *now*?

Mr. Gibbons dimmed the house lights as kids took the stage. It was hard to see anyone unless they were down in front or right next to you. A few people were even surrounded by a dim, red halo of light from exit signs at either side of the stage. Madison's eyes scanned the room.

Where were Ivy and her drones—Phony Joanie and Rose Thorn? *Down in front, right side of the room, talking to Mrs. Montefiore, the musical director.*

Aimee? *Down in front, mingling with another girl in Dance Troupe.*

Hart?

"Finnster!" Hart cried out of nowhere, and plopped into the seat right next to hers. He had been calling Madison that stupid nickname for years. He'd also been sitting behind her the whole time.

"Hello," Madison said. She was so surprised, she swallowed a great big gulp of air.

"Is this seat taken?" Hart joked, but of course he'd already made himself comfortable, leaning back and perching his sneakers on the row in front. "Hey, I wanted to ask you a question about the science homework."

"Ummm," Madison started to speak. Suddenly, without warning, she was out of the seat, pushing past Hart's legs, dashing up the aisle, heading out of the auditorium, running away.

Thunk.

The assembly doors banged open. Madison squinted. The light was brighter in the hall. The air was different, too. She leaned up against a giant trophy case and took a deep breath.

Inside the case were trophies for everything from

football to public speaking. Madison looked inside at all the names. This school was so much bigger than middle school; sometimes it felt overwhelming. Inside there was also a small display of autumn leaf art from the nature club and a bulletin board where the honor roll would be listed after the first marking period.

"Madison?"

She jumped and saw a boy standing near the water fountain.

"Drew!" Madison said, amazed. "You scared me. What are you doing out here?" Her voice echoed off the tiled walls and floors.

"You look wicked pale. Are you okay?"

Madison leaned past him to take a drink of cool water. "I'm okay. Just jumpy. Nervous about . . . you know . . . the audition."

"Me too."

"You are?" Madison asked.

"Yeah." Drew was looking at the floor.

"So what song are you gonna sing?"

"Oh no. I'm not auditioning," Drew said. "No way. I'm gonna work backstage instead. You know, lights, sound, that kind of stuff."

"Really? How did you learn about all that?" Madison asked.

"My older brother, Ben, did that in high school," Drew said.

"You have an older brother?" Madison was

intrigued. She didn't know too much about Drew's family except that he was super rich.

"Ben's from my dad's first marriage," Drew said. "He's in college now. We're not close, really."

"Oh," Madison said. Something in Drew's voice said to stop asking questions.

"Why don't you work backstage, too?" Drew suggested. "Why don't you ask Mr. Gibbons?"

Maybe Madison could work on the play *and* still be part of the group?

She smiled. "You think?"

"Yeah. Well. I gotta go." Drew shoved his hands inside his pockets and walked back inside the auditorium.

Madison followed. She could barely see her way down the aisle the moment the darkness enveloped her again. The only light now was a yellowish beam onstage, where one girl sat singing on a stool, holding a single high note. She sounded like an angel. Madison took a seat and watched until the girl had finished her song.

She was Lindsay Frost, and she'd been in Madison's class since first grade, but Madison rarely noticed her. The only time Lindsay spoke out in class was to ask for a bathroom pass.

Right now, however, Lindsay *and* her voice were making quite an impression on everyone.

"Thank you, Miss Frost," Mr. Gibbons said when Lindsay had finished her song. "I think I can speak for everyone when I say that was delightful."

"Even if she *can* sing, she's still a freak," someone whispered in the row directly ahead. Madison knew the voice. *Ivy Daly.*

"I can't believe she crawled out of her hole to try out," Rose Thorn whispered back. "As if she thinks she'll get in."

"As if," Phony Joanie said.

"*Fat* chance, right?" Ivy laughed at her own stupid joke. She always made cracks about the way people looked. It was one of the things that put her on the top of Madison's enemy list.

Before Madison knew what she was doing, she leaned forward. "Why don't you guys just shut up?"

Ivy whirled around. "Why don't you make me?"

"Shhhhhhhhhh!" Mr. Gibbons shushed them from down in front. "Keep it down, ladies, or you're out of here."

"Yeah, keep it down, Madison," Ivy said so everyone else heard. Rose and Joanie laughed.

Madison clenched her fists. She wanted to grab Ivy's pretty red hair and yank it out handful by curly handful until Ivy Daly was as bald as a big old bowling ball.

But Madison kept her cool.

She had something very important to discuss with Mr. Gibbons.

After Lindsay's song, a few other kids got up

onstage and tried to outdo one another. One kid even got up there and juggled while he sang.

Madison could feel the pound of a pulse behind her knees and on her wrists. It pounded more with each audition—the idea of her getting up there. It was like someone had turned her treble dial all the way up to the highest setting.

By the time she approached Mr. Gibbons, Madison was afraid she might not even be able to speak. Her mouth was dry, too.

"Not everyone is cut out for singing," Mr. Gibbons told her when they spoke. "I think I know what would be just perfect for you, though. . . ."

Madison's body hummed when he told her what she'd be doing.

She was bursting to tell someone her good news.

```
From: MadFinn
To: Bigwheels
Subject: Something Important to Tell
You
Date: Thurs 28 Sept 5:31 PM
```

Me again. Where are you? I know you are probably just busy again or your server is down again. But I still wish you would write! I was hoping that you would pick up the e-mail I sent yesterday and write back. Did you get it? Are you ok?

20

Didn't you tell me once you hated
acting? You didn't like people
pretending and being fake. Well,
after today, I *totally* agree.
What do you think about stage
managers?

THAT'S ME!

I just walked up to the advisor and
told him I was too nervous to go
onstage, and he said there was
other stuff for me to do. I have
to collect a few props and help
with line readings in case people
forget and organize their
costumes.

It should be a blast, don't ya
think?

Please write. I'm waiting!
Yours till the stage manages,

MadFinn

As Madison was signing off on her e-mail, an
Insta-Message popped up.
    It was Fiona, a.k.a. Wetwinz. The pair ducked
into a private room to chat.

<Wetwinz>: I didn't c u at the end
  of Wiz, what happened????
<MadFinn>: I didn't try out
<Wetwinz>: what??
<MadFinn>: I didn't try out
<Wetwinz>: WHY?
<MadFinn>: im gonna be stage manager
  instead
<Wetwinz>: oh
<MadFinn>: I told aimee all this on
  the phone didn't she tell you
<Wetwinz>: Why?
<MadFinn>: I really wanted to do
  that. How was ur audition?
<Wetwinz>: I WUZ SO NERVOUS!!!!!!!!
<MadFinn>: Egg said you have a
  reallygood voice
<Wetwinz>: Egg did? What a QT! What
  else did he say
<MadFinn>: tell me how ur audition
  was
<Wetwinz>: no tell me more about
  Egg :>)
<MadFinn>: what about Ivy?
<Wetwinz>: she'll get a good part
<MadFinn>: probably
<Wetwinz>: her voice cracked during
  that one song though
<MadFinn>: what else?
<Wetwinz>: time 4 dinner
<MadFinn>: DON'T BE NERVOUS L8R

Madison realized how happy she was *not* to be in Fiona's shoes right now.

She was happy not to be nervous anymore.

Madison had started the school day feeling like such a mess, but she was a long way away from "mess" now. She felt the same kind of calm that comes when a rainbow appears after a storm.

After the computer hummed and shut down, Madison crawled right back into the safest place in the world, under her quilted blankets. Phinnie crawled in beside her. Madison could feel his wet nose on her arm.

Soon she'd be asleep, and she'd be that much closer to tomorrow.

Closer to her debut as stage manager of *The Wiz*.

"Don't push me!" Aimee shrieked when some kid with a backpack nearly mowed her over. They were standing in the hallway before seventh-grade lunch.

"Sorry," the kid said, pushing his way through anyhow. "You're the one in the way."

A very large crowd was trying to see the bulletin board on the second floor by the faculty elevator. There, on a piece of Mr. Gibbons's light blue paper, was posted the official cast of "Selections from *The Wiz*."

"Don't be nervous," Madison reminded Fiona as she locked arms with her. They gently nudged their way to the front.

Madison tugged Fiona's hand. "I can't believe it—look!"

"I can't believe it, either." Ivy groaned as she read the list. Her drones groaned, too.

Fiona just giggled.

Selections from *THE WIZ*
FIRST REHEARSAL: FRIDAY, SEPT. 29
3:00 PM in MAIN AUDITORIUM

CAST

Auntie Em	Roseanne Snyder
Toto	Chocolate (Mr. Gibbons's dog)
Dorothy	Lindsay Frost
Uncle Henry/Gatekeeper	Suresh Dhir
Evillene the Wicked Witch	Fiona Waters
Addaperle the Good Witch	Aimee Gillespie
Scarecrow	Thomas Kwong
Tin Man	Walter Diaz
Lion	Dan Ginsburg
Glinda the Good Witch	Ivy Daly
The Wiz	Hart Jones
Munchkins and Winkies	Zoe Bell, Beth Dunfey, Douglas Eklund, Lance Gregson, Joan Kenyon, Rashida Lawrence, Chet Waters, Tim Weinstein

CREW

Lights and Sound	Wayne Walsh and Class 9 Tech Club
Tech Assistants	Andrew Maxwell, Joey O'Neill
Choreography Assistant	Aimee Gillespie
Dance and Music	Mrs. Montefiore
Piano	Mr. Montefiore
Sets and Scenes	Mariah Diaz and Class 9 Art Club
Stage Manager	Madison Finn
Faculty Advisor	Mr. Gibbons

Ivy looked at the list. "Well, I didn't get Dorothy, but at least I got a big part. Glinda's a big part, right?"

Poison Ivy got the goody-goody princess role, Madison thought. It figured.

"I have to go talk to Mrs. Montefiore right away," Ivy said. She flipped her hair and walked away.

Fiona was *still* giggling. She'd gotten a good part, too. Better than she'd expected. "I like the way Evillene sounds."

Aimee waltzed over. "Oh my God, this is amazing—you got a lead! You totally rock, Fiona! And I get Addaperle! And a dance solo! And choreography assistant! I am sooooo psyched."

Fiona looked a little embarrassed by the attention, but she couldn't stop herself from beaming. Madison thought she looked more like a model than ever at that moment.

Egg, Drew, Chet, Hart, and even Tommy Kwong, king of drama club, bellied up to the bulletin board next. Madison watched them searching for their names on the blue list. Chet picked at his ear nervously. Egg bounced up and down like a jack-in-the-box. Drew, of course, played it quieter than quiet because he already knew what he was doing, just like Madison.

"Hey," Drew whispered, catching Madison's eye. "Congrats."

Madison grinned. "Yeah."

Drew slunk over to Egg, and the two of them pretended to bow down to Hart Jones. He'd been cast as none other than The Wiz himself, so he deserved the royal treatment.

Across the hall, Tommy Kwong celebrated his part with just as much fanfare. He was already practicing floppy-armed scarecrow antics, to the amusement of a group of girls who'd gotten chorus parts. As they oohed and aahed, Madison shimmied closer to Aimee and Fiona.

"I can't believe Poison Ivy is Glinda the Good Witch!" Aimee said.

Fiona's smile was wider than ever. "And I'm the *evil* witch," she said dreamily. "It's all pretty kooky."

They all laughed, and Madison gave Fiona a giant hug, one of those hugs where you don't let go right away.

"I am so glad you came to Far Hills," Madison told her.

"Excuse me." A girl walked up to the trio of friends and tapped Fiona on the shoulder. "Congratulations. You were so good at auditions."

"Thank you for saying that," Fiona said gently. "I'm sorry, I don't know you. I'm new. I'm Fiona Waters."

Madison recognized her right away. She was Lindsay Frost—the girl on the stool with the angel voice. Lindsay introduced herself. She wore an over-sized black sweater and chunky barrettes shaped like hearts.

"You were great at auditions," Madison said. "Everyone was mesmerized." She glanced up at the list again. Lindsay had been cast as Dorothy.

"Gee, thanks," Lindsay said. "I've been taking singing lessons and singing in choir since I was in first grade. And I love L. Frank Baum's books more than anything."

"Frank who?" Aimee and Fiona asked at the same time.

"Duh, you guys know," Madison said. "The guy who wrote the real Oz books."

"Don't you know them? In *Ozma of Oz*, Dorothy helps to save a queen. It's great," Lindsay said. "And there's this character named Princess Langwidere who wears a different head each day. I can loan you my copies if you want."

"Oh," Aimee said, still not knowing what they were really talking about but pretending that she did. "Oh yeah. Those books."

"Oh yeah," Fiona added. "Those books are kooky."

Aimee snickered when Fiona used that word again.

"Well," Lindsay said. She tugged down on her sweater. It was all stretched out and baggy around her middle. "I have to go to my next class now.

You're in English with Ms. Quill, right, Aimee? Maybe I'll see you around."

"Maybe," Aimee said as she walked away.

"Thanks again, Lindsay!" Fiona called out. She turned back to Aimee and Madison. "She seems nice."

"For a geek," Aimee said.

"Aimee!" Madison yelled at her. "Sometimes you can be so harsh."

"Well, it's the truth, isn't it?" she defended herself. "Isn't it?"

"The truth is," Fiona chimed in, "you sound like Ivy when you say stuff like that."

Aimee looked a little hurt. She didn't want to be like Poison Ivy.

"How well do you know Lindsay, Maddie?" Fiona asked.

"Well, she's been in our grade forever," Madison said.

"But we're not *really* friends," Aimee clarified.

Fiona and Aimee wandered off to their next classes, but Madison went in a different direction. She thought about how someone who had seemed so invisible could suddenly steal the spotlight from Ivy Daly and her drones.

It was an interesting development.

That night was Madison's weekly dinner with Dad, a night she looked forward to all week long. Ever since

Mom and Dad had gotten the "Big D" last year, Madison had reserved Thursdays just for him—except for the one dinner when he brought his new girlfriend, Stephanie, along.

Tonight she couldn't wait to spill the beans about the show.

Dad picked Madison up a little bit late, as usual. Being late usually made Mom rant and rave about how inconsiderate he was, which Madison hated. Mom didn't seem to be bothered tonight.

"He's here! I'm going!" Madison cried out when she saw Dad pull into the driveway. Phinnie wailed, "Wawoooooo," as Madison closed the front door. He hated good-byes even more than Madison did.

"So," Dad said the moment Madison hopped into the front seat and buckled up. "Tell me all about the auditions for the play and don't leave anything out, not one detail."

As Madison explained, Dad shook his head and chuckled lightly to himself.

"What's so funny?" Madison asked.

"You're a chip off the old block, you know that?" Dad said. "When I was a kid, I remember getting so sick whenever I had to do anything in front of other people. I had a terrible case of stage fright. I couldn't even stand up in the classroom. All the kids would laugh at me. . . . It was bad news. Puke city."

"Puke? Gross, Dad. You? Really?"

"You bet. So I guess you can chalk this one up to

genes, Maddie. Blame your old dad for your case of nerves. Sorry, kid."

Madison reached over and touched his shoulder. "I don't mind, Dad. Not really. Besides, now I'm stage manager."

They arrived at Dad's downtown Far Hills loft just in time to see the last innings of a baseball game between the Mets and the Braves. Next to computers and collages, Madison loved baseball. She got *that* from her dad.

"Did you see that?" Dad yelled at the television set. "That was a strike! What? Is the ump blind?"

Madison was setting the dinner table for two while "Finn's Fantastic Meatballs" heated up in the oven. It was really just Swedish meatballs with noodles, but Dad named all his recipes. He even baked Madison Muffins once. They were supersweet.

"Hey, Dad, I forgot to ask—can you help me with my computer assignment tonight? I have a test coming up."

"Double play!" Dad yelled at the television. Then he turned to his daughter. "Did you say 'test,' Maddie? Didn't school just *start*?"

"Yeah, well. Time flies when you're in junior high. Will you help?"

Dad laughed and walked into the kitchen. "Of course I'll help." He kissed Madison's head. "I'm really proud of you, young lady. Have I told you that lately? You are a bright, smart . . ."

"Dad," Madison moaned. "Don't start. Please."

"Start what? Isn't it acceptable for a father to be proud of his little girl?"

"Yeah, but you get so sappy. You and Mom both do that. Anyway, sit down. Dinner's served." Madison set the serving dish on the dining room table. "Oh and for the record, Dad, I'm not a *little* girl."

Dad laughed. "I know that, honey," he said. "Believe me, I know."

When the baseball game ended in overtime, they finally logged on to Dad's computer. It was fancy, streamlined with a monitor edged in polished steel. Dad always had the highest-quality equipment. Plus he upgraded a lot.

"Let me quickly show you my new Web site," Dad said as he punched a few keys. When the computer turned on, a picture appeared.

Unfortunately it was Stephanie, Dad's new and annoying girlfriend.

"Oh," Madison said, staring at the screen. "It's her."

Just then, the screen dissolved into another picture. This one showed Madison and Phinnie. It was taken last year during a snowstorm.

"It's not just her. Look, Maddie." Dad punched a few more keys. "Most of my screen savers are photos of *you*."

Madison watched as the picture of her and Phin

in the snow dissolved into her school photo from last year, which then dissolved into a photo of Dad on water skis, and then into a photo of Madison waving from the inside of Dad's car.

The screen finally dissolved for the last time into wavy lines, and Dad's site booted up. A giant blue logo appeared with the words FINN FRONTIERS.

"That's my company," Dad said proudly. "Well, my newest venture." Dad had started and stopped a whole bunch of businesses in the past ten years. Mom called him a snake oil salesman sometimes, but Madison wasn't sure she knew what that meant, exactly.

"Wow, that's neat-o," Madison said. The logo rotated around and around, leaving a trail of blue "dust" on the screen.

Madison was prouder than proud that her dad was so "with it" where technology was concerned. She didn't know any other parents in her class into computers the way he was.

"Let's tackle your computer homework now," Dad said, exiting his company's screen. "I think we make a good team."

Madison agreed.

 Hart

     Just got back from Dad's. I have a
Swedish meatball stomachache. I also have
Hart on the brain.

I talked to The Wiz a.k.a. Hart for a little while after science class. Every time I see him and talk to him alone now is like a big deal, I can't help it.

Can you say CUTE? Plus, he stopped me in the hall, not the other way around. What does that mean? I congratulated him and he congratulated me and how dumb is that? He will make THE BEST Wiz ever in the history of *The Wiz*.

I think Ivy likes him, too, which stinks. She always flirts and she will probably find a way to make herself the center of attention in *The Wiz and* get Hart, too. Aimee's right. She's not just playing a witch in the show. She is a real witch.

What would Bigwheels do right now? I bet she is popular with guys. I'm just guessing. Maybe she can help me with the play *and* with Hart.

That is, if she ever writes back.

Chapter 4

Madison thought about Bigwheels all weekend long. Something was obviously wrong. Her keypal had never taken this long to answer an e-mail.

But Sunday morning, when Madison checked her mailbox for like the twentieth time, it appeared.

```
From: Bigwheels
To: MadFinn
Subject: Re: Something Important to
Tell You
Date: Sat 30 Sept 11:58 PM
It's late. Not like there's anyone
for you to tell, but still don't
tell anyone I was up this late, ok?
I had trouble sleeping, so I went
online. I'm really not allowed on
the computer after ten.
```

My life is a little strange these
days in case you didn't notice.
Can't really describe why. Just is.
I haven't even been writing poems.
I haven't been writing you. I'll
tell you later. I have to go with
my grandfather tomorrow. Scratch
that. It *is* tomorrow. Whoops. I
have to go today, Sunday.

Sorry for being out of touch. I
hope your play is working out. I
think that guy you're crushing on
sounds nice.

Meet me Monday at GOFISHY, ok? I'll
be there around five. Don't forget.

Yours till the hot dogs,

Bigwheels

The e-mail from Bigwheels took Madison by BIG
surprise. She wasn't sure how to respond to
Bigwheels when *Bigwheels* needed advice. What do
you do when your secret online friend has a problem
and you can't tell anyone in the real world about it?

Madison wished she could ask Aimee, but Aimee
didn't even know Bigwheels existed! When Aimee
called that night, Madison decided to keep her
online secret and to talk about clothes instead.

36

"Have you decided what to wear to the first rehearsal?" Madison asked.

"Oh my God! Wearing? I don't know what I'm wearing! Am I supposed to wear something special?" Aimee sounded like she was in a panic. "What are *you* wearing?"

Madison sighed. "I asked you first, Aimee."

"I don't know. What are you wearing?"

Aimee talked in circles sometimes. It was like she was dancing even when she asked questions, bobbing back and forth.

"Why don't you just wear your flared pants," Madison finally said. "The blue ones."

"Maddie, those don't look good on me."

Even if Aimee couldn't figure out what to wear, she'd *always* have an opinion about what *not* to wear.

"Wear your gray sweater, then," Madison suggested.

"You're kidding, right?" Aimee scoffed.

The next morning, Madison was the one who had to laugh when she met Aimee on the way to school. Aimee had on the blue, flared pants with her gray sweater tied neatly around her neck. Madison had opted for a long black skirt, sneakers, and a purple cardigan sweater with little flowers across the top.

After classes ended, Madison was the first one into the auditorium for rehearsal that afternoon. She sat right down in front, waiting for Mr. Gibbons and all the other students who were picked as cast and crew to take their seats. The room seemed completely different today. It wasn't dark like before. The whole stage shone with bright white light that washed out the curtains and the floor, making it a warm and inviting place. Instead of nervousness, the room was brimming with excitement.

"Everyone settle down, please!" Mr. Gibbons said as he walked in. "I'm sorry to be late. But please don't use this as a reason for *you* to be late to rehearsals, okay?"

Madison turned around and raised her eyebrows in Egg's direction. He was late to everything.

"Now to begin our first meeting, I'd like to thank you all for being a part of this production," Mr. Gibbons continued. "As Will Shakespeare said, 'The play's the thing.'"

Madison smiled to herself.

"We're only doing a few numbers from *The Wiz*, so in all fairness the lines and songs have been divided up equally. I want all students to have an equal opportunity to really shine. I hope you—*no*—I *know* you will."

From the middle of the auditorium, a loud kid named Suresh stuck his fist in the air and yelled, "Yesss!" Everyone laughed.

"Okay, now, settle down." Mr. Gibbons chuckled. "We've got a lot of work ahead of us, and only a very short time to do it."

Mr. Gibbons explained that the seventh graders would be working with ninth graders in the school's tech club and art club to get things done. Madison was happier than happy to hear that. It meant working with Mariah Diaz, president of the art club and Egg's older sister. Aimee and Madison both felt that having Mariah around was like having an older sister of their own—and Egg didn't mind sharing.

Kids began flipping through the script pages. Madison could hear Ivy and Rose counting up how many lines they each had. Joanie was complaining that she hadn't gotten any kind of lead part.

Mr. Gibbons called everyone in the cast up to the stage to line up in a single row across, but it turned into an instant fiasco.

No one could get it straight. Kids were nudging and shoving all over the place. Finally Mr. Gibbons blew a whistle to get them to STOP! He wanted them in order by height. Simple? No. That took *another* five minutes to figure out.

Meanwhile the crew stayed seated out in the audience alone. The ninth-grade tech and art clubs had left the room, so the only backstage people remaining were Madison, Drew, and Joey O'Neill, a seventh-grade kid everyone called "Nose Plucker."

Sitting in the audience was like being on an island and looking over at the mainland. Madison started to get that sinking feeling again. But now she wasn't just sinking into pillows or seats or anywhere else.

She was just sinking.

Lindsay Frost was up on stage, slouching in her baggy jeans and T-shirt, her hair pulled back in the same barrettes she'd worn at auditions. She was standing right next to Poison Ivy, all decked out in low-slung pants and a short-sleeved sweater that had a kitty-cat decal on it. Madison saw the pair as the sun and moon of seventh grade, opposites traveling in the same sky.

When Mr. Gibbons asked them to pair up, Ivy left a two-foot space between herself and Lindsay. Ivy didn't want to be paired off with *her*.

Madison knew the real truth: Poison Ivy would much rather be in orbit with her own drone rather than someone she considered "uncool."

But none of it mattered in the end because Madison could see that Lindsay was oblivious to Ivy—and everyone else around her. She didn't seem to care about kitty decals or who was standing where.

Mr. Gibbons clapped as Mrs. Montefiore, the music teacher, played a few scales. She asked the now assembled line of kids to join.

"Vocal warm-ups, boys and girls!" she said. "Do, re, mi . . . That means you, too, Miss Daly. Come along now. Mr. Diaz, turn and face front NOW!"

Drew leaned over to Madison. "Aren't you glad you're down here and not up there?"

Madison nodded. "I guess."

But inside she felt differently.

Mr. Gibbons explained that on a stage, the place between the actors and the audience is called a fourth wall. It's what separates real life from the life of the play.

Right now, Madison felt like the wall was separating her from her friends.

When rehearsal ended, Madison felt much better. In a snap, her whole group was back together again by the lockers.

"Let's go hang at Freeze Palace," Egg said, looking at Aimee, Madison, Fiona, Chet, Drew, and Hart. "Come on, it's only four o'clock!"

"Cool," Hart said. "I gotta be home around five, though."

"Oh, Chet, we don't have to be home, do we?" Fiona asked her brother.

"I can't go, Egg. I have too much homework," Drew said.

Aimee suggested they go hang out at her dad's store, Book Web, instead of the ice cream place. The bookstore was closer to school.

"You could do homework, Drew," Aimee said. "My dad has three new computers in the cybercafé part of the store."

"Yeah?" Drew asked. "Are you going, Madison?"

"Yeah, Maddie, are you going?" Fiona asked, tugging on Madison's purple sweater.

Madison grabbed her orange bag. "Yeah. Let's go."

"Let's boogie." Aimee twirled around and pushed open the school doors.

Madison was gladder than glad about how things were working out.

Going to Book Web with the cast was a chance to break the fourth wall and be with her friends. Maybe she could even spend a little time with Hart?

Bigwheels would approve.

Chapter 5

"Hey, Daddy." Aimee kissed her father as they walked into his bookstore.

Aimee's oldest brother, Roger, was behind the Book Web counter, helping a man choose a book for his granddaughter. Roger was working there while he saved money for graduate school. He wanted to be a professor.

Other than that, the store wasn't too crowded.

"Is it okay if we hang out here for a little bit, Daddy?" Aimee asked.

Mr. Gillespie nodded and extended his hand. "Hello, Walter. And Andrew. And Maddie. And you're Fiona, right?" He introduced himself to Chet, too, and shuffled the group over to a large table near the back of the store. It was lodged between two giant bookshelves overflowing with used paperbacks.

After a chorus of awkward thank-yous, Mr. Gillespie disappeared into the back room.

Madison sat down first, then everyone else filtered over and squeezed in around her. The table really wasn't big enough for all seven of them, but they would make it fit. Madison couldn't believe it when Hart ended up squished on one side of her.

"Sorry," Hart said when his knee knocked hers.

Madison covered her cheeks because she was afraid she might be blushing.

"Okay, so what did you guys think of the first rehearsal?" Aimee asked the table. "I mean, I think Mr. Gibbons is so nice."

"Rose is a babe," Egg said.

Aimee slugged him. "Rose? Egg!"

"Finnster, what does Mr. Gibbons have you doing as stage manager?" Hart asked.

Madison could feel his breath, he was so close.

"Um, well . . ." Madison tried talking, but the words were lodged in her throat like grapes.

"That's great that your sister is helping with the set and costumes, Egg," Fiona piped up. "She's so glam."

"Glam?" Egg laughed so hard, he started to cough. "Don't make me laugh."

"She is, Egg!" Madison yelled. "Glamorous in her own way."

"This is boring. Let's go over to the computers," Chet said all of a sudden. Hart thought that was a great idea. As he jumped up to join the others, he kicked Madison, but she didn't mind.

Egg stood up. "We can go online from over there, too. Mr. Gillespie gave me the passwords."

Before the boys could move to the cyber part of the café, however, a woman rushed over and blocked their path.

"Well, hello," she said. "Aren't you all in my daughter's class?"

It was Mrs. Daly, Ivy's mother.

Everyone grinned back at her without saying a single word. Poison Ivy was right behind her.

"Ivy tells me your class is doing *The Wiz*," Mrs. Daly gushed. "That must be so much fun!"

No one said anything, but Mrs. Daly kept right on talking.

"I was in *The Wiz* in junior high, too—isn't that funny?" Mrs. Daly said. "Ivy, don't you want to say hello to your friends?"

"Hello," Ivy said curtly. She turned back to her mother. "Can we go now?"

"*The Wiz* is a great show, Mrs. Daly," Hart said. "I'm Hart Jones. I'm in *The Wiz* with Ivy."

"Oh really?" Mrs. Daly said, impressed.

"Hart's not in *The Wiz*, Mother," Ivy said, perking up for a moment. "He *is* The Wiz." She smiled right at Hart but avoided all eye contact with the three girls at the table.

"Actually, we're *all* in the play," Hart said,

gesturing to Madison, Aimee, Egg, Chet, Fiona, and Drew.

Everyone said hello. That's when Ivy's smile disappeared.

"Can we get your book and just go, Mother?" she said.

"Okay, dear." Mrs. Daly let out a deep sigh. "Good-bye and good luck to all of you. I can't wait to see it."

"Mother, let's GO." Ivy grabbed her mother's arm. Even though she was leaving, Ivy made a point of looking over her shoulder. She smiled at Hart one last time as she walked away.

Madison wanted to scream.

"Maybe we should have asked Ivy to stay and run lines with us?" Fiona whispered as Ivy and her mother walked away.

"What?" Aimee said. "I don't think so, Fiona. I mean, oh my God, she's usually so nasty to us, so why should we—"

"She's not nasty; she's cute," Chet said to Egg. All the boys laughed knowingly, even Hart. Ivy might be the meanest girl in class, but she also had the best hair and showed her perfect belly button whenever she had the chance. Boys loved that.

"Hey, check this out." Hart pointed to a page in his script. "In this scene I wear a big mask. And Fiona, you have to wear bad-witch makeup. Egg, are you gonna wear tinfoil as the Tin Man or what?"

Egg clapped him on the shoulder. "Ha, ha, ha, Hart."

Drew snorted.

Madison couldn't take her eyes off Hart. She wondered if she would be the one to help him put on his mask before the show.

She hoped.

Talking about all the costumes also made Madison think of her prop list. She went back through the script for items.

Crystal ball.

Lion's whiskers.

Special silver slippers.

Even with Mariah and the art club's help, Mr. Gibbons would have a lot of preparation to do—and Madison would be the one helping him do it. The role of stage manager now seemed way harder than just playing one part or singing one song.

"Wow, they're cutting a lot out of the original show." Hart flipped through the rest of his script pages. "'Selected scenes' means we lose half the songs."

Drew checked his watch for the tenth time. "Don't you guys have a test tomorrow? I do."

"Yeah, me too," Hart said. "I gotta fly."

"Is it five o'clock already?" Madison asked. She suddenly remembered her chat plans with Bigwheels. "I better get home to . . ."

She wasn't about to tell everyone there about

how she really had to hurry home to go in a special chat room to see what was wrong with her online friend's life.

". . . to walk Phinnie," Madison finished.

"Can't Phin use the dog door?" Aimee asked.

"Who's Phin?" Hart asked.

"Her pug," Fiona answered.

"The Finnster has a Phin?" Hart joked.

Egg mocked Hart. "Finnster has a Phin?" he said in a singsong voice.

"Hey, what about Blossom? She's a great doggy, too," Aimee boasted. She had a girl basset hound that loved to play with Phin. Madison and Aimee always joked if you put their two dogs together, they would make the ugliest, smushed-faced, floppy-eared pups.

"Are we staying or going . . . ?" Chet asked. "Or talking about *dogs*? Hello?"

Aimee shrugged. "*I'd* like to keep doing *The Wiz*. You guys have other places to be, obviously."

"People to see, places to go . . . " Egg cracked.

"Aimee," Fiona said, "*I* can stay a little longer if you want. We can still go over lines, just you and me."

Madison felt funny about leaving when she heard that. For some reason she didn't want to leave Aimee and Fiona alone. If she walked away, would Madison miss something important? She'd already missed the cast lineup and the singing rehearsal. She didn't want to miss anything else.

Egg was walking away. "Later, Aim." He nodded in Fiona's direction.

"Later, Egg." Fiona grinned right at him.

"Yo, Wicked Witch of the West." Chet waved his hand in front of his sister's face like he was waving her out of some kind of trance. "See you home."

"IM me, Maddie!" Fiona said, ignoring her brother.

"Call me later, 'kay?" Aimee called to Madison.

Madison waved to the pair. She was still reluctant to leave, but Bigwheels would be waiting.

The walk home went by slowly without Aimee and Fiona there to gossip. The streets were empty, the air was chilly, and the sun was beginning to sink in the western sky. Her bag weighed a ton and pulled heavily on her shoulder. She'd brought home her math textbook. She had the same test Hart did.

Since she was alone, Madison took a shortcut through the backyards of the houses just behind Blueberry Street, snagging her purple sweater as she tripped through a neighbor's garden and slid over a rock wall. It was still quite light out, but soon the sky would get darker and darker until all the pink disappeared.

With each stride, Madison secretly wished she were back at Book Web with Aimee and Fiona, even though she didn't have lines to memorize. Was being picked as stage manager less like being cast in the show and more like being cast *aside*?

"Stop over-thinking," Madison told herself.

Phin welcomed her home with a loud bark as soon as Madison walked in the door. She gave Phin a big hug, and the dog responded with a snort. Sometimes it was hard for pugs to breathe when they got overexcited.

Mom had left a note on the counter, explaining how she ducked out to do grocery shopping, so Madison grabbed a root beer and ran up to her room. The clock by her bed said almost half past five. She had to log on to bigfishbowl.com—fast. She went into the main fishbowl to find her keypal.

```
        SHARK (Moderator)
        MnMrox411
        TellMeAStORY
        Wohl_Consol
        ChuckD4Ever
        PrtyGrrl88
        12345Slim
        Brbiedoll
```

```
<TellMeAStORY>: get out
    MadFinn has entered the room.
<Wohl_Consol>: I mean it
<TellMeAStORY>: u lie
<PrtyGrrl88>: Hey MadFinn A/S/L?
```

Madison didn't like it when kids in the chat room waiting room asked for her A/S/L, which meant age, sex, and location. It made her uncomfortable, even with SHARK in the room. What if some creep-o was in the room, pretending to be some kid? Mom once told Madison some horror stories just so she'd stay safe.

The stories worked.

```
<PrtyGrrl88>: Finn . . . A/S/L?
<PrtyGrrl88>: Wohl . . . A/S/L?
<MnMrox411>: Who likes rap? Rap
    RULES
<PrtyGrrl88>: This room bites
<SHARK>: Watch your language
    PrtyGrrl88
PrtyGrrl88 has left the room.
Bigwheels has entered the room.
<Bigwheels>: MadFinn!
<MadFinn>: Let's go ASAP
<Bigwheels>: *poof*
```

Madison followed Bigwheels into GOFISHY. She was dying to hear what Bigwheels had to say.

```
<MadFinn>: HEY
<Bigwheels>: i missed u
<MadFinn>: me 2
<Bigwheels>: im sorry again bout the
    other day
<MadFinn>: no prob but whats
    wrong???
<Bigwheels>: %-(
```

<MadFinn>: wuzup? y r u sad?
<Bigwheels>: mom & dad
<MadFinn>: what happened?
<Bigwheels>: they're splitting up
<MadFinn>: IDGI
<Bigwheels>: it's a long story
<MadFinn>: can u tell me
<Bigwheels>: they told me they're
   separating
<MadFinn>: whoa
<Bigwheels>: I am in total shock
<MadFinn>: :-c
<Bigwheels>: my little sister
   doesn't even know
<MadFinn>: what did they tell u???
<Bigwheels>: they didn't say much
   just that they don't need time
   apart whatever that means
<MadFinn>: whoa
<Bigwheels>: your parents split up
   right?
<MadFinn>: yes
<Bigwheels>: how did u feel when
   they told u?
<MadFinn>: <rrr>
<Bigwheels>: it's so weird
<MadFinn>: I know
<Bigwheels>: what am I supposed to
   feel?
<MadFinn>: I'm sorry
<Bigwheels>: I'm just sad

52

```
<Bigwheels>: my mom is moving out
<MadFinn>: really?
<Bigwheels>: yeah usually the dad
    leaves right?
<MadFinn>: my dad did
<MadFinn>: hello?
<MadFinn>: Bigwheels?
<Bigwheels>: I have to go
<MadFinn>: can't you talk more? I
    want to know everything
<Bigwheels>: I have to go PAW and
```

Bigwheels signed off without even saying a real good-bye. Madison didn't know what to think.

She couldn't believe it.

Bigwheels's parents were splitting up just like Madison's parents had?

It was one of those moments when having an online friend didn't feel quite right. Madison couldn't reach out to give Bigwheels a hug. Her keypal was miles away.

But far away or not, Bigwheels was in trouble. The distance and the online separation didn't take away from that. Now Bigwheels needed Madison, not the other way around.

And Madison wanted to help.

Chapter 6

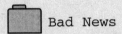 Bad News

I should have expected Tuesday would be bad news before I even got to rehearsal. Like when Bigwheels told me online last night about her parents. I should have known then. I figured seeing Fiona, Aimee, and everyone else at rehearsal would fix it. NOT.

Rude Awakening: It's hard to look at the bright side of life when you're sitting in the middle of a dark auditorium.

I couldn't stop thinking about Bigwheels all day.

Thankfully, things got way better after rehearsal ended. Aimee surprised me tonight around six when she came over with a new CD she bought. We danced around my room a

little. I am the worst dancer on the
planet, but that's ok. She got a letter
from one of her summer camp friends, too,
so we read it together while she French
braided my hair.

    I guess her glad erased my sad.
    I hope I stay this way.
    We have SUCH a busy week.

At Wednesday's rehearsal, Lindsay Frost walked into the auditorium and tripped over someone's backpack. She went flying into a row of seats and landed on her stomach.

She said she was fine, but Mr. Gibbons rushed her off to Nurse Shim.

It really *wasn't* a big deal. But after Lindsay left the auditorium, a few of the other cast members started buzzing about the whole thing. Ivy was plotting how she would become Dorothy once Lindsay had to drop out.

The Wiz seemed to be bringing out the worst in some of Madison's enemies *and* even her friends.

Lindsay came back a little while later with nothing more than a bump on her arm, an achy tummy, and a bruised ego. Mr. Gibbons was relieved.

So was Madison.

The idea of Ivy becoming the new Dorothy gave her the jeebies. The enemy would have more time to flirt with Hart if that were true.

"I am so embarrassed about tripping," Lindsay

confided in Madison during a break. "Was everyone laughing at me?"

Madison didn't know what to tell her. She shrugged. "I don't think so."

"I get so, so, SO nervous," Lindsay said. "The nurse told me I should go home and rest since my arm was hurt, but I didn't want to leave. This is too exciting, being in this show and all. Everyone is so nice."

"Yeah." Madison didn't know what to say.

Doesn't she get it? Everyone is NOT so nice.

Lindsay's arm looked like it had a dent in it. Madison kept nodding.

At the very end of rehearsal, Mr. Gibbons and Mrs. Montefiore asked Lindsay if she felt well enough to come onstage and practice "Ease on Down the Road," the song for Dorothy, the Scarecrow, the Tin Man, and the Lion.

There was a lot of commotion in the room, and no one was paying attention at first to the singers and dancers except for Madison. She might not have known what to *say* to Lindsay, but she knew she liked to *listen* to her.

Up on the stage, the cast in the other parts of the song goofed on Lindsay every time she moved. She did look a little off balance, but they were making way too big a production out of her being awkward.

Who cared how she moved? Lindsay *sounded* better than anyone in the auditorium.

"Look," Aimee said to Madison and Fiona. "I feel so bad for her. Does she know how *dumb* she looks?"

Fiona giggled. "It's her pants."

Being a mediocre dancer was no reason to be made a laughingstock, was it? Madison couldn't do a pirouette or a jazz turn, either.

"Her clothes are so lame," Aimee said. "And she's kinda klutzy. She should not be in a dance number. Definitely not."

Fiona nodded in agreement. "I see what you mean about the way she dresses. I wonder if that's why she's always alone. . . ."

"What are you guys talking about?" Madison asked. "She has a great voice. Why do you have to say stuff like—"

"It's not like we think she's a bad person or any-thing, Maddie," Aimee said. "She *can* sing, I admit it. It's just that she's different, right, Fiona?"

Madison knew what Aimee really meant. And it made her just a little sad.

The next afternoon, during Thursday's practice, Mr. Gibbons split the cast into smaller groups so characters could rehearse different scenes simultane-ously. He sent the chorus members to the music room with Mr. Montefiore, other main characters stayed in the auditorium, and the crew stayed behind to tape the stage, label props, and do other backstage tasks.

Real-life cousins Hart and Drew joined members of the ninth-grade tech club to organize lighting and sound effects. They tested different-colored gels over the spotlights during Hart's solo "So You Wanted to Meet The Wizard." Green was the coolest-looking gel because when light shone through it, the green gel made the whole stage look like a rain forest. It reflected an eerie glow off Hart's face.

Madison thought he made a perfect wizard. *Perfect*.

One of Madison's key responsibilities for the day was to prompt lines for kids who forgot. Egg missed all his cues, but no one said anything. Even drama king Kwong spaced on a few bars of his song. Not one peep.

But when Lindsay forgot a few of her lines, *everyone* ribbed her. During the "Ease on Down the Road" number, Dan the Lion called her "Blimpie."

Madison was uncomfortable when she heard that, but Lindsay wasn't fazed. She didn't seem to care about anything people said behind her back or to her face. She sang her solo as beautifully as ever. Other people looked right through Lindsay like she was plastic wrap, but Madison was starting to see all of the things Lindsay had inside. She might be a different kind of friend, but something about her was special.

Mariah arrived in the auditorium at four o'clock.

She and Madison went into a room together back-stage to work with the home and careers teacher, Mrs. Perez. A group of kids was assembling some of the costumes.

"Excuse me." Mrs. Montefiore poked her head into the room where they were working. She needed to use the old practice piano in the corner so the three witches could run through their solo numbers.

Mrs. Perez moved her fabric, sequins, and other assorted garments into the corner. "Okay, we'll finish over *here*."

With everything that was going on in practice, it became difficult for Madison to focus on clothes. How can you help glue sequins on shirts when your best friend and worst enemy are singing scales ten feet away from you?

The only clothes Madison could seem to pay attention to were the ones on Ivy and Aimee. They were both wearing platform sneakers, canvas pants, and multicolored power bead bracelets. Aimee's blond ponytail perfectly matched Ivy's red one.

"Maddie!" Aimee called from the piano. "You're gonna love this. Listen up."

Madison waved over as if to say, "Yeah, sure, whatever."

"Maddie?" Aimee was raising her voice like she always did when she talked way too fast. "Didn't you hear what I—"

"Aimee, we ALL heard what you said," Ivy

quipped. "Uh . . . could you talk a little louder?" They were semi-snotty words, but she didn't say them in an obnoxious way. Ivy actually sounded like she was kidding around.

Ivy never kidded around like that.

"Oops! Bigmouth alert!" Aimee joked. "But is it me or . . . YOU?"

She made a funny face and Ivy laughed—one of those deep belly laughs. Their ponytails shook from side to side.

"Takes one to know one!" Ivy spit out, laughing.

Ivy never laughed like that.

Madison didn't see what was so funny.

"Now, remember how we did it last time, Addaperle. . . ." Ivy said.

"You bet, Glinda," Aimee said back.

Was this really happening? This trio should be sparring, not singing. And definitely not *smiling*.

Fiona leaned on the piano the whole time, laughing as hard and as long as Aimee and Ivy. Listening to their laughter was like coming down with chicken pox.

Please go away, Madison told herself. She itched all over.

"Tut, tut. Let's start, girls." Mrs. Montefiore hit a few piano keys.

Mariah also tapped Madison on the shoulder and reminded her they had a lot of work to do and not a lot of time to do it. She handed her a bag of big blue beads and asked Madison to string them on a long piece of cord. Madison sat down with her legs crossed and pulled the cord with both fingers. She could bead *and* keep her eye on the singing witches at the same time.

Mrs. Montefiore played Ivy's solo number from the end of the show next. But halfway through the introductory melody, she stopped abruptly.

"I just got a wonderful idea," she said. "Aimee, I want you and Ivy to sing this one as a duet. You're together in the scene. I think it makes sense. And your voices do sound lovely together."

"But it's my solo," Ivy barked.

Aimee rolled her eyes. "Solo, polo, rolo . . ."

They were kidding around again.

"Miss Daly," Mrs. Montefiore said. "Most solos have been turned into group numbers. This is about working together. To-geth-er."

"Can't Fiona sing, too?" Aimee asked.

Mrs. Montefiore shook her head. "Just do it the way I am asking, please. And Miss Waters is not in this scene, Miss Gillespie. She's the bad witch Evillene. At this point, she's dead."

Fiona giggled. "Oh yeah, I forgot."

Ivy tilted her head to one side like she had her head in an imaginary noose.

"Yeah." Fiona laughed even though it was a creepy gesture.

Mrs. Montefiore banged her fist on the side of

the piano for attention. She plinked out a few more piano chords that sounded a little out of tune, but Ivy and Aimee's voices trilled right along into the first stanza.

"'Believe what you fe-eeeee-el,'" they started to sing again. "'Because the time will come arooooooooound . . .'"

As they got louder, Madison had to admit that they *did* sound good together. Not as good as Lindsay, but better than Egg. By the second verse Aimee and Ivy were standing so close together at the piano, they looked practically attached.

"'Believe in the magic that's inside your heart,'" the pair harmonized. "'Believe what you seeeeee . . .'"

Madison couldn't believe what *she* was seeing at all.

"Pssst!" Mariah leaned down to speak. "Señorita Finn, how are those beads coming along?"

There were only seven blue beads on the cord. *Whoops.*

"Madison!" Mariah said. "Mrs. Perez is gonna throw a fit. What's your problem?"

Madison wanted to point at Ivy and Aimee and yell, "THEM!"

Instead she slid another bead onto the string.

For the rest of the day, Madison couldn't get the faces of Aimee and Ivy singing and smiling out of her head. And when Aimee didn't return Madison's phone call that night, it only made her feel worse.

Friday, Madison was feeling more of the same.

She didn't see Aimee all morning, which wasn't unusual since they didn't really have that many classes together, but her imagination started doing back flips.

What if Aimee was being nice to Ivy outside of rehearsal, too?

What if they were all laughing together right now?

What if they decided to become best friends and the joke was on Madison?

When Madison didn't see Aimee or Fiona at lunch, either, she got more upset. And although she ate with Egg and Drew that afternoon, Madison barely said a word the whole meal.

Mr. Gibbons took time to go over the master prop list with Madison during the day's rehearsal, and by then Madison was really bummed out. Luckily, his compliments temporarily put her in a better mood.

"What a great job you're doing," he praised. "*The Wiz* wouldn't be the same without you."

"Thanks, Mr. Gibbons," Madison replied sheepishly. She was pleased that at least her stage manager duties were working out. She wished doing good prop work would translate into an automatic A on all of Mr. Gibbons's English assignments. That would be something else.

"Gotcha!" Aimee shrieked as she came up behind Madison during the rehearsal break.

Madison nearly leaped out of her sneakers.

Aimee threw her arms around Madison's waist. "Where have you been?"

"Where have *you* been?" Madison asked.

"Me? You're the one who's so busy, you can't call me." Aimee poked at Madison's side. "I wanted to play you that song again from my new CD. It is so awesome, I can't stop listening to it."

"You called? When?" Madison asked.

"Last night. Before I walked the dog."

"But—"

"I left a message with your mom, but she said you were on the computer. I wanted to see if you wanted to walk Phinnie, too."

"You did?"

"Yeah!" Aimee was dancing around while she talked.

"I didn't get any message," Madison said.

"What? Did you think I blew you off or something?"

"No. Of course not." Madison paused.

"So what else is new?" Aimee asked, twirling around.

"I heard you doing that duet with Ivy yesterday."

"Oh yeah? What did you think? Pretty good, huh? Mrs. Montefiore is a big pain, but you know what? Ivy has a good voice, so it's actually working out," Aimee seemed pleased by the whole thing.

"Are we talking about the same Ivy? *Poison* Ivy?"

"Yeah, Poison Ivy. But she's really not so bad as far as the show goes. You know, when we're singing. She has a high voice. We were practicing today together during lunch."

"Oh?" Madison looked up at Aimee. "You had lunch with Ivy? Alone?"

"No," Aimee said. "Fiona was there."

"I wondered where you guys went."

Suddenly Aimee saw the sad, left-out look on Madison's face.

"I'm sorry," Aimee said. "I should have told you. I forgot. Things are busy since *The Wiz*. . . ."

"You really had lunch with *Ivy*?" Madison said for a second time.

"It's just 'cause of the play, Maddie. We're in the play. You know how it is."

Madison realized she *didn't* know how it was.

From across the auditorium, Mrs. Montefiore and Ivy motioned for Aimee to go over to the piano. Everyone was standing there: Egg, Hart, Fiona, Lindsay . . .

Everyone.

"Why don't you come over too, Maddie?" Aimee said.

Madison thought about it. If she went over to the piano, she'd be right there, crammed together with all the other seventh-grade singers, even Poison Ivy.

Maybe around that crowded piano, she'd really and truly feel like a part of the cast.

Madison put down her stage manager clipboard and started to walk over.

"Uh, Madison," Mr. Gibbons called out. "I need you to run down to the basement and get me some small props. Here's the list. Can you do that for me, please?"

"Right now?" Madison asked.

"Of course. We need to do a little set painting later on, and I want to get things ready. Just ask Mr. Boggs for the key to the basement space. He'll help you."

"But I have to—" Madison started to say, looking over at the piano. Mrs. Montefiore had already started to play.

"Maybe Drew can help you," Mr. Gibbons suggested. "He's up working on the lighting board."

"Forget it," Madison said, walking out of the auditorium. "Just forget it. I'll be fine by myself."

She turned around once at the auditorium doors to look back and see everyone singing at the piano.

Not even Aimee seemed to notice she had gone.

Chapter 7

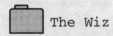 The Wiz

Rude Awakening: Why do they call it a play when it's so much work?

Friday Mr. Gibbons made me go into the hideous dark dungeon that is our school basement. It was like walking into a bad movie. Mr. Boggs, the janitor, wasn't around, so I started looking through boxes on my own.

BIG mistake.

There was a spiderweb near the boiler room that was bigger than my head.

Now, I love animals of all kinds and I don't really mind spiders, either. Most people don't even realize how good spiders are because they eat all the bad bugs. But that web freaked me.

Mr. Gibbons keeps sending me around the
school building to get all these things he
needs. Most of the time, I bring these
"props" up, and the box just gets shoved in
the corner of the stage. He isn't even
using all of them!!!

I thought being stage manager was
important. And fun. But it's mostly just
hard work. And I'm running around doing all
this stuff like I'm invisible or something
while everyone else sings and dances. The
show feels like a nightmare sometimes—with
the spiders *and* without.

But I didn't give up on the school
election Web site, I didn't give up when I
fell off a horse at camp two summers ago,
and I *won't* give up on *The Wiz*.

Madison couldn't remember a weekend that
whizzed by faster than this one. All day Saturday she
worked to cross off items on the prop and costume list.

Mom was a huge help. Madison was luckier than
lucky to have a mom with connections through
Budge Films. Mom called a few friends from a costume company, and they agreed to loan Far Hills
some of the more complicated costumes like the
Lion suit and the Tin Man's limbs, even in smaller
"junior high" sizes.

Saturday night, Mom had to run over to the Tool
Box hardware outlet at the mall to buy lightbulbs
and a new broom. Madison tagged along.

"Look at all this stuff," Madison said as they walked in the store. Madison's brain nearly blew a fuse when she saw an entire wall with just hammers and spied paint cans piled into pyramids. There was even a special aisle just for nails.

Normally, a hardware store would make Madison say "Boring."

Something was different today. Being stage manager made her think differently.

Against one wall were samples of floor tiles. A sign on one bin read SALVAGED LINOLEUM. Madison plucked out some yellow squares. They glistened when the light hit them the right way.

"Mom," she said. "Do you think we could use these for the yellow brick road?"

Mom gasped. "What a *great* idea, Maddie."

In addition to the tiles, Madison found a bowl that looked like a fortune-teller's crystal ball when you turned it upside down, a tin can for the Tin Man, and a clear plastic rod that could double as a magic wand for Glinda.

"You could decorate that, too," Mom suggested.

"With glitter glue, maybe," Madison said. Every new idea she had was leading to two or three other new ideas.

The Finn living room turned into a prop room once they got home and unpacked the bags.

"Just think, Maddie, two weeks ago you weren't

even going to be a part of the show, and now look." Mom pointed to piles.

Later on, Madison went online to surf the Internet for even more brilliant ideas. Bigfishbowl.com had a search link on its home page. She plugged in some key words to see what interesting sites would turn up.

When Madison entered the word *wizard* into the search engine, it gave her the addresses to an odd assortment of destinations. One link sent Madison to a Wizard of Oz fan club page, while another page linked up to a role-playing game page on magic. She even found the hyperlink for a page on "Muggles Who Like Harry Potter and Other Wizards." She was having so much fun surfing the Net that she lost complete track of time.

More than half the items were crossed off her prop and costume list now. Was she finally mastering this stage manager thing?

Sunday afternoon Madison couldn't wait to tell Dad about all the props. She went over to his place, but they didn't do as much talking as she'd hoped. Madison might be sailing along with work on the show, but she had gotten way behind in her *home*work. Once Dad found that out, he sat her down in his dining room to finish. Dad couldn't believe that Mr. Gibbons would load up his students up with homework during rehearsals for *The Wiz.*

But he had.

She spent two whole hours reading *Diary of Anne Frank* and writing a short essay at Dad's dining room table.

When Monday morning rolled around, Madison was *still* working on her diary assignment. She'd just about finished when Mom asked her to help load the car to bring the yellow brick road tiles and other props to school.

"I'm sooooo stressed out!" Madison said as they motored over to Far Hills. Rushing in the mornings usually meant rushing all day long, too. She would be a little late to Mrs. Wing's first-period computer class.

Luckily Mom had written an excuse note. Mrs. Wing was cool about the whole thing. Mrs. Wing was usually cool about everything.

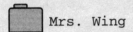 Mrs. Wing

My English essay is DONE! I feel so happy being in computer class now. Not just because I get my work done so much faster than everyone else and can go into my own files like now, but because of my teacher. Being around Mrs. Wing just makes me feel smarter.

Great news! Mrs. Wing told me at the start of class that she would help me make the programs for *The Wiz*. I told her I wanted to design the cover. It'll be like making a collage, and I love making

71

collages. I never know when I start, what
words and pictures will end up together.
Mrs. Wing couldn't believe it when I told
her I kept all my files on the computer and
off. She says we can scan the collage at
school and then print out final copies for
the copy center.

We started talking about *The Wiz* page
for the seventh-grade Web site. Mrs. Wing
says she'll post pictures online after the
show ends. When rehearsals end, I'll be
working more on the Web pages in my free
time. Principal Bernard told Mrs. Wing he
wants Far Hills to be tech connected.
(That's what he calls it, anyway.) So next
semester we'll be doing more "cybrarian"
work, like logging information and making
homework databases.

Mrs. Wing had on the most excellent scarf
with orange polka dots today, and she doesn't
even know that's my favorite color! Mom would
say that's good karma. She believes that

"What are you writing?" Egg asked.

Madison clicked off her monitor. He was giving
her the evil eye.

"Nothing," Madison said. "Nothing . . . except an
e-mail to Rose saying you think she's HOT."

"You what?" Egg said.

"Shhh!" Madison warned. She didn't want to get
in trouble. Luckily Mrs. Wing hadn't heard or seen
them. "Egg, I was kidding. Relax."

"Tell me what you wrote NOW," Egg said. He gave Madison an Indian sunburn by grabbing her forearm with both hands and *twisting*. . . .

"Owwwwch," Madison squeaked. She looked down at her now beet-red forearm. "That hurt."

The bell rang and Drew walked over to Madison and Egg.

"Are *you* singing today, Tin Boy?" Drew asked.

"Hey, quit the Tin Boy jokes," Egg said. "I'm working on dance steps with Aimee, I think."

"How's Aimee doing with all that?" Madison asked. "I haven't really seen much of her choreography."

"She's wicked bossy," Egg huffed.

"She is not," Madison defended her.

"All girls are bossy," Egg shot back.

"I'm going to tell your sister you said that." Madison pinched him.

"Like she would even care," Egg said, rolling his eyes.

The boys hustled out of the computer lab with Madison behind them. She was on her way to see Egg's sister at that very moment.

Mariah and Madison had been excused from their second-period classes so they could meet about the play. It wasn't a big deal since Madison's second period was Mr. Gibbons. He said she could make up the work later. Mariah had her second period free.

Madison couldn't wait to tell Mariah how she and Mom had collected so many key props over the weekend.

She was prouder than proud.

"Buenos días!" Mariah said when they met up in the newspaper room.

"Buenos días," Madison answered back. "I love the new hair color."

Mariah had painted streaks of red all over her head. She liked to change the color just enough so she made an impression—but didn't get sent to Principal Bernard's office. In addition to a dress code, Far Hills Junior High had rules about dyed hair, pierced body parts, and even tattoos. The rule was: DON'T. One time Mariah had a henna tattoo on her shoulder and she'd been sent home to change into a shirt with longer sleeves.

"It's fuchsia, actually." Mariah ran her fingers through her hair. "Madison, you would look awesome with blue—or maybe even green streaks. Ya wanna try?"

Madison chuckled. "Uh . . . NO."

She was daring with her ideas, but when it came to her hair, Madison wasn't brave at all. She didn't even like getting a haircut.

"I have to meet with the eighth-grade prop person at the end of this period, so we better hurry." Because she was president of the junior high art club, Mariah had extra responsibilities. She was always doing extra work for the club, for shows, and for teachers she liked. Sort of like how Madison felt about Mrs. Wing.

"Okay, let's start." Madison pulled out her list and named all the things she was able to gather.

"Check you out," Mariah said. "Art club is painting the set backdrop after school today. I got four teachers to help and the shop teacher volunteered, too. Did I tell you? We're painting it to look like Broadway. A New York City skyline."

The tribute to Mrs. B. Goode would last three separate evenings, but they'd use the same backdrop for all three shows. The first performance was *The Wiz* selections. The following night, the eighth grade was doing selections from *Guys and Dolls*. The next night would be the ninth grade doing a medley of New York City tunes. Madison was pleased since a city backdrop made an ideal Emerald City.

"You're so good at this," Madison said. "And you're so good at being an artist."

"Well, I don't know about *that*." Mariah smiled. She pointed to her head. "I mean, I do paint my *hair*. You're artistic, too, you know."

Madison blushed.

"Anything bizarre happen at rehearsals yet?"

"Well . . ." Madison said softly. "Rehearsals are fine."

"Come on. What's the matter?"

"Oh, nothing. I'm just not used to it, that's all."

"Used to what?"

"Well, sometimes I don't really feel like *I'm* a part of the show. I know I'm helping, but I still feel so helpless. Like every time we're at rehearsal, Mr. Gibbons makes me go down to get something in the basement or tells me to go deliver papers to the administrator or has me sit and prompt lines all by myself in the audience. Meanwhile everybody else is goofing around and having a great time."

"Being stage manager is hard," Mariah said. "People think it's way harder to stand up onstage and sing a song—"

"It *is* hard to get up onstage and sing," Madison chimed in. "I know I get all panicky whenever I try to do that."

"Yeah, but it's still not as hard as what we do, right? Like planning costumes and making sure all the set pieces are where they should be. Where would Mr. Gibbons be without us doing all this?"

"It just makes me feel . . ." Madison wasn't sure how to say it. "I feel so out of it."

"I hear ya. Kids in my class think I'm out of it, too, just because of the way I dress—" Mariah joked.

"But you dress great," Madison interrupted.

"Yeah, whatever." Mariah shrugged it off. "The point is, they don't get it."

"Get what?"

"*It!* Wait until you get to be a freshman like me. Then it really starts to stink. You never know what's happening. You're like the oldest in some ways, but then you're the youngest in other ways."

Even though she was only two years ahead, Madison really looked up to Mariah. But was it really going to get *worse* as she went along in junior high?

Madison did NOT want to believe it.

"No matter what happens during the show," Mariah said as she walked out, "just remember this. It'll all go back to the way it was when the show ends. So don't stress about the jerks. Like my brother." She winked.

Madison sighed.

"Look, Madison, you're the glue, right?" Mariah said.

Madison gave her a blank look. *The glue?*

"Think of it like this," Mariah tried to explain. "You're the one holding *The Wiz* together, okay? So you're the glue."

It sort of made sense. Mariah's words repeated like a recorded message inside Madison's head.

You're the glue. You're the one holding it together.

Whenever rehearsals felt bizarre or she felt out of it, Madison could take that message and play it again.

Maybe being the glue could be her secret weapon against Poison Ivy?

Maybe it could even get Hart to notice her more?

That night, Madison wanted to talk about *The*

Wiz and "being the glue." Madison didn't like how important ideas could happen when there was no one to share them with.

Mom was under a deadline, so she wasn't talking much.

Aimee and her brothers were off at some family dinner in another town.

Fiona's line was busy.

Madison checked her e-mailbox. She'd been unlucky in e-mail lately, but every time she opened it anew, she held her breath for an extra beat—just in case. It had been a few days since she'd checked. Madison didn't like the idea of deleting messages even if they meant nothing. But she had to eliminate some things.

	FROM	SUBJECT
✉	Wetwins	Surfing the Net Games
✉	Boop-Dee-Doop	Spring Clothes ALL NEW
✉	JeffFinn	Fw: FW: This is so funny!!!
✉	Webmaster@bigfis	discussion boards working
✉	Postmaster	Nondeliverable mail

Nothing in her mailbox made Madison feel any more "with it" than she'd felt hanging with Mariah at rehearsal. It was all e-junk, mostly.

There was a super T-shirt sale at one of her favorite online stores. *Nah.* DELETE.

Dad sent a lame joke about a duck. DELETE.

Fiona's brother, Chet, had written about a Net newsletter he wanted to create, reviewing Web sites and computer games he liked. *Not into it right now, maybe later.* DELETE.

Bigfishbowl was starting up a new area of bulletin boards where kids could safely post messages. *Worth checking out.* SAVE.

Finally Madison saw an e-mail that was returned to her. She had originally sent it to Bigwheels last week. Even worse than getting no e-mail was learning that e-mail you sent didn't arrive.

Madison would have to write another e-mail to Bigwheels right away.

Maybe *this* one would get delivered.

Chapter 8

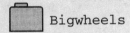 Bigwheels

So I sent Bigwheels this long, long,
long e-mail that started out talking about
boys and school and ended up talking about
how I felt when Mom and Dad had the Big D.

Funny how that subject always comes up,
isn't it?

Bigwheels is feeling bad and I hope I
can be helpful. So she IMed me back right
away and we went to GOFISHY for a chat. I
thought, here is the moment when I could
make even more of a difference. Yes!

But she left in the middle of talking!
She hasn't e-mailed me again, she hasn't
IMed me either.

Do I give terrible advice?

Maybe having a friend online isn't the

same as having a *real* friend. Is that why I can't help her? Is Bigwheels a real friend?

Madison got to the lunchroom later than usual Tuesday afternoon.

Gilda Z slopped sloppy joes onto soft buns.

"Cheese or no cheese?" Gilda asked.

Madison placed her tray on the counter. "No cheese, please," she said, and moved along down the line with her plain sloppy joe. They were all out of strawberry yogurts, so she got banilla instead—vanilla and banana mixed. She'd missed *all* the good lunch selections.

After paying for her food, Madison turned into the noisy cafeteria and inspected the room for her friends. She started back toward the orange table in the rear. To her surprise, all her friends were sitting there.

Plus Ivy, Rose, and Joanie.

Madison almost dropped her tray.

"Maddie, over here!" Fiona chirped, shoving over so Madison could sit down. But there wasn't any room on that side. All the boys were on that side. Madison walked around to the other end of the table.

There wasn't any room there, either.

"I guess I'll sit over there," Madison said, moving toward a green table behind the orange one where everyone else was sitting.

Aimee quickly stood up. "No! Maddie, you can

fit! Ivy, can you move down a little? You too, Rose."

Ivy and Rose both pushed their trays down and made room so Madison could sit next to Aimee. They didn't do it quietly, but they moved. Down at the other end, Egg, Drew, Chet, Hart, and Dan, the kid who was playing the Lion, were too busy playing spitball hockey to even look up.

Never in her life did Madison imagine she'd be sitting at the orange table in the back of the room between her best friend and best enemy. But as her gramma Helen always told her, "Never say never to anything."

"Where were you?" Aimee asked. "Why are you late for lunch?"

Madison shrugged. "I had to help Mrs. Wing."

Ivy interrupted. "She's that computer teacher, right?"

Madison nodded and snapped open her yogurt top.

"That's nice for you, I guess . . ." Ivy said. She leaned right over Madison's tray to talk to Aimee. "Did I tell you that Mrs. Montefiore said we could go ahead and do a dance with our solo, Aimee?"

"What solo?" Madison asked.

"Oh, our duet," Ivy clarified, sipping a juice. "Didn't you hear us singing it the other day?"

Rose piped up. "It'll be the best number in the whole show, Aimee. Your choreography is really good."

Madison couldn't believe Rose would ever compliment Aimee on her dance, but she did.

"You and Rose and Ivy are all dancing together?" Madison asked.

"Yeah," Aimee replied.

"Well, I'm not really that good," Rose mumbled. "But Aimee's helping me out."

"You are *too* good," Aimee told her.

Madison looked over at Fiona desperately.

Was this really happening?

"Madison, what are *you* working on for the show?" Ivy asked. "I don't see you at rehearsals much."

"I've been busy with stage managing, Ivy," Madison said. She couldn't believe Ivy was sitting *this* close. Madison could tell she was wearing make-up.

"Noooooooooo!"

Across the table, Hart let out a wail. He'd lost his spitball hockey game.

"That wasn't a penalty. Egg, you stink!" he cried.

Everyone stopped talking.

Hart looked around with a bashful smile.

Madison glanced over at Hart for a second and thought she saw him wink. But seventh-grade boys absolutely don't wink, especially not in the middle of lunch with a million people around, do they? Madison wasn't so sure.

The mere thought of Hart winking in her direction

83

made her feel better about being at the table.

Ivy jostled Madison's arm, and the yogurt cup almost tipped onto the sloppy joes.

"Oh, sorry, did I do that?" Ivy said.

Madison wanted to pour banilla on Ivy's head.

"Hey, Ivy," Egg yelled across the table. "We heard a rumor."

Hart spoke up, too. "Yeah, Ivy, we heard a rumor. Are you having the cast party?"

Fiona was spacing out. "I haven't heard anything. Is it true?"

"Well . . ." Ivy said coyly to the boys only. "Maybe."

Madison turned to Poison Ivy. "*You're* having the cast party?"

"Well, my parents said it was okay," Ivy said, flipping her hair. "So I guess the rumor is true. It should be great."

"Cool," Chet said.

"Is it a cast party, Ivy?" Drew asked. "Or is it cast *and* crew?"

"Huh? I don't know," she said. "Cast, I guess. And crew. I haven't really decided."

"Well, it really isn't for you to decide," Madison muttered.

"Excuse me?" Ivy said.

Phony Joanie clucked her tongue. "I think only people who are really in the show are supposed to go to a cast party, like actors and the director."

"That's not true!" Fiona said. "It's for everyone. It's for your family and friends who aren't even in the show if you want it to be."

"Well," Joanie said. "That's not the kind of cast party I've been to."

Madison knew that Phony Joanie had probably never been to a single cast party in her entire life.

"A cast party is for everyone, even people who are behind the scenes," Aimee said, looking right at Madison.

"The crew—I mean, Madison and Drew—can come," Ivy snarled. "If they really want."

She said that like it was the last thing in the world she wanted to happen.

"Hey, does anybody have a dollar I could borrow?" Dan interrupted. "I wanna get another dessert."

"You already had two desserts," Chet said. "Like, slow down, Lion Man."

"I can't help it. I'm hungry," Dan said, grabbing a half-eaten brownie off Chet's tray. "Fine, I'll eat yours, then."

Aimee laughed, but her smile disappeared when she looked over at Madison. "What's that on your shirt?" she whispered.

Madison looked down.

Splat.

The whole time she'd been eating her lunch, her sloppy joe had been slopping. There were orange blotches in three different places.

Rose and Joanie snickered.

"Here." Fiona handed Madison a wet napkin across the table. "You can't even tell that you spilled it."

"I can't believe I just did that," Madison said aloud.

Ivy snickered, too.

"Is something funny?" Madison turned to her.

Ivy held up her hands in front of her face and shook her head as if she hadn't laughed.

"Is something wrong?" Madison asked.

Ivy stood up and grabbed her tray. "Not with me. What about you?"

The boys got up to go when Ivy stood. Madison wondered if they did that on purpose.

Even Hart got up. "Looks like this party is breaking up," he said, grabbing his backpack.

Egg, Chet, Dan, and Drew followed.

Madison wanted to shout out, "Good-bye, Hart," but it was too late. The boys were halfway out of the cafeteria without turning back.

Ivy and her drones were right behind him.

"*That* was totally awkward," Fiona said to Madison. "Why did you get all weird with Ivy?"

"Because she was being a jerk," Madison said.

Aimee nodded. "I guess. A little."

"You guess? A little? I thought you were my friends," Madison said.

Aimee leaned in. "What are you talking about?"

"If you were my friends, you would not be sitting here at our table with the most popular, most obnoxious, most EVIL people in the school."

"Maddie, it's really not that bad. Why are you acting like this? I mean, it wasn't even a problem having lunch all together—until you came over."

"What's *that* supposed to mean?" Madison said.

"You—you know what I mean," Aimee stammered.

"You just sat there," Madison said. "While she and her drones laughed at me."

Fiona shrugged. "She wasn't *really* laughing, Maddie."

"Then what was *really* happening?" Madison tried in vain to mop away the sloppy joe on her shirt, but the stains just got worse. "What a mess!"

"Maddie, we're your best friends," Aimee explained. "We were just hanging out."

"Whatever," Madison said, wiping some more at the sloppy joe stain.

"Madison, don't you believe us?" Fiona asked.

Madison realized she *did* believe them. They were her best friends. But she was still angry. Really angry.

"I don't mean to be weird." Madison sighed. "It's just that I couldn't believe I would ever find you eating lunch at the same table—at *our* orange table— with Ivy Daly."

"It's just that Ivy has been pretty cool." Aimee

put her arm around her best friend. "About the show, I mean."

Madison was *really* trying to understand.

"She's being so nice to me and Fiona," Aimee said.

She's being so FAKE. Don't you get it?

She wanted to say that out loud but decided not to say anything.

The three friends got up and started to leave.

"Madison, wait!" a voice yelled from the other side of the lunchroom. It was Lindsay Frost. "I have something to ask you," she said.

"Hi, Lindsay," Fiona said.

Aimee waved hello and then said to Madison, "We'll wait over there."

"I'm so glad I caught you!" Lindsay was talking fast. Madison noticed that her hair wasn't combed. She even had a sloppy joe stain on her sweater. It was kind of gross. Madison looked down at her own shirt.

"You spilled lunch, too, huh?" Lindsay smiled, pointing at Madison and then back at herself.

Madison held her hands over her blotches. "No, not really."

Were all eyes in the lunchroom on them?

"Um, did you say you had a question for me?"

"Yes! I was looking for you earlier. I wanted to see if you had time to practice lines with me later," Lindsay said.

"Later?" Madison asked.

"Before or after rehearsal, I guess. Or if you have a free period."

"Oh," Madison said. She couldn't take her eye off Lindsay's sloppy joe spot. Did her own shirt look as bad as Lindsay's sweater?

Aimee and Fiona were standing over by the exit doors, waving and waiting.

"Well, can you help?" Lindsay asked again.

"Well," Madison started to answer. She was about to say, "Yeah, sure, yeah, I'll go," but then Aimee make a face. A funny face.

Lindsay was oblivious as usual. Madison wanted to run.

"I'm sorry," Madison blurted out suddenly. "I'd really like to help . . . but I can't. I have so much work for the show and I'm really behind in my classes and maybe we can do it tomorrow?"

"Oh." Lindsay shrugged. "No, that's okay. Don't worry about it. I understand. I'll see you at rehearsal. Another time, I guess."

As Lindsay walked away, Madison hurried over to Aimee and Fiona.

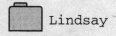 Lindsay

Rude Awakening: Popularity is a war I can't win.

I watch the other kids onstage and I wonder what's real and what's not. People

89

can be such fakers, and when they're
singing and acting it's even worse. Even
people you thought you knew.

That fakeness just continues right off
the stage into life, doesn't it? I should
have helped Lindsay today when she asked
me. But I didn't. Dissing Lindsay was more
embarrassing than spilling sloppy joe on
myself in front of Hart and everyone else.
It was way more embarrassing than anything
I've done lately. How could I be so
un-nice?

Even when I think I can rise above the
whole mind trip about what's popular and
what's not, I *still* get sucked in by what
other people think. I care what they think.
Does that make me a bad person?

What happened to being the glue and
holding everything together like Mariah
said? I am so not holding ANYTHING together
right now.

I can't figure out where I fit in.

Chapter 9

The morning of the first dress rehearsal, Madison got up extra early to get a head start on some positive vibes. She was up at five-thirty, to be exact. A case of major nerves can sometimes be the best alarm clock in the world.

Phinnie made a snuffling noise and curled into a tighter ball when Madison stretched and slid out from under the covers. But ever so quietly, Madison perched by the bedroom window seat to watch the sun come up like a piece of tangerine candy.

More than anything else in the entire world, Madison wanted to do a good job in *The Wiz*. As she looked out at the sky she made a wish for that . . . times two . . . with sugar on top . . . crossing her fingers just to be sure. Superstitions couldn't be proved; Madison knew that. But they didn't hurt.

"Please don't let me mess up," she said aloud to the sky. "Please don't let me miss any cues or drop any props. Please let *The Wiz* be the best show ever."

By the time the dress rehearsal started, she was readier than ready to watch that wish come true.

"Let's get this show on the road!" Mr. Gibbons yelled. He motioned up to the mezzanine to Drew and Wayne, who were running the lights, to begin. "Is everyone almost ready back there?"

This was the true test. Everyone always says a bad dress rehearsal is good news for the real show. Madison wanted to believe that *both* could be fantastic.

Mariah rushed into the dressing area. "Has anyone seen Toto—I mean, Chocolate?"

Mr. Gibbons had brought in his own dog, Chocolate, to be in the early scenes as Dorothy's dog, Toto. The poor animal had only been at one rehearsal so far and had been so traumatized by the lights and the music that she'd peed onstage.

A low barking noise was coming from behind one of the curtains at the far end of the stage. Mariah heard it first.

"Bad girl, Chocolate!" she exclaimed as she retrieved the mutt from between a heavy fold of fabric. The dog had gotten tangled up back in the curtains and was shaking like a windup toy.

A missing Toto is not a good omen, Madison

thought, crossing her fingers again. She went back into the dressing room.

"Hey, Finnster!" Hart cried as Madison entered the dressing room.

He was decked out in a purple flowing cape and carried his mask in hand. The mask, constructed out of papier-mâché by the ninth-grade art club, was twice the size of Hart's real head. It was more like a monster head really, with giant sunken holes for his eyes and red feathers at the top that looked like flames shooting out. It was attached to a broom handle so Hart could hold it up in front of his face during the early Oz scenes—just before Dorothy and the others discover that The Wizard is a big faker.

Egg was standing nearby. "Hey, Hart, that's a good way to get girls."

"That's real funny, Tin Boy head," Hart said as he held up the mask. "Hey, what do *you* think, Finnster?"

Just as he said that, the mask came detached from its handle.

"Hart!" Madison yelped. She leaned forward and caught it.

"Whoa," Hart said. "That was close. But now what am I supposed to do? Lift it up like this—"

"No, let's fix it." Madison ran over to the prop shelves and retrieved some twine and duct tape that other people in the crew left around just in case anything needed to be tied up or reattached. The mask was repaired instantly.

"Madison, can you help me, too?" Fiona said.

On the other side of the prop closet, Fiona was searching for her witch hat, which had been mysteriously misplaced.

"It was here a little while ago," Madison told her. "I double-checked my entire list. Are you sure you didn't pick it up?"

Fiona looked frazzled. "No, I swear. Well, maybe. Oh, I don't remember. It's so busy back here and—"

"Is someone missing a witch hat?" Mariah said, walking toward Fiona.

Madison breathed a sigh of relief. "Don't take it off, Fiona, okay?"

Fiona really could be the world's biggest space case.

Peeking through the curtains, Madison could see Mr. Gibbons hunched over the piano with Mr. and Mrs. Montefiore. They were reviewing the order of song numbers. Mr. Gibbons had rearranged and shortened the *Wiz* tunes with the music department. For now the piano played, but for the real show, they were adding drums, cymbals, and a trumpet. Those band members just weren't expected at rehearsal today.

Madison had set up a bench with a script on it so she could easily cue missed lines. She saw Ivy leaning over the script, flipping pages to find her parts.

"Ivy, you need to go finish getting dressed," Madison said.

Ivy kept looking through the pages.

Madison moaned. "Why don't you go look at your own script, Ivy? We're starting in a few minutes and I need to—"

"Look, I don't come on for a few songs, so I have plenty of time to get in costume," Ivy said. "And I need to look at this script now. I left mine in my locker."

Madison shook her head. "No." She grabbed the script. "Get dressed."

Ivy looked steamed. Had Madison really said that?

Rose and Joan walked over. They'd heard everything.

"You can use my script, Ivy," Rose said. "I'm not stingy, like some people around here."

The three enemies skulked away.

"How do I look?" Lindsay asked. She modeled her braid-in pigtails and gingham jumper. She was carrying Chocolate in her arms. He was still shaking from the curtain incident.

"You're the perfect Dorothy," Madison said. "That's a great costume."

"Thanks," Lindsay said.

"Do you have everything else you need?" Madison asked.

Lindsay nodded. She stuck out her pinkie.

"What's that for?" Madison asked.

Lindsay smiled. "For luck. I'm very superstitious, aren't you?"

"Hey, Madison." Mariah poked her head out of the dressing room. "I have to help the Munchkins lace up their green shoes, so I'll be back here. Are you okay by yourself?"

Madison smiled. "I think so."

"She's totally in control," Lindsay said as she walked to the other side of the stage for her entrance. "Thanks again, Maddie."

Madison wasn't exactly in total control, even though she wished she were. Frantic cast members had her surrounded. There were other teachers and crew people around, but everyone seemed to need *Madison* to help.

Help!

Tommy's scarecrow stuffing was coming undone. Madison stuffed it in and tied a new knot in his costume to make it all better.

Dan's lion suit was a little too big and he kept stumbling around, bumping into people and things backstage. Madison unzipped his paws and rolled up his leg fur.

"We'll figure it out after rehearsal," she told him. "This will work for now."

"My wand is missing!" Ivy screeched. She practically spit the words into Madison's face. "Aren't you supposed to keep track of the props, Madison?" She said Madison's name like it tasted bad.

"Yes, but you wanted to be in charge of your own props, remember?" Madison reminded Ivy that she was the one who didn't want anyone near any part of her costume. She'd made that perfectly clear during rehearsals, so Mr. Gibbons told her she could keep her stuff separate from the rest of the cast's as long as she kept track of it.

"But you're the prop person and you're supposed to know what to do, right?" Ivy snarled.

"I do know what to do," Madison said. She walked away, leaving Ivy there alone in her Glinda outfit with an expression of utter disbelief.

"I'm going to tell Mr. Gibbons," Ivy threatened.

Madison didn't care. "Have you seen Aimee?" she asked Mariah.

Five Munchkins looked up at Madison and pointed toward the backstage bathroom.

"Aimee?" Madison called out. "Are you in there?"

A muffled voice from behind the door squeaked, "Yes."

It was Aimee, but she didn't sound like herself.

"Aimee? Are you okay?" Madison rattled the knob. "Can I come in?"

The door unlatched and Madison walked inside. Aimee was leaning up against the sink.

"Aimee, what's the matter?" Madison asked. They were looking at each other in the mirror reflection.

Aimee shook her head. "I have cramps. Bad ones."

Madison rubbed her back. "Did you eat something weird for lunch?"

"Not those kind of cramps." Aimee lowered her voice so Madison could barely hear. "I have my period."

Madison didn't know what to say. She and Aimee had never really talked about this. Madison hadn't gotten hers yet.

"What should I do?" Aimee asked.

"You want me to tell Mrs. Montefiore that you have your period?" Madison asked.

"Noooo! Don't tell anyone," Aimee said. "I'll be okay. I better just get into my costume."

"Are you sure?" Madison asked.

Aimee put down the toilet seat and sat. She grabbed at her stomach and took a deep breath. "Cramp," she whispered.

"Aimee?" Madison was worried.

But a heartbeat later, Aimee stood right back up. "I'm fine. They come and go, you know?"

Madison realized she *didn't* know. Not one bit. She was eager to get older and wiser, but Madison could definitely wait for her period. She wasn't ready to enter the world of cramps.

"Aimee, are you nervous, too?" Madison asked before walking out.

"I don't get nervous. I don't get all weird when I

have to go onstage. I go onstage all the time at dance camp. Why would right now be any different than then? I just think—"

Aimee paused and took a deep, deep breath.

"I've never been so nervous, Maddie," Aimee finally admitted. "I don't want to mess up. All those dance steps and—"

"Aimee, you'll be great," Madison said. "You know you'll be great. You always dance great, no matter what. Even with cramps.'"

Aimee looked straight into Madison's eyes. "You're the best."

"The Munchkins are waiting," Madison joked.

As she walked out of the girls' bathroom, Madison was so lost in thought that she almost smacked right into Tommy Kwong. Once again, he'd come unstuffed. Madison restuffed.

"Madison!" Mariah yelled. "There's someone outside from the local paper. They want to take a picture of everyone in the show. Mr. Gibbons wants you and everyone else on the stage."

Sometimes the local paper ran human-interest stories about school events like this. This article was going to be about Mrs. Goode's twenty years at the school and her various contributions to the Far Hills community. They wanted photos from a dress rehearsal so they could run the piece the day of the show. They'd be doing separate pieces on the seventh-, eighth-, and ninth-grade performances.

Mr. Gibbons had turned up the house lights. "Uh, can I get everyone out here, please? All the seventh-grade cast members onstage."

The Montefiores stopped playing. Madison and Mariah helped to corral the witches and Winkies onto the set. They were standing in front of the city backdrop, and it looked so magical. The yellow linoleum squares twinkled when the lights hit them in just the right way.

"Okay, now let's line up," Mr. Gibbons asked the cast.

Amazingly, everyone got into rows and the photographer asked everyone to stand closer. Madison crossed her arms and watched everyone come together. It was so exciting!

Fiona waved her over.

"Here," Fiona said. "Get in the picture! Stand next to me!"

Aimee put her arm around Madison's shoulder when she slipped in.

"Hold on!" the photographer yelled. "Would the Tin Man please straighten his tin hat?"

Egg fixed it.

"No, no—I need the Munchkins to be in the same group, please," he said raising his camera up to his eye again. "Yes, that's better."

Mr. Gibbons yelled out, "Dan, would you please roll down your lion feet?"

Madison helped.

"Okay." The photographer made little hand motions to tell kids to move in, move out, and then move in again. "Would the boy playing the Scarecrow please check his straw?"

Madison looked over at Tommy. Mrs. Perez needed to work on that costume a little more.

"Okay, now everyone smile," the photographer said, lifting the camera up once more.

Mr. Gibbons suddenly stepped in front of the camera. "Wait! Ivy Daly isn't here. Ivy? How could we be missing Ivy?" he yelled backstage. "Madison, where did Ivy go?"

"I'll get her," Mariah said, running to the back. Madison was very glad she didn't have to go.

In a second, Ivy was onstage, apologizing. She had *finally* found her Glinda wand.

"Now are we ready?" the photographer asked once more.

Everyone smiled.

"Wait! I'm sorry, but who is the girl in the second row? The one in between the two witches?"

Madison knew he was talking about her.

"She's our stage manager," Mr. Gibbons said.

"Could I ask you to please step out of the picture, miss? This is just for cast members wearing costumes."

Madison felt everyone's eyes on her. "It's okay, Madison," Mr. Gibbons reassured her. "You can be in the next round of photos."

Madison slowly walked to the side of the stage.

"Thanks!" the photographer cried. "Now, *Wiz* cast, please say 'Oz!'"

Madison blinked when the flash went off and got dizzy. The photographer kept taking picture after picture, posing the group in different arrangements. He even took shots of Addaperle, Evillene, and Glinda by themselves. The three of them looked great in their costumes.

By the time Madison got into the photo, the photographer only had a few shots left. She posed with Drew and the Nose Plucker. Madison knew *she* wouldn't make the paper, but she tried not to let it bother her. The cast and crew photo might make it into one of the trophy cases in the school lobby.

When the picture-taking hubbub died down, the cast finally started their opening number. The actual dress rehearsal took about twice as long as it should have, but it finally ended around six-thirty, to loud applause from Mr. Gibbons. He gathered everyone onstage for a little postperformance pep talk.

"You guys were great," he said. "See you back here on Monday."

"That's it?" Egg said.

Mr. Gibbons nodded. "That's it. Good job. Now get your gear and get home." Because it had gotten late, he kept it real short.

Kids were pulling off their costumes in a hurry, so Madison and Mariah kept running from place to place backstage. They had to make sure that props were returned, capes were hung up, and all the caps to the makeup tubes were twisted on tight.

When she was finished running around, Madison had lost track of Aimee and Fiona. They weren't in the dressing room, the bathroom, or the auditorium.

"Have you seen Aimee?" Madison asked Dan.

He played dumb and put on his Lion voice. "Duh, which way did dey go?"

Madison laughed as she walked away. Dan was a dork, but he was funny.

She bumped into Lindsay at the auditorium entrance.

"Hey, did you see Aimee or anyone else?" Madison asked her.

"Nope," Lindsay began. "Yeah! I did see Aimee. She was headed out with her stuff like five minutes ago. Fiona was with her, I think."

Madison sighed. *They'd left without her?*

"You know, Madison, you really should have been in those photographs," Lindsay said. "I mean, you're the most important person in the show."

"Yeah, well . . ." Madison mumbled. "No biggie."

"Still, I hope you know how psyched we all are. Everyone thinks you're a great stage manager."

Madison scratched her head. "Thanks."

"I mean it," Lindsay said.

"That's really nice of you to say that," Madison said. "I mean, you don't have to."

"I know. So you wanna walk home together?" Lindsay asked her.

Just then, Aimee ran into the auditorium. "Oh my God, Maddie! I felt a little sick and I went down to the nurse's office to see if anyone was there. I'm so sorry, but I couldn't find you! Fiona's waiting outside. My brother is coming with the car."

Lindsay started to walk away. "I'll see you guys later, then."

Madison looked at Lindsay and then Aimee and then over at Lindsay again. "Want a ride?" she asked.

Aimee jumped in. "Yeah, come with us."

Lindsay looked at Aimee. "You sure?"

Aimee smiled. "Of course, I'm sure."

Madison turned to Lindsay. "Come on, let's go."

Chapter 10

From: Bigwheels
To: MadFinn
Subject: Hi
Date: Sat 14 Oct 10:15 PM

Thanks for sending a copy of your school program cover for *The Wiz*. I downloaded it and it looks so cool.

I am feeling ok now. My mom and dad are seeing a counselor I think. I guess I have to wait and see what happens. The only problem is that I can't get all my homework done and I'm worried about my grades. Do you study hard? I just have so much more homework than I had last year. I think teachers believe in cruel and unusual punishment. My brain hurts.

Send me more e-mails about the
play. How is the guy playing The
Wizard? Do you still like him?
Thanks again for being my keypal
and for your advice. It's nice
having you out there.

Yours till the home works,

Bigwheels

Even Bigwheels had trouble at school. It was just
another thing they had in common. She sounded
like she was in better spirits since her last e-mail.
Maybe Madison really did help her keypal. Maybe
she should make Bigwheels her own special collage
about being smart. Bigwheels said she liked the *Wiz*
cover, which meant she'd probably *love* a collage of
her own.

Madison rummaged through the piles on her
floor for the right words and pictures. She found a
cartoon of a computer and some pictures of flowers
her mom had taken in Thailand on a business trip a
while ago.

It was nice to take a break from all things related
to *The Wiz*.

The house was so quiet. Mom was out running
errands and then taking Phinnie to the vet for his
regular checkup. Madison almost never missed Phin's
trip to the vet, but she made an exception this once.

106

Mom said it was okay for her to sleep in after the busy week.

Madison thought about staying under the covers. But she wasn't about to waste valuable time alone— *sleeping.*

She turned the stereo volume in the living room to its highest setting. She could feel the bass vibrate inside the wood floors as the radio played America's Top 40. As her frozen waffles popped out of the toaster, Madison sang along even though she couldn't sing. She liked the part of the radio show where people called from all over the country to dedicate songs to people they loved. One day Madison would call with her own song request. She'd dedicate her song to Hart.

When the radio show ended, she went into Mom's office to boot up her computer. This was the best part about being alone in the house. She could sit at Mom's workstation and imagine that *she*, Madison, was the real-life film producer. She was Madison Finn—making an important call, dashing off a quick memo, taking a meeting.

Madison loved the idea of being important.

She also liked the idea of being just a *little* sneaky.

Mom didn't like it when Madison played video games, so she had strict rules about computer game time and kept all the games on the shelf in her office. But with Mom gone, Madison could play. Today she installed Troll Village, the not-yet-released video game software Mom got from someone at Budge Films.

In Troll Village, Madison had to trick all the trolls in the town in order to become sheriff and rule the area. It was like the Wild, Wild West with saloons and horse stables, only the gunslingers weren't wearing cowboy hats. They had pink, blue, and neon yellow troll hair. Madison could sit and play for almost an hour without moving a muscle. She wasn't sure she even blinked when she played.

When the phone rang, Madison jumped so suddenly that she pressed the mouse accidentally and eliminated one of her troll's seven lives.

Whoops.

"Hello, Finn residence." She answered the phone in a special way just in case it was a work-related call for Mom.

There was silence on the other end of the line.

"Hello, is somebody there? Who is this?" Madison knew *someone* was on the line.

"Maddie, is that you?" It was Drew Maxwell.

"Drew?" Madison asked. "Is that *you*?"

"Yeah. What's up?"

"Um . . . not much."

Madison took the game off pause and played while she talked on the phone.

"How's your weekend?" Drew asked.

"Um . . . fine." Madison had no idea why he'd be calling her.

"I didn't see you after the rehearsal. I wanted to tell you that all your stuff looked good."

"Uh-huh." Madison was half listening now.

"What do you think about the lighting?" Drew asked.

Madison had turned back to her trolls, so she didn't really hear.

"Maddie, are you there?" Drew asked again. "Did you like what we did with the footlights?"

"Yeah," Madison mumbled. "Oh, sure."

She couldn't get the least bit excited about talking to Drew. Ever since they'd been helping Mrs. Wing out with the Web site at school, Drew had been hanging around Madison nonstop. She felt bad because he wasn't always sure what to say. She was half afraid he might say something mushy.

There was nothing worse than the vacuum of silence on the phone between them. Like now.

Drew coughed.

Madison coughed.

"So, anyway," Madison said. "I sorta have to go."

Drew gulped. "Are you coming over today to watch the movie?"

"The movie?" Madison didn't know about any movie.

"Yeah, the movie."

"What movie? Where?"

"At my parents' guest house. We're renting the original *Wizard of Oz* and everyone's coming over to watch it."

Madison was confused. "Everyone? Like who?"

"From the play," Drew said. "We said we'd watch the movie, remember? You were there."

"No, I don't think so."

"You don't know about the movie?"

"No," Madison said again. "No one told me there was a movie." She was repeating herself like a parrot.

"Whoa," Drew moaned. "I guess Fiona forgot to tell you. She told me she'd ask you. I think. Yeah. We were talking about renting the movie the other day, and then I asked my mom if we could do it because we have that big-screen TV. You know the one in the guest house?"

"Uh-huh." Madison felt the exact same way she felt in first grade when she was the only person in class who wasn't invited to Willie Walker's birthday party. Mrs. Walker said the invitation had gotten lost in the mail, but Madison never believed it.

Drew was still talking. "And so everyone just sort of invited themselves. Egg has a big mouth—you know that."

"Uh-huh." Madison grunted. *So why hadn't Egg told her?*

"I guess we forgot to ask you."

"I guess." Madison grunted again.

"But you were *always* totally invited."

"Why didn't you ask me yourself?" Madison asked. "I mean, we only see each other all the time

110

these days at the play and in computer class, too."

"Uh—uh—uh . . . I know. . . . B-B-But . . ." Drew was stammering a lot now. He did that when he got real nervous. "I'm SORRY," he said. "I swear I thought one of the girls was gonna ask you. Fiona said she would. I SWEAR."

"What time does it start?" Madison asked.

"Three," Drew said. "Well, can you come?" he asked. "I mean, now that you know?"

"I have one question," Madison said. "Will Ivy Daly be there?"

"I don't think so," Drew said.

When Drew confirmed that Ivy would *not* be at the screening, Madison agreed to come over—no problem, no hard feelings attached.

Drew sounded relieved when he said good-bye. Madison was relieved, too, that the conversation was over.

As she hung up the phone, she felt freakier than freaky. Mom and the dog walked in the moment she put down the receiver.

"Grrr . . ." Phinnie nuzzled Madison's foot.

"Will you take him for a *w-a-l-k*, please?" Mom asked as she kissed Madison hello.

"Wanna go out?" Madison asked. Phin panted as she grabbed the leash and raced him to the door. Of course, Phinnie won—sliding to the finish. Whenever he ran anywhere too fast in the house, he'd skid across the polished floors.

Madison walked around the block in a trance. She was trying to remember everything in her closet, row by row. She had no idea what she was going to wear to Drew's place. Once she changed out of her sweatpants and oversized T-shirt from her dad's alma mater, she had to put on something cute. Boys were going to be there. Hart was going to be there.

"Will his mother be home?" Mom asked Madison when she came back from the walk. Mom didn't like Madison going places without chaperones.

"I think . . ." Madison suddenly worried that Mom might not agree to let her go. She considered lying, but then admitted she really wasn't sure. "I think so," Madison said again, wishful.

Mom finally said that Madison could go.

"Thanks, Mom. This could be a very important movie, you know."

"Okay, honey bear," Mom said with a nod. "Now go change. It's after two-thirty."

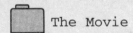 The Movie

```
     I was the last person to get there.
     It's weird to (1) not get invited in the
first place and then (2) walk in when
everyone else has already been there for a
while. It's like I had a neon sign on my
head that said, "By the Way, I Was Invited
at the Last Minute."
     I always have over-thoughts—today I was
the afterthought.
```

Right away Aimee and Fiona made room for me between them on the floor, so it got better. Plus Fiona said it was all her fault for not asking me. She just spaced. After that it was pretty much normal for a while. Egg wouldn't shut up; Drew was being Mr. Nice as always. His mom made all this popcorn and it was *everywhere* on the floor.

And then the doorbell rang. Of course it was Ivy. She decided to come at the last minute. Drew was nice to her, too. All the boys were. She was wearing this shirt that was way too tight and jeans that were too tight, too.

I could almost pretend she wasn't there if I sat with my back to her. But when we paused the tape for snack break, Aimee got up to go talk to her. I couldn't believe that! Even Fiona thought that was a little weird.

Hart wasn't there. I wonder why? Lindsay wasn't there, either. I guess no one remembered to invite her, either.

It's bad enough that Ivy has to win things like elections and play parts, but suddenly it's like she has to win *people*, too. When she and Aimee started singing their duet just for fun, I wanted to RUN.

Tonight when I see Dad for dinner, I know he'll say I'm over-thinking this whole Ivy thing. After all, it is just one play. But what if this isn't a temporary thing? Aimee's brothers all told her there are

MAJOR changes in seventh grade. What if changing *friends* is one of them?

But how do you just *forget* to invite your BFF to the movies?

After feeling snubbed at Drew's, the last thing Madison was prepared to deal with was Dad's girlfriend, Stephanie. But Dad invited her along for dinner, despite Madison's protests.

"I want you to be nice," Dad pleaded. "Please."

Madison tried. Dad seemed so blissed out when he was around Stephanie. He smiled nonstop and made even more dumb jokes than usual.

And Madison had to admit, Stephanie really was nice. It was just hard to see another person sitting across the table from Dad where Mom used to sit.

At dinner, Stephanie told Madison how she'd been an actress all through college. She was so enthusiastic, which took Madison by surprise.

"You were?" Madison asked.

Stephanie nodded. "I think being in a show is a terrific way to find out more about yourself. When you act, you can become anyone or anything."

"And what about being offstage?" Madison asked. "Being a stage manager?"

"Well." Stephanie leaned in a little closer to Madison and whispered, "Then you're in charge—of you, of the cast, of everything."

Madison noticed Dad's expression as he looked at

Stephanie. His eyes were shiny like wet marbles. He couldn't stop staring.

It was embarrassing.

Madison didn't remember if Dad ever looked at Mom that way. She tried to search her memory banks like she searched on the Internet, thinking of specific "search" words to see if they'd trigger any memories: *love, dinner, kiss.*

But she came up empty. *No matches found.*

That night before bed, Madison fished through her piles of files, pictures, and words about theater, acting, taking charge. She thought maybe she could make Stephanie a collage, too?

She'd do one for Bigwheels first . . . then one for Stephanie.

Madison shut her eyes tight. What she really needed was sleep.

The play was only days away.

Chapter 11

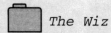 *The Wiz*

I learned how to sew a cape. Actually, I sewed part of Hart's cape. Mrs. Perez really sewed most of it. But still, it's like a part of me will be with him during the show. How cool is *that*?

Tuesday. Boring. I am so busy, I barely have time to write. I have like two hours of homework and it's ten o'clock already. We had another dress rehearsal today. It was forty-eight minutes exactly. Didn't stop for anyone. One funny part was when Ivy forgot her line in one of the songs and I had to cue her. She was MAD about that.

Thursday. Wow. Final run-through. We cleaned the stage afterward. Aimee's dances are so great. It's better that Rose is in the dance numbers because when they dance side by side, Aimee blows her away. Aimee has been so busy practicing, we haven't really talked. Fiona has a cold, but it actually makes the bad-witch voice better. Egg is good, too. We're all GREAT! *The Wiz* is GREAT!!!!

On Friday, Madison logged online before breakfast. With *The Wiz* on the horizon, she was feeling ultrasuperstitious. She decided to go to bigfishbowl.com for a little help. Just before every major life event Madison would visit "Ask the Blowfish" on her favorite Web site.

Right now was no exception.

Site members were instructed to ask a yes or no question on-screen, directing their question to an all-knowing blowfish that looked like a puffy gumball with fins. When she typed her question and hit ENTER, a bubble popped up with the answer. The answers were like wacko fortune cookie fortunes, and Madison knew the way the answers appeared was random, but she believed them, anyway.

She wanted to believe.

Madison typed: *Will the play be good tonight?*

The fish blew a bubble with its answer. "Things will go swimmingly."

Madison was very encouraged.

Will everyone like the show?

The fish said, "The tide is high."

Madison was still encouraged. She had to ask the next question.

Will Hart talk to me tonight?

The fish said, "Beware of sharks."

Madison couldn't believe a blowfish could possibly be SO right. It was like the computer knew about Poison Ivy. *She* was the shark, after all.

Madison asked one more question.

Does Hart like me?

The fish said, "The tide is high."

Madison was thrilled to hear that . . . but then she realized that the blowfish already gave that answer once.

"But it's still a positive," she told herself.

She checked her mailbox, too, while she was online and found an electronic card waiting there. It was better news than what the blowfish delivered. On it was a picture of some kind of cartoon wizard.

```
Make a Wish
You're a "wiz" at whatever you do!
Thought this was funny! Hope every-
thing goes well backstage. Write
soon.
Yours till the leg breaks,

Bigwheels
```

Madison closed her laptop and went down to the kitchen. She'd hang with Phinnie while she ate her cereal. When she'd finished eating, Madison got down on the floor beside him and rubbed his belly. Phin was snoring, curled up by the dishwasher. His shallow little breaths were so peaceful.

Dogs have a way of telling a person everything will be okay just by lying there. Madison read somewhere that dogs never forget. Even if someone is gone for a year, once he or she comes back, that dog will sniff and love and be a friend just like before. When a dog does that, people know they're home.

"I have to go, Maddie! Do you want a lift to school?" Mom said, walking into the kitchen.

Madison couldn't pass up a ride this morning. It was raining.

Was rain a good omen or a bad one?

"We're off to see *The Wizard*," Mom joked as they pulled out of the driveway.

When Mom said, "Wizard," all Madison could think of was Hart.

Everyone in homeroom cheered when Mr. Bernard made his morning announcements about the show.

"To all the students at Far Hills who are participating in the revues from classes seven through nine, thanks for all your hard work. You have made this a very special week, especially for Mrs. Goode, who has devoted much of her teaching career to helping Far Hills students. I ask that all teachers and counselors please take into consideration that students who are

119

participating in the show be given special . . ."

Listening, Madison felt better instantly. She wouldn't stress about her work right now. She couldn't. She had to concentrate on the play.

It would have been nice if Madison's science teacher, Mr. Danehy, had been in agreement with Principal Bernard. While the majority of the seventh-graders could think of nothing else except *The Wiz*, Mr. Danehy thought it was important for the seventh graders to be thinking about tsunamis and sound waves.

During last period, he announced a science test out of the blue—on waves of all kinds.

"Test Monday. No exceptions," he said, stepping into the science storage closet for a moment. No one, not even Hart, was ready for a test.

When Mr. Danehy was out of sight, Chet stood at the front of the room and suggested that they go into his desk to steal the test so everyone could get an A and make Mr. Danehy bonkers. Egg thought that was a great idea, too. But Madison reminded them both that they probably didn't want to get caught and be expelled, right?

"Expelled?" Egg said.

"Hey, I was only kidding," Chet said.

When Mr. Danehy reentered the class, the students pleaded for mercy in rounds like "Row, Row, Row Your Boat."

"Please, please, change the date?"

"Mr. Danehy, we have play practice."

"*The Wiz* is over soon."

"Well," Mr. Danehy said, standing in the back of the class with his arms folded against his chest. "I see."

Everyone breathed a sigh of hope when he said he would *think* about changing the test date. Thinking about it was better than nothing.

Two hours before the show was supposed to go on, before anyone had on costume or makeup, *The Wiz* cast and crew gathered together backstage. Mariah and Wayne were there, too. It was pep talk time. Mr. Gibbons had something very important to tell everyone.

"So here it is, kids," he started out. "The moment we've all be waiting for, right? *The Wiz* is here."

"Yes, I am, Mr. Gibbons," Hart called out. "I'm right over here."

That got a big, nervous laugh.

"We had only a short time to pull together and do this, cast—"

Drew interrupted. "And crew, Mr. Gibbons. Don't forget."

"Yes, Drew, cast *and* crew. And I am wowed by how well you all worked together as a group."

Madison looked over at Aimee, who was sitting to her left, across the room at Ivy, and then over by the door at Lindsay.

Fiona leaned over to the right and whispered in Madison's ear, "Are you nervous?"

"Big time," Madison whispered back. "Are you?"

"Big time." Fiona stuck her arm inside Madison's. "Remember when you told me not to be nervous? That day when the cast was posted?"

They looked over at Aimee together and she pointed to Mr. Gibbons, who wasn't looking in their direction at the time. He was talking too much tonight. He must be nervous, too.

Aimee made a goofy face like she was pretending to scream silently. "Help me!" she mouthed the words. Madison and Fiona almost lost it when she did that.

"So, kids." Mr. Gibbons turned back toward them. "When you get inside the auditorium, there will be lots of activity. We're the class leading off the program, and that's a big responsibility. I want you to be careful, pay attention . . . and HAVE FUN."

He turned to Mrs. Montefiore, who had a few words to say. "I will lead vocal warm-ups backstage. After which everyone can get dressed and ready to go. Understood?"

Everyone nodded.

Ivy raised her hand and talked at the same time. "Do we come out for standing ovations? How do we line up for our curtain call?"

"That's assuming people are clapping." Mr. Gibbons laughed.

Good one, Mr. Gibbons.

"Actually that's a good question, Ivy. You'll get applause after each of your songs. And for the final number, you'll all stay in place and take one last bow."

Lindsay had her hand raised, too. "Mr. Gibbons?" she asked.

"Lindsay!" he said. "One more question?"

"What do I do with Chocolate in between scenes again? Did you say something yesterday about cookies?"

"I almost forgot!" He reached into his pocket and pulled out some Liver Snaps. "Chocolate loves these. One after each scene should keep her happy."

Everyone was twittering . . . chittering . . . more nervous than ever by now.

"So go on out there and break a leg, everyone!" he shouted.

The cast and crew burst into big whoops and claps.

Madison heard Ivy whisper to Rose as they walked out of the room, "Gee, I hope fatso doesn't eat all the Liver Snaps for herself." She couldn't believe Ivy could say something so cruel after all the hard work Lindsay had done.

"Hey, Finnster!" Hart called across the room. "Wait up!"

Madison felt her stomach flip-flop.

"Hey, Finnster, have you seen my Wiz cape? Mariah told me you guys did something to it."

Madison grinned. "We sewed on silver stars."

"Whoa, that sounds cool," Hart said. He ran his fingers through his brown hair. Madison could almost smell his shampoo.

"Um, excuse me . . . Hart?" someone interrupted.

It was Poison Ivy. Madison thought she had already left the room, but here she was.

"Hey, Ivy," Hart said with a sweet smile.

Madison loved watching Hart smile, but only when it was directed at her—not her enemy.

"I just wanted to make sure I told you again about getting to the cast party," Ivy told him. She was speaking directly to Hart and ignoring Madison completely. "At my house. I can give you a ride if you don't have one. I know you said your parents had to go straight home."

"I'm grabbing a ride with Drew's parents," he said, still smiling.

Ivy flipped her red hair and touched his arm. "Okay, see you later, then."

She touched his arm.

The cast shuffled into the practice room with Mrs. Montefiore. Time was flying by. Madison was just going through the motions while visions of Ivy reaching out to Hart filled her head.

Vocal warm-ups lasted ten minutes, and then Egg led the group in a round of tongue twisters. Mr. Gibbons said those made you limber all over and think fast on your feet. Aimee, Rose, and some other dancers were off in a corner, stretching their arms and legs, too.

"Señor Hart?" Mrs. Perez was standing across the room, holding his purple cape. "Come put on your costume."

It was time for *everyone* to get into the auditorium and get on their costumes. Madison realized she'd better head backstage to help the singers get into their Tin Man, Lion, and other suits—fast. The Munchkins had to be covered in green face and hand makeup, too.

On her way backstage, Madison heard one of the techies say something about there being a lot of people in the audience.

Madison went to look for Aimee and found her applying lipstick in a back room. Aimee was so happy to see her, she couldn't stop talking to take a breath.

"I just called my house to tell everyone I saved seats down near the front for them and my mother told me that your mom is riding with them—can you believe that?" Aimee blabbed.

"Really?" Madison was glad to know her mom would sit with the Gillespies instead of Dad. That took some of her worrying away.

"How are you doing, Maddie? You look funny."

"Hey, I'm not the one dressed up like a witch," Madison said.

"Is your dad bringing his new girlfriend tonight?" Aimee asked.

Madison shook her head. She didn't think Stephanie would be there. But like Gramma Helen said, "Never say never." *Oh boy.* It would be hard enough handling Mom versus Dad without another person there.

Aimee looked over at the clock. "Fifteen minutes!" she shrieked, and ran into the bathroom to pee.

Show time!

The play really had turned out to be "the thing."

It was the thing that turned Ivy, Aimee, and Fiona into witches, made Madison into a manager, and would now reunite Madison's parents.

Madison wondered how she could be the glue that held the play together and yet feel so unglued herself. She had spent a better part of the last three weeks e-mailing Bigwheels back and forth about what to do if the Big D was looming at her home. But Madison had NO ideas about what to say or do. Not really.

The idea of Mom and Dad, and even Stephanie, sitting in the audience at the exact same time made Madison want to run far, far away.

Only there was nowhere to hide. Not now.

The show must go on.

When Madison walked into the auditorium just before the show, she couldn't believe her eyes. The set looked more bright and alive than ever before, with painted skyscrapers sparkling along the back wall of the stage.

The room was packed with screaming junior high school students. Madison had never seen the auditorium like this. She felt a magnetic pull from all of the energy in the room.

At her feet were piles of programs, stacked up for distribution when people were seated. Mrs. Wing had pulled together all the individual flyers from *The Wiz* and the other class shows and made one fat, twenty-page program. They were using it for all three nights of performances.

Madison was thrilled to see her own collage

copied on a page inside. She compared it to the pages from the other classes. An eighth grader had drawn a sketch for the *Guys and Dolls* section, and the director copied a New York City postcard for the ninth grade.

There had been no room for student biographies, but everyone's name was neatly listed, along with the names of everyone that had painted the set or helped with lights. Ivy had raised a little bit of a stink about this since she wanted to be as much of a show-off as possible. "She probably wanted a full page all to her own," Madison mused, "with a full-color photograph and the caption 'Look at me, I'm so great!'" But the program only had her listed once.

Madison, on the other hand, found her name listed *more* than once at the bottom of the crew page.

Stage Manager and Props	*Madison Finn*
Costumes and Makeup	*Mariah Diaz, Madison Finn*
THE WIZ Program Design	*Madison Finn*

In a short section in the back, Mrs. Wing had also included a long list of thank-you messages from the school administration and parents. Each family had to pay ten dollars to have their greeting printed, and the money defrayed the costs of refreshments and other set expenses. It was fun to flip through and see what people had to say.

♥ *Congratulations to all members of the cast, especially Fiona and Chet. We're so proud of you. Mom and Dad*

♥ *Way to go, cast and crew of* THE WIZ—*you've got the chemistry for success! From 7th, 8th, and 9th grade science dept.*

♥ *Mr. Gibbons and the entire cast—you rock! Break a leg! Mr. and Mrs. Montefiore*

♥ *Felicitaciones y buena suerte en el futuro, Walter and Mariah. Con amor, Mom, Dad, and Nannie Conchita*

♥ *Best wishes to the seventh-grade STARS from Mrs. Goode. How can I thank you all?*

Aimee's family had paid to have the entire back cover of the program so it could be a congratulatory message *plus* an advertisement for her dad's cyber-café and book store. Aimee was tickled when she saw the message, *To Our Dancing Queen, Love, Mommy, Daddy, Roger, Billy, Dean, Doug, and Blossom.* Madison read through all the thank-you messages and saw one for Ivy, Rose, and even Dan the Lion—but didn't find her own name anywhere.

Mr. Gibbons was directing kids on where to stand, sit, and hang out. Madison couldn't find Mrs. Perez or Mariah anywhere, but Lindsay was nearby.

"Isn't this awesome?" Lindsay asked. She had on her full costume.

"Yeah, it is," Madison said, still a bit distracted.

"I can't believe how many people are out in the lobby already," Lindsay said. "I went out to see."

Madison thought about Mom and Dad again. "How many people are out there?"

"They sold like three hundred tickets, Mrs. Montefiore told me. Imagine if they had seventh, eighth, and ninth grade performing on *one* night?" Lindsay said.

"Have you seen Mariah Diaz anywhere?" Madison asked.

"Mariah?" Lindsay asked. "You mean the one with the red streaks in her hair? She's back doing Munchkin makeup, I think."

Backstage was a full-blown disaster. At first, Madison didn't see anyone she recognized, which was a little intimidating. The backstage area was a crush of teachers, techies, and other kids in all kinds of weird makeup.

Ivy and her drones appeared suddenly out of one girls' bathroom. Ivy was all decked out in her Glinda garb, wand in hand.

"Madison!" she yelped. "Where are we supposed to go?"

Madison wanted to say, "Ivy, why don't you just go HOME." But she didn't. She pointed to a side area of the stage where she now saw half the cast gathering. Fiona waved.

"You need to go over there," she said to Ivy as she waved back. "Over by Fiona and the rest. And break a leg."

"Thanks . . . I guess," Ivy said.

Madison laughed to herself. She knew the super-stition was to say, "Break a leg" for *good* luck, but that wasn't what she *really* meant. Madison was standing there focusing all her energies on the pos-sibility that maybe Ivy actually would break one of her legs. It wasn't a nice thought. Then again, she hadn't had too many *nice* Ivy thoughts lately. She looked down at her hands and noticed how she'd chewed off all her nails this week.

Mr. Gibbons appeared, clapping for everyone's attention.

In a few minutes, the curtain would be going up.

Madison could hear the Montefiores playing the introductory music for the evening. She peeked out between the curtains and saw a sea of parents flow-ing down the aisle into the assembly seats. It was definitely a full house tonight. Madison still couldn't spot Mom or Dad, though. She'd have to wait and face them after *The Wiz* was over.

Principal Bernard led off the evening with a short speech about Mrs. Goode's commitment to Far Hills Junior High. He cracked a few jokes that got big laughs from the parents in the audience.

Madison held her breath. *The Wiz* was here. This was real.

"Pssst! Finnster!" Hart whispered, coming up behind Madison. "Whaddya think?" He had on the purple cape with silver stars.

"Wow," Madison gasped. "You look so . . . cool."

"You think?" he said nervously. "Thanks, Finnster. Cool." He leaned over and touched her arm when he said that.

He touched her arm.

Madison could feel the pink in her cheeks. She felt anything but cool right now. "You're welcome," she quivered as he walked away.

Her heart was pounding—hard.

"AND NOW, PRESENTING CLASS SEVEN AND SELECTIONS FROM *THE WIZ*."

Lindsay clung to Chocolate as she walked onstage in her Dorothy costume, followed by Rose Thorn as Auntie Em and Suresh as Uncle Henry. When the lights went up, Lindsay started to sing without hesitation. Her song was originally supposed to be Auntie Em singing alone, but Mrs. Montefiore made it a duet, just like she'd done with some other songs. It was as angelic as ever.

Madison darted over to help Mariah, the Munchkins, and Aimee get onstage for the next number. Lindsay's great singing gave her a jolt of energy.

Aimee spun onstage in the "Tornado Ballet."

She wasn't onstage alone for too long, but it was close enough to a dance solo to make her happy. She was wearing a purple leotard with yellow lightning bolts sewn on the side.

Every song and dance number seemed to go more smoothly than expected. The seventh grade was getting laughs and applause in all the right places. A superstitious Madison couldn't help but think that the "bad rehearsal" theory really was true in their case. The cast and crew dress rehearsals had been minor disasters, but this real show was a smash.

"Mariah." Madison found Egg's sister standing backstage in between a Dorothy-and-Scarecrow song number. "Do I need to do anything else right now?"

Mariah just smiled. "We did it. We're four songs away from the end." She leaned over and squeezed Madison's hand.

Madison watched the rest of the numbers standing in the wings, in that space between backstage and onstage. She felt like she was hovering on the edge of a cliff, the air electric with movement and sound. Madison stood in the folds of a black curtain, holding her marked-up cue script and watching the action. Occasionally she wandered backstage where people needed help with costumes or makeup touch-ups and visited the prop closet to make sure everything was still in order for the final scene. But mostly Madison stayed right there in that in between space until the end of the show.

She was in the middle of *everything* there, and she liked it.

"Ease on Down the Road" was one of the best numbers. Dan the Lion took a header during his dance part, but it was so funny, people thought it was a planned part of the show. Egg didn't have the best singing voice, but he was also getting a lot of laughs. Tommy Kwong, as usual, was a hit. His floppy Scarecrow got rip-roaring cheers.

Fiona's song as the evil Evillene got a roar of applause, too. She looked fantastic in her gray makeup and black hat. Mariah had helped her to affix a fake nose, too, with a giant, bulbous wart on the tip. Casting the nice girl as the bad witch had been a fun choice by Mr. Gibbons, and Fiona was surprisingly good at hamming up the obnoxious parts. Madison didn't ever want to see Fiona being anything but spaced out and sweet in real life, however. There were enough witches at Far Hills already.

Glinda and Addaperle's duet was a success. When Ivy and Aimee rushed offstage, Aimee danced right over to give Madison a big, sweaty hug.

"How was I?" Aimee asked. She was bouncing all over the place.

"You're all wet," Madison said.

"I know, I'm sweating. Can you see it?" Aimee raised her arms for Madison to check.

"Nope," Madison said. She wanted to tell Aimee that her performance had been so amazing—and she wanted to tell her how much she loved it. But right now, everything else was on hold for the last musical number. They would talk more later.

Lindsay Frost was up next.

As Lindsay belted out her solo, the last song in

the show, "Home," Madison listened for the response inside the auditorium.

It suddenly got quieter than quiet.

In a place jammed with chatty junior high schoolers, parents, toddlers, and faculty, *that* said everything. For a brief moment, Lindsay wasn't labeled a "geek." She wasn't in Poison Ivy's shadow. All eyes were on her—front and center.

Lindsay Frost was the most popular.

Just before the last song started, as Mrs. Montefiore clinked her opening chord, Madison saw a slow haze drift across the stage. It lifted up all the music—and then Lindsay's voice—up and out into the auditorium. Madison could actually see dust lingering in the light beams like magic powder.

The show had cast a powerful spell on the seventh grade, and it would stay with Madison and everyone even after the curtain fell. Madison watched the entire cast and crew rush the stage for bows, leaping into the air and screaming with the excitement that comes when the show is finally over.

"Wooo-hoooo!" Egg yelled out. He and Hart were high fiving all over the place.

As the curtain bobbed back up, the seventh graders finished taking their group bows, and Ivy and Aimee presented Mr. Gibbons with flowers. Madison was right there, in the corner of the stage, watching them. But this time, she didn't mind seeing her enemy and friend doing something together.

That was their job—and she knew hers.

She knew where she fit in. She really had been the glue.

Fiona and Aimee grabbed Madison to go out toward the lobby as the crowd dispersed. Families were waiting to greet everyone there.

"I can't wait to see my parents!" Fiona squealed.

"All of my brothers came—could you die?" Aimee said.

Madison gulped. It was the Mom-and-Dad moment of truth.

She rushed off with her friends to the front of the building and searched the crowd. She searched for Mom on one side, and Dad on the other. What would she say to them? What if Stephanie *was* here?

"I'll never find them!" she said. The lobby was packed.

Then, over by the table with the soda and brownies, Madison saw Mom's cobalt blue coat.

She was talking to Dad.

Chapter 13

"Slow down, honey bear!" Mom gasped as Madison zipped over.

Madison almost crashed into the table with little cups of water on trays.

"Whoa, Maddie," Dad said, opening his arms to shield her from the table's edge. He gave her a big hug. "Guess you're a little excited?"

"Yeah, well . . ." Madison didn't know what to say. "How long have you guys been talking?"

Mom and Dad turned to each other and smiled.

"Your father got here on time for the start of the show, Maddie. Can you believe it?" Mom said.

Dad shifted from foot to foot. "I'm not sure I believe it, Frannie," he said to Mom. "Must be your influence."

"I really enjoyed the performance," Mom said, changing the subject. "Especially Aimee and Fiona and . . . who's that other girl? Your old friend Ivy. They make great witches."

Madison couldn't believe Mom liked the witch part best.

"I liked the props," Dad said. "And the set and the costumes and . . . let's see, what else did *you* do, Maddie? I liked that best."

"Aw, Dad," Madison said.

"Did you see our note to you in the program?" Mom asked.

Madison made a face. "Note?"

Dad opened the program. "Yeah, I think it's somewhere here in the middle." He pointed.

♥ *Madison, we love watching you "ease on down the road"*
   to success in everything you do! Great job!
   Mom, Dad & Phinnie

Madison stared at the page and then at her parents. "Thanks . . ." she whispered.
They hadn't forgotten.

Hart was standing only a few feet away. Madison saw him talking to two women, one who looked like she might be his grandmother.

"Hey, Finnster!" Hart said when he saw Madison looking.

"Hey, Hart."

"This is my *ya ya*," he said, introducing the older woman. He seemed sorta embarrassed. "Uh . . . that

138

means 'grandmother' in Greek," he added.

The old woman had a sweet face with soft wrinkles all over.

"Ya Ya," Hart said. "This is Madison. Remember I told you, she's the one who made the cape."

"Ahhh, yes." The old woman took Madison's hand in hers and squeezed. Her hand was covered in smooth lines, too. "Hart tells me you did the costumes. You must be so very proud."

Hart's mother was there, too. "Madison Finn? Is that you? I haven't seen you since before we moved!" She reminded Madison about a time when she slugged Hart in the playground back in first grade. "Things have changed a lot since then, right?" Mrs. Jones laughed. "It's so nice to see you two together again. Are your mom and dad here?"

Hart and Madison both looked down at the floor. Parents could be so clueless. She reintroduced Mrs. Jones and Ya Ya to her mom and dad.

"Nice to meet you, Hart," Mom said. When no one was looking, Mom leaned over and whispered to Madison, "He's cute, Maddie."

Madison blanched white. "Mom!" she gasped softly, praying that Hart hadn't heard.

Mom winked and leaned in. "I know, I know. I won't say any more."

Dad and Ya Ya were talking about Greece the whole time. He'd lived over there for a year when he was a kid.

Meanwhile Hart disappeared to the other side of the room with Chet and Egg. They were talking to Rose and Joanie.

Madison wanted to gag.

She watched the hordes of people swirling around the room: mothers and fathers and sisters and brothers and students from all the grades in Far Hills Junior High. Everyone was buzzing in a figure eight from the brownie table to the auditorium doors to the parking lot.

Except Madison's parents.

Her mom and dad stood in the same place—next to each other the entire time. If she didn't know any better, Madison would have thought that her parents were still together. They were standing there like they always did for her whole life, laughing and nodding like nothing would ever come between them.

"Maddie!" Fiona shrieked from a few feet away. She hurried over. "Can you believe it's over? I am so bummed."

"Yeah," Madison said, glancing at Mom and Dad again. Endings *were* sad.

Aimee came over right after that, trailed by Mr. and Mrs. Gillespie and the entire Gillespie brotherhood. Roger, Billy, and Dean congratulated Madison and chatted up her parents. Doug, the Gillespie ninth grader, qickly disappeared, looking for a few of his friends.

"Do you want a ride to the cast party?" Aimee asked, hugging Madison's shoulder.

Madison pulled away. "The cast party?"

"Yeah!" Aimee said. "Oh my God, it should be great. Everyone is going."

Madison couldn't believe it. In the chaos of the crowd and Mom and Dad's reunion, she had forgotten something so important.

The cast party.

At Poison Ivy's house.

"*Everyone* is going to be there." Fiona giggled. She was looking around the room. "Including Egg. He's going, right?"

"Fiona!" Aimee said. She still cringed whenever Fiona brought up his name, which she did at every opportunity.

"Ivy didn't exactly invite me," Madison said. "I don't know if I—"

"You're invited, Maddie! *Everyone* is gonna be there," Aimee said.

"But Ivy and I—" Madison started to say.

"Forget Ivy," Aimee declared. "The cast party is the absolute best part of the show, Madison. It's the whole point. If you don't go, I won't go."

"It's just that—"

"Maddie, it's a cast party, not *her* party! She may be a good witch in the play—"

Fiona interrupted. "But she's a bad witch in real life."

141

They all laughed.

When Madison slipped backstage again to get her orange bag, she bumped into Lindsay. Lindsay was sitting at one of the mirrors in the dressing room, brushing out her hair.

"Oh," Lindsay said, surprised to see Madison in the mirror's reflection. "I was just getting ready to go home."

"Home? What about the cast party? You have to go to the cast party. Everyone's going to be there," Madison said.

"Nah, I don't think so." Lindsay sighed.

"But you're Dorothy! You're the star of the show!"

Lindsay smiled. "Yeah, of the show, maybe, but not the party. I don't feel like it. In case you didn't notice, I don't exactly have a million friends."

Madison sat in the chair next to Lindsay. "What do you mean? You have friends."

Lindsay ran the brush through her hair again. "Forget it."

"You have friends, Lindsay. I'm your friend."

Lindsay turned to Madison. "That's nice of you, Madison. But I know we were just friends during the show. It's okay."

It was definitely NOT okay.

Madison thought about Aimee and Ivy pretending to get along during *The Wiz*. Was she doing the same thing with Lindsay?

"Lindsay, you have to come to the cast party. Come with us."

"Us?"

"Me and Aimee and Fiona."

"That's okay. *Really.* You go."

Madison stood up again. "You sure?"

Lindsay nodded. She pulled her hair back on both sides with her heart barrettes.

"You should really wear your hair down," Madison said. "It looks better that way."

Lindsay looked into the mirror. "Really?" She took the clips out.

"And you should really go to the party, too," Madison added.

Lindsay stood up and started to pack her bag. She shook her head. "Maybe another time. I'm just not into it. Not tonight."

"How are you getting home?" Madison asked.

"I'll just walk."

"By yourself?" Madison cried.

Lindsay laughed softly. "I always do."

"Where are your parents?" Madison asked.

"They don't come to these things," Lindsay said simply. "But it's okay."

It was definitely NOT okay.

Lindsay started to walk away from the dressing tables. "See you later, Madison. Thanks again for everything."

Madison waved her arms up. "Hey, wait! I still

143

really think you should come to the party. Won't you just come for a little while?"

"Maybe." Lindsay waved and disappeared into the bathroom.

Madison got her own bag and went off to find Aimee, Fiona, and her ride to the cast party. She was disappointed that nothing she'd said seemed to help with Lindsay.

Aimee was standing out in front of the school building, spinning around. Her brother Roger was pulling the van up. Fiona stood nearby, chatting with Mr. Gibbons. He had Chocolate on a leash.

"Fantastic," the teacher said, clapping Madison on the back. "What fine work, Madison. Just grand."

Roger pulled up, and they all got into the van.

"Good-bye, Mr. Gibbons," Aimee yelled out. "See you at the party!"

Madison sank into the backseat and stared out the window as they pulled away. *The Wiz* was over. She felt relief and sadness at the same time.

"Lindsay didn't want to come?" Fiona asked.

Aimee nodded. "Yeah, where is she?"

Madison shrugged. "She went home."

"Hey." Aimee nudged her brother. "What reeks?"

Roger's van smelled funny, like old socks. Fiona and Madison pinched their noses and Aimee fanned hers.

"I don't smell anything," Roger said. He opened

the window and a rush of cool, fall wind blew in.

"That's better, stinky," Aimee said. Fiona and Madison were laughing in the backseat.

"You guys were dynamite onstage tonight," Roger said, peering into his rearview mirror to see Madison and Fiona in the backseat. "And offstage, too, Miss Stage Manager."

Madison felt herself blush a little. Just like Dad, Roger knew how to say the right things. If she had to have a runner-up crush on anyone in the whole world, it would be Roger Gillespie, with his stinky car and all.

When they arrived at the Daly house, Roger could barely get into the driveway. There were too many cars dropping off kids and parking at the side of the road. Everyone really *was* there.

When the three friends walked into Ivy's front hallway, it was like walking into a magazine spread from *House Beautiful*. Mrs. Daly had little china dishes set out on each table with peanuts and other snacks. The dining room table was decorated with flowers and punch bowls. Everywhere she looked, Madison saw food, people, and more food. Mrs. Daly was floating from room to room, making sure the guests were eating. She had on a witch hat like the ones from *The Wiz*.

"Hey, Madison!" Drew came over and said hello to the three girls. "There are these little pizzas inside, and everyone is hanging out in the den."

Aimee answered for everyone. "Thanks for the info, Drew."

Chet bounced over with Hart in tow.

Hart.

"Hey, Finnster!" he said. "Hey, Aim and Fiona."

Madison couldn't take her eyes off him. He wasn't wearing his glasses, and he looked cuter than cute. As he walked toward the food, Madison started to follow, but then she heard a familiar voice. A voice she didn't expect to hear.

Lindsay?

She turned to see Lindsay hanging up her coat in the front hall closet with Mr. Daly's assistance. Her hair was down like it had been in the dressing room.

"Hey, look who's here!" Aimee saw her, too.

"She looks different," Fiona said. "What's different?"

Madison smiled. *Everything* was different. Lindsay had taken Madison's advice and turned up for the party.

As Madison rushed over, she noticed people staring at Lindsay. Wearing her hair down had made all the difference.

Lindsay looks *pretty*, Madison thought.

The house was filling up quicker than quick. Kids crammed into the different rooms, while a fleet of teachers made their way to the hors d'oeuvres table. Madison overheard Mr. Gibbons asking Mrs. Wing what she thought of cheese puffs and spinach dip.

146

Mr. and Mrs. Montefiore had already taken a seat at the Daly piano and were playing a jazzy tune.

Aimee came over to Madison and Lindsay. "Let's go scope out the action in the other room," she said.

"Okeydokey," Lindsay replied. She tugged on her black cowl-neck sweater.

They both followed Aimee out the door.

"Maybe the party won't be so awful after all," Madison said to Aimee, smiling.

Chapter 14

Chet was showing everyone at the party how he could balance a spoon on the end of his nose. Aimee tried, too, but kept dropping it.

Drew and Egg were busy throwing peanuts into their mouths. Egg flicked one over toward Hart.

"No way, man—I'm allergic to peanuts!" Hart said.

Madison made a mental note. She'd have to add that information into her Hart file—NO PEANUTS.

"Come on, you guys," Madison said. She wanted some punch.

"Did you hear about Mrs. Wing?" Fiona said.

"What?" Madison said. She couldn't believe she didn't know something about her favorite teacher.

"I heard that her husband is a spy," Fiona said.

"Get OUT!" Aimee laughed.

"Seriously," Fiona continued. "Or a detective. Anyway, he's supposedly really cute."

Madison knew Mrs. Wing's husband would be cute.

"Didn't they just get married or something?" Aimee asked.

Madison's head spun. There were so many things she knew nothing about.

They all walked over to the drink table. Mrs. Daly had food and beverage stations set up all over her house.

Madison looked for Lindsay as Aimee poured her a drink. Lindsay was right there on a sofa, talking to a techie and another teacher, Mr. Lynch. He was the faculty advisor who helped set up the show's light board.

"Excuse me." Poison Ivy pushed Madison to the left to get a cup of pineapple punch. "Having a good time?" she asked, smirking.

Madison shrugged. "Sure," she said.

"Really?" Ivy said, sipping her punch.

"Um . . . where's the bathroom?"

"We have three," Ivy shot back. "You can use the one down there next to the den."

As Madison wandered out of the bathroom, she made her way into the Dalys' den. She was attracted to all the books. Shelves had been lined with leather volumes, and an antique spoon collection hung framed on one wall. Silver frames gleamed like they'd been polished this morning.

Everything felt a little untouchable, kind of like Poison Ivy herself.

Madison saw a photograph of Ivy that must have been taken back when they were in second grade. The photo seemed so familiar, and it took Madison a moment to realize why.

She'd been there.

In the picture, Ivy was seated on a log and her head was thrown back, midlaugh. Madison remembered that *she* was the one who made Ivy crack up that day. She had been standing just outside the frame of the photograph when it had been taken. Back then, Ivy and Madison knew how to make each other crack up on command.

Madison remembered everything about that day, from cherry ice cream cones to sitting on the log in the photo, making frog noises.

"Hey!" Aimee burst into the den, talking a mile a minute. "Oh my God, Maddie, what are you doing in here? You have to come into the living room and see what Hart Jones is doing. He knows these magic tricks and it is way cool. Come on!"

Madison followed Aimee back into the bustle of the party. A bunch of kids and teachers had gathered around the coffee table. Hart was kneeling down.

"Okay, Egg, pick a card," he was saying. "Any card."

Egg cracked, "What is that, a fixed deck or something?"

"Just pick a card, man," Chet said.

Egg pulled a card out of the deck and looked at it. He put it back again. After shuffling the deck, Hart went through each card until he reached the jack of diamonds. He looked up at Egg.

"No WAY! How did you know that?" Egg said.

Everyone laughed.

Madison watched as Hart did the trick again for Egg's sister, Mariah. Once again, he identified the right card.

"He's like a real wizard," Fiona said. Hart had put on his purple cape with the stars again as a joke.

Madison wished she had the nerve to go over and do the trick with Hart, but she didn't. She just watched as he flashed the cards to the rest of the group.

"Hey, Madison." Lindsay came up to her, smiling.

"Hey." Madison grinned. "I'm glad you came to the party, Lindsay."

"I was leaving the building and Mr. Gibbons saw me walking away. He said he wouldn't let me go home alone, so he gave me a ride over. He's so nice."

Madison nodded. "It's a fun party. Are you glad you're here?"

"I'm really here because of you," Lindsay said softly. "You were right about everything. So thanks for that. Thanks for being a real friend."

Madison couldn't help but smile.

Ivy was perched on a chair across the room. She announced, "Sundaes in the kitchen! Does anyone want ice cream?"

Everyone hustled in. No one would turn down homemade sundaes. Mrs. Daly had hot fudge and whipped cream and a whole lineup of toppings, on the counter. Ivy was waving an ice-cream scoop around like it was a magic wand.

As fate would have it, Madison ended up in the ice cream line next to Hart.

Magic.

"Cool tricks you were doing in there," she said.

"Thanks, Finnster," he said. "My dad got me magic lessons for my birthday last year. I know a pretty cool rope trick, too. I'll show you sometime."

"Hello, Hart." Ivy appeared with a bowl of ice cream. She handed it to him. "If you want toppings, they're all over there."

He grabbed the bowl and walked away. "See ya, Finnster."

Ivy looked at Madison and tilted her head to one side. "Having fun yet?" she said. "Everyone says my party is great."

Madison didn't want to be rude. "Everything's great, Ivy."

Ivy shrugged. "I know." She walked away.

Aimee was standing away from the ice cream and sauces. Madison went over to talk to her.

"No ice cream, Aim?" she asked.

Aimee shook her head. "Nope. I have to watch what I eat. I don't want to get all bloated."

Aimee was always worrying about her body. She said she needed to be careful because of dance. She wanted to look good in her leotard. Madison thought she looked just fine.

Fiona wasn't worried about anything, however. She had piled ice cream, caramel sauce, and nuts in a bowl and was headed across the room toward Egg. She'd probably be back for seconds, too.

"Look at that," Madison said to Aimee when she saw where Fiona was headed. "Look who Fiona is sitting with."

"Oh my God!" Aimee said. "What do you think they're talking about?"

"I dunno."

Now it was Aimee and Madison's turn to giggle.

"Pssst! Look at that guy over *there*," Aimee said. She nodded in the direction of a tall kid with a crew cut. He looked like he had an earring. He'd been one of the techies who'd helped to rig Emerald City and some of the other set pieces, including the oversized trees Mom helped get.

"He's in ninth grade, isn't he?" Madison asked.

Aimee raised her eyebrows. "So?"

Madison pushed her friend. "Aimee, I can't believe you."

"I'm gonna go talk to him," she said.

153

Madison watched as Aimee approached the nameless ninth grader. She didn't stop smiling once. Aimee sure knew how to get a guy's attention. Madison wondered what magic was involved in that.

The party kept up until almost nine-thirty. Madison didn't see Lindsay again, so she figured she must have left.

Fiona was hanging out with Chet, Egg, and Drew on a sofa, talking about computer games. Fiona was sitting right next to Egg. Madison wondered if they *would* start dating. She pushed that out of her thoughts real quick.

"Guess what?" Aimee suddenly reappeared with a giant smile. She said that her brother Roger would be coming to pick them up in a few minutes.

"What happened to that ninth grader?"

"He was nice," Aimee said, not revealing much detail.

"So what are you gonna do?" Madison asked.

Aimee shrugged. She had no idea what she would do. It was just fun to flirt.

"You know what?" Aimee asked all of a sudden. "You're a great friend!"

Madison was surprised. "Why are you saying that, Aimee?"

"Because. You're so nice. To me. To Lindsay. . . ." Aimee's voice trailed off. "Seventh grade just stresses me out and I'm not so good at being nice. I know that."

"You're great, too," Madison said, wrapping her

arm around Aimee's shoulder. "You're my best, best friend."

Aimee had a big grin on her face. "We made it to junior high, Maddie. We used to talk about this. Parties. Boys. All of it. And now . . ."

Madison sighed. "We're really here."

With arms locked, they glanced around the room. Madison had come this far and now she wished she could just go a little more. If only she could flirt better! Madison hadn't spoken more than five words to Hart since the party started. And even when she did speak, Ivy always showed up in the middle of it.

Drew came strolling over to Madison. "I just wanted to say good-bye," he said. "So, good-bye." Just like that, he walked away, before Madison had a chance to say anything. He and Egg and a bunch of other guys left, too.

Where was Hart?

Madison, Fiona, and Aimee grabbed their coats and bags and walked toward the front door. Just when she thought she'd missed seeing her crush, Madison spotted him. He was standing in the living room—and she saw him but knew he hadn't seen her yet because he didn't yell, "Finnster!"

There was another reason he didn't say anything. Ivy Daly.

She was hunched over, leaning on a desk right next to him. She was scribbling something on a pad of paper.

Was Ivy giving Hart her number?

Madison turned right around and ran straight through the front door, scuttling out of the Daly house so fast that Aimee and Fiona could barely catch her.

Once they were inside Roger's van, Madison didn't say one word about what she'd seen, even though Aimee and Fiona suspected that something had suddenly gone very wrong.

Madison wouldn't tell. It was a *secret* secret—next to the files, next to Bigwheels.

How could Ivy have given Hart her number?

Madison asked herself that question at least ten times. She wondered why she liked the real-life Wizard so much that it made her sides ache. She couldn't list reasons. It wasn't about lists. She just FELT it.

That's what *The Wiz* was all about, anyway, wasn't it? You had to hold on to your dreams. Especially the dreamy ones like Hart.

Madison gave Mom an enormous hug when she walked in the door at home. Mom and Phin had been up watching TV and waiting for Madison's return. Phinnie waddled over, half asleep, too. He yawned.

"Well?" Mom asked curiously. "Talk! How was the party? How's that cute boy?" She wanted the whole scoop—and nothing but the scoop.

Madison filled Mom in on the food stations, the magic tricks, and the rest. Then she yawned, just like

Phinnie had. No talk about cute boys tonight, Madison explained.

"I have to go to bed, Mom."

Phin followed Madison up to her messy room. He made himself comfortable on her bed pillows as she opened her laptop. Madison hoped that maybe this was one of those late nights when Bigwheels would be online when she wasn't supposed to be. She logged on to bigfishbowl.com.

It was a busy Friday under the sea.

And Bigwheels *was* online.

```
<MadFinn>: You're here!!!!
<Bigwheels>: what a surprise how
   cool
<MadFinn>: (((Bigwheels)))
<Bigwheels>: thx whassup?
<MadFinn>: FIRST how r ur parents
<Bigwheels>: :-Z LOL
<MadFinn>: No! I mean with splitting
   up
<Bigwheels>: kewl
<MadFinn>: still together?
<Bigwheels>: sort of
<Bigwheels>: I'm not so worried
<MadFinn>: @—)—(—
<Bigwheels>: is that a flower???
<MadFinn>: yup
<Bigwheels>: thanks for advice it
   helped sooo much
```

\<MadFinn\>: really?

\<Bigwheels\>: totally

\<MadFinn\>: I had our cast party
tonite

\<Bigwheels\>: and? What happened with
your crush?

\<MadFinn\>: CUL8R

\<Bigwheels\>: what?

\<MadFinn\>: he's seeing someone else
I think

\<Bigwheels\>: bummer

\<MadFinn\>: me and boys are 100%
hopeless I swear!

\<Bigwheels\>: that is SO not true

\<MadFinn\>: what about u?

\<Bigwheels\>: hopeless LOL

\<MadFinn\>: how is school 4 you?

\<Bigwheels\>: I have a HUGE english
essay due and I'm writing on The
Lost Princess of Oz. You inspired
me.

\<MadFinn\>: I did?

\<Bigwheels\>: GTG

\<MadFinn\>: are your parents
watching?

\<Bigwheels\>: Mom just found me on
the computer

\<MadFinn\>: whoops

\<Bigwheels\>: guess they weren't
sleeping

\<MadFinn\>: bye

```
<Bigwheels>: WB
<Bigwheels>: *poof*
```

Before she closed down her computer, Madison had to get into her files. So much had happened tonight, and she couldn't risk forgetting any of it.

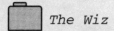 *The Wiz*

So it's over. The sky didn't fall in on my head, the stage didn't collapse, and no lives were lost during the making of this show. I would say the only thing that *was* lost during *The Wiz* was my nervousness.

Rude Awakening: Just when you feel like you're on a yellow brick road to nowhere . . . something great happens.

I'm not quite sure what I expected from Oz. Sometimes I do things because everyone else is, or I like people (or DON'T like people) because everyone else does. I want to be liked, too. But meeting Lindsay changed my feelings. I don't even know if I will stay friends with Lindsay after this, but I will try.

I think that I am a combo of every character in the play right now. I've gotten smarter, I felt more stuff in my heart, and I also got braver. I hate to admit that parents are right, but they are—sometimes. Dad would be glad to know that I learned all these things from doing the play. His pep talks worked lots. So did Mom's.

> The characters in *The Wiz* couldn't get
> through Oz without friends and the same is
> totally true for me. My list includes old
> friends like Aimee, new friends like Fiona,
> and even friends that I didn't expect like
> Lindsay Frost. And online friends. I can't
> forget Bigwheels!

Madison signed off and shut down her computer. If she didn't get some sleep soon, she'd be destroyed tomorrow. She wanted to be in good spirits for dinner with Dad and Stephanie and for hanging out with her friends. Plus, she had so much homework to catch up on. Luckily, Mr. Danehy had agreed to move the big science test a week later.

Phin was just as pooped as Madison. He jumped up into bed with her.

"I can't go through Oz without my friends," Madison cooed into her pug's ear. "Not even my animal friends, right, Phinnie?"

He snuzzled close, looked up at her with his wet brown eyes, and snorted.

It was a doggie "yes."

Madison closed her own eyes.

Dorothy was right when she said there was no place like home. There was no place like Madison's house right now.

Especially under the covers—the safest place in the whole world.

Mad Chat Words:

%-(	Sad and confused
:-c	Bummed out
:-Z	Sleeping
QT	Cutie
CUL8R	See you later
A/S/L	Age/sex/location
ASAP	As soon as possible
IDGI	I don't get it
<rrr>	Anger
PAW	Parents are watching!
(((Bigwheels)))	Cyberhug to . . .
Kewl	Cool
@--)--(--	Rose (flower)

Madison's Computer Tip:

Sometimes when I'm on the computer, a whole hour can go by and I don't even realize it. **Time flies when you're online. Keep an eye on the clock and don't forget your friends.** I try to make special times (like during study hall or after dinner) for answering e-mail, chatting, writing in my files, surfing the Net, homework, and other stuff. I don't usually do all those things at once. I try to remember to spend *real* time with friends and not just Insta-Message time.

Visit Madison at www.madisonfinn.com

Book #3: *Play It Again*

Super Quiz

Now that you've read the story . . . how much do you *really* know about Madison and her friends?

1. Who is Mrs. Montefiore?
    a. The soccer coach
    b. The assistant principal
    c. The musical director

2. What color hair does Ivy Daly have?
    a. Brown
    b. Black
    c. Red

3. Where do Madison and her friends run into Ivy and her mother, Mrs. Daly?
   a. The Cyber Cafe
   b. Freeze Palace
   c. Outside Far Hills Junior High

4. Who are real-life cousins?
   a. Chet and Fiona
   b. Madison and Aimee
   c. Drew and Hart

5. Who plays the role of Dorothy in *The Wiz*?
   a. Ivy Daly
   b. Lindsay Frost
   c. Roseanne Snyder

6. What role does Dan Ginsburg play?
   a. The Tin Man
   b. The Wizard of Oz
   c. The Cowardly Lion

7. Where does Madison get inspired to make a yellow brick road?
   a. The tool store
   b. The library
   c. The arts-and-crafts store at the mall

8. What is Bigwheels's big news for Madison?
   a. Her parents are splitting up.
   b. Her parents are moving.
   c. Her brother has ADD.

164

9. What role does Mrs. Perez have in the play?
    a. She's the school custodian.
    b. She keeps track of rehearsal times.
    c. She makes all the costumes.

10. Why is everyone upset with Mr. Danehy?
    a. He scheduled a test the week of the play.
    b. He gave a killer pop quiz after lunch.
    c. He kicked Madison out of his classroom.

11. How does Mr. Gibbons tell the cast to keep Chocolate, the dog playing Toto, happy during the show?
    a. Scratch the back of her head.
    b. Give her Liver Snaps.
    c. Pull her tail.

12. Who plays the Wicked Witch?
    a. Ivy
    b. Fiona
    c. Aimee

13. What surprises Madison the most about the announcement in the program that is dedicated to her?
    a. It's printed in red ink.
    b. It takes up half the page.
    c. It's written by both Mom *and* Dad (and Phin, too!).

14. What does "(((Madison)))" mean?
    a. Madison's feeling squished.
    b. Give Madison a big hug.
    c. Don't mess with Madison.

15. What does Hart do at the cast party to impress everyone?
    a. Performs magic tricks
    b. Stands on his head
    c. Sings a song

16. Which of Madison's friends is a member of the Spanish Club?
    a. Aimee
    b. Fiona
    c. Elena

17. What famous Shakespeare saying does Madison's mom quote?
    a. "Love is a many splendor'd thing."
    b. "The play's the thing."
    c. "To be or not to be, that is the question."

18. Which of the following items is not wedged inside the frame of Madison's bedroom mirror?
    a. A picture of Hart
    b. Her mother's business card
    c. A pink ribbon from Lodge 12 at Camp Chipachu

19. What is Madison's favorite sport to watch with her dad?
    a. Baseball
    b. Football
    c. Ice-skating

20. What is the name of Madison's dad's newest business venture?
    a. The Finn Foundation
    b. Finn Frontiers
    c. The *Finn*ish Line

21. In whose honor is *The Wiz* being performed as a tribute?
    a. Mrs. B. Goode
    b. Mr. Seymour Clearley
    c. Mrs. Amanda Huginkiss

22. Who has a sister named Mariah?
    a. Fiona
    b. Aimee
    c. Egg

23. Which play will the eighth graders be performing?
    a. *A Streetcar Named Desire*
    b. *Guys and Dolls*
    c. *Romeo and Juliet*

24. Which of Aimee's brothers does Madison have a small crush on?
    a. Roger
    b. Frank
    c. Benjamin

25. What does Hart call his grandmother?
    a. Grandma
    b. Granny
    c. Ya-Ya

BONUS QUESTION:

Who is Madison's new friend after the play ends?
    a. Lindsay
    b. Hart
    c. Chet

Answers:
1c, 2c, 3a, 4c, 5b, 6c, 7a, 8a, 9c, 10a, 11b, 12b, 13c, 14b, 15a, 16b, 17b, 18a, 19a, 20b, 21a, 22c, 23b, 24a, 25c

Bonus Question: a

How well do you know Maddie?

24–25 correct: You might as well pack your bags and move to Far Hills, because you are a *Madison Finn* fanatic!

20–23 correct: You could totally be Madison's BFF, because you know her inside out!

17–20 correct: You think Maddie's pretty cool, and you'd have fun hanging out with her.

14–16 correct: You know a few things about Madison, and you're interested in finding out more about her.

13 or fewer correct: You didn't quite catch all those details about Maddie, but don't worry—there's still lots of time to learn.

Like Madison Finn, author Laura Dower is an only child, enjoys her laptop computer, and drinks root beer. Laura has written more than 60 books for kids. She lives in New York with her husband and two children.

Visit Laura at www.lauradower.com